# THE SILVERY PATH:

## The Underworlds

Also in the series:

No Way Back: The Underworlds

Taken With a Dark Desire: The Underworlds

Rejecting Destiny: The Underworlds

# THE SILVERY PATH:
## The Underworlds

# Dennis Scheel

This is dedicated to my dog Yoshi, who recently succumb to illness after a slipped disc. You are always in my heart, we went through so much and I will always miss you!


Thanks to the edit by Diane Ash and the cover by MiblArt.

# Chapter 1- A New Beginning

Den, Denida's human form, trotted from his grandparent's house with a smile painted across his face. He admired the sunny sky before skipping down the road, humming to himself.

*He's barely grown.* Odin clenched his scepter. "We have to do it within one week." He glared in through a window, then turned to Loki. "I'll leave the task to you; don't fail me."

Loki chuckled. "Why bother? They're lowly humans."

"I want to expedite Henna's prophecy. We have waited in this world long enough. This is your chance to show me that I can rely on you, Loki."

"But what I still don't understand is: why? Isn't that kid Henna's chosen one?"

Odin adjusted his grip on his scepter. "His soul form is, not the boy, but certain events must fall into place to achieve Henna's desired outcome, instead of a less desirable one."

"Understood." Loki smirked.

"You must use dark magic to kill the boy's grandmother within one week. I can't specify how important that is."

Loki's eyes widened. "To frame Lucifer?"

Odin sighed. "Aren't you attentive today." He leaned closer to Loki. "Correct."

***

A curtain of snow coated Dynasty like a veil. Christmas decorations adorned the grounds.

Denida and Nina stood on Dynasty's balcony, waving at a crowd with Dan, Susan, and the Colonel behind them, ringing in the New Year.

Denida kissed Nina on the cheek. *She's so radiant in the snow.*

Fireworks exploded brilliantly as the clock struck midnight. The sky lit up with a spectacular magic stroke humming, "Happy New Year!"

Nina hustled to the fireplace as soon as they ventured inside.

Dan smiled as he approached Denida. "A new year, and a new beginning."

*He has no idea…* Denida smiled. "Funny you should say that, my friend."

Dan frowned. "Why?"

Denida scratched his forehead. "It's a new beginning, as you said; the Underworlds have united again, and Heaven and Hell remain at bay. Things are good."

Dan glanced at the Colonel, who remained focused on his chat with Susan.

"Claus is still away from our word, out of sight and out of mind," Denida continued.

Dan nipped his lip. "What are you getting at?"

Denida licked his lips. "I need you to be my vice president, Dan."

Dan gasped. "Me… but why?"

"You're very capable, and I need to focus on-" Denida's eyes trailed to Nina. "Nina and I need time." He poured two glasses, stepped up to Nina, and handed her one, gazing deeply into her eyes.

***

The Colonel barged through the door to Dan's office. Dan sat behind one gargantuan stack of papers, but similar piles filled the whole office, leaving just enough room for a narrow path to his desk. Dan held a single page in his left hand and a pen in his right. "You've been in charge for a few weeks, now. I'm surprised you're not more caught up, Dan." *Crap.* "- I mean, Vice President, Sir." The Colonel saluted him.

Dan lifted his head. "Colonel, what's the matter?"

The Colonel removed his beret and wiped his forehead. "Something terrible has happened."

"Bad enough to interrupt my work?"

"Yes, Sir. We've detected dark magic on Earth."

Dan struggled to process the Colonel's words. After a moment, his pen slipped from his hand, falling to the floor with a clink, shattering the silence. "Are you sure? Denny's magical shield around Earth should protect it."

The Colonel nodded his head. "Yes, but-"

"Denny brought Heavani to the Devil, in exchange for his word that demons would never-" Dan slammed his fist on the desk. "Of course, it's happening now, just as Denny is leaving." He stood hunched over the desk. "Send the task force to deal with it, ASAP!"

The Colonel put his beret back on and marched out the door, where the Commander waited for him.

"You." The Colonel frowned, glaring at the Commander.

"Yes, Sir." The Commander maintained eye contact.

"We have permission to investigate the dark magic, so you'd better behave yourself."

The Colonel led the Commander to the Gate, from which they journeyed to Earth, to reconvene with the task force.

The Colonel surveyed their surroundings, then flinched. "How was anyone able to bypass the barrier and use dark magic here?"

The Commander shrugged. "It came from the little house down there."

The Colonel squinted at the house. *I should use my soul form, so that humans won't see me.* "Acknowledged." He strolled down the road, his focus flicking between the buildings he passed on his way to the house. When he arrived, his eyes widened, as paramedics hastily departed through the front door with a gurney. *Did somebody die?* He glanced back at the Commander, then continued inside the house.

The Colonel gasped and quivered like his knees had turned to mush. He bolted from the house and leaned up against a wall.

The Commander ran up to him. "Colonel, are you okay?"

"We've got a serious problem."

The Commander stepped back. "Sir?"

"There are pictures of Lord Denida's human form in there." The Colonel rubbed his forehead. "I have to interrupt Denida's vacation. There's no other way." He hurried to the Gate to return to the Underworld's HQ, where he marched straight past Dan's secretary to enter his office, but the stacks of paper from earlier stood alone in the empty room.

*Where did he go?* The Colonel plopped down in a chair, rubbing his forehead. *Denida's office, maybe?* He jumped to his feet and stepped out.

The secretary in front of Denida's office greeted him with a smile. "Hello, Colonel. They are expecting you."

*They?* The Colonel's eyes widened as he trudged through the doors.

"John..." Denida stepped up to the Colonel and shook his hand. "- just who we needed."

"Needed, for what?"

"Something feels off. Dan said he sent you to investigate the Darkness appearing on Earth?"

"Affirmative, near your human form..." The Colonel lowered his head.

"Tell me more."

The Colonel flinched. "Someone used dark magic to kill one of Den's relatives, Sir."

Dan gasped, lifting his chin from a stack of papers. "Are you serious?"

"If the Darkness killed them, then Lucifer is behind it." Denida bared his teeth.

The Colonel pursed his lips. "Yes, Sir."

Denida ran his fingers through his hair. "Guess I'll need to return to Hell, after all." He put his hand on the Colonel's shoulder. "Dan's in charge until I get back. Can you check on Nina for me?" He lifted his ring to his lips, then vanished from the room.

"Where's-"

Dan lifted his hand. "Nina's at Dynasty with Angel."

*Oh, her horse...* The Colonel spun around and marched to his car. *At least I get to see some beautiful greenery.*

"John, welcome." Dynasty's butler opened the car door and saluted the Colonel.

The Colonel nodded. "Lady Nina is with Angel?"

The butler scratched his cheek. "Correct, at the stables."

"Thank you." The Colonel stalked to the stables, where Nina stood, brushing Angel. The Colonel cleared his throat.

Nina turned to the Colonel. "John, what brings you here?"

"Denida instructed me to check on you."

Nina threw the brush into the bucket at her feet. "Why? I thought he wanted to spend time with me, to focus on us, for once."

The Colonel tapped his palm on his trousers. "Something... came up."

"Again?" Nina approached and poked the Colonel's chest. "Well, you can tell him he needs to finish that up and get ready for some time away. I'm finding it hard to stay here without Daniel." She shoved past the Colonel.

*Denida won't like this...*

*Lucifer's mansion.* Denida rubbed the ring on his finger, which guided him on his trek. Darkness surged through the air in Hell, creating thick black fog. As he neared the mansion, the mist thinned.

Denida peered back before pushing on the door, finding it locked. *The hell?* Denida stepped back and scrutinized the building, seeing that it stood as majestically as always. Finally, he gritted his teeth and thrust his arm forward, forcing the doors open with magic. He strolled into the dark hall ahead of him. Denida paused, glancing around. *It's never been in disrepair like this.* Denida ran his fingers across a fist-sized dent in the drywall.

He marched down the corridor to a pair of double doors and thrust them open.

Dust and cobwebs covered every centimeter of the room. Filth littered Lucifer's throne. Dim light glimmered from the back room.

Denida slowly approached the next door, glancing at the throne as he passed. As he stood before the next room, he peeked through the threshold. Lucifer sat on the floor, staring up at a mural of Heavani. Darkness engulfed him like a cloak.

"Luci?" Denida's voice cracked hoarsely.

Lucifer jolted up, the Darkness clinging to his body. "Hello, Denida." Contempt saturated his tone. "Our business is done," he hissed and stormed out of the room with Denida in tow.

Denida hurried after him.

Lucifer whipped around so suddenly that Denida stumbled. "- unless you have returned to Hell to join me in my war?"

Denida could see Lucifer's eyes filled with rage and emptiness. "What war?"

Lucifer's crimson eyes sparkled. "Heavani died; God will pay!"

"Wait." Denida lifted his hand. "Pay, how?"

"Exactly the way Henna wanted." Lucifer smirked. "His death, and all of Heaven's."

"If you go to war, you won't have time to focus on new souls."

Lucifer clenched his fist. "I… don't… care. You're no longer welcome in Hell!" He slammed his fist into Denida's chest, and Darkness surged from it. It encircled Denida, thrusting him out of Hell.

Denida clenched his fist, using all the ring's power to eradicate the lingering Darkness, which still encased him. He closed his eyes against a sting in his heart from the massive amount of energy he used. Denida arched his neck and peered around, realizing he now stood outside of Heaven's Pearly Gates.

*It's worse than we thought. I must talk to Gabriel.* He hurried to Heaven's Gate, only to pause and rest his hand on his chest. His meager stamina slowed his stride.

Saint Peter shot Denida a death stare as he approached. "Halt! You're not allowed inside."

Denida waved his hands. "I just need to-"

A white light surrounded Saint Peter's silhouette, and his eyes glowed intensely. "I said no," he hissed. "Come closer at your own peril; I dare you."

*I'm not strong enough after expelling that Darkness.* Denida withdrew with his hands, before spinning around and strolling toward the Gate outside Heaven.

Denida knelt beside the Gate, stroking the cloud's surface.

"Didn't it go well?" A woman with rainbow eyes manifested beside Denida.

"Queen Henna," Denida turned his eyes from her to the cloud. "What are you doing here? Our dealings are done."

Henna sat beside Denida and glared at him sternly. "Are you certain of that? You have yet to fulfill my prophecy."

"No, we're done."

Henna smiled. "You'll listen if you want to avoid more casualties. Most of the souls in your Underworlds have split souls, with some of those souls connected to a human on Earth. You know from Claus what happens when any of those connections, or their human forms, die."

Denida caressed the cloud under his hand.

"Have you already forgotten how strong Claus became after his other soul forms died?"

"Enough of this." Denida gritted his teeth and jumped to his feet. "I know what you are."

"What I am?" Henna frowned.

"God, Gabriel, and Lucifer's goddess…"

Henna rose with an irritated expression. "That's not all I am. Someday, you will understand." She waved and disappeared with a rainbow flash.

Denida gritted his teeth. *Henna remains at large.* He clenched his fist, and his Underworlds ring teleported him back to his office. He fell to his knees, but swiftly staggered out to his secretary.

"Sir?" The secretary's eyes widened.

Denida grabbed ahold of her desk to pull himself up. "I need to see the Colonel, ASAP."

Denida fell into his chair, recuperating, waiting for the Colonel.

"Denny?" Nina lounged on a couch in Denida's office and smiled widely.

"Nina?" Denida's ears burned. "What are you doing here?"

"I figured I would seek you out, since you're so preoccupied. Why do you need to see the Colonel?"

Denida sighed. "Henna…"

"No, it's time to move past that. We need to focus on us, remember?"

"I know, but-"

"Don't you want to work on our relationship?" Nina crossed her arms.

"*Beep*," the intercom sounded. "The Colonel and Master Sergeant Susan are here."

"I do, and I will, after this, I swear." Denida bent over and pressed the intercom button. "Let them in."

The Colonel saluted Denida. "You wanted to see me, Sir?"

Denida slammed his desk so forcefully that some pencils rolled onto the floor. "Henna!"

Susan and the Colonel exchanged a glance.

The Colonel licked his lips. "I thought we weren't dealing with her, anymore."

"We are, now. She is up to something, and Lucifer's preparing for war with God. We must maximize our security measures."

Susan stepped forward. "Can't you persuade Lucifer to-"

Denida shook his head. "He exiled me from Hell."

The Colonel gasped. "I thought you were on his good side?"

"We made a deal; I'd bring him Heavani, and he'd protect our human forms on Earth."

Susan stayed rooted to the spot. "What does this mean for the Underworlds, and everyone on Earth?"

Denida rapped his knuckles on the desk. "Everything is about to change."

Susan rubbed her palms together. "Maybe you should talk to Henna. Didn't you say she knows everything that happens?"

"Maybe you're right." Denida turned on his heel. *Wait, would Henna get anything out of this?* He froze midstride with a heavy sigh, then strolled over to Susan and rested his hand on her shoulder. "She won't help. Besides, she doesn't know everything. She allegedly sees all the possible futures that can occur, but doesn't know which course fate will take. That depends on our choices."

Susan tilted her head. "We'd still be better off after talking to her than we are, now."

Nina cleared her throat and stepped in between Denida and Susan. "The Henna debacle is over."

"Sir." The Colonel saluted Denida. "I'll rally our security detail." He marched out of the office.

Susan followed him, only to pause after a few steps, and spun to face Denida. "Sometimes, we have to do what we don't want to. You told me that once, Denny. If you know where she is, go."

"You're right." Denida kissed Nina's cheek. "I'll walk you out." He held the door for Susan. "I'm sure she's at her planet with two suns."

Susan paused just outside the office, and her eyes narrowed in confusion. "That's habitable?"

Denida nodded. "Yes, but she's that world's only resident, now." He scratched his temple. "I forgot to tell the Colonel to report day-to-day operations to Dan. He's using Claus's old office."

"I heard about that, but I didn't know you were retiring?"

Denida laughed and leaned against the wall. "I'm not, but with all this going on, I don't have time to devote to the Underworld, so he's my acting vice president."

Susan waved as she strolled down the hall.

Denida examined the ring under his glove. *I guess I have no choice but to talk to Henna.* He frowned at Nina and opened his mouth to speak.

Nina shook her head at him, as a composed sadness wrestled with bitter acceptance for control of her lips.

With a sigh, Denida closed his eyes and clenched his fist, teleporting away.

Denida's eyelids fluttered, only to squint against the sunlight from the twin suns reflecting on a castle's glassy façade. Denida raised his hand to his forehead and rushed inside to escape the direct light.

The castle's grand interior stood as bare as Denida remembered it from the last time he visited Henna.

"Welcome back, Denny." Henna appeared behind Denida.

Denida spun around in shock.

Henna smiled with her rainbow gaze. "I'm glad you had a change of heart."

"I didn't."

"Then why have you come? Did you miss me that much?"

Denida folded his hands together. "You can see the future."

"Not exactly." She leaned in and met Denida's eyes. "Didn't Lucifer's story tell you that much?"

"I want to know more." Denida wrinkled his brow.

"Think of it as a big tree. When a choice is made, fate branches and new options appear. The choices you make determine your future."

Denida lifted his finger. "What options will Lucifer's war lead to?"

"The end, one way or another."

*Yikes*. "I need to know how to end this with as few casualties as possible," Denida hissed.

"And you think I can help you with that… or that I want to?"

Denida bared his teeth. "If you want my-"

"I'm not Lucifer. I don't need to make a deal with you, to get your help. You will bring the end to God, Lucifer, and Gabriel in time; Destiny ordains it."

"Destiny, my ass. I care about protecting souls, so I intend to prevent this catastrophe. I've had enough of your galactic mumbo jumbo." Denida's eyes flared. "Goodbye." He teleported away.

# Chapter 2- Demons Appear

The Colonel sat in front of a cluster of seven monitors, which displayed live feeds from robots across the Underworlds. Naphtali spoke to the Colonel from World Eight's feed.

"Things will be different with Dan in charge, won't it?" Naphtali asked.

The Colonel shrugged. "I sure hope not. Denida left him in charge, so it shouldn't be that bad. Thankfully, we don't have any demons running amuck anymore."

"Yeah, everything's better, now." Naphtali smiled widely.

"I wonder…" The Colonel scratched his head. "- if this 'war' of Lucifer's will change that."

Naphtali's smile froze. "War?"

"The one against Heaven."

Naphtali gasped. "Lucifer wants war with Heaven? I thought God and Lucifer would always just have a private power struggle between themselves."

*Why does it matter?*

*"Beep,"* a monitor a few screens away flicked on.

The Colonel tilted his head. *Earth?* "Just a sec, Naphtali." He approached the monitor.

"Is anyone there? Demons are attacking us!" a soldier stared in the camera with wide, bloodshot eyes, as a demon tackled him, terminating the feed.

*How can demons be on Earth?* The Colonel wiped a bead of sweat on the back of his neck.

"John!" Naphtali hollered.

The Colonel blinked out of his daze and hurried back to World Eight's feed.

Naphtali sat hunched over at the monitor, drenched in blood.

"What happened to you?"

"Demons," Naphtali murmured. "Inform Denida."

The Colonel nodded. "Are you okay to get cleaned up and-"

Naphtali spun around to a scuffle. A pair of demons slammed him into the feed, cutting the signal.

"Naphtali!" The Colonel punched the keys and shook the monitor. "Work, dammit!" After a few minutes of his eyes growing wide with concern, he jumped up and ran out, sprinting though the offices, eventually slamming through a door. "Dan!"

"What is it, now?" Dan put laid his pen on his desk and frowned.

"Demons… Naphtali needs our assistance. It's not just Earth."

"Naph…" Dan leaned back in his chair with a pensive expression.

"On World Eight, the former demon," the Colonel reminded Dan.

Dan lit up, but bit his lip with concern. "Why are there demons in the Underworlds? I thought Denida ended that invasion."

"Lucifer threw Denida out of Hell. He doesn't give a rat's ass about Denida's deal, anymore."

Dan nodded. "All's fair in war, I guess… but why come to me? You're the head of the military, so you can send aid on your own."

"Have you forgotten how many worlds we have to go through to get to Underworld Eight? Get in touch with Denida, so we can use his ring."

Dan buttoned his jacket. "Follow me to the lab."

The Colonel saluted and accompanied him.

Upon entering the lab, Dan picked up a chunk of a Gate's central unit.

The Colonel glanced at his watch. "Sir, pardon me, but is now really the right time for some weird experiment?"

Dan ran his hand through his hair. "I don't get it. I was able to split the Gate's material to use a chunk of it for the time machine. Now, I can't..."

The Colonel frowned. "How would that help us with the demons?"

Dan slammed his fist on the table. "If we could make a ring like Denida's, we could send them straight to-" Dan's mouth hung agape. "Henry showed me, so I thought maybe I could, but I just remembered that Henry was Henna. She only wanted Denida to..."

"What are you talking about, Sir?"

Clarity relaxed Dan's features. "I can't make this myself. Head through the Gates, for now. I'll send Susan to Earth to ensure Denida's human form's safety and inform Denida to join you with his ring ASAP."

"Yes, Sir." The Colonel saluted and departed the room. He continued through the building until he reached the military division, where the Commander and Susan sparred together.

"Just the two I was looking for."

Susan gawked at the Colonel.

The Commander seized his opportunity and swept her legs. "Losing focus in a battle is a death wish; you should know that, Susan."

"Commander," the Colonel's voice resonated sternly. "Your dirty tricks are unprofessional and unfit for a skirmish."

The Commander's face soured. "Sorry, Sir." The Commander wrinkled his nose and extended his arm to Susan, pulling her to her feet.

Susan and the Commander saluted the Colonel. "Sir."

"Commander, we must go to another underworld to assist with a demon invasion. Gather supplies."

The Commander rolled his eyes. "We're going to finish the match, then-"

"Negative. It's a direct order!"

The Commander arched his neck. "I don't think it's that important that we go right this second."

"Can it, or face the consequences of insubordination." The Colonel turned to Susan while the Commander sauntered away. "Your orders are absolute while I'm away. Dan needs you to contain the demon uprising on Earth. I'm counting on you to keep the mission on track."

"Sir." Susan saluted.

"At ease." The Colonel followed the Commander and caught up to him at the task force barracks. The Commander informed the troops of their upcoming mission.

The Colonel marched around the room and scoped out the troops, finding their rucksacks already packed for their departure. *I never realized it before, but the Commander's not bad at motivating his soldiers...* "Commander, let's proceed through the Gate."

"The one next to us, Sir? Or to Earth?"

The Colonel shook his beret and smacked it on his leg before putting it back on. "We need to get to World Eight." He buckled a knife onto his belt before proceeding through the door.

"What-" The Commander sped to intercept him. "Sorry, Sir. We have to traverse several worlds?"

"Affirmative."

The Commander swallowed. "How will we get back? The Gates are all one-way."

"Denida will help us with his ring when we're ready to return, but we can't wait for him, now."

*I'd better bring one of these devices that can charge a Gate instantaneously, just in case.* The Colonel grabbed one of the devices lying next to the Gate. "It's time." He turned to the operators. "Charge it up!"

The Gate sparkled with a flash. The Commander shifted on his feet and faced the Colonel. "Sir-"

The Colonel clenched his fist. "Yes, let's move it, on the double!" He paraded the troops to the Gate. The Commander hurried to catch up, barely making it before the Gate teleported them and instantly powered down.

Several birds flew overhead when they exited through the other Gate.

The Colonel's eyes followed the birds, as the uniformed men and women continued toward a giant building, which the Commander could just barely see through the trees. The Colonel pointed at it. "That's our destination."

The Commander increased his pace to catch up to the Colonel. "Requesting permission to speak, Sir."

"Granted."

"Are we going to have to fight demons?"

The Colonel peeked at the Commander. "We have before…"

"But that was to defend the Underworlds. I don't think fighting is the right course of action, Sir."

"Well, we're not throwing them a tea party!" The Colonel bared his teeth at the Commander. "It's an order from the vice president. You will follow our orders, or do you wish to face a court-martial?"

The Commander lowered his head. "No."

"Good, then?" The Colonel spat.

"Sir, yes, Sir." The Commander saluted and slammed his other hand against his pants.

The Colonel smirked. "Forward, march." He led the troops around the trees to the building he had pointed out earlier. "Halt!" The Colonel instructed as soon as they reached the building's guards. He strolled to the front of the patrol unit and saluted one of the guards.

The guard's eyes widened, and he ran to open the doors. "Want us to lead you up to your office, President?"

*President?* The Colonel's eyes widened. *What is he- of course. The leader is one of my other souls.* "Negative. Soldiers, forward, march!" He surged through the doors with the troops tailing him. The Commander tagged along behind them.

The Colonel glanced at the directional signs inside and continued up an elevator. When he exited it, two guards saluted him and swung the doors open, letting the group pass.

The Colonel stopped in front of the president, who sat behind a wide desk with a puzzled expression on his face. "John, why are you here?" The president lowered his pen to the desk.

"We must use your Gate to continue into the next world."

The president's eyes turned to the troops, and then flicked back to the Colonel. "Sure, John… but why do you have so many soldiers with you?"

"One of the Underworlds needs our help." The Colonel sighed deeply and anger tainted his tone. "- to fight demons!"

The president stood. "Follow me." He guided them to the Gate.

The Gate stood in the center of another room and lit up as they entered.

*It's powered on, good…*The Colonel turned to the president. "Heaven and Hell are going to war, and the demons might appear here, next, so you should prepare your military forces."

"What… a war?" The president's eyes widened, and he examined the troops. "Thank you for the heads up."

The Colonel winked and saluted the president. "Forward, march!"

The soldiers marched through the Gate, followed by the Colonel. The Gate teleported them to the next world. They appeared on a grassy hilltop. The Colonel tapped the Commander's shoulder. "We're going to see another version of me in this world."

"Another?" The Commander wrinkled his forehead. "Why are there so many of you?"

"That's an interesting question." *I'll have to ask Denida about that the next time I see him.* The Colonel shifted his feet and turned around. "The castle's next."

They trampled down the hill, nearing a castle.

"Halt!" a guard outside the castle held up his hand. "What business do you have, here?"

*I'll let my face do the work…* The Colonel stepped forward and saluted.

The guard shook his head. "Looking like our colonel won't get you in. I ask again: what is your business, here?"

"We are from another Underworld."

The guard shrugged. "Nothing important, then. Leave."

"Hold on a minute." The Colonel stepped forward.

The guards cocked their rifles.

"I said leave!" The first guard approached, closing the gap between himself and the Colonel.

*No… we can't stop here.* The Colonel removed his beret. "I'm John, a Colonel, who has experience with fighting demons. I'm not trying to impersonate your leader. I'm his soul counterpart from another world and you will regret not letting us through."

The guard drew his sidearm.

The Colonel grabbed the barrel and pulled it closer to his chest. "If you kill me, my troops will kill you. We won't leave until we see your colonel."

The guard tightened his grip on the gun, while examining the troops. After a moment of hesitation, he lowered his weapon. "I'll take you, but your troops are to stay put out here."

"Affirmative." The Colonel snapped his fingers. "Commander, you're in charge."

The guard led the Colonel through the castle to his own colonel's office. He turned to the Colonel outside the room. "You'd better be good, if you know what's best for you." He knocked on the door. When an "Enter," echoed from within, he stepped inside with the Colonel.

"Sir." The guard saluted. "This soldier says he's from another Underworld."

The colonel leading this world's army glared at the Colonel next to the guard. "What's your name?"

"I'm a Colonel and the name's John…"

"Well, I'm a colonel too, so calling you John might be easier. What can I do for you, John?"

"We're from Lord Denida's world," John stated matter-of-factly. "You must know him."

The colonel behind the desk glared. "We?"

The guard cleared his throat. "This guy has more soldiers with him. They're still outside."

The colonel at the desk clenched his fist. "Bring them in here already, Soldier."

The guard nodded and scurried out of the office.

"So, you are the famous Colonel whom Denida spoke so highly of?" The colonel leaned back in his chair.

"And you're a colonel too, who's also in charge of an Underworld." John winked. *We do look similar…*

"And I assume you're here for a reason?"

John grunted. "Demons have been spotted in an Underworld. We're on our way to assist." His eyes remained locked on the door, before returning to the colonel at the desk. "You should prepare for a demon invasion, just in case."

The colonel jumped out of his chair and trudged over to John. "Why here? Denida assured me that by joining forces, those cretins would never come back."

"Lucifer is in an all-out war with Heaven; everything has changed."

The Commander trekked inside with the rest of the troops.

John smiled at the boss. "If you can't protect this world, just use the robot to send a memo to Denida, but we need the Gate, if you don't mind?"

The colonel's gaze intensified. He gestured at a picture on his desk, showcasing a younger Denida and John. "Denida gave me that to show me how much he values his friendship with you, and it meant a lot to me to see his respect for his military leader, especially one who happens to be my soul counterpart." He sighed, and a subdued smile crossed his lips. "The Gate's downstairs; follow me." He led them to the Gate, which shone as vibrantly as the last one.

"Sir." John saluted. "Good luck." He ventured through the Gate with the others in tow.

As soon as they stepped through the Gate, locals swarmed the troops and gazed at them.

The Colonel clapped, trying to get the crowd to disperse. "Nothing to see here, just a normal military unit."

The crowd gasped and stared, mesmerized, when they noticed the Colonel.

"Sir, we should continue," the Commander interjected quietly.

The Colonel snapped to attention. "Yes, we need to go see Nina."

"Nina?" The Commander frowned.

"Denida has informed me that Nina's soul counterpart leads this world," The Colonel remarked.

"Ms. President is at the castle," one of the bystanders announced.

The Colonel and the Commander exchanged a glance.

"Sir, yes, Sir." The Commander saluted and strode to gather the soldiers.

They all marched through the town, approaching the castle, which seemed architecturally antiquated compared to the rest of the city. The townspeople stepped out of the way but continued to stare and chatter among themselves.

*What a strange world…* The Colonel exhaled a sigh of relief when he finally reached the castle.

"Colonel?" The guards dropped their guns and swarmed the Colonel.

"Yes?" *This world gets weirder and weirder by the second…* "We need to see the president."

"Yes, Ms. President will be happy to see you, too." The guards directed them inside the castle.

A younger-looking Nina sat on a throne inside a spacious room, tapping her hand on the armrest. Her eyes widened at the sight of the Colonel. "That's not possible… you died."

*A teenaged Nina, how about that.* The Colonel furrowed his brow. *Died? What is she… oh, everything makes sense, now.* He shook his head. "I'm not your colonel; I come from Denida's world."

Nina cracked her knuckles. "Denida, yes. You must be one of the other soul parts of our late colonel."

"You know about the others?"

"I've heard of them. From what I've seen, most souls get split across several Underworlds, so their soul power isn't too strong. Denida's probably as powerful as he is because his soul is whole."

*That makes sense…*

"Then the Colonel must be weak, seeing as he's in all the Underworlds," the Commander chuckled. "But why is Denida so special?"

"I think I'm still too young to know that." Nina rose with a smirk.

The Commander stepped closer. "That didn't stop you from knowing about the soul energy…"

"You need the Gate to continue your trek, right?" Nina tapped her lips. "It's next to the time machine." Nina sauntered past them, only to stop at the door. "That's how I learned about soul energy; the time machine showed us."

Nina led them to the building that housed the Gate. "Lieutenant Colonel, these guys need to use the Gate," she instructed a soldier bearing a lot of medals, who stood next to the threshold.

He turned to salute them. "Welcome, I'm Lieutenant Colonel Anderson. Do follow me." He strolled through the building, over to the dim Gate that stood on one side of the building.

"Get the device from the time machine. These guys need to use the Gate." Anderson commanded a soldier, who hurried to fetch it.

The Commander turned his head to track the soldier Anderson had ordered. His eyes followed the soldier as he ventured into a heavily guarded area.

"Time… machine?" The Colonel stuttered. "You were serious?"

Nina smirked. "We're experimenting with it."

"No!" The Commander pushed through the crowd to reach the Colonel and Nina. "Your former president stopped that experimentation for a reason. Why would you start it up again?"

Nina raised her eyebrows. "Times have changed."

"Have you forgotten what happened before?" The Commander clenched his fists. "You need to stop this before it becomes a disaster," he hissed.

The soldier returned and inserted the device into the Gate.

"We do us… you do you." Nina waved. "Do take care in the next Underworld."

The Commander's muscles tensed.

"Commander, stand down! We're leaving," The Colonel rested his hand on the Commander's arm.

The Commander sighed and relaxed. "Yes, Sir."

The Colonel saluted. "For the record, I also disapprove of you using the time machine, but as you said: you do you…" He turned to his soldiers. "We're guests. Behave yourselves."

The Commander shook his head. "You know this will end badly, just as well as I do, and they will be defenseless when it goes sideways… especially if demons show up here."

"That's not our concern," the Colonel insisted.

"You know Denida will be against this."

The Colonel stared at him sternly. "We're going, and that's an order, Commander."

The soldiers stepped through the Gate, with their two commanding officers still talking behind them.

The Commander peeked at the heavily guarded area around the time machine and gritted his teeth.

"Think fast!" The Colonel tilted his head and pushed the Commander forward.

"Sir." The Commander steadied himself as the last of their soldiers marched through the Gate. "I'm sorry." He grabbed the Colonel's hand and forced him through the Gate. The Commander jumped back out of the teleportation stream as soon as the Colonel was through.

On the other side, the Colonel turned back, awestruck, as the portal faded. *He deliberately stayed behind?*

# Chapter 3- Beginning of the End

Denida knelt behind Nina and rubbed her shoulders.

Nina sipped a drink, while watching her horse, Angel, grazing next to them on the outskirts of the forest near Dynasty. She squinted with a tranquil smile. "More to the left." She rested the glass on her lap and hunched forward.

Denida focused on her other side.

"Ouch," she hissed. "Not so hard."

*Crap, she's not enjoying this. I shouldn't have tried...* Denida retracted his hands. "Sorry."

Nina glared at him, put the glass on the ground, and rested on her stomach. "Maybe you can try now, unless you're deliberately trying to disappoint me?"

"Of course not," Denida insisted.

Nina smiled. "Good."

Denida resumed rubbing Nina's back until she turned over, took Denida's hand, and stroked it. "This is nice."

Denida leaned in close and kissed her. She folded her arms around him and pulled him close.

Angel moseyed farther away. He grazed until dusk, when Nina whistled for him, and he returned to them.

With Angel close again, Nina rested her head on Denida's chest, stroking his hair. "We should spend more time together, like this, just us."

"I always want to. Work has just been extremely busy, lately."

"Maybe…" Nina's fingers trailed down Denida's chest, next to her head, and she fell into a slumber under the sunset's orange glow.

***

Nina strolled down a road on a misty night. She wandered into a garden behind a house. *I don't want to go there. No, stop!* It was as if a string pulled her to continue onward, despite her best efforts to stop her legs from walking. The sky darkened under an ominous, crimson cloud.

A spear rested in a bloody pool on the grass.

Nina cautiously reached for it. When her fingers coiled around the spear, thunder roared in the distance.

"Why didn't you come for me, Mommy?"

The spear fell from Nina's hand. "Daniel?"

Daniel touched the wound on his chest. "She impaled me and took my heart. Why didn't you stop her? Didn't you want to save me?"

"I did." Nina trudged toward her son. "Dad and I tried to find you. We searched everywhere. We even went to Henna's world to see you, remember?"

Daniel lowered his head. "But only Dad came for me when I was alive… when I needed you."

"I was on my way. I would have done anything for you," Nina pleaded. "Please believe me!"

Daniel stared Nina in the eye. "Then why aren't you doing more?" Flames engulfed him.

"Too late." Medusa jabbed Nina from behind and ripped her heart out.

***

Nina sprang up, startled, her face glossy with sweat.

*Nina?* Denida sat up and stroked her back. "Did you have a nightmare?"

"Yes…" Nina rubbed her eyes. "We should get away, just the two of us, away from all these bad memories. We need to find each other again."

"I don't know." Denida flinched. "The Underworld-"

"Dan is helping you lead our Underworld, now. You need some rest, too. Isn't it about time we focus on us?"

*She's right… Dan has things under control, and Nina needs me more than he does, now.* "Where do you want to go?"

"Away from this Underworld." Nina licked her lip in thought. "Didn't Henna give you an entire planet just for yourself? You said it's gorgeous and that only you can get there."

"Craym?" Denida frowned. "That planet is desolate, at least when Henna hasn't been summoned."

"We won't summon her. I want you all to myself." Nina smiled vividly.

"If you're sure you'll be okay with the isolation, I guess we can go there. Let's stop by Dynasty to pack."

Denida clenched his fist and returned to Dynasty with Nina, using the ring. He kissed her cheek. "I'll get our stuff." He stumbled up the stairs.

The butler stood at the foot of the stairs, beside a phone on a round table. "Sir." The butler extended the phone in his hand for Denida as he hurried to the stairs, but Denida just passed him like he didn't see him.

***

Nina frowned at the butler. "I'm here, but we're about to leave. Do you need something?"

"Susan is on the phone…"

*Not more Underworlds crap. We're on vacation now, even though it feels strange to go away with Denny without our son with us, anymore…* Nina exhaled heavily. "I'll take the call."

"You?" The butler's voice quavered. "But… she asked to speak with Denida."

Nina stepped around the butler and snatched the phone. "Susan?"

"Nina? I'm looking for Denny," Susan's voice sounded.

 "I can take a message, but he's busy right now." Nina rolled her eyes.

"Demons have invaded Naphtali's world. The task force went to assist, but they can't return without Denida's ring."

"They're the task force. I'm sure they can manage."

"No!" Susan raised her voice. "The demons are completely unhinged with Lucifer's war against Heaven. I'm on my way to Earth to keep watch over Sus and Den and stop the demons from advancing."

"Nina!" Denida called from the top of the stairs.

Nina's eyes widened. "I gotta go. I'll pass on your message to Denida, and he'll take care of the task force. Good luck, Susan, and be careful." She slammed the phone down and ran to the stairs, almost stumbling into Denida.

Denida frowned. "Were you talking to someone?"

Nina licked her lips.

"Nina?"

Nina shook her head. "No one. You pack everything?"

Denida lifted his arms, brandishing two full duffel bags. "Unless you want even more clothes?"

"I'm sure that'll be fine." She kissed his cheek. "Teleport us away."

Denida handed her one of the bags, pulled her into his embrace, and clenched his fist. His ring glowed brightly with a silvery shade, teleporting them to Craym.

They appeared on a planet surrounded by flowers, stretching out in all directions around them.

"Wow," Nina gasped. "There must be a flower for every color of the rainbow, here."

Denida bent over with his hands on his knees, catching his breath from the exertion of using the ring. "Yes, well… that's Craym for you." He sighed heavily, standing up straight. "Come, I know a house we can use." He led Nina out of the greenery and passed some houses on a quiet street.

*Denida wasn't exaggerating, after all; there's no one here.* Nina stared at the empty houses they passed on their trek to the one Denida insisted would be fitting.

Denida stopped in front of two grand estates. They bathed in the sunlight, which seemed even more vibrant than the sunlight back home.

Having observed the vibrancy, Nina turned her focus to the sky. *Oh, right... the two suns Denida mentioned...* "Why are there two suns, anyway?"

Denida shrugged. "I wish I knew. Neither Lucifer, Gabriel, or..." He shook his head. "No one told me. Anyway, this house is awesome. I remember it from the memories Lucifer showed me."

Nina followed him inside, expecting to see cobwebs and dust coating everything, but the house was as clean as if it had been lived in yesterday. "What?" Her mouth hung wide. *Why isn't there any dust?*

"Dust mites are too filthy to exist in her world," Denida said into Nina's thoughts. He ran his hand down her arm and helped her with the bag. "This way, Sweetie."

Nina let him take the bag she'd forgotten was still on her shoulder and trailed behind him, taking her time to examine the estate. Her eyes fell on a picture frame, stopping her in her tracks. *Is that Lucifer as a child?* She reached for the picture of a young boy between an older man and woman.

"Sweetie, why aren't you-" Denida stopped when he saw her holding the frame.

"This is the house the Devil grew up in?"

Denida glanced at the frame and flinched. "Yes, the young boy, Azal, lived here with his parents. Azal became Lucifer when Shaddai became God." He wrapped his arms around Nina and rested his chin on her shoulder. "That's in the past, though." He took the picture and set it back down on the counter. He reached for Nina's hand. "Time for us."

***

Susan approached the school on Earth with several troops close behind, but a block from their destination, they encountered a gory sea of bodies wearing Underworld soldier uniforms sprawled out on the ground. Every single corpse sported a hollow chest and chewed up heart. A deafening silence filled the air.

Susan knelt to examine the remains of one of the soldiers. She ran her fingers down his face to close his eyelids as she exhaled deeply.

A demon lunged from out of nowhere and thrusted his fingers into the torso of one of her fellow soldiers, who cried out in agony.

Susan sprinted to the injured soldier as fast as she could and slammed the demon to the ground.

The demon's eyes flared red. He effortlessly shoved her away, sending her flying back into a tree with so much force that all the tree's apples fell to the ground with a series of loud thuds. By the time the last apple hit the ground, screaming demons charged Susan's soldiers and tore them limb from limb.

Susan watched the grisly scene unfold through blurry vision. Dread roiled in the pit of her stomach, but she bit her lip to force herself back to her senses. Her eyes spotted the demon who initiated the attack, strolling casually through the carnage in her direction.

"Welcome to your new hell, Missy." The demon lifted her by her throat and propelled his hand at her gut.

*No…* Susan's eyes fell on the collapsing soldiers. A surge of adrenaline rose through her and she grabbed the demon's free hand. "No!" Susan spat in his eyes. "It's not over, yet." She headbutted the demon.

The demon released Susan in his shock.

Susan spun and sprinted down the road.

The demon shook his head. "After her!" he commanded.

The other demons gave chase.

Susan ran into a crowd of humans rushing through their morning commute.

The demons chased Susan, but when she disappeared into the crowd, the demons busied themselves with killing the humans all around them.

*Yikes…* Susan turned in terror at the first human's scream. *What? They're killing… humans… but how can they do that with Denida's magic seal?*

Susan raced down a side road and scampered inside a building. *It should be safe, here. I have to get to Denida's human counterpart… but how?* She slowly slid the door open ajar, but the screams had only grown louder, so she slammed it again, barricading it with her back.

Susan's heart thundered in her chest. She drew in a deep breath. *Colonel… what would you do? Wait, I know.* Susan closed her eyes and shifted from soul form into a tangible human form. *Now the demons may not notice me… as long as they don't try to kill me, too.*

Susan tore the door open and walked outside, deliberately avoiding eye contact with the demons. *I need to find a way around the school… maybe I should walk in an arc to create distance between us, but still pass them.* She continued down the road until the screaming subsided enough to satisfy her, before turning down a side road.

Several demons stood chit-chatting in front of Susan. "They have to be here somewhere," one of them remarked.

*They? Are they still looking for me, or are there others, too?* Susan stood frozen, hiding behind a car.

"Sus," a red-haired girl whispered, waving her over from behind a car.

Susan stared, confused. *Me?* She peeked at the demons once more, before slowly approaching the girl.

The girl ran behind a nearby building. "Why are you out here? They could see us."

Susan opened her mouth, but it just hung wide, unable to speak.

"C'mon, let's return to the others before it's too late."

"The… others?"

"You know, at the school?" The girl frowned.

*School*? Susan nodded. "Yes."

The girl weaved between abandoned cars like a professional athlete. She stopped in front of a sizable brick building and knocked on a side door. "Open up; it's Kate!"

A "*click*" indicated that someone inside unlocked the door, and it swung open. "Hurry!" A boy with long white hair waved them inside. He locked the door and added several additional padlocks. "Den is out in the main room with the others."

*Den… Denny? It can't be. Here?* Susan stepped back until she reached the wall. Then, she quickly closed her eyes and transformed back into her soul form.

"Huh. Where did Sus go?" Kate frowned. "Guess she already went out to the others…"

Susan's entire body trembled with nervous energy. Following Kate to the common area took her focus, but she relaxed when she saw other students sitting around the room.

"There you are." Kate waved at Susan's human form, who sat among the other teens.

"Yeah?" Susan's human form wrinkled her forehead. "Where else would I be?"

"Outside with me."

"Are you crazy? No way I'm going out there."

"Yes, *way*," Kate insisted. "I saw you over near the demons."

"Huh?"

A boy sitting next to Sus knocked on the table. "Enough bickering. You saw the demons; what are they up to? Do they have any idea where we are?"

"Of course not, Den. I would have told you if they were coming."

Den shook his head and leaned back in the chair. "We need to-"

"… stay vigilant." Sus smiled at Den teasingly.

He looked away with a red face. "… Yes."

*Why isn't Nina here with Den and Sus?* Susan watched her human form interacting with Denida's human form. Their interaction mesmerized her, piquing her curiosity. *How do they know each other? And why isn't he at the old school?*

Den stretched. "It doesn't matter; I set up traps, so they'll be in for a rude awakening if they find us."

*This is so surreal… I need to get back to the Underworld.* Susan marched out of the room and shut her eyes with a deep breath, but nothing happened. *What? Why can't I teleport?* She clenched her eyes and focused extra hard, but it yielded the same result.

*No… no… no.* Susan sprang through the wall, and ran out to the road, but stopped immediately when she reached the curb. She had locked eyes with a demon.

"My, if it isn't my dear Susan, the one who got away." The demon smirked. "Showtime!"

Susan peered back at the school. *This can't end well… I need to bluff my way out of it.* "You mean the one who will get reinforcements to come and crush you?"

The demons sneered. "How? You should know by now that the Darkness has been strengthened by all the souls we've harvested here. It's even stronger than Denida's spell and has laid a curtain over this town. It's ours and you're trapped."

Susan swallowed. "The Gate," she hissed.

"Oh. Do you mean the Gate that can also bypass Denida's seal and let you escape? Do you really think we didn't take care of that? You are stuck and your soul is mine." He smirked.

Susan bared her teeth. "There's no other way!" She spun around and sprinted back to the school. She passed through the walls into the hideout Den and the other humans had settled into.

Den and Sus sat playing cards when Susan returned.

"Demons!" Kate screamed.

Den flicked his fingers. "Let's lure them; get the trap ready."

*What's the trap they're talking about?* Susan watched them with intrigue as Den plodded into a computer room filled with monitors. *Interesting, they have video feeds of the school grounds.*

Kate appeared on one monitor, nodding at the camera, and pointing at the demons.

Sus grabbed a walkie-talkie. "Kate, we're ready. Lead them into the trap."

The demons noticed Kate's walkie-talkie.

Kate dashed across the playground, screaming, and waving her arms.

Den followed Kate from one monitor to the next. He rubbed his cheek uneasily. "It's time!" He hustled to the gym, moments after the demons chased Kate into it.

Sus rushed past Den, but halted as she reached the demons. They slammed the door open and dashed into the gym.

"Now!" Den yelled into his walkie-talkie.

A boy, who had allowed Sus and Kate into the school, jumped out from a bush, smashed the door shut, and locked it with four padlocks. "Done!" he hollered into the walkie-talkie.

"Same here," Kate's voice sounded in the boy's walkie-talkie.

Den issued a thumbs up. "Well done, Jakob."

Jakob kicked the door triumphantly.

Kate sauntered over from the other end of the building and whistled, waving her hand.

Den tilted his head, they reconvened with Kate.

Kate winked. "Let's find out why these things are killing everybody."

"Damn right!" Den followed her to a room with a security feed of the gym.

The demons rattled the doors at both exits. Then, they turned to one of the demons standing in the center of the room and shook their heads.

"What's your plan?" the demon hollered. "I'm an archdemon. Keeping me barricaded in here is only a temporary solution!"

"Why are you killing everybody?" Den asked over the intercom.

"Why not?" the archdemon chuckled. "The time has come for the final confrontation, so the Darkness needs as many souls as possible to crush the angels."

*Interesting.* Susan stepped closer to the monitor.

"Then leave us alone and kill the rest of the humans!" Den screamed into the intercom.

Susan startled and faced Den.

The archdemon sneered. "Why would I ever do that? Susan is here, not to mention Denida's human form."

Den frowned. "Deni...da... how would you know that name?"

"What's wrong?" Sus stood in the doorway, wearing a confused gaze.

*Crap... they can't know...*

"Besides, what do you intend to do to stop us? We can always summon more demons to attack you on the outside. Unless of course... you have an ace up your sleeve?"

Den nipped his lip. "Maybe we should just get out of here. There was this school I used to attend, which is so small that they would never think to look for us there."

*No... that's...* Susan inhaled deeply before exhaling again, reverting to her human appearance. "Hello, Den. The stories are real, after all. You're Denida."

Sus approached Susan cautiously. "What… are you?" She poked Susan.

"I'm your soul, who is supposed to watch over you, but I'm also a soldier." Susan pressed the button to speak into the intercom. "Hey, Demon Scum, missed me? Guess what; I do know how to kill a demon."

"You're bluffing," the archdemon wrinkled his nose.

"How would you?" Den eyed Susan quizzically.

"Shouldn't you know already?" Susan tapped her forehead and smiled.

"This can't…" Den ran his fingers through his hair and shook his head. His determined gaze rose to Susan. "Shoot their eyes to release their souls."

Susan nodded in affirmation.

Den turned to Jakob. "Get the BB guns, we need to shoot them in the eye to kill them."

"But how do you-"

"We don't have anything else. We have to try it."

Jakob pulled several BB rifles out of a cabinet of confiscated belongings and handed one to Den. "What do you want to do with these?"

Den tapped the intercom. "So, how do we find common ground?"

Jakob wrinkled his forehead. "I thought you wanted to use the guns?"

"I do," Den insisted. "I'm not asking to be friendly; we have to get close enough to shoot them."

"Maybe the attic?" Jakob shrugged.

"Perfect." Den gestured over his shoulder for everyone to follow him.

Susan trailed them upstairs. They stopped in the crawlspace, able to see the gym from the attic vents.

Den quietly slid a vent's loose panel aside to create an opening. He loaded some pellets into his gun. "On my count, aim for the eyes, but I take the first shot."

He lifted the gun to his left eye, clenching his right eye, despite not being able to see through it. "Three... two... one... shoot!"

The pellets struck the demons in the eyes. A dark shade wisped from their eyes as they slumped to the ground.

"See, I told you." Susan gloated. "I didn't think those guns would be enough, but I knew how to kill them, after all."

Den lifted his head. "Does this mean all my fantasies are real?"

"They're not just..." Susan sighed. "Yes, they're real."

Den handed her the rifle and stared out the window. Several demons charged the school. "Just what I expected. The archdemon called for backup. Let's get out of here before it's too late!"

# Chapter 4- Reaching Naphtali

"Sir." The Colonel saluted his counterpart in the next Underworld, a general.

"John?" The general mirrored the greeting. "What brings you here?"

"I need to use the Gate, Sir."

The general eyed the troops next to the Colonel. "If you insist." He smiled at a younger man next to him. "I'll take them to the Gate. I'll be back soon, Mark."

The general guided them to the Gate.

The Colonel increased his pace to march next to the general. "Mark's your son?"

The general hummed.

*Maybe a family might've been nice.* The Colonel scratched his chin. *It's great that at least one version of my soul decided to live that sort of life.*

When they reached the Gate, he stopped, waving his hand at the Gate. "Here you go."

The soldiers continued toward it.

The Colonel nodded with a smile, but the general cleared his throat. "Is there a reason you asked about Mark?"

"No. Denida just mentioned…"

"Denida helped reunited us. He seemed to be grappling with losing his son, just like I struggled with losing my wife. How is he doing?"

"Denida's doing better and…" The Colonel pinched the bridge of his nose. *I still don't understand how Henna could show them Daniel's soul, but a least they got their peace.* "The past is just that, the past."

"What do you mean?"

"Denida has accepted what happened; he and Nina are at peace now."

"Good. Happy trails." The general saluted.

"Just watch yourself; dangerous times are approaching."

The general lowered his hand. "Dangerous?"

"The Gates-"

"Yes," the general grumbled. "I know how dangerous they can be…"

The Colonel returned the salute and accompanied his soldiers through the Gate.

They appeared outside of a Gate on a hilltop.

"Forward, march!" The Colonel led his soldiers to the robot's location. *We're getting close, now.*

A woman in a military outfit stood in front of a checkpoint, which led into a high-security area.

"Master Sergeant Susan!" The Colonel hollered.

Susan spun around. "Colonel, you mean. How can I assist you?"

"Halt!" The Colonel saluted. "Colonel Susan, Ma'am, I'm a colonel from Denida's world. We need to use your Gate to the next world."

Susan glared at the soldiers. "Negative. No one goes there without the High Sorcerer's approval."

"Then I'd like to request an audience," the Colonel asserted.

Susan rolled her eyes and turned to the guard at her side. "Tell them that a colonel from Denida's world is here." She waved her hand, indicating the secure building. "There you go. They know Denida and can guess why you're here, but don't hold your breath; it's unlikely that they'll-"

"Susan," a young man identical to Dan appeared. "The High Sorcerer is expecting him. I'll take the Colonel to the Sorcerer."

"Alright, Dan." Susan saluted.

The Colonel followed Dan. Magic soared overhead until it struck a forcefield. The field deflected the blow back at the caster. *It's almost like we're back with Denida, fighting magic…*

"In here." Dan held a door.

The Colonel licked his lips. "A lot of magic here…"

"It's the Holy Grounds. They are practicing."

"Who? Practicing for what?"

"Welcome, John. I'm the Warlock. What are you here for?" A middle-aged woman stood inside the Holy Grounds.

The Colonel clenched his fist. "Ma'am, I'm seeking permission to use the Gate."

"The High Sorcerer is expecting you. Follow me."

"Yes, Ma'am." The Colonel peered back at Dan. "Coming?"

Dan shook his head. "This is as far as I go. The Warlock will take you the rest of the way. Good luck!" He closed the door.

*He is a strange one in this world.*

"Colonel?"

The Colonel rushed to the Warlock. She led him to the High Sorcerer and whispered something into the Sorcerer's ear.

"*Interesting,*" The Sorcerer muttered. "Colonel John, you have come, after all."

The Colonel frowned. "Do I know you?"

"You don't know me, but I know you." The Sorcerer stood. "One course of Destiny prophesized your arrival. In that version of fate, you were coming to see Naphtali. Is that why you're here, now?"

*Naph? Oh, that's the next world.* The Colonel gasped. "Who, or rather, what are you? How can you know what fate has ordained?"

The Sorcerer lifted his hand and an image of the Colonel sitting in front of the monitors manifested. "The beginning of the end has begun." The Sorcerer approached a door in the back of the Holy Grounds, but stopped before he reached it. "Your soldiers are awaiting your arrival at the Gate. The Warlock shall take you."

"This way, Colonel." The Warlock lifted her hand.

"No!" The Colonel stormed after the Sorcerer.

The Warlock materialized in front of the door. "You don't wish to do that."

"Yes, I do."

The Warlock folded her hands and raised them to her lips. "Do so, and the Gate will become off-limits."

"I understand," he paused. "We need to go back. My soldiers are still near the first Gate."

The Warlock nodded. "Like the Sorcerer said, we've already brought them to your destination. I'll bring you to them." She led the Colonel out to the courtyard and across the Holy Grounds to the Gate.

Dan stood in front of the Gate with the troops.

The Warlock gestured for them to proceed through the Gate.

As soon as the Colonel and his unit appeared in the world on the other side of the Gate, demons met them in a world enveloped in inky Darkness.

*This is not like what it looked like when I talked to Naphtali. Can it have changed this much already?*

"I've found more soldiers." A demon pointed at the Colonel and his troops, before charging at them.

The Colonel reached for his sidearm, but somehow the gun got stuck in the holster. He lifted his eyes. The demon had almost reached him. "Fire!" he commanded, only to register the ongoing sound of gunfire. His troops were already fighting their demonic combatants. *Crap…*

The demon slammed the Colonel against the Gate and headbutted the Colonel, making him drop to his knees in the dirt.

The demon leered at him with a repulsive stare. "Time to join the Darkness." His hands swirled with Darkness, as he raised one of them and clenched it.

A spear impaled the demon. "Sorry to ruin the party!" Naphtali ripped the spear out and reached into the wound to rip out his heart. He threw it on the ground and helped the Colonel stand.

"My troops…" The Colonel stared at them, relieved. Naphtali's soldiers had joined to assist them in their effort to dispatch the demons, just as Naphtali had done for him. "Are you sure you need my help?"

Naphtali's eyes turned bleak. "I do. Demons keep coming. My troops are waning by the hour. Darkness is filling this world again."

The Colonel tugged at his gun again, releasing it from its holster. His eyes widened. *How is it suddenly free?* "Where's the innkeeper? Is he okay?"

"The other side of the world is covered in Darkness again, so we're holed up at his inn."

"Who's leading these demons?"

"Leading?" Naphtali snorted. "If only someone were leading them. The demons keep coming from Hell and I've yet to see any real leadership behind the attacks."

"But there must be archdemons, right?"

"Nope, let's go before the next wave comes." Naphtali strode away.

*Not a single archdemon?*

"Colonel, we need to get away from this Gate. The demons seem to flock to it for some reason," Naphtali raised his voice.

The Colonel growled and spun around. He approached the Gate's main unit and pulled it out. "They are likely trying to enter the other Underworlds, but can't anymore."

Naphtali scratched his forehead. "I doubt it; they don't need the Gate to enter our worlds. Besides, the Gates are one-way, remember? Let's go." He wrung his hands.

The closer they drew to the inn, the thicker the air became. By the time they were at the inn, the air had lost its opacity, surrounding them oppressively.

"In here." Naphtali held open the door while his eyes fixed on the sky. "Hurry; the Darkness is growing."

"It's getting stronger." The innkeeper hunched over the counter. "My, my… the man with you, who looks like me, has something useful. Is that the device from the Gate?"

"Yes, Sir." The Colonel placed the device on the counter. "Denida taught me that this is made of a very unique material that contains strong magic. I don't know if the demons can use it, but we're better safe than sorry," he boasted. *I hope the other Underworlds we've already visited confiscate their devices in case the demons come to them, too.*

The innkeeper ran his fingers over the material, intrigued. "We can't stay here much longer. The Darkness will find us soon."

The Colonel turned to Naphtali. "Do you still have the robot with a feed to my underworld?"

The innkeeper raised his head from the device. "It's in the back room."

"Show me!"

The innkeeper brought the Colonel to the robot, and turned its live feed on. "There you go."

The screen on the robot pulsed with static for a few minutes before a face appeared.

"Sir." A soldier from the Colonel's underworld appeared and saluted.

*Where's Susan?* "I need to talk to Denida, Private."

The soldier shook his head. "Impossible, he hasn't come back yet."

"Sergeant Susan, then?"

"She's still on Earth, Sir."

The Colonel exhaled deeply. "When one of them returns, inform them that I must talk to them ASAP." He removed his beret and ran his palm across his forehead.

The innkeeper gazed at the Colonel. "So, you're the one who is me in another world?"

The Colonel rolled his eyes. *Do you really want to chit-chat now, of all times?* He marched out of the room to regroup with the others.

Naphtali shrugged. "Nothing?" He tossed the Colonel a duffel bag. "We need to go before they find us."

The Colonel inspected the bag. "But where do we-"

The front door flew off its hinges and demons swarmed the inn.

The soldiers assumed their offensive positions in a semicircle around the Colonel and Naphtali.

"Kill them!" A demon stomped over to the counter and retrieved the Gate's device. "One down," he snickered.

*No, we can't allow them to take that.* "Get the device." The Colonel pointed at the demon at the counter.

The demon bore a gloating smile and pushed his fist forward. The rest of the demons charged at the soldiers before they could reach the demon at the counter, who turned and exited the inn.

The Colonel rushed after the demon. "Stop!"

The demon sneered. "You're far from home, Colonel." He spun around. "You aren't as smart as they say; it's unwise to follow an archdemon, especially all alone."

"He's not alone, Bael." The innkeeper left the building.

"Hand over the device." The Colonel took a step forward, confronting the demon.

"That won't happen. I'm here to collect these." Bael glared at them. "But two versions of the Colonel, not good!" He raised his eyebrow.

The Colonel aimed his gun at Bael's eyes. "Give me the device, or else."

"I'm an archdemon; you need to remove my heart to kill me. My eyes won't be sufficient," Bael gloated. "I'm surprised you didn't know that having trained under Little Evil, and all…"

"That can't be true; Denida killed-"

"Did he kill an archdemon, or was it just a regular demon?" Bael lifted the device above his head. "No matter… say goodbye to this." The device faded from his hand.

"*Bang, bang, bang!*" The Colonel squeezed his gun's trigger repeatedly. The bullets blasted into Bael's eye sockets.

Bael chortled and teleported to the innkeeper. "Miss me?"

The innkeeper clenched his fist and punched Bael's head.

Bael flinched, thrust his arm inside the innkeeper's gut, and ripped out his beating heart.

The Colonel raced over to grab the innkeeper as he collapsed, catching him just before his body hit the ground, but the innkeeper's face remained empty. The Colonel felt a tingle in his fingertips, followed by a surge of energy welling up within him. *Wait, did his death make my soul stronger?*

"Guess you're the only one left." Bael winked.

The Colonel bared his teeth and slowly laid the innkeeper on the ground. "If the eye is insufficient, maybe I should try what you suggested." He unsheathed his knife from his belt and lunged at Bael.

Bael grabbed the Colonel's hand with the knife. "You think you, the insignificant human, can kill me? I don't think so." He glared menacingly at the blade.

The knife grew so hot that its shiny blade turned red followed by its hilt, forcing the Colonel to release his grip. The Colonel staggered back, cradling his hand.

"Guess I get to kill two Colonels today." Bael surrounded himself in a swirl of Darkness as he approached the Colonel.

The Colonel scoped his surroundings, noticing a glass bottle on the ground. He grabbed it and smashed it against the wall and shards of glass fell. "No, only one."

Bael slowly stepped closer, unfazed by the Colonel's broken bottle. The closer he drew, the more prominent the Darkness became.

*Shouldn't he be worried?* The Colonel's eyes filled with concern as he trembled in apprehension. He clenched the bottle tighter.

"That won't keep you safe." Bael gloated. He reached the Colonel, who thrust the bottle at the demon. The bottle vaporized as soon as the Darkness surrounding Bael touched it. Bael clamped his fingers around the Colonel's throat and lifted him off the ground.

The Colonel thrashed with all his might.

Bael, smirked, continued lifting him and tightened his other hand into a fist. He thrust at the Colonel's chest, only for Naphtali's arm to stop him.

"Long time no see…" A flicker of a smile appeared on Naphtali's face. "-although I wish we'd never met."

"Naph!" Bael released the Colonel, who plummeted to the ground.

Naphtali's eyes wandered over to the innkeeper. He stepped in front of the Colonel.

"The Darkness always wanted to get its demons back, especially the ones who escaped with the Dark Angels. This must be kismet." Bael winked.

"Then, the Darkness won't like me killing you." Naphtali flung balls of energy at the demon.

Bael crossed his arms, using the Darkness to shield him. The Darkness devoured the dark projectiles, which increased its strength.

Naphtali continued swinging his hands, hurtling fireballs at Bael instead, but the Darkness extinguished them.

*At least the fireballs aren't strengthening the demon...* The Colonel's troops rushed outside, having finished with the demons inside, and one soldier handed him his dagger. The Colonel whistled at Naphtali. "Let's go; we won't be able to beat him, now!"

Naphtali flinched before turning to join them.

The Colonel peeked at the innkeeper. *Someday, I shall avenge you...* The Colonel turned his eyes to the cloud of Darkness.

Naphtali prodded the Colonel's shoulder gently. "Let's go." He guided them through the world, which grew increasingly darker as they ventured farther.

*We're approaching the darkened side of the world.* "Where are-"

"We need to hide from the demons in the best place we can, in plain sight."

"Where?" the Colonel asked.

Naphtali winked. "Denida mentioned a place close to the Gate, where he met with Lucifer once. Of course, they would never consider checking for us that close to the second Gate..."

As they neared the Gate, a house came into view. The Colonel and Naphtali led the troops inside.

Mice ran across creaky floorboards and cobwebs coated the walls.

*Guess no one's been here for a long time. Maybe Naphtali has a point, after all...* The Colonel wiped dust off a chair and sat down. "What now?"

"I don't know…" Naphtali peered out the curtains.  "Maybe we should leave this world, but the next world is Hell. and if this world is full of demons, I can only imagine what Hell will be like."

# **Chapter 5- The Past**

The Commander stared at the Gate. *I hope I won't face a court-martial for this…*

Anderson cleared his throat. "Ma'am, what do you want to do with him?" He frowned at the Commander.

Nina shrugged shoulders. "Just power up the Gate and send him on his way!"

"You can't. It needs time to recharge." The Commander folded his arms. "Until then, you're going to listen to me when I'm telling you that using the time machine is a *horrible* decision."

Nina rolled her eyes. "That's your opinion."

The Commander marched up to her. "No, I know it is. Denida used time machines more than once, and things always went south. If you need another example, look what happened to your own president!"

Nina flinched. "You knew him?"

"Negative." The Commander stood in front of Nina. "But Denida told us stories about how dangerous Claus was and how using the time machine created conflicts in the past that ruined the future. There's a reason you need the Gate's power to use it."

Nina lifted her finger. "You've got a point." She pointed at Anderson. "Take the device back to the time machine. We're losing time where we could bring him back."

"What?" The Commander's eyes panned from Anderson to Nina. "How am I supposed to use the Gate?"

"You're not." Nina reached for the Commander's hand. "We're going to use the time machine, now. You're welcome to join us if you wish."

"What's so important that you need to use it?"

Nina bared her teeth. "We need to set this world right again." Nina followed Anderson.

*Again?* The Commander pursued them. He stopped abruptly when he reached the other side of the building, where Nina entered another expansive room.

A mechanism as majestic as the Gates stood in the center of the room. Colonel Lieutenant Anderson affixed the device to it. "It's ready, Ms. President."

"Did you set the timer?"

"Yes, Ma'am." Anderson handed Nina a trinket so small that it could fit into her pocket. "Just press this to return to our current time after you've saved him."

"Finally, he will see the woman I've become." Nina smiled at the Commander, who still stood in the threshold. "Do you wish to join us?"

The Commander shook his head in defeat. "*When* are you going and why?"

"For me to know and you to find out, Commander." Nina turned to Anderson. "Charge it up; I'm going."

The Commander shifted his feet before turning to Anderson, who turned on the machine. The Commander rushed over and reached for the switch.

Anderson swept out the Commander's legs and aimed his sidearm at his face. "Move, and it will be the last thing you do!"

"Good job, Lieutenant Colonel. You're in charge until I return," Nina smirked and walked into the time machine's portal.

"Now we wait for her to return." Anderson retracted his gun.

The Commander raised his brow. "Where has your president gone, Sir?"

Anderson tapped his foot. "To our former president..."

"But he died?"

Anderson nodded solemnly and closed his eyes for a few seconds. "President Nina wanted the time machine to go back to a time before Denida appeared and witnessed the former president's death."

The Commander peered at the time machine. "But why isn't she back, yet? It is a time machine, so shouldn't she be able to return to any given time?"

"Yes." Anderson peeked at his wristwatch.

"Demons killed the last president, you know. She might be in danger!"

"She can-"

"You're a soldier, aren't you?" The Commander raised his voice. "It's your job to keep your commanding officer safe."

Anderson spun to the dashboard and typed something. He raised his sidearm and pointed it at the Commander. "Let's go."

"Me?" The Commander's eyes widened.

"There's no way I'm leaving you here." Anderson pushed the Commander through the machine.

After exiting the machine, the Commander rubbed his nose and scoped out his environment. "Where's Nina? Didn't we travel to the same time?"

Anderson stared at his wristwatch. "Crap," he snorted. "I must have done something wrong. We're an hour late..."

"Well, she's not here, now..." The Commander rubbed his forehead. "Wait, Denida is coming to this world, soon. I know where he'll be."

Anderson glanced around. "Maybe we should just wait."

"Why? There are demons here, and she would be in danger if they got to her."

Anderson sighed and nodded. He followed the Commander through the Darkness-filled world.

The Commander hunched behind a boulder on the way to the castle and signaled for Anderson to do the same. "The Darkness is thick because demons are patrolling the area."

"Then let's just go around." Anderson stood up.

The Commander grabbed Anderson's sleeve and yanked him down. "No," he hissed. "The Gate is on the other side of the cloud."

"But demons…"

The Commander glared sternly at Anderson. "What if they've captured your president?"

Anderson bared his teeth. "You're right; let's go." He rose quickly.

The Commander pulled him down again. "I know you want to protect her, but we must move strategically so that *we* don't get caught."

They tiptoed into the dense, black cloud.

"This way," a feminine voice echoed from somewhere in front of them.

*Nina?* The Commander glanced at Anderson, only to notice the lieutenant colonel slowly trailing behind him. *I must make sure that voice didn't come from a demon.* He hurried to Anderson. "Wait here; I need to check that our path is clear."

The Commander followed the voices with his head down.

Demons stood around something, but they cleared the way for another demon, revealing Nina in the center of their circle. The new demon folded his hands, and a black flame enveloped them. "You will give us Little Evil?"

Nina giggled. "Yes, you can have him."

"You're certain he'll have the ring?"

Nina brushed hair out of her eyes. "Yes, but you must grant me permanent control of this world in exchange for him." She gritted her teeth. "As for the sitting president…"

The demon shook his head. "He's already met his demise." He lifted his hand above his head, strengthening the black flame. "It's too late to back out, now. We'll devour your world in one-"

"I'm not backing out." Nina stared resolutely.

*Is she trying to bargain with the demons? I need to get to Denida before they reach him and change the course of history!* He retreated to Anderson.

"Status?"

A lump formed in the Commander's throat. *Should I inform him of his president's dealings? No, we might not get to Denida in time.* He gazed toward where he saw Nina.

"Sir?"

The Commander sighed. "I can't join you… but your president is over there." He tilted his head forward. "I have to save my own president."

"Thank you, Sir." Anderson saluted and hurried to where the Commander had been.

*I've got a bad feeling about this, but maybe Denida can help…*

The Commander surged through the Darkness. The farther he traveled, the thinner the cloud around him became until it was nonexistent. Buildings lined the streets, but the giant Gate in front of the Commander stood surrounded by greenery.

*Time to wait for Denida…* The Commander marched in the direction of the Gate.

A hand grabbed the Commander from behind as he approached the Gate and flung him to the ground.

A demon appeared with eyes as dark as charcoal.

The Commander reached for his pocket and withdrew his combat knife. He staggered to his knees and prepared to lunge. They charged at each other, meeting halfway.

The Commander thrust his knife, but the demon's Darkness coiled around the blade, making it as slippery as butter. The knife slid from the Commander's grasp. He dropped to his knees and dug through the dirt to retrieve the blade.

"Too late." The demon clenched his fist and swung it forward, sending the Commander flying across the ground until he slammed into a tree.

*No, it can't end here…* The Commander gasped for air and tried to stand but collapsed with an agonized groan.

"Going somewhere?" The demon snorted.

The demon waved his hand and a dark shade shot out of it. The Commander froze with terror as it struck his forehead and he tumbled lifelessly to the ground.

***

Nina hunched over the Commander and laid her hand over his nose. *Still alive…* She turned to the demon. "You failed; he's still alive."

The demon flinched and stared nervously at an archdemon next to Anderson. "Master Zar?"

"Wait!" Anderson scurried to Nina. "Ma'am… President, you can't."

Nina glared at Anderson. "I won't let anyone stop me."

Anderson lowered his eyes to his feet, before abruptly raising his focus again. "Collateral."

"I guess." Nina strolled to the Gate. "They should be here, soon."

Zar teleported next to Nina. "If you are deceiving us in any way, you'll pay for it with your life."

"I'm not," Nina hissed. "Ask the Commander; he knows Denida's coming."

"We shall see." Zar forced her to her knees in front of the Commander and ran his finger across the Commander's forehead.

The Commander's legs jerked, and he opened his eyes, which immediately fell on Nina. "Have you had second thoughts about allying with demons?"

"Of course not," Nina scoffed. *What an idiot.* She couldn't suppress her grin. She raised an eyebrow at Zar. "We have an understanding."

"With him?" the Commander stuttered. "You do know who that is?"

"Of course, he's the one who can give me what I want."

Zar raised his palm. "She already knows that I'm a demon, if that's what you're asking."

"Denida," the Commander grunted.

Zar's eyes shot to the Commander.

The Commander trembled. "Nina, that demon killed your president."

Nina shrugged. "Really?"

"Yes!" the Commander yelled.

Zar rubbed his hands together and smirked. "I can't wait for Denida to arrive so that I can do the same to him."

The Commander wrinkled his nose. "Denida? Why would he come here?"

*No, no, no...* Nina grabbed the Commander and rammed him up against a tree trunk. "He's coming, and you know it." She shoved him again. "Tell the truth."

"Madam President, how can I? I've wasn't here when that happened this time."

*He's right; only Denida and Dan were here. Did I enter the time wrong?* Nina released her grip.

Zar's eyes flared. "What you need to remember, my dear Nina, is that a demon can read thoughts." He snorted. "I warned you that you would regret deceiving me." He extended his hand, which started to swirl with Darkness. It cast fragments of Darkness at a fixed point near them. A hole manifested in the Darkness-infused air, from which even more demons appeared.

"Kill them," Zar commanded. "Nina, as you draw your last breath, I want you to bear in mind that, I will kill your world's president because of you."

Nina shook her head. "You said you already did that!"

Zar raised his brows with a devious snort. "Haven't you learned not to trust a demon?"

Nina swayed to the side and ran to the Commander, with the demons right behind her. She yanked him along with her, not slowing down as she darted away. Anderson used his gun to shoot at the demons to slow them down.

"You caused this. You shall be tortured … but the president's death comes first," Zar's voice rang in Nina's thoughts as she retreated, not pausing to look back.

The demons halted their pursuit after a minute.

"Madam President!" Anderson called. "They've stopped chasing us."

Nina ran her hands through her hair and slammed her fist into a brick wall. "He… he," she muttered under her breath.

The Commander straightened his shirt. "What did you expect from a demon? Of course, he'd break his word."

"Only because you made him think Denida isn't coming!" Anger tightened in Nina's chest.

"What do you think will happen if he gets Denida?" The Commander shrugged. "We're in the past. Denida is the one who helped you kill them. He can't do that now that you have changed the course of history. There is a reason you shouldn't mess with time travel!"

*Smartass!* Nina threw a punch at the Commander, but he jumped back.

"You're just a little girl, playing with the adults, Nina. You tried and failed. Let's go back to the present."

"No!" Nina lunged, striking the Commander's face. "Not until you tell them the truth."

*"Bang!"* Anderson fired his gun into the air, stopping the altercation. "Ma'am, telling Zar won't make him honor your deal; he's a demon. More importantly, if we go back now, the present will have changed."

"You're right." The Commander rubbed his jaw. "Denida has to kill Zar and convince Nina to lead this world in order to fix everything."

*Won't be enough...* Nina sighed. "But we changed it..."

The Commander shook his head. "Negative. Zar doesn't believe Denida will appear. We just have to ensure the right events occur, or-"

"Or what?" Nina raised her voice.

The Commander shrugged. "You'll get a Claus future, where demons rule your world."

Nina's teeth clenched as if she were about to say something, but no words came out. Instead, she shut her eyes. *He's right.* "How, then? Do you know what happened, here?"

"Yes, Denida showed my colonel and me, so that we could learn from it."

Anderson frowned. "Then, he *did* appear around this time?"

"Denida and Dan appeared at the Gate and snuck through the haze to the-" The Commander paused midsentence. "We need to move fast; time is of the essence."

"Where to?" Nina asked with tense self-restraint.

"Where you first met Denida..."

*The hell? Where did I first- oh yeah.* "The president. We gotta save-"

"Nina, no!" The Commander grabbed her shoulders. "Zar has certainly gone directly to him."

"I'm not giving up; I'll go myself, if I have to." Nina stomped past them into the dark abyss.

# Chapter 6- Pursuing Nina

*According to what Denida showed us, there are demons in that haze.* The Commander stood in front of the dark air around the castle. "Nina probably went through that. We can follow her or take a longer route, but demons will appear."

"You said we might not survive if she messes with history." Anderson gritted his teeth. "We have to follow her."

The deep haze eclipsed most of the light as soon as they entered it.

Anderson walked a little faster because the Commander kept watch for a demonic sneak attack, but Anderson froze as a flicker of light emanated from the Darkness straight ahead. "Mr. President?" Anderson charged ahead.

*Not again.* The Commander darted after Anderson. Within a few steps, he spotted several figures in front of him, so he crouched and snuck closer.

"Maybe the light came from this guy." A demon tossed Anderson into a crowd of chattering demons.

*What am I going to do?* The Commander gawked.

"I saw it, too, but I don't know where it-"

"Shut up!" The demon leered at Anderson and kicked him in the gut. "You're on restricted land."

*This is bad.* The Commander unbuckled his belt and approached them. "Let him go." He rested his hand on his sidearm.

"Oh?" The demon who'd spoken grabbed Anderson by the throat and lifted him off the ground. "We can do to him whatever we please."

"Not on my watch." The Commander lifted his gun and fired it. The bullet tore through the demon's left eye, and Anderson slumped to the ground beside the demon.

The Commander crept to Anderson and helped him up. They marched onward, but the cloud now shrouded everything. A swarm of demons patrolled the castle grounds.

Anderson charged past the Commander with his gun still in hand.

"No." The Commander extended his arm to try to block him. *This won't end well...*

Nina stood up from behind a bush and waved her hand, which made Anderson halt in his tracks. He saluted and crouched behind the bush beside her. She peeked at the Commander as he neared them. "Your Denida arrived. The colonel has him in the barn."

The Commander surveyed the courtyard. He spotted a barn on the far end of the grounds, beyond the castle. "Good, they should leave for the castle soon."

The barn's doors slid open. The colonel stealthily led Denida, some troops, and an even younger Nina through the haze, as they approached the castle's front door.

Nina's intent gaze followed her younger self.

Denida walked through the door, as it wasn't even there.

"Guess everything's proceeding as planned," the Commander remarked.

"Not good enough," Nina bared her teeth. "We can still improve the present." She jumped to her feet.

"No." The Commander grabbed her shirt and yanked her back down. "We can't change *anything*, no matter how badly you want to."

"I can still stop Zar, with or without you." Nina headbutted the Commander, making him collapse to the ground. She clambered to her feet and ran toward the castle.

Anderson shifted his weight as he wrenched his focus from Nina's back to the Commander grunting on the ground.

The Commander ran his hand across his forehead. "Damn, that hurt…" His eyes met Anderson's. "Still want to follow her?" He snickered. "Life is full of choices; this is your opportunity to make a good one."

"She's my president."

"So?" The Commander frowned. *Ouch!* As soldiers, we usually just follow orders…." His shoulders slumped. "I disobeyed my colonel to stay here and protect you two. That was my choice. What's yours?"

"I can't," Anderson turned away.

"If that's your wish, follow your president, even if she isn't acting like one."

"I know she's acting foolishly, but I can't just leave her to die."

"We won't." The Commander brushed dirt off his trousers. "We must stop her before she messes with the intended course of events. I want you to remember this, so that you don't let her screw with fate again." He took Anderson's pistol and handed it to him. "Come on; time's a wasting, Soldier."

The Commander shuffled to the door, watching the demons carefully, to avoid putting himself in their crosshairs.

Anderson tailed the Commander. When they entered the castle, he cleared his throat. "This colonel of yours taught you well."

*Denida showed me where the president's body was. Nina must be there.* The Commander rushed farther into the castle. He stopped suddenly outside a room, where he drew his sidearm and sauntered into the room with the gun pointed straight ahead.

A body laid in the middle of the room, surrounded by blood spatters.

The Commander holstered his gun and turned to Anderson.

"Where's President Nina?"

*He's right; she's not here. If she's gone after Zar, Denida had better kill him soon.* The Commander's eyes creased with worry.

He dashed through the doorway and saw Nina and Zar walking out of a door across the room, only to see him backing into the room again with a cocky grin. Nina sprang after him, slamming the door wide open in her haste.

"I've got you now!" Nina waved a spear at him.

"Have you come to see me kill your president? You're too late and you brought this on yourself," Zar snickered.

Nina's eyes flared. "Denida is here. We can still make a deal."

Zar gloated. "I'm already aware of that, so I don't see why I need you, anymore." He rubbed his hands together and a dark glint appeared between his palms. "Anything else?"

Nina slammed the spear against the floor. "Why would I? You owe me."

"I owe you?" Zar mocked.

"Nina!" Anderson pushed past the Commander, who grabbed him before he was out of reach.

"No." The Commander yanked Anderson behind him. "That's a demon."

Nina lifted the spear. "You're supposed to die here, but I can save you."

Zar rubbed his hands together once more, enhancing the dark sparkle. "I already killed your president. Now it's your turn." He charged at her and thrust his hand into her guts. "Toodeloo, little witch." Zar ripped her heart out and spun around to fling the heart at the Commander, whose eyes were wide with shock.

Anderson scooped the heart up and bolted to Nina's body. He knelt before her and held the heart to the cavity in her torso.

Zar levitated off the floor. "Enjoy." He blew a kiss at Anderson and teleported away.

The Commander neared Anderson with increasingly slow steps.

Anderson sobbed with his head on Nina's stomach.

The Commander rested his hand on Anderson's shoulder. "We should return to our time."

Anderson clenched his fist, before picking up the spear. "No!" He poked the sharp end. "I'm going to kill Zar!"

The Commander shook his head. "No, Denida will kill him, just as he's supposed to. This..." He tilted his head to Nina's remains. "- must be her destiny, too."

Anderson shook his head violently. "I'll do it myself."

"You?" the Commander snarled. "I doubt you know where he went. And how? Denida almost died, but you think you can beat him?" He shook his arms emphatically.

"You know where he is."

The Commander rolled his eyes. "I know how Denida killed Zar, but he never showed me where." He approached Nina and withdrew the device to control the time machine from her pocket. "I am going back, Lieutenant Colonel. Are you coming?"

"I'm taking her back for an honorable burial." Anderson lifted Nina in his arms.

The Commander exhaled deeply and pressed a button on the device, teleporting them back to the present. He yanked the main unit out of the time machine.

Anderson carefully laid Nina on the ground and closed her eyelids with his index and ring fingers.

"I told you time travel was a bad idea."

Anderson gritted his teeth. "You'd better shut your trap if you know what's good for you. We need to bury her and-" He stormed over to the Commander and snatched the time machine's main unit. "- after that, I will go back and correct this disaster myself."

The Commander rolled his eyes. "I told you; it won't work. You can't undo a death. Denida already tried something like that and-"

"I don't give a rat's ass about your president. Nina is dead, so I'm in charge around here." Anderson whistled for two soldiers, who hurried over. "Lock this man up."

They grabbed the Commander by the arms and dragged him outside. They locked him in an empty cell in an adjacent building.

The Commander could hear taunts from the other cells.

"*Clang, clang.*" A middle-aged man grinned from the cell next to him. "Welcome, babe. Why don't you give me some sugar?"

"Sugar?" The Commander approached the front of his cell.

"Yeah." The prisoner beckoned.

The Commander sauntered closer to the bars. "Okay…" He ran his hand up the man's face and rested it on his cheek. His smile froze, and he yanked the fellow prisoner's face into the bars before shoving him back. *I don't have time for this; I need to find a way out of here.* He plopped down on his cell's bunk bed.

"What the hell, Man?" The prisoner kicked at the bars. "Just you wait," he threatened. "You're gonna get into an unfortunate accident in the courtyard."

*Courtyard?* The Commander approached the bars, where he could see the man. "When?" he demanded.

"Your death will be-"

"Yeah, yeah." The Commander grabbed the bars. "But when will the guards bring us out?"

"Not until noon tomorrow. Come to think of it, I might just kill you in the showers today, instead."

The Commander turned away and paced around his cell before returning to the bars. "We're both here, so wouldn't it be better if we get along?"

"Not until you pay for what you did."

*Not happening.* The Commander returned to his bunk bed and closed his eyes.

"*Clank, clank, clank.*" A guard ran his gun's barrel across the prison cell's bars. "On your feet."

"It's time!" The guy in the next cell cheered.

The Commander rubbed his eyes and stood up. "The courtyard?"

The guard stopped in front of the Commander's cell and glared at him. "No, just a shower for you, filthy scum." He continued down the row of cells, before spinning around and pressing a button. "Line up, kids!"

The Commander stepped into the row of inmates, and they marched across the building on the guard's command.

The inmate in front of him winked. "Payback's coming."

"It's not-"

"There's no time like the present."

The guard smacked his gun against the doorframe outside the showers. "Quiet."

The prisoners filed into the shower, while the guards stayed at the entrance, guiding them inside.

The Commander started undressing. An older man covered in wrinkles passed him with a persistent glare. *What's his problem?* He grabbed the soap and entered a stall. The Commander turned on the faucet and cold water dripped down onto his chest. *Crap, it's freezing.*

"*Creak,*" the stall door slid open and the prisoner from the adjacent cell stood buck naked in front of him. He held a towel in one hand, and soap in the other. He wrapped the towel around the soap and swung it, striking the Commander in the face. The assault continued until the naked guy suddenly smashed into the wall and fell to the stone floor. Water dripped over his skin, now accompanied by soap, running down his back.

The towel fell from his hand, and the soap slid across the wet floor.

The Commander froze with shock. The old, wrinkled man had a towel wrapped around the assailant's neck, like a garrote. His face tensed as he tightened the towel. The more the prisoner thrashed, the harder the old man squeezed until the prisoner's neck snapped, and he fell lifeless.

The Commander clenched and lifted his fist.

"Don't worry. The name's Trey. Let's get out of here before the guards discover him."

The Commander stepped over the body and followed Trey to the queue heading back to the cells.

More prisoners lined up behind them.

"A prisoner is dead!" someone hollered from within the shower.

Several guards rushed to the stall, while the rest hurried to the front of the queue.

"That neighbor of yours was always trouble," Trey whispered. "- but not anymore." He winked.

*Trouble?* "You knew him?"

"It's a small prison, so-"

A guard jabbed Trey's side. "Shut up! Everyone, get back to your cells."

The guards shoved the prisoners back into their cells.

The Commander stared at the empty cell next to his. *This didn't help me find a way out...*

Anderson cleared his throat. "Howdy, Commander. Enjoying the accommodations, I hope?"

"You here to release me, yet?"

Anderson shrugged. "Not until you help me get Nina back."

*Not this crap again.* "She's dead."

"Just tell me the exact time your president entered our world, and I'll do the rest." Anderson raised his brow.

The Commander shook his head.

"Maybe you need more time here." Anderson glared at the next cell. "Then again, you might end up like that guy."

The Commander charged forward and reached through the bars, grabbing Anderson's arm.

Anderson pried the Commander's hand away. Instead of releasing it, he yanked it farther out, pulling the Commander up against the bars. "You can stay here, then." He spat in the Commander's face before releasing him.

Anderson retreated with a vicious glare. "I will bring her back, with or without you; you'll see. If I need to kill your president, so be it." He strode off.

The Commander rubbed his wrist, staring down the corridor after Anderson. *I have to get out of here before he screws us all over.*

Several guards appeared. They continued past the Commander's cell and stopped at the one beside his.

A man cleared his throat. "Prepare this cell for the next inmate." One guard stepped in front of the Commander's cell, while the others entered the neighboring cell. The guard tapped his knuckles on his pants.

"Hey, Lieutenant Colonel Anderson was here. Do you know him?" The Commander leaned up against the bars.

The guard's face tensed so much that all his wrinkles showed his real age. "President Anderson, you mean."

The Commander flinched. "Nina's been buried already?"

"We're done, Warden," a voice echoed from the adjourning cell.

The warden nodded into the adjacent cell before turning back to the Commander. "Not that the likes of you would care, but yes, she's been buried."

"But..." The Commander gasped.

"Don't worry; he instructed me to execute you ASAP, so you will die this weekend." The warden raised his brow. "Having spoken to you, I can see why he wants you dead." He turned away.

"Wait!" The Commander clenched his fists around the bars. "Kill me if you want, but you have to stop him from messing with time."

The warden trounced away, followed by his guards.

"If Denida dies, everything changes. You have to listen to me!" The Commander dropped to his knees and clutched his temples.

A guard kicked the Commander's back. "Think about what you want for your last meal."

# Chapter 7- Nina

*Nice weather, today.* Nina meandered through the empty town with Denida, intertwining her fingers with his.

Denida caressed her hand for a few moments before releasing it. He ran into a meadow, only to return with a single rose. "I know it pales in comparison to your beauty, but it's the best I could find."

Nina smelled the rose and stared straight ahead. "What's with that castle?"

Denida's smile froze. "Bad news."

"We should go check it out."

"No," Denida retorted. "It's nothing."

Nina raised her arms. "But it's made of glass."

Denida exhaled deeply. "It's not glass. It may be pretty, but that's Henna's castle. I don't want to go there, and neither should you."

*Interesting.* Nina sniffed the flower and took Denida's hand, leading him back to their borrowed house. She rubbed Denida's shoulders. "You should get some rest; that was a long walk."

Denida shook his head. "No, I'm fine."

Nina patted his back. "Fine, but at least let me prepare you some tea." She entered the kitchen and brewed a cup of tea. Nina tiptoed back into the room to peek at Denida, who sat in a chair, resting his legs.

*It's ready.* Nina brought the cup to a countertop. Her fingers hovered over it, and she muttered a chant while stirring the tea. Satisfied, she lifted the cup and brought it to Denida. "Alright, here it is." She smiled tenderly.

Denida let the aroma sink in before he took a sip, then another. He blinked slowly. "What? I don't-" The cup dropped from his hand to the floor, and he slumped over in the chair.

Nina grabbed a rag to clean the water and set the cup on the table. She stood, gazed at Denida, and laid a blanket over him. *There, you should rest well, while I check out that castle...*

Nina ventured to the castle and stopped outside its doors. *It's menacing up close.* She swallowed and proceeded inside. The expansive halls glowed with all the colors of the rainbow. Despite the beauty, an eerie silence drew Nina's attention to the obvious lack of life.

"Nina." Henna materialized in front of her. Her voice echoed throughout the empty corridors. "What brings you to my perfect home?"

Nina stepped back. "I... I..."

"Where's Denida?" Henna asked matter-of-factly.

"He's at the house, where-"

"You know you are not welcome here."

Nina shook her hands. "Denida doesn't know that, and I used a drowsy spell on him, so that I could come here."

Henna's rainbow eyes became even brighter than usual. "I'm not concerned with Denida knowing where you are. Daniel perished, so it's time to focus on him again, and you're not supposed to be here. If I need you, I'll come to you. You never seek me out." She squinted.

*Screw that, I want Daniel back.* "No," Nina hissed. "I had to come. Is Daniel okay?"

Henna lifted her eyebrows. "I told you that our new deal's terms involved you getting your son back after you finished my bidding."

Nina shifted on her feet. "I'm working on that, so can't I just see that he's okay?"

"I've never failed you, have I? You can perform strong magic and are in a role of power, no? All you need to do is complete the task I've asked of you, and Daniel will be yours again."

"So, you won't show him to me?" Nina raised her voice.

Henna shut her eyes and tilted her head. She teleported behind Nina and thrust her hand inside her, and her hand glowed with a silvery light. "I made you and I can destroy you and your son."

Nina lifted her hands in defeat. "I'll keep Denida here."

Henna retracted her arm. "Make sure you do." She strolled away. "But don't use any spells on Denida, again. Use a potion next time, if anything. He's capable of strong magic, so spells won't work on him for long. In fact, you'd better get back before he wakes up." She raised her hand.

*It worked this time…* "Wait!" Nina yelled.

Henna turned to Nina inquisitively. "Yes?"

"I'm close to Denny, and I know from experience that he's not special enough for all of this. The Devil doesn't even give a rat's ass about him, anymore."

"And how would you know any of that? You're just a measly human whose sole purpose is to keep Denida away from his real soul mate." Henna shook her head.

Nina clenched her fist. "It's too late now. You *need* me."

"Need you?" Henna smiled widely. "What for? I knew it was a possibility that you would fail me. I have prepared for the scenario wherein you'll never see Daniel again. The question is, have you?" She grinned. "Your twin would've been much better bargain with so much less drama and defiance."

Nina looked to the side. "What twin? I don't have any siblings."

Henna raised her palm and blew air on it, forming a silvery image before her. Within the image, two younger versions of Nina played together.

***

The girls ran across a playground, where they climbed up a slide.

Henna watched the girls. *Time for their destinies to align with fate…* She approached the playground, her appearance changing into a child version of herself. "Hi, girls."

They glanced at each other.

"Who are you?" one of the girls asked.

"I'm Henna, and who are you?"

"I'm Nina. This is my twin sister, Nylah."

Nylah grasped Nina's hand. "Let's go." She attempted to pull Nina away.

"In a second." Nina dug her heels in to resist Nylah's pull.

Nylah drew in a deep breath that raised her shoulders. "Nina, we've never seen her around here before; she's a stranger. Let's go!"

"It's alright. I'm the same age as you," Henna interjected. "I just wanted to talk to you."

"We don't want to hear anything you have to say." Nylah tugged her sister's hand again.

Nina jerked free. "How about you let me decide for myself, for once?"

Nylah froze with a hurt expression on her face, which faded in an instant. "Fine." She dropped Nina's hand as if it were on fire. "But I'm telling Mom about this, tonight." She turned and ran across the sand to the other side of the playground.

Nina bit her lip. "Sorry about that; Nylah can be that way sometimes."

Henna nodded. "It's good that you can stand up for yourself."

"I really should go after her." Nina dashed over to her sister.

Henna followed them.

Nylah patted Nina's back and glared at Henna. "Let's go."

Nina bit her lip. "Sorry, Nylah has always been strong-willed…"

Henna's eyes widened. "But not you?"

Nina shook her head. "Not really, but I'd better go with her." She ran after her sister.

*So, fate's taking that course… Nina, not Nylah…* Henna strolled after them. "I've got something you may like."

"Yeah? Are you leaving?" Nylah snarled.

"Something a lot more intriguing." Henna reverted to her adult form, and the world around them froze in its place.

Nina clenched her sister's arm.

"What is this?" Nylah yanked her arm free and approached one of the kids, who'd stopped his swing set ride mid-pump. She poked his cheek and turned to Henna. "What are you?"

Henna's smile widened, her rainbow eyes shining. "Why don't I show you?" She raised her arm. Their surroundings vanished and, in their place, a cloudy surface formed.

Nylah watched, intrigued. "Where are we?"

"This is the only entrance to my world; it never stays in the same place." Henna approached the Gate. "Where we are now isn't as important as where we're going." She sauntered over to a side of the giant Gate and blew on it. A speck of silvery dust exited her mouth and caressed the Gate, powering it on.

Nylah clutched Nina's hand. "We're *not* going in there."

Henna spun around. "No, Nylah? Are you certain that you don't wish to see what I can show you? You already saw what I can do. Do you really want to go home, never seeing what lies beyond the Gate?" She lifted her gaze to Nina. "What about you? Do you wish to return home, too?"

Nina tugged her hand free. "No!" She marched through the Gate.

Henna extended her arm to Nylah. "Wish to join us, my dear?"

Nylah shot Henna a vicious stare. "She's my sister; I'm not leaving her alone with you." She shoved past Henna and stomped through the Gate.

Henna chuckled. *They chose my favorite course of destiny.* She joined them inside the Gate.

"Th-this isn't r-right," Nylah stuttered, watching a strange crowd of people wandering through a world that looked nothing like the playground they'd left.

Nina ignored her and continued into the crowd, intrigued.

"Why don't you think so?" Henna stopped next to Nylah.

Nylah shrugged. "Something feels off."

"Perhaps it might help to know what this place is."

Nylah's eyes widened and shifted to Henna.

Henna's smile broadened. "This is where dead souls reside."

Nylah gasped. "Dead souls?"

"When a soul dies, it comes to this world, one only I can enter."

"This place is awesome." Nina sauntered up to them with a smile. "It's so intriguing; the people and buildings look like they're from all over."

Henna clapped her hands loudly. "If you find this place interesting, you will like this, too," She smirked at Nylah. "- both of you will." She rubbed her hands rapidly, and a silvery light emanated from them. It enveloped them, and an image formed.

An older version of one of the girls wandered down a path.

"Is that…" Nylah pointed at the woman.

"You're twins." Henna shrugged. "It could be either of you. Destiny is like a tree. You can always choose a different branch. I only know what happens on the paths, not which one you will choose."

Nylah clenched her fist. "Then why are you show-"

"Henna," the woman in the image remarked.

An identical Henna appeared in the vision and folded her arms. "Hello, Nina."

"I have fulfilled your desires. Denny is on his way to complete your prophecy."

The image of Henna ran her finger over her upper lip. "I know. Have you come for your reward? Do you want me to make you a goddess?"

The older Nina rubbed her hands greedily. "Yes, I have waited for this forever, and what I want-"

Henna flicked her fingers. The greyish cloud around them vaporized along with the image. "This is but one possible outcome."

Nylah peered back at where the image had been. "But that's Nina's destiny. What are you offering me? Heck, what is your price, and what do you want us to do for you?"

"That was just one version for only one of you." Henna winked at Nina. "This, you see, is my world. You saw what I can do. I can make you both goddesses or grant you your every desire."

"You didn't tell us your price," Nylah hissed.

"I want you to help me with someone."

Nylah rolled her eyes. "Take us back home."

"Wait." Nina stepped in between them. "What exactly will you give us?"

"Nina," Nylah hissed.

"No, Nylah. Let's hear her out." Nina batted her eyelids at Henna. "Well?"

Henna loosened her fist and blew into it. The silvery dust that she exhaled from her lips flew over Nina and Nylah, and in a split second, they appeared back on the playground where Henna first encountered them. Henna's gaze met Nina's. "What would you like?"

"How did you do that?"

"You gotta be kidding me!" Nylah threw up her arms.

***

"Remember?" Henna smirked at Nina when the image faded.

Nina exhaled deeply. "Nylah, yes. I haven't thought about her in gosh… before Denida."

"I know." Henna chuckled. She wanted it that way."

"She?" Nina gasped. "My sister? That's impossible."

"Think so? You'd be surprised." Henna's rainbow eyes grew in intensity. "I'll show you. After you agreed to help, I knew she would want to, too. She just needed an extra nudge."

The image reappeared.

***

Nylah jogged down a path, looking older, like a young adult. She stopped, sitting down with her head between her legs, heaving in deep breaths.

"Hi Nylah, long time no see."

Nylah raised her head from her legs. She swiftly lowered it again. "What do you want, Henna? Nina's already agreed to help you."

"I'm here to see you."

Nylah bared her teeth. "There are Dark Angels here. All you did was endanger her."

Henna shrugged. "Nina made her choice, but she'll be fine. The Dark Angels don't kill her in any of her possible futures."

Nylah wiped some sweat from her forehead. "What do you want?"

"You could have what your sister-"

"No!" Nylah shoved past her and resumed her jog, running as fast as her legs could bear. When she reached her house, Henna stood at her front door, waiting.

"You are very displeased with your sister, no?"

"I disagree with what she's doing. This world is just as doomed as she is. Whatever power you can grant her isn't worth it."

"Are you sure about that?"

"Yes." Nylah spat on the ground.

Henna stared at the trail, then back up at Nylah. "Let me show you one last thing. If you still insist, I'll leave you alone. Deal?" She held out her hand.

"Showing me my future won't-"

"I would never insult your intelligence like that."

"Still…" Nylah walked up to the house.

"If you still say no, I'll retract my offer to Nina!" Henna called as Nylah passed her.

Nylah paused, turning her head with a chuckle. "Alright, do your best." She reached for Henna's hand. As soon as her hand held Henna's, they teleported away.

Nylah examined their surroundings as they manifested somewhere else. They stood in a field, where an eight-legged horse grazed. "Where have you taken me this time? A future with genetic manipulation?"

"That's just my horse." An elderly man with a patch over his eye approached them. He stopped next to Henna and bowed. "My queen, what brings you hither?"

"Nylah, meet Odin of Valhalla. I'm sure you've heard the legends about him, no?" Henna smiled.

Nylah's stony face filled with questions as she scrutinized Odin, but she quickly turned back to Henna. "Come on; you really expect me to believe that you're introducing me to a god?"

Odin cleared his throat. "The goddess made me who I am. I shall serve her until the end of time."

Nylah bit her trembling lip as her eyes settled on the strange eight-legged horse again. "The goddess?" Her attention drifted to Henna. "You?"

Henna nodded. "Odin was a citizen from my own world until fate chose him to become a god."

"No." Nylah shook her head. "I don't believe this. You can do some magic, sure. But a god, no way."

"Well-"

"I'm not listening to any more of this drivel; just take me back! You told me you would leave me alone after this and bring Nina back. Odin of Valhalla is nothing but a myth for people to believe in."

Henna met Odin's gaze. "Show her."

Odin lifted his arm, and a scepter appeared in his grasp. He slammed it into the ground. Their surroundings changed, revealing crowds staring at them.

A man with a giant hammer hanging on his belt approached them and bowed to Odin. "Father."

"Seen enough, or do you need more to believe me?" Hanna frowned.

Nylah shook her head. "Only a few people follow his religion. Do you have God following you, too?"

Odin's face paled. He spun and approached his horse without a word.

"God is the reason I'm still here. He killed me. I'm here to set things right, so that I can return to my world in peace." Henna shrugged. "Remember the future I showed you and Nina? I can see the path you can take to help us, and I know that our desires will never have a chance to come to fruition without you."

"That's why Nina joined you?"

Henna peered at her fingers. "No, I never showed her any of this. She just wanted the power I could grant her."

Nylah clicked her tongue against her teeth. "Power?"

"I'm the ultimate goddess of this world. I made everything you see, so yes, I can grant her power."

Nylah gazed at Odin. "As well as make someone a god?"

"If they so desire, yes."

Nylah gritted her teeth. "But Nina is already helping you. You want me to take her place?"

Henna bent her fingers, making everything around them disappear. "Nina is operating in the soul realm; you would not. I want you on Earth with your and Nina's human form."

Nylah grunted. "If you want that, I have a condition."

Henna wrinkled her forehead. "Making demands, now?"

"Only one: I don't care about my sister. I doubt she even thinks about me. We haven't talked for a long time, so please make everyone forget me. If you can achieve that, we've got a deal."

"That's easy." Henna flicked her fingers, sending them back to the Underworlds.

"Nylah!" A girl ran up to her. "Where've you been? I was looking for you."

Henna shut her eyes, only to open them again with her rainbow color shining. She lifted her palm. "Nylah, away," she whispered, blowing out a gust of silvery ash from her lips.

The girl in front of them stood, bewildered. "Who are you?" She spun around and strolled off.

Nylah clicked her tongue against her teeth. "Can I see how Nina is doing before we go?"

"Your wish is my command." Henna stalked onwards, with Nylah following close behind.

Nina stood next to an older man with a stony expression. "I want to help you fight Danyel and the rest of Dark Angels. I have access to the info you need, so you can trust me."

"I don't know," the man hesitated.

"Colonel, they wouldn't suspect me; I have an innocent face." Nina took the Colonel's hand and held it up to her chest.

"See, she is doing well." Henna smiled.

"What is she doing? Why would she…"

"She has started her mission for me, as you will on Earth."

Nylah spat on the ground. "And what exactly do you want from us?"

"Destiny is ripe; my prophecy shall unfold in the next few years-"

Nylah sighed loudly. "Get to the point."

"The child I prophesied to bring an end to Shaddai, Azal, and Gabriel has been born. I need you to ensure that he does not meet his destined soulmate."

"Why?"

"I've seen the possible destinies. If he meets her, he won't follow his ordained path. Nina will be distracting his soul, and you will make sure he doesn't get close to his soulmate on Earth."

"How?"

"You will control your human from inside her; come."

Nylah's eyes tightened at the sight of Nina. "Bye, Sissy." She grabbed Henna's hand, and they teleported to Earth.

***

"Nylah… th-that's-" Nina held her hands over her mouth. "Why are you telling me, now?"

"It serves a purpose, but as you can see, even if you fail me, your sister is my contingency plan." Henna looked down the vacant castle's hall. "You are to handle Denida's soul side, and your sister will monitor his human form from inside your human body."

Nina gaped. "But how?"

"My magic can enable oddities, including granting you and your sister abilities that you shouldn't have, unless you've forgotten?" Her eyes turned rainbow. "So, return to Denida before your sister accomplishes her mission, first." Henna flicked her fingers, and Nina appeared in front of the house.

*The hell?* Nina gazed around.

"Nina?" Denida approached her from the garden, rubbing his forehead. "What happened? I don't remember, but I have an odd feeling."

Nina hurried over to Denida and helped support him. "Let's get you inside."

# Chapter 8- The Escape

The Commander tugged some of the bricks, scuffed the floor, and shook all the bars in his cell. *There's no way out of here. I should have followed the Colonel instead of getting caught up in this mess.*

"You have until Sunday evening, Mister." A guard leered through the bars.

The Commander stood up straight. "As a soldier, I will face my end with dignity."

The guard rolled his eyes. "Whatever you say. I guess that means you don't care about getting some fresh air in the courtyard?"

*Maybe I can escape from there.* "I do." The Commander straightened up.

The Commander strode into the crowd and moved to the brick wall around the courtyard's perimeter. He slowed down as he gently ran his hand over the wall as he paced.

"Hey." The old man from the shower strode over.

The Commander paused and retracted his hand. "Trey, right?"

Trey nodded. "I heard what they'll do to you-"

The Commander shook his head. "I'm not giving up just yet."

Trey peered over his shoulder and leaned in. "Good, because I can help you escape."

"Really?"

"Yes," Trey whispered. "I can't do it alone, but with another pair of hands."

The Commander pursed his lips. "How?"

"Do you remember your neighbor?" Trey chuckled.

"You killed him," The Commander snarled.

"His body will be transferred to the morgue."

"And?" The Commander shrugged.

"You're not listening. The morgue is downtown."

"Wait; you planned this?" the Commander raised his voice.

Trey hushed the Commander and casually waved at the guards staring at them. When the guards turned away, Trey faced the Commander. "Come with me."

They moseyed through the courtyard, until Trey stopped in front of a few inmates lifting weights. "He was a bad seed, but this is an opportunity for both of us." Trey shot the Commander a severe expression. "We have to decide now if we're going to take this chance; the body leaves at dawn."

"I will be executed Sunday, so affirmative, but how can we possibly escape with the body? There must be a security detail."

"Time's up!" A row of guards opened the prison door. "Line up," one commanded.

"I'll let you know, tonight." Trey sped over to the queue.

*Tonight, how?* The Commander followed Trey.

"No, you don't." A guard cocked his gun at the Commander. "Your line is over there." He nudged the Commander toward his own queue.

*Not good.* The Commander gazed back at Trey, as he was led back inside.

*Two days… what am I going to do?* The Commander rubbed his hands together and slammed his fist into his cell's wall. He slid to the floor with an enormous sigh.

*** 

The Colonel stared through the shades over a window in the shack. "They can't sense that you're a former demon?"

"No," Naphtali whispered. "Once a demon, always a demon. Why do you ask?"

The Colonel retreated from the window. "Denida was cocky enough to try to get out with his demonic form. I was wondering if we could try that, too."

"To outsmart the demons?"

The Colonel knelt in front of Naphtali. "To use the Gate before Bael gets us. We can't beat them ourselves, and Denida might be-" He shook his head. "He's not here, so something must be awry in our world, too."

"Are you nuts?" Naphtali slammed his fist on the table. "That Gate leads to Hell!"

"Do you have another idea? Bael rendered the first Gate out of commission."

"I swore I'd never to return to Hell." Naphtali's eyes shone with horror. He shook his head. "We can't just sneak in, either; there are too many of us."

*That's true.* The Colonel tapped his chin with his palm.

"I can avoid the demons, here." Naphtali shrugged. "I would rather do that forever than go back to Hell."

"Where there's a will, there's a way. Can't we all masquerade as demons?"

"No." Naphtali scowled.

The Colonel returned to the window. *Bael...* "Bael!" he hollered.

"What about him?"

"He can get us to the Gate."

Naphtali spun out of his chair and rushed to the window. "No, we can't let him find us."

"We're out of options. Think fast, everyone!" He charged to the door and wrenched it open.

Bael stared at the sound, and his eyes darkened instantly.

The Colonel's gaze soured as he rushed back inside.

Bael pursued the Colonel. He thrust his arm forward, sending a wave of energy in the direction of the door, making it fly off its hinges.

"Wait!" Naphtali crossed his arms into an x-shape, creating a forcefield between Bael and everyone else. "You don't want to run this place! This is the Dark Lord's inn."

"The Dark Lord only cares about one thing now: strengthening the Darkness." Bael swung his arms left and right, making portals appear throughout the room. Demons started streaming into the inn from the portals. "I told you I would get you, and now I can," he snarled. "Kill them."

The demons spattered Naphtali's forcefield with dark magic attacks.

Naphtali flinched. "There's too many."

"Aim for the eyes!" the Colonel yelled. He fired his gun and his troops followed suit.

Bael grunted and stroked a circle in the air with his hands, while muttering a chant. His spell created a wide, dark ball. When it was darker than a black hole, Bael grabbed it, spun around, and chucked it into the room. It created a vortex, filling the room from the floor to the ceiling.

The soldiers gunned down many demons, but twice as many appeared from the vortex. They burst through Naphtali's forcefield effortlessly.

The soldiers shot them as quickly as they could.

*We need to kill Bael.* The Colonel aimed his gun, but the multitudes of demons made it impossible to target Bael, so he grabbed his knife and charged into the crowd. He impaled every demon he encountered in the eye. Through the sea of demons, he saw Bael standing in wait.

"Little Evil's colonel… I shall enjoy this." Bael snickered.

"Too late." The Colonel lifted his gun and emptied the magazine. The bullets shredded Bael into skin and holes, yet he remained standing, as if time had halted his demise.

Bael's eyes blackened to the shade of charcoal, and his face shifted into that of another demon before he tumbled to the ground.

*What?* The Colonel knelt beside the body. "It wasn't him?"

"Dark magic." A demon stepped on the floorboard.

The Colonel spun around with his gun raised.

The demon's eyes darkened, and his face transformed into Bael's.

The Colonel squeezed the trigger. "*Click.*"

Bael shrugged. "What a shame; you've used all your bullets."

The Colonel dropped the gun and grabbed his knife. "I don't need them." He thrust it forward, but it banged against an invisible cone.

"You really thought it would be that easy? Denida sure knows how to pick them." Bael rammed his arm forward, creating a gust of wind, sending the Colonel flying across the room, smashing straight into his fellow soldiers.

Naphtali rushed to The Colonel's side.

"Evil always wins." Bael clenched his fist and turned his focus to the demons. "Grab them!"

***

"Ouch!" The Commander opened his eyes against piecing pain.

A guard retracted his leg from kicking the Commander's back. "Stay awake, Soldier Boy. Death shall befall you soon enough." He stepped past the Commander.

Rows of footsteps clinked on the floor as they passed the Commander's cell and stopped in front of a neighboring cell.

The Commander approached the bars. "What's going on?"

The guard locked the cell and wordlessly glared at the Commander. He marched past his cell.

"Hey!" The Commander rattled his cell's bars.

"You should stay quiet." Trey's face pressed up against the neighboring cell's bars.

"What are you doing here?"

Trey issued a thumbs up. "I convinced the guards to move me to this cell. I told you; time is of the essence."

The Commander's fingers coiled around the bars. "But how do we-"

Trey hushed him. "Quiet, give me some time." He waved his hand and banged on the bars before extending his arm again. "Let me know if anyone's approaching, okay?"

*What a strange request.* "Sure," The Commander's voice shook.

"Good to hear." Trey stepped out of view.

The Commander watched the row of cells, staring intently for so long that he rested up against the bars. He peeked at Trey's cell occasionally. *What is he doing that requires privacy?*

"*Clunk.*" A low, mechanical rumble followed by a sharp "*click,*" sounded behind the Commander, who swiftly spun around. His eyes traveled to the cell's back wall, where a brick next to the toilet had fallen from the wall.

*What the...* The Commander crawled next to the toilet and examined it. Another brick fell and hit the floor when he reached it. He picked up one of the bricks and clutched it tight, ready to strike. He spotted a flicker of movement through the hole created by the bricks.

"Get back," Trey's voice emanated from the dark hole.

*Trey?* The Commander retreated.

Trey emerged from the hole. He waved his hand. "Follow me."

The Commander shifted his weight to his other foot.

Trey crept out of the hole. "Come on; we must hurry."

"How did you dig that tunnel so fast?"

Trey rolled his eyes. "The cellmate beside you was preparing an escape, so he dug this."

"And you killed him?" The Commander bared his teeth.

Trey lowered his head. "He shafted me. After all the help I gave him, he was going to escape by himself..." He sighed deeply.  "- leaving me to take the fall for it. I've been here for too long, to have it almost be all for naught..."

"And how would you know that? I doubt he would willingly tell you," The Commander mocked.

Trey wiped some sweat from his forehead. "I overhead him talking to another inmate about a plea deal that would frame me."

The Commander strolled over to his bed and adjusted the covers to create the appearance of a person on the cot. "Alright, I'm ready to give your plan a go."

Trey crawled into the hole.

The Commander took a piece of linen with him and cautiously followed Trey. When he entered the hole, he spun around, rolled up the cloth, and blocked the tunnel's entrance with it before creeping after Trey.

After a long crawl, a light appeared at the end of the tunnel.

Trey slowed to a halt. "We must get in the hearse outside before it leaves." He increased his pace to the exit, where he snuck out behind a car.

*He sure is frigid for a civilian.* The Commander crept down behind the car.

Armed guards patrolled around the hearse as a guard loaded the body into it.

The Commander gritted his teeth and turned to Trey. "We have to get in that hearse?"

Trey nodded. "When we can find a way around the guards" He nipped his fingertip.

The Commander shook his head. "That's easy. They're guards; I know how they think."

A guard slammed and locked the hearse's back door and stowed the key in his breast pocket.

The other guards waved at him and walked back into the building.

*Only one left.* The Commander ducked as the last guard approached them.

"Is someone there?" The guard squinted.

The Commander and Trey slithered to the other side of the car.

"Weird," the guard remarked. "I was certain I saw something." He turned and strode a few steps before stopping and spinning around. Apparently certain he was alone, the guard focused on his hand. "Appear." He lifted his hand.

A bright glow emanated from the guard, but a dark cloud grew above where the Commander and Trey hid.

The guard raised his gun and sprinted over to them. "Howdy! Trey, you're a little far from where you belong." He glared at the Commander. "And who might you be?"

The Commander bit his lip. *That's magic.* "I…"

The guard rolled his eyes. "Trey, I thought you canceled the escape plan?"

Trey shrugged. "I needed to modify it." His eyes trailed to the gun. "Our deal still stands?"

The guard holstered his gun and reached for his shirt pocket. "Of course." He walked to the car and opened the door for them.

Trey climbed in, followed by the Commander.

The guard lifted his eyebrows with a flicker of a smile before shutting the door.

Silence filled the hearse's dark interior. "How do you know that guard?" the Commander broke the silence after a few minutes.

"Being in prison as long as I have allowed me to make some alliances."

"Why did we sneak up if you knew him?

Trey nodded. "I had to be sure he was still on my side."

*He sure planned this well.* The Commander coughed and crouched next to Trey. "What did you do to land yourself in prison?"

"That piece of-" Trey gritted his teeth. "I mean, there was this cop, Claus."

*Claus, again?* The Commander grunted. "I understand. If it's the same Claus, we've dealt with his soul counterpart in our underworld. He's a bad apple." He shrugged. "Our president, Denida, insisted Claus could be good and led him to one world where 'he could do no harm,' he said."

"What!" Trey banged his fist into the floor.

"*Bang, bang,*" sounded on the side of the car.

"You'd better stay silent." The Commander lifted his hand. "As for Claus, our president wanted to repay him for saving us from a demon."

Trey shook his head. "Our president took care of our version of Claus."

"Yes, then you elected Nina to be president after him, with her lieutenant colonel following her blindly."

"Excuse me? What lieutenant colonel?"

"Lieutenant Colonel Anderson…"

Trey's foot scraped against the car's floor as he stood up. "Wait; he's the one who wants you dead, isn't he?"

"He wants to go back to the past to save Nina, but she died; he can't change the course of time."

"We can't worry about that, yet." Trey shook his arm. "We'd better hide behind this body for now."

They hunched down behind the body and waited until the car started moving.

"*Creak,*" it sounded. "Open up the garage, so we can get this corpse out of here."

"*Rumble.*" The car jerked into motion.

"We can't be out already?" The Commander shifted nervously and turned to Trey.

"Don't worry; I coordinated everything," Trey whispered.

The car came to a halt, and the front door clicked open, only to slam again.

"*Cluck,*" the rear door's latch clicked.

Trey jumped to his feet, only for the Commander to yank him down. "Not yet, it's too soon," he breathed.

The door burst open, and light streamed into the hearse.

The warden jumped into the car and tore off the blanket covering the body.

"Looking for something?" The driver asked. "I guarded this hearse all night; there's nobody in there."

"We have two escapees, so we're checking everything." The warden glared at the driver. "And we're going to get them and anyone who may have helped them."

"Hope so."

The warden laid the cover over the body again. "They must have had help from the inside, so anyone who knows anything will be executed for treason."

"They deserve nothing less." The driver clenched his fists.

The warden ran his finger over the sheet. "Anything you wish to tell me?" His eyes fell on the driver, who shook his head.

The warden climbed out of the car and approached the driver, staring into his eyes for a long minute. "Alright." He smacked his trousers. "Let him go!"

The driver smiled while the security guards next to the warden closed and locked the car doors.

Trey and the Commander looked at each other silently for what felt like an eternity. The low roar of the engine interrupted their silence.

The Commander's gaze remained fixed on the rear door, while they rode for the next hour. The car trembled on uneven terrain and the Commander lost his footing, but he put his hand on the floor to steady himself. *Are we on a dirt road?*

The car came to a halt and the engine turned off.

"Uh oh." The Commander lowered his head behind the body.

Keys rattled in the car door, and it opened, lighting up the dark hearse. "Trey, it's safe."

Trey tapped the Commander's shoulder and straightened up. He exited the vehicle. "Freedom!" He drew in a deep inhale and sighed contentedly. "How I've longed for the fresh air."

*As if he's never been in the courtyard.* The Commander crawled out and rubbed his forehead, before facing the driver. "How do I get to the palace?"

"All work and no play," Trey chuckled. "I can take you; I knew the former president."

"I need to get going before they suspect anything. Good luck, Trey." The driver shook Trey's hand and hurried back to the car. He turned it on and sped down the dirt road.

Trey coughed. "What will you do when you get to this Anderson fellow?"

"He can't be allowed to hurt my president in the past; it'll ruin everything."

"So, you will…"

The Commander shot Trey a stern glare. "Either he gives this up willingly, or I will have to force him to."

Trey smirked. "Just what I wanted to hear. You helped me escape, so I'll return the favor.

# Chapter 9- Anderson

*Finally here.* The Commander decelerated and checked his surroundings.

Trey increased his pace, passing the Commander.

"Trey," the Commander hissed.

Trey ignored him, but whistled and waved to a soldier standing watch.

"Trey, you're back!" The soldier embraced Trey.

*They know each other?* The Commander caught up to them as they hugged each other warmly. He cleared his throat.

Trey nodded. "Sorry, where are my manners? Commander, this is my old friend." He turned to the soldier. "Could you help us see Anderson? He's the president now, right?"

"Yes, he took over after Nina tried to…" The soldier peered over his shoulder. "- she tried to bring your dad back, but failed. Anderson went back to try again."

The Commander stepped in front of Trey. "Father? You're the former president's son?"

"Yes." Trey waved his hand dismissively at the Colonel, his eyes never leaving the soldier. "You can let me inside Anderson's chambers. He will return, no?"

The soldier shifted his weight onto his other leg, then back again. "I… I don't-"

"For old time's sake?"

"Sorry, I can't." The soldier hurried back to his post. "Please leave and don't come back."

Trey frowned, finally turning his attention to the Colonel. "Follow me. I know another way in." Trey whirled around and followed the building's exterior wall.

"Hang on a second." The Commander sprinted in front of Trey to block his path. "How can you be the president's son? Denida never mentioned anything about the president having a son. In fact, as far as I'm aware, the former president nominated Nina because they had a father-daughter relationship." The Commander stomped his foot. "When Claus went back in time to revoke Nina's presidential status, he locked the president up, alone. Surely, if the president had any family members, Claus would've imprisoned them, too."

"Dad was… I did something."

"What?" The Commander raised his voice.

Trey leaned against the wall and arched his neck. "It was a long time ago. Claus was a cop, as you probably know, but he was also my childhood friend." He pushed himself off the wall and folded his hands. "I believe I should show you, instead." Trey shut his eyes and inhaled deeply. "The past." A cloud enveloped his hands and he thrust them outwards, creating a magic screen, on which an image formed.

*** 

A younger Trey strolled down a store aisle with a six-pack under each arm. He put them down on the counter with a clatter and pounded the counter with his fist. "Come on; I don't have all night."

"Hold it!" Claus appeared and grabbed Trey's hands. He rummaged through Trey's pockets and confiscated candy bars, which he threw onto the counter. "Lookie here." Claus cuffed Trey.

"What the hell do you think you're doing?" the clerk demanded.

Claus flashed his badge. "I'm a cop. I'll take this punk in." He put the candy bars in his pocket and grabbed the drinks before jerking Trey out of the store. He trekked to his car and threw the confiscated items in the backseat before gently pushing Trey onto the passenger's seat.

Claus plopped down in the driver's seat, inhaled deeply, and glared at Trey. "Free yourself." He tossed Trey the keys to the cuffs and started the engine. Claus sped down the road while Trey removed the cuffs and reached for the beer.

"It worked like a charm." Trey took a sip from the can.

Claus's shoulders slumped. "Doesn't it always?" He stopped at an intersection and tilted his head. "But are you sure this is a good idea? Your father is bound to find out, someday."

Trey rolled down the window and tossed the empty can out of the car. "What's he gonna do? I'm his son, and he's always forgiven me before."

"I know, but I'm a cop, now. I can't just-"

Trey slammed his foot down on the accelerator.

"What are you doing?" Claus swerved to avoid the cars in front of them.

Claus reached over and turned on the siren while he whipped down a side road.

Trey kept the gas pedal to the floor.

Claus jerked the car into a garage complex, where he kept the wheel turned as far as possible to the right, driving in repeated circles.

Trey jerked back to his side of the car, and Claus swiftly pressed the brakes, bringing the cruiser to a halt. Claus yanked the keys from the ignition and turned to his friend. "What the hell-"

Trey chuckled and raised his finger. "Remember who my father is." He smirked.

Claus gritted his teeth. "You can't keep using that excuse. Isn't it time to grow up?"

"Why?" Trey grabbed a candy bar from Claus's pocket and chomped down on half of it. "Fun without consequences is the best."

"Why?" Trey bit his candy bar. "Fun should *never* end."

Claus started the car's engine again. "We should go back to your father."

"Now? But we just-"

"Yes, now," Claus hissed. "I have to report to work soon."

***

"Wait." The Commander waved his hand. "What was that? Claus was good, and you were an irresponsible bra- I mean, immature?"

Trey wiped some sweat from his forehead and laughed. "No, you're right. I *was* a brat, and he was my childhood friend."

"Did he imprison you?"

Trey nodded. "He quickly rose through the ranks. My father was impressed. He always wished I was more like Claus."

The Commander ran his tongue over his teeth. "Sorry, go on."

Trey inhaled deeply and let out a heavy exhale before wrinkling his brow and pointing at the image.

***

Trey lied on his bed, repeatedly tossing a ball up in the air and catching it when it fell.

The president grabbed the ball. "Are you even listening to me?"

Trey rolled his eyes and sat up. "You gave me this lecture before, Dad. I'm tired."

"Tired?" The president flung the ball at the wall. "You should grow up, like Claus has. The time for childish antics is over."

"Ahem." Claus knocked on the doorframe. "Sir, if I could have a moment?"

The president shut his eyes with a sigh. "Claus, what is it?"

"There have been some reports…"

"About what?"

"You'll have to see it, yourself."

The president shot Claus a condemning glare. "Tell me now, so that I can get back to my son."

"The reports are about your son," Claus snickered.

*The hell?* Trey glanced at his friend, his heart aching as if it had been ripped from his chest.

The president studied the look they exchanged. "Burglaries, again?" He rested his hand on his son's shoulder.

Claus shook his head. "More serious than that, so important that even you cannot protect him, Sir."

"Seriously?" The president eyed his son. "We have an-"

"Murder is more important than our friendship." Claus reached for his handcuffs. "Get on your feet."

*Murder?* "But I haven't-"

"Wait." The president stepped in front of Trey. "Maybe he didn't do it. He hasn't been convicted-"

"I'm sorry, but there are witnesses, Sir.

The president retreated.

"Dad?" Trey bore a worried gaze as his Claus cuffed Trey's behind his back.

The president stood stunned into silence.

Claus pushed Trey in front of him.

"What the hell, Claus?" Trey planted his feet.

Claus tugged at Trey, but he refused to budge. "What?"

"What are you doing, Claus? You know as well as I do, that I haven't killed anyone."

"Do I? What I know is that you're under arrest." Claus grabbed Trey by the neck. His nails dug into Trey's skin. "And you will do as I ask."

Trey gritted his teeth and stomped onward, stopping at the police car, only for Claus to shove him into the backseat.

*Dad, please help me.* Trey noticed his dad watching from a window. When their eyes met, his father turned away.

Claus sat in the driver's seat and drove down the road. "It's a shame, really."

Trey sat with his eyes closed as thoughts raged in his mind. *Why would anyone say that they saw me commit murder? And several people, too…* "I don't get why they would accuse me."

Claus grunted.

For the next few minutes, Trey just stared at Claus.

The car stopped in front of a jail. Claus turned to Trey. "I know why."

"You know what?"

"Remember what you asked? You wanted to know why they said that you killed him."

Trey gasped. "Well, don't keep me waiting!"

Claus gloated. "Because I told them to."

"What?" Trey banged against the side of the door.

"You can't get out. You've become an obstacle to my career, so I had to do something." Claus grinned maniacally.

Claus stepped out of the car and waved to some other cops. "I don't think I can handle this one myself. He's upset that he got caught."

The cops joined Claus in removing Trey from the vehicle.

"No, he set me up!" Trey screamed hysterically.

"That's what everyone claims," one of the cops remarked.

***

Trey maintained his balance by leaning on the wall. "Father never answered my calls and avoided my trial. The silver lining was that prison made me more mature."

The Commander shook his head. "Every single one of Claus's forms across the Underworlds have been conniving, so I'm not surprised."

"Yes, but now you can see how I'm so familiar with this world, so you can trust that I know a secret way into the castle."

The Commander tailed Trey along the wall until they stopped at a portion of the building's façade that appeared cracked and grimy with age. "Is this it?"

Trey peeked over his shoulder. "Not yet, just follow me." He strode along the wall for a few more minutes before kneeling abruptly and beckoning the Commander to follow.

"What's wrong?" The Commander knelt beside him.

"We need to get in there." Trey pointed at a storage shed.

The Commander shrugged as he spotted several maintenance men around the outbuilding. "You could just use magic."

"Against innocent people?"

"Desperate times." The Commander frowned, and his eyes fell on Trey. "Is there another way in?"

Trey peered at the sun. "We still have time. Let's see if work calls them away."

*We don't have time for that.* The Commander surveyed the ground. "Follow my lead." He reached down and grabbed a stone, which he tossed with all his might. It soared through the sky and shattered one of the main building's windows.

The workers jumped up and scurried over to the window to investigate.

"Now!" The Commander sprang to his feet, and they darted for the shed. Once inside, the Commander scanned the room and grabbed a broom to barricade the door. Now safe, he heaved a sigh of relief. "What now?"

"I... I." Trey's eyes panned the shed's interior. "Maybe I remembered wrong?"

"You've got to be kidding. Hurry up and remember before we get caught!" The Commander cupped his ear to the door.

"It's been so long." Trey idly traced his fingers along the wall, until his hand slipped behind some gardening tools, and he stopped dead in his tracks. "I think it's here."

"It looks rundown." The Commander hurried over and pushed a rack of supplies away from the wall, revealing a wooden plank.

Trey helped the Commander pull it aside, revealing an entrance to the castle. "See?  I used this passage all the time as a kid." They stepped into a dark room.

"We need to get to the throne. Would that be in your father's room?"

"I'll lead the way." Trey turned the corner, only to duck behind the wall.

A maid grabbed some cleaning supplies before strolling out the door that he'd entered through.

"I'd better lead. Stay close." The Commander cautiously ambled forward. He peered around the corner before continuing.

Only a few soldiers patrolled the castle's rooms, so the trek to the chamber continued smoothly.

Anderson had made himself comfortable in the father of Trey's old chambers. Sketches and notes about Denida littered the walls, creating an uncomfortable air of obsession and madness.

The Commander examined the walls, especially one specific wall with big letters scribbled in the center. *He's still trying.*

"Another inmate said Anderson had some obsessive tendencies, but this is a bit much." Trey shook his head. "What do we do now?"

"We wait." The Commander paced over to the desk and rummaged through its drawers. *Nothing of interest.* His focus panned across the walls again. *Perhaps that's everything Anderson's considered, so far.*

They continued searching every nook and cranny of the room in the following hours, confirming that the only information about Denida was, in fact, on the walls.

"*Clack, clack, clack.*"

"Someone's coming!" The Commander grabbed Trey and ran to the bathroom.

The doorknob turned, and Anderson entered the room. He tossed his jacket on the bed and sauntered to the wall to jot down a note.

"Nice homey touch you have here, covering the walls with paper. You look like a loony-bin." The Commander waved at Anderson.

Anderson charged the Commander, shoving him up against the wall on the other end of the room. He swung at the Commander, aiming for his guts.

The Commander reached for Anderson's fists, but his combatant punched him so fast that he couldn't catch them.

"Halt!" Trey clenched his fist, spun in a circle, and thrust his arm at Anderson. A small gust of wind flew across the room, slamming Anderson up against the wall.

Anderson's attacks ceased, and he clung to the wall for a moment, before tumbling forward.

"You," Anderson sneered. He grabbed his gun and aimed it at Trey's sweat-drenched head. "Your father should have had you executed, but no matter; I'll enjoy doing that for him."

"Shouldn't you… um … focus on getting Nina back?" The Commander squinted.

Anderson's frigid gaze shifted to the Commander, but he kept his gun trained on Trey, focusing on him again within a second. "Getting to your president is harder than I first anticipated, but I can see why everyone wants that ring of his."

"You saw Denida?"

"I tried to shoot him, but it's like that accursed ring warned him."

"So, it's not too late." A smile surfaced on the Commander's face. "You need to stop exploiting time travel. It's impossible to bring Nina back."

"Trey, you should have stayed out of this." Anderson tightened his grip on the gun. "Now you will have another murder to answer for." He whipped the gun to the Commander.

Trey wiped his forehead and charged Anderson, causing his hand to shake so his shots would miss. The bullets struck the wall behind the Commander.

Anderson swung at Trey, who deflected the blow. As Trey smacked Anderson's face, Anderson pulled his gun again. The men wrestled over the gun with all their might, but it slipped from Anderson's grip.

Anderson lunged at Trey, knocking him down and wrapping his hands around Trey's throat. He growled as Trey struggled to breathe.

"Stop!" The Commander touched the gun to the back of Anderson's head. "Let him go."

Anderson lifted his arms. "There, don't do anything rash."

Trey coughed and crawled away. "What… happened… to you?"

The Commander circled in front of Anderson. "It's over, now. You will never go back in time again."

"You think you can stop me?" Anderson hissed.

The Commander cocked the gun. "This is an order: stand down, Soldier!"

"Dad sure surrounded himself with immoral people." Trey returned from the bathroom and approached them, stopping in front of Anderson.

The Commander glanced at Trey from out of the corner of his eye. "Your father didn't know Anderson; Nina did…"

"As far as we know," Trey mocked.

Anderson bared his teeth as his eyes followed the Commander's hand, but he addressed Trey. "I know who you are, but your father is dead."

"Same as your president. Are you suggesting that I should do as you have been, and try to change history?" Trey rolled his eyes. "I don't live in the past."

Anderson shook his head. "Nina already tried that and paid with her life."

The Commander switched the gun to his other hand. "Let's all just take a deep breath; this isn't getting us anywhere. The device to the Gate, please?" He extended his hand.

Anderson pushed himself up off the ground. "Want to follow your Colonel to his death?"

"Through the Gate," the Commander asserted. "- not to death. So where is it?"

Anderson reached for his back pocket and held out his hand with a clenched fist. "I left it with the Gate. Here's the key."

The Commander approached Anderson's hand.

When the Commander stepped away, Anderson grabbed the Commander's arm, pulling him forward, and ripping the gun from his grasp.

"Too slow! And you were a Commander?" Anderson gloated. "As I said, it's time to join your colonel in death."

Trey clenched his fists and closed his eyes, sweat appearing on his forehead. In an instant, his eyes opened, and he threw his arms out. A whirlwind appeared and hurtled toward Anderson, scooping up all the furniture in its path and volleying it with its haste.

Anderson fired at Trey, but the gust deflected the bullet's trajectory. Anderson bared his teeth and squeezed the trigger as fast he could, emptying the magazine.

The wind ripped the gun from Anderson's hand before it sucked him up.

"Uh oh." The Commander lifted his arms to shield his face.

Trey closed his eyes and let out a sigh, disbanding the whirlwind. Everything collided and dropped, forming a giant pile on the floor.

The Commander meandered over to the heap of furniture, where he knelt and put his fingers on Anderson's eyelids and closed them. *I'm sorry it had to end this way.* He gazed at Trey. "Magic again?"

Trey hunched over, gasping for air. "Unfortunately. At least he won't kill Denida, now."

# Chapter 10- Reaching the Colonel

The Colonel glanced at the demons surrounding them. "Why keep us alive?"

"You can have your freedom." Bael snickered. "All you have to do is give me your soul, Soldier Boy."

The Colonel scoffed. "Where are you taking us?"

"I'm not taking you anywhere." Bael gloated. "My demons are taking you home to Hell. You get to endure the same torture Denida knew so well."

Naphtali thrashed, trying to escape.

Bael smacked Naphtali's cheek. "Calm down, Naph. You'll be home, soon."

Naphtali shook his head. "You should want to take me back, yourself. You can show everyone that you're the one who managed to capture an escaped demon."

"You aren't as important as you think." Bael tapped the device in his hand. "They're taking you because I need to put this back and modify the Gate you entered through, so that we can go harvest millions of souls across the Underworlds."

The demons escorted the Colonel, Naphtali, and the soldiers through the dark edge of the world, where the second Gate stood.

*They can change the direction of the Gates?* The Colonel peeked at Bael, heading in the direction of the first Gate. *Denida, where the hell are you?*

The demons tailed their captives, not paying them much mind. A dark cloud around the prisoners guided them forward.

More demons appeared in front of them as they neared a massive building housing the second Gate. Demons hurled slurs and taunts as the prisoners passed them.

Naphtali sighed heavily beside the Colonel. "This is my worst fear coming true, you know, but if we're being brought in as new arrivals, we'll be just a few of many." He gritted his teeth. "How many souls do they want? There could be thousands of demons there that we have-"

"Time to escape?"

Naphtali shot the Colonel a cold glare. "I doubt it. Hell is covered in Darkness, which watches everything."

"You escaped," the Colonel stated, his voice shaking with uncertainty.

Naphtali spat on a boulder as they passed it. "Not alone, Denida and the other Dark Angels aided me."

*Crap.* The Colonel glared at the demons and clenched his jaw as adrenaline began pulsing through his veins like fire. He spun and rushed through the crowd of soldiers. "Time to end this!" He slammed into the edge of the cloud, but it was like crashing into a wall.

The dark cloud halted its forward motion and ensnared the Colonel. The Darkness intensified and fully engulfed the Colonel.

*I... can't... breathe...* The Colonel reached for his throat, gasping for air.

"Stop!" Naphtali screamed.

"Why should we?" one demon snarled.

Naphtali lifted his hands. "Master Bael won't be happy if you kill him."

The demon in charge grunted and waved his hand, lifting the Darkness from the Colonel, who collapsed. "Move it." The demon yanked the Colonel back to his position next to Naphtali.

The cloud started floating onward again.

"That felt-"

"I know." Naphtali supported the Colonel. "The Darkness is a barrier. We can't escape."

"But demons can pass through it, so you should be able to."

"That requires advanced dark magic, which I never learned." Naphtali sighed.

The demon from before smirked at the Colonel, and waggled a condescending finger at him.

The demons led them inside the well-guarded building and stopped in front of the Gate. They bowed to a dark figure standing watch. "Master Bael wanted these souls brought to Hell, Master."

The demon spun around and gestured at the Gate. "Lead them through."

They nodded solemnly.

Naphtali's bloodshot eyes darted around constantly, and cold sweat glistened on his face.

"It will be okay," the Colonel assured him.

Naphtali swallowed and nodded before turning his bloodshot eyes to the Gate. The first row of soldiers vanished through the Gate. With each step, Naphtali's breathing became increasingly labored.

The Colonel's eyes widened as they exited the Gate in Hell. *Where are all the demons?* The reality of a sparsely populated Hell quickly replaced the Colonel's mental image of a hellscape teeming with evil.

Naphtali clenched the Colonel's arm. "The Darkness is stronger than the last time I was here." He grimaced. "By a lot."

The dark cloud led them to a crowd of souls, which stretched as far as the eye could see. Condensed Darkness hovered in the sky above the masses.

The Colonel tilted his head to Naphtali. "You think Lucifer is here?"

"Heh," a booming laugh rang from the sky, echoing throughout Hell.

"Hahaha," the laugh rang from the sky, echoing throughout Hell.

"Get out of my way." A man with red eyes shoved through the crowd. "I'm an archdemon; let me through!"

The dense cloud wrapped around the archdemon and took the shape of an individual, but it only had a body shape without a face. "One who has failed us."

A ring of fire shot up around the archdemon, forcing the colossal crowd to retreat. Souls shoved into each other, just to avoid it.

"She knew how to kill us."

"Liar!" The fire intensified and turned blue from the heat. "Humans wouldn't know how to do that."

"She wasn't human; she was from the Underworlds," the archdemon insisted.

The flames subsided, and the Darkness swept into the sky. It crashed into the archdemon's body and an image of the archdemon's last memory formed in the atmosphere. It rewound, starting with a group of demons falling on the gymnasium floor and ending with them being shot in their eyes.

"Bael must have been right," the Colonel whispered to Naphtali.

"Hey, demon scum!" a taunt sounded from the image.

"Susan?" The Colonel spun to the image.

The dark cloud leapt from the archdemon's body and hovered before the Colonel. "You know who that is?"

"Damn right, I do. That's Master Sergeant Susan from my Underworld, and she's going to kick your ass."

"But she's on Earth." The cloud intensified, enshrouding the Colonel. It took the shape of two piercing grey eyes, the only light in the dark cloud.

"Of course, she went to Earth, just to stop you." The Colonel smirked.

"So, you intended, but she will succumb, just like you." The cloud flew to the archdemon. "Vormath, go bring me their souls, especially this Susan's. Fail me again, and your soul will perish."

Vormath chuckled eerily. "Shall I kill Denida's human side, as well?"

The eyes turned red. "I don't need Denida's soul, so just kill him for good."

Vormath's smile widened. "As you wish, Master." He bowed and vanished with a puff of smoke.

***

Trey strolled beside the Commander. "Are you sure we should follow your colonel?"

*Why would he ask that?* The Commander frowned.

"You said you opposed his orders to stay here. He could court-martial you, but you are more than welcome to stay here."

"Denied." The Commander peered at Trey. "I appreciate your offer, but my colonel will understand."

Trey inserted the main device into the Gate. "What if he doesn't?"

"Every action has consequences," the Commander remarked matter-of-factly.

Trey shook his head. "That's just-"

The Gate sprang to life, illuminating the room. "Finally, it's on."

Trey saluted. "Good luck, Commander."

The Commander tapped his fingers on his trousers. "Are you going to be okay, here?"

"Yes, I need to bring order back to this world."

The Commander nodded and saluted before stepping through the Gate. The first thing he saw were sparrows gliding through the sky. He ventured down a nearby road.

The Commander crept behind some shrubs. *I'd better be careful or... wait!* He rushed forward, stopping a few paces from the oncoming troops, but his wide smile faded quickly. *I don't recognize these people, but their leader looks just like the Colonel. Maybe he's another soul counterpart.* He saluted quickly. "Colonel, Sir?"

The soldiers cleared the way and the man the Commander had spotted stepped forward. "General, you mean." He pointed to his stripes. "Colonel, do you know him?"

An unfamiliar colonel among the general's troop slid out and surveyed the Commander, before turning to the general. "No, Sir."

"General, Sir, my apologies for the confusion, but you look identical to my colonel."

The general's eyes widened. "Are you talking about John?"

"Yes, I was a part of his troop, but…" The Commander pursed his lips.

"But?" The general frowned.

"I had to stay behind to fix something."

"And that-"

"Dad." A boy stared at the general intensely. "We need to get to the Gate ASAP."

The general exhaled heavily. "You're right, Mark." He scratched his head. "Can you take him to the Gate John departed through?"

"Of course, Dad."

The general turned his attention to the Commander. "That's where you're heading, I presume?"

The Commander nodded and followed Mark, while the others continued in the opposite direction.

After a few steps, the Commander cleared his throat. "May I inquire about something?"

Mark stopped and turned around. "We really need to hurry so I can get back to the others, but what is it, Commander?"

"You don't look like a soldier, so why were you going to the Gate with those troops?" the Commander asked.

Mark pursed his lips and sighed. "There are two reasons, if you must know."

"Let's hear them."

"Claus abused the Gate's power before, so my dad, the general, figured we should check on both Gates, now."

*Sounds like the general lets his son tag along on lots of missions. Must be nice.* "Hm, and the other reason?"

"That's…" Mark arched his neck to stare at the sky. "Mom is buried there."

"Your mom?"

"Isabella, yes. Claus killed her during his reign here."

*Just as I thought, Claus has always had an evil streak.* "I see. I'm so sorry."

"Don't worry." Mark waved his arm dismissively. "Anyway, it's not much farther."

Mark strolled to the castle and led the Commander to a room with a Gate standing at the ready. "This is the Gate your colonel left through."

The Commander smiled and patted Mark on the shoulder. "Thanks, Kid." He darted to the Gate, but stopped, frozen in front of it, and peered back. "Sorry for interrupting you and your dad's time." He waved with a hint of a smile and marched through the Gate.

Rain splashed the Commander's face as soon as he exited on the other side. The downpour turned the dirt path on the hill into a trail of mud.

*Dammit.* The Commander lifted his hand over his forehead and trudged down the road. Mud squelched under his soles and completely covered his boots by the time he reached the town at the base of the hill. As soon as the town was close, he rushed over to the side of a building, taking cover from the rain.

"At last!" The Commander beat the rain out of his jacket.

"Another soldier." An older man puffed on his cigarette. "You get separated from the others or something?"

"The others?" The Commander furrowed his brow.

The man tilted his head up the road. "The others went to the Holy Grounds."

The Commander peered down the road. A giant wall stood at the end of the street, obstructing something. "I guess that's where I'm going, then. Thanks!" He hustled down the road, weaving between buildings, seeking shelter from the rainfall. When he reached the wall, he lifted his arm to shield himself from the downpour and sped across the open ground to a checkpoint.

"Halt!" a guard lifted his hand, preventing the Commander from reaching shelter from the rain. A light flicker swayed around the guard's hand. "What is your business, here?"

"I… can you let me…" The Commander stepped closer.

The guard spun his hand, expelling a bolt of lightning, which struck the ground next to the Commander's foot. "Don't move."

*Magic here, too?* The Commander retreated with his arms up. "I don't want to cause any trouble; I'm just looking for my colonel."

"Colonel?" The guard stepped back, watching the Commander intently. He reached for his cellphone, but when he couldn't find it, he glanced at the table beside him and reached for a different one. "There's another mysterious person here and he's asking to see the colonel."

The Commander let his arm slide to his side. "The colonel is coming?"

"She's on her way." The guard waved his hand.

*She?*

The giant gateway opened, and three individuals stepped through: two-foot soldiers, who stopped beside the guard, and a woman in officer fatigues.

"Susan?" The Commander gasped with shocked rattling his voice.

The guard thrust his hand forward, and another lightning bolt struck the ground. "Show Colonel Susan some respect."

*Fascinating, I'm meeting one of Susan's soul counterparts, here.* "Ma'am." The Commander saluted. "I'm looking for my commanding officer."

"Your-"

The Commander nodded. "Denida's colonel, Ma'am."

Susan saluted. "You're Denida's commander? Welcome. Soldier, stand down." Susan gestured to the guard for the Commander to join them under the side of the building.

The Commander hurried over to Susan.

When he stood beside them, she tilted her head to one of the soldiers next to her, who lifted his hand and blew on it, drying the Commander's clothes instantaneously. "I bet you've guessed your colonel has already left." Susan met the Commander's eyes. "Why are you still here?"

The Commander straightened up. "I had to fix something a few underworlds back, but I need to rejoin the Colonel, now."

Susan's gaze widened. "I'll take you to our High Sorcerer to see if we can send you to the next underworld."

Susan guided him through the gateway into the Holy Grounds.

The Commander stopped abruptly in amazement, staring at the clear blue sky. "But how?" He pointed up.

Susan chuckled. "We're on the Holy Grounds; it doesn't rain, here." She raised her eyebrows. "Follow me."

Susan strode onward, until she reached two wide doors. She knocked loudly on them, before standing still in wait.

"Enter!" a female voice rang from within.

Susan pulled the door open and encountered a woman with an expectant grin standing inside.

"Susan?" The woman's eyes acknowledged the Commander next to Susan before returning to her. "Another one of Denida's soldiers?"

"Ma'am." The Commander stepped forward and saluted.

The woman smiled. "Warlock is fine."

"Warlock, I need to use your second Gate to follow my colonel."

Susan nodded. "Yes, we need to see the High Sorcerer. May we have an audience?"

The Warlock scrutinized the Commander. Finally, she turned and shook her head. "That's unnecessary; you have our permission. Take him to the Gate."

Susan nudged the Commander forward and they began walking at her quick pace. She nodded at the technicians next to the Gate. "I hope you find your colonel in good health."

"Colonel Susan!" one of the technicians yelled. "I only just inserted the device a second ago, and it powered on."

Susan stepped closer and raised her hand to block the Gate's bright light. Dark figures appeared in the brightness from the Gate, and four demons stepped out, followed by a bigger one. The four men spun to the techs and ripped out their hearts.

"Fresh souls," The demon standing still at the Gate raised his arms. The Gate powered down. "You two look important. Howdy-Mowdy there, I'm Bael. Could you direct me to the first Gate?"

"Are they…" Susan's wide eyes turned to the Commander.

The Commander shuddered. "You're a demon?"

"Not just any demon," Bael gloated. "I'm Archdemon Bael."

*Has he met the Colonel?*

Bael tilted his head. "Colonel? Do you mean the guy with Naphtali? I sent them and all their soldiers to Hell." His crimson eyes glinted.

The Commander gritted his teeth. "You'll pay for that!" He spun to face Susan. "Colonel, you'd better get your troops on high alert."

"Because of them?"

The Commander glanced at her. "Now!" He pushed Susan out the door and turned to the demons.

"You've got guts, just like that colonel of yours, but it failed him." Bael waved his hands to command the demons. "Kill him."

Two demons approached from different sides.

The Commander checked them out cautiously, then grabbed a chair and smashed it over the one on his left. He charged the other one, banging him into the wall. With that demon stunned, the Commander tightened his grip around the demon's throat and squeezed with all his might.

The last three demons darted over and jerked the Commander away from his victim.

"Uh oh." Bael bore a maniacal smirk as he approached the Commander. "I would kill you, but it will be more fun to tear your soul out in front of your colonel."

# Chapter 11- Seeing the Earthly Nina

*It's secure, now.* Susan waved for the kids to follow her down the road.

"We can't stay out here. The demons will find us," Den insisted.

*I know.* Susan rubbed her eyes. "We're out of options. They've already surrounded your old school, so we can't even hide out there."

"We can go to my house," Kate suggested.

"Your house? No, they would check there." Susan's eyes widened. "But they wouldn't know where her house is."

"Her?" Sus and Den asked in unison, eyes locking.

"You know, her." Susan smiled at Den. "Nina's farm is nearby." She escorted them down backroads to a dirt path on the town's outskirts. After a few minutes, they reached a small farm.

A guy with greasy dark brown hair stood outside, smoking a cigarette. "The cops should take care of it, Nina." He spun around, grabbed a pitchfork beside him, and waved it at them. "This is private property."

"Jakob!" Susan yelled.

"Yes?" both the guy with the pitchfork and the guy next to Kate answered.

"Um… handsome Jacob." Susan pointed at the guy with the pitchfork.

"Handsome Jacob? I could get used to that." He put the pitchfork down. "How can I help such a pretty lady?"

"If he's the handsome one, what am I?" the other Jakob grunted.

"Tall Jakob?" Sus teased.

"We are hiding from-"

"Oh, sweetie," Handsome Jacob smirked. "We'll call the cops."

"The police won't be able to handle them." Den frowned.

Den?" Nina approached them. "It's you!"

Susan clapped her hands. "Pay attention; the demons are dangerous and they're not from here. I've dealt with them many times where I'm from."

Handsome Jacob dropped his cigarette butt. "You're from my heart. I've longed for our destined rendezvous; it must be kismet."

*Jesus.* Susan rolled her eyes. "No, I'm from another dimension, the Underworlds. I knew about this farm because Nina's human form is here."

"Really?" Kate frowned.

Susan nodded. "Yes, I've come here as part of my job."

"And what job is that?" Nina blinked.

"I'm here to protect you."

"That seems to be going so well, judging from the looks of you." Nina shoved past Handsome Jacob, only to halt a step from Susan. "So, Miss…" She bit her lip. "You know my soul form?"

"Soul?" Susan swallowed.

"Yeah, you said human form and mentioned being from another dimension." Nina lifted her eyebrows.

Susan's lips started to quirk upwards into a smile, but she turned away before it formed. "I've known Nina for years. We were on Earth a few months ago, chasing after Jack. So yes, I know her well."

"Is my soul doing well?"

"Yes, she is. I'm a soldier from the Underworlds, with a sworn duty to protect Denida and his wife."

Den grabbed Sus' hand. "Well, if they don't want us here, we can just-"

"Bye." Nina waved and headed back to the farmhouse.

"Wait!" Susan rushed after Nina. "We should stay close together."

Nina flipped her hair. "More people, more trouble. No thanks."

*How can she not want to be close to Den? They're connected.* Susan's disbelief forced her to gather her thoughts before she could respond. "I need to protect you and Denida," she repeated, sounding much less self-assured of her duty, now.

"Denida?" Nina's eyes drifted past Susan. "You mean Den is-"

"Denida, yes."

Nina clicked her tongue against her teeth with a soft smile. "In that case, you'd better stay. Besides, Handsome Jacob would be disappointed if his 'kismet' left," she joked.

"Thanks, let's get inside before anyone sees us." Susan sped up to the building, peeking back from in front of the door. "Hurry up!"

Den trailed after Sus.

Nina gazed at the sky, while slowly rubbing her hands together, before following everyone else inside.

"So why aren't you in the Underworld?" Nina crossed her arms, assessing Susan.

"I came to fight the demons."

"By yourself?" Nina followed up swiftly.

"Yes, I-"

"Then why not go back for reinforcements? We can stay hidden, here."

*That's a lot of questions.* Susan gritted her teeth. "I can't; the demons dismantled my escape route."

Nina surveyed the room, and her eyes fell on Den. "Denida would send aide to protect his human form, right? So, can't we wait for that?"

*She's damn good at guessing. Something's off with her, but what?* "I suppose…" Susan mumbled.

"We used to go to the same school, right?" Nina meandered over to Den.

Den swallowed. "Yes, you remember me?"

"Of course." Nina grabbed Den and Sus' hands. She smiled as her eyes fell on Den, then on Sus.

Den looked at Nina's hand holding his and swallowed. "The school is surrounded by demons, now."

"We know." Handsome Jacob approached. "Nina and I barely escaped. Luckily, she swept us away."

"Swept?" Den stared, confused.

"The demons didn't even see us leaving." Handsome Jacob gloated.

Susan parted the shades to peek outside. "Is there anywhere we can hide? Somewhere the demons won't find us if they search here?"

Nina shrugged. "I don't think so. All we have is the barn and what you see in here."

Susan arched her neck and tapped her knuckles on the windowsill.

"Why do you ask?" Nina batted her eyelids.

"We need safety."

"Safety?" Nina rolled her eyes. "Thanks, but we're fine; your handsome little Jacob and I have been fine."

"Yeah, about that…" Susan tilted her head. "I know you and something isn't right."

Nina grinned. "You know me? I've never met you before."

Susan peered around the room before her eyes fell back on Nina. "But I know Nina and you're just… not like her."

Nina shifted to her toes and back. "I don't know what to tell you; this is who I am."

Susan grunted. "I've experienced an imposter pretending to be someone else before."

Nina gasped. "Well, if you don't trust me, you can leave, but I'm staying far away from those things."

Susan turned her attention to the window, spotting the barn. "You've got horses out there?"

Nina inhaled deeply. "A few, I'll show you." She led Susan out to the stables.

"So, you like horses?" Susan checked out the horses as she passed them.

"When you grow up on a farm, they're kinda hard to avoid." Nina waved her arm. "Those are all our horses, or 'that's all folks,' as they say." Nina giggled at her own cleverness.

Susan petted a horse. "We could hide out here. Demons avoid livestock. Animals tend to get upset around the Darkness."

"Let's tell Den." Nina spun around and hiked back to the door.

"- and the others," Susan mumbled. She stalked after Nina, but as soon as she left the barn, her focus landed on several oncoming cars. She clenched her fists. "Expecting company?"

Nina licked her upper lip. "Go inside; I'll deal with them." She stepped out to the road with her arms crossed.

Susan darted inside.

Handsome Jacob jumped to his feet. "Hi, my beauty. Did you miss me as much as I-"

Susan shoved past him. "Think fast; demons are approaching."

"Here?" Den raced to the window. "What about Nina? Is she going to be okay?"

"We've gotta go!" Susan rushed to the window and reached for Den's arm.

Den jumped back. "No, we can't just leave her. I'm not leaving!"

Susan bared her teeth and stared out the window.

The cars stopped in front of Nina. Their doors sprang open, and a man exited the vehicle closest to her. He rubbed his palms together. "Howdy, Nina."

"Isn't that the demon we shot?" Den lifted his finger. "We'd better help-"

"Wait." Susan grabbed Den's hand. "Let's stay still for now. Nina wanted to handle it." She turned to the window.

The archdemon closed the distance between himself and Nina. "I believe some friends of mine are here. Would you be a dear and take me to them?"

Nina waved her hand dismissively. "And you think I'd tell a perfect stranger if they were here?"

"That's quite an easy matter to address," the demon smirked. "My name is Archdemon Vormath. You have a woman from the Underworlds here. I can sense her spirit." Vormath sniffed.

Nina shrugged. "Nobody's here except Jacob and me."

"Liar, there's a strong odor." Vormath tilted his head and sniffed the air. "Wait, are you also an-"

Nina charged at Vormath, ramming him into the car. She spun around and dashed through the front door.

Den and Susan scurried from the window to the foyer to meet her.

"They know you're here. Follow me." Nina sprinted through the house and out a back door, where she immediately turned left, and ran inside a storage garage for the farm's vehicles. Nina gestured to a van.

"It works?" Susan peeped.

"Yes, I've used it to sneak out before."

"Put it in neutral and let the two Jacobs push it out so they won't hear us." Susan poked her head out to steal a glimpse at the house. The demons had already started rummaging through it.

Vormath was the only demon still near the cars. He repeatedly banged his fist on a car's roof.

Susan turned to the van, raised her finger to her lips, and shushed the group. She mimed for the two Jacobs to start pushing the car.

Susan focused on Vormath, while the others pushed the car down a dirt road.

Susan peeked over her shoulder. *It sure takes time…*

"They're gone!" Demons swarmed out of the house.

"Really?" Vormath clapped his hands and lowered his forehead. Darkness enveloped him, and he shifted his eyes, staring right at Susan. "There!"

*Crap.* "Start the car!" Susan sprinted behind the car with the demons in hot pursuit. "Come on." She waved her arms at the Jacobs, who looked at each other confusedly.

"Babe, where are you going?" Handsome Jacob asked, while Tall Jacob followed her and climbed into the van with Susan and the others.

"Jacob, come on!" Nina screamed from the van.

"But the car?"

A bat flew over the field. A dark aura surrounded it as it hovered above Handsome Jacob. It transformed into Vormath, who dropped to his feet and grabbed Handsome Jacob by the throat. "What a nice specimen."

Nina bared her teeth.

"Nina, you should have bet on a winner, not those weaklings. This one's life is forfeit because of you." Vormath thrust his arm inside Handsome Jacob and ripped his heart out. He raised his hand with the heart. "Want to try a bite?"

Nina grabbed a wood plank intended for an upcoming repair.

Susan stepped in front of her. "No, Nina. He's a demon; that's what he wants."

Nina shoved her aside, jumped out of the van, and charged at Vormath.

Susan shot up and rushed to the door.

"You…" Nina's eyes glowed furiously.

Vormath threw Jacob's body in front of her feet. "This is what happens when you cross a demon." He bore a wicked smile.

Nina knelt and kissed Jacob's forehead. "You're right; one shouldn't mess with a demon. I was warned about that."

"By Susan?" Vormath frowned.

"Heh," Nina scoffed. "Susan? That petty girl, don't make me laugh."

"What is she doing?" Susan peered out the door.

Vormath scratched his nose.

Nina glanced back at Susan manically. "So…" She licked her lips. "You want to know who warned me?"

"Whatever." Vormath shrugged. "I would rather have your friends' souls."

"Sorry, the queen doesn't want anything to happen to Denida, yet."

"The q-queen?" Vormath stuttered.

"She taught me how to avenge the life you just took."

"You?" Vormath sneered. "A human beating an archdemon? Impossible."

"You'll be impressed, then." Nina's eyes glinted.

Vormath plunged his fist into the sky, creating a cone of Darkness around him and a pentagram on the ground. "Too late," he boasted.

"Darkness," Nina thrust her arm forward and fired a silvery beam. The beam smashed into the cone, tinting its surface silver.

"You think white magic can beat me?" Vormath laughed. "The Darkness on Earth is stronger than that, and it's only growing now we're here."

Nina lowered her hand, covering it with the other, only to extend it again, creating a silvery beam with twice the strength of the first one. It pummeled the cone, creating a tiny hole.

Vormath's eyes widened. He swiftly clenched his fists, expelling Darkness from his fists to fix the hole and reinforce the cone.

Nina inhaled and exhaled slowly, focusing all her strength on her last burst of magic, which crashed into the cone with enough force to shatter it.

"But how?" Vormath screamed in disbelief.

"There is something stronger than your petty Darkness." Nina stepped closer.

"Was that magic?" Den gasped. "Susan, how is that possible?"

"Silvery…"

"Huh?" Den nudged Susan's shoulder. "What?"

Susan shook her head, her eyes locked on Nina and Vormath.

A pentagram appeared on the ground around Vormath and Nina, and a dark cloud appeared above them. Vormath raised his arms as he shapeshifted into a demonic shape.

Nina continued stepping closer, unphased.

Vormath shook his left hand and thrust it forward, sending a black flame hurtling toward Nina.

Nina sidestepped, but the flame still licked the side of her shirt, burning her sleeve. She charged forward, ignoring the flames, but as soon as she neared Vormath, a dark haze appeared where he stood. A bat burst into the air across the pentagram and transformed back into Vormath.

Nina spun around. She hissed and beat out the flame on her shirt with her palm. She eyed Vormath as she dropped to her knees.

Vormath shifted and clenched his fist, ready to strike.

Nina slammed her open palms on the pentagram. The ground lit up with the same silvery shade she had fired before, disintegrating the pentagram.

Vormath stepped back. "No." He shook his head, and his eyes landed on Susan. "You." His pupils darkened. He transformed into a bat and darted through the air to the van.

"Drive!" Susan commanded and slammed the door shut.

Nina lifted her hand, creating a barrier, which the bat smashed into. She lowered her arm and sauntered up to Vormath.

The van stopped as demons strode down the road, blocking their exit.

"What do we do?" Tall Jakob asked.

Susan gazed out the window to check for Vormath. *Did she stop him?*

"Susan?" Sus joined in.

"Wait." Susan lifted her hand.

"Why don't you come down?" Nina stomped her foot.

Vormath's magic ceased, and he reverted to his human form. He crashed to the ground.

Nina smiled. "So small and worthless, how nice."

Vormath's eyes flared red, and he lunged.

Nina raised her hand.

Vormath smashed into an invisible barrier.

Nina's face turned cold as she thrust her hand inside Vormath's gut. She squeezed his still-beating heart a few times before ripping it out.

Nina shoved the heart into her mouth and took a huge bite out of it. She stood and turned, facing the van. She marched down the road, stopping before she reached the van, and waved at it. "It's a shame it had to come to this; I wasn't supposed to show my true colors."

Nina stomped her foot, expelling a wave of silvery magic that vaporized the demons blocking the road. She winked at Susan. "This is fun, though."

"Go!"

"Go!" Susan stomped down on Jakob's foot, accelerating down the road.

Den looked out the window and back at Nina.

Nina stood, waving, with a huge grin on her face.

# Chapter 12- Destiny Forms

*How interesting that they're in Azal's house, on my planet, where Shaddai killed me.* Henna leaned on the windowsill outside, watching as Nina nursed Denida.

"Ouch!" Nina's hand shot to her forehead.

"What's wrong?" Denida attempted to sit up in the bed.

"I don't know. I just had a strange feeling, like something changed?"

"Maybe spending time away from Dynasty was a bad idea."

"No, not that." Nina placed her hand on Denida's. "I just haven't gotten enough rest; that's all." She stretched. "I'm going to get some water. Shout if you need me." She walked into the kitchen and drank a glass of water.

"How is he?" Henna's reflection appeared in a window, next to Nina's.

Nina twirled around to Henna. "Fine, I'm taking care of him."

Henna tapped her finger on her cheek. "I'm going to Earth to see your sister. Shall I pass on a message?"

"Nylah? I thought I was never to hear about her again."

"You aren't supposed to, but she made progress with Den. A possible fate is starting to take form."

"I'm decades ahead of her; Denida thinks I'm his soul mate."

*So, you think.* Henna stared at her fingers as she fiddled with them. "You and your sister are both here for a reason. You both have a destiny to fulfill."

"And I will succeed." Nina planted her hands on her hips.

Henna's eyes shone as she smiled. "I hope so, for your sake." She vanished, surging through dimensions. Many versions of fate's intertwining paths appeared ahead of her until she landed and materialized on Earth. She could hear screams in the distance. *I guess Azal chose that destiny, after all. Soon he won't be called the Prince of Darkness, anymore.* Henna approached a dirt road, scuffed up with tire tracks, and noticed Nina's human form. "Ahem."

Nina turned to Henna. Her mouth opened as if she was about to say something, but she ground her teeth instead. "I…"

Henna slowly shook her head. "I already know what you chose to do."

"I had to avenge Jacob." Nina bared her teeth.

"I had hoped you would've been smarter than this, Nylah."

Nylah kicked the dirt. "Are you here to end me?"

"No," Henna stated matter-of-factly. "You can still help, not in the way I had hoped, but…" She folded her hands. "Susan's soul and human forms are both here."

Nylah grumbled. "I don't like that girl."

"You were stationed here to keep them apart. You'll do your job, unless you've lost interest in divinity?" Henna raised her eyebrows. "You failed me this time. It would be a shame to have to show you what happens if you let me down again."

"It's too late; Susan saw me perform magic, so she knows something is off."

Henna surveyed the field. "Demons are here, so there are solutions."

"Involving demons? But I just killed some of them."

"You'll have to figure this out if you don't want your sister to outpace you. She's alone with Denida's soul form, as we speak."

"No," Nylah hissed. "I'll find a way."

"Then I will anticipate your success." Henna clasped her hands. "Until the next time." She vanished and flew through the dimensions until she appeared in Valhalla.

"My Queen." Loki bowed. "What brings you here?"

"You." Henna extended her hand.

Loki grinned at her hand.

"I would like you to help me, which will also help you."

Loki simpered and grabbed her hand.

Henna traveled through dimensions with Loki and stopped at a specific world.

Loki examined their surroundings. "Where are we?"

"I brought you to an Underworld, the Wild West."

Loki's eyebrows creased in befuddlement.

"Claus is here. He's mischievous, like you. He can help Denida reach his potential."

"Isn't that too much interference?"

Henna glared. "We're just helping Destiny follow the right path."

Loki tapped his finger on his trousers. "And what good will I get out of assisting him?"

"Help me, and you'll see." The rainbow shade in Henna's eyes brightened. "You don't want to be in Odin's shadow forever, do you? I can grant you the means to surpass him."

"Okay." Loki sneered.

"Just get Claus to Earth."

Loki shrugged. "But where is this Claus of yours?" He turned to Henna, only to find her vanishing.

Henna appeared outside Azal's estate. She sauntered through the door and into the living room, where Denida was still resting. "Hello, my child."

As soon as she spoke, Denida's eyes turned dark, and his face cold. He propped himself up. "Henna, let me guess; you've come to try to involve me in another scheme?"

"I only came to check on you. I see you are not feeling well."

Denida climbed to his feet, leaning against the wall to steady himself. "You're up to something."

"Do we have company?" Nina froze in the doorway when her eyes met Henna's.

"Hello, Milady, I'm Henna. Who might you be?" Henna approached the door with an extended hand.

"I'm Nina." Nina surveyed Denida. "You really shouldn't be up, Denny." She passed Henna to approach Denida.

"Ah, Denny's wife, how nice to finally meet you." Henna's eyes met Nina's.

Nina took ahold of Denida's arm, trying to ease him down.

"No." Denida shoved Nina behind him. He clenched his hand with the ring. "You're not welcome here, and don't call me Denny!"

Henna's gaze fell on the clenched hand. "I just wanted to say hi. I'll leave you to your recovery." Henna shifted her focus to Nina before backing out of the room. She levitated back to her castle, standing high above everything else in rainbow radiance.

*I will await Nina here. Maybe I should see how Loki's doing in the meantime.* An image of Loki pacing through a town formed in front of her.

***

*Where would this Claus person be?* A horse-drawn carriage passed, before Loki crossed the road and meandered through a saloon's swinging doors.

All eyes turned to the door.

"Hi, how are y'all?" Loki waved.

A row of men approached, encircling Loki. "You're not welcome here." The man closest to Loki reached for a gun holstered on his belt.

Loki turned his sight to the other patrons around the man. "Are you sure you're talking for everyone?" he smirked.

"Either you back out of here, or we will escort you out by force." The guy squinted.

Loki rolled his eyes.

The man drew his gun. "Last chance."

"*Bang!*" rang from the stairs. A man with a shiny star on his chest stood on the top step. He descended the stairs. "Are you gentlemen causing trouble, again?"

The hooligans surrounding Loki stepped back, as the lawman approached. They snuck a quick peek at their ringleader.

"Not you again, Claus." The ringleader spat on the floor.

"Yes, me. Or would you rather deal with Sheriff Robert?"

"Let's go." The leader rushed to the door with his cohorts.

"Claus." Loki bowed. "Sheriff," his eyes fell on the writing plastered upon the shiny star. "Just the man I was looking for.

Claus polished his badge with his sleeve. "Yes, a sheriff saved your sorry hide."

"Denida's Claus. I'm Loki, and I can-"

"I'm not interested." Claus's face turned expressionless. "Have a wonderful day!" He tilted his hat and marched outside.

*No, you don't.* Loki dashed after him. "I didn't get to say thanks."

"I was just passing through this town." Claus arched his neck and mounted a horse. "There's a competent sheriff here, who can help you with your problem." He brought his horse to a gallop and trotted down the road.

*We're not done, yet.* Loki untied a horse fastened to a post and climbed onto it. He pursued Claus. *He's so far ahead already.* Loki rested his hand on the horse's side. Energy emanated from his hand to the horse. The horse increased its stride, allowing Loki to catch up. He lifted his hand from the horse's side to the reins. "Hello again, Claus."

Claus gaped. "How-"

"We didn't finish our chat."

"No!" Claus yanked the reins, halting his horse. He dismounted it and reached for his gun, aiming it at Loki. "There's no way you caught up to me that fast."

Loki rested the reins in his left hand. "I used magic. You must remember how that feels?"

"Magic?" Claus reinforced his hold on his gun with his other hand and stalked over to Loki. When he reached Loki's horse, he yanked Loki off of it and spun him around, cuffing his hands behind his back. Apparently satisfied, Claus forced Loki to his knees.

Loki wore a wide grin when Claus faced him. "Are you do-"

"Shut up!" Claus demanded. "I'll ask the questions. Are you a demon?"

"Demon?" Loki mocked. "I'm better than those petty creatures. Insults know no bounds, you know?"

Claus released his grip and stepped back. "If not a demon, then what are you?"

"Demons are not the only beings who can use magic, you know. There exists magic stronger than dark magic."

Claus shook his head. "White magic doesn't hold a candle to dark." He stowed his gun, pushed Loki forward, halting next to his horse, and rummaged through his satchel.

"Claus?" Loki leered. "White and dark magic are just bastardized versions of the true magic: silver."

Claus frowned, eyeing Loki.

The cuffs shone brightly and disintegrated. Loki lifted his arms and rubbed his wrist.

Claus grabbed his revolver and pulled the pin back, keeping his eyes on Loki. "Freeze, Demon!"

"I don't see why the queen thinks you and I are alike." Loki shuddered. *Maybe it was an insult?*

"What queen?"

"The one who foretold these events."

"One wrong move, and you're dead." Claus shook the gun and tilted it at the second horse. "We're going to my boss. You will ride in front."

"I already listened… to Henna." Loki mounted the horse.

"You can tell Robert all about that. You might be my lucky catch." Claus approached his horse. "We're going-"

*Maybe we are alike, after all.* "To the second Gate, I know." Loki flashed Claus a smile before making the horse canter.

Claus followed Loki, watching his every move.

As the horses passed the settlement's outer wall, Loki stared at the huge Gate. *No way.* He stared with his mouth slightly agape. *I never thought that the Gate Henna mentioned to Odin would be here, of all places.*

"Hey!" Claus yelled. "Wake up, already."

Loki spun around with wide eyes. "Why is Henna's Gate here?"

Claus grumbled. "I don't care about your nonsense. We're going up that hill." He titled his head to indicate a curve in the path.

"To see Robert?"

"The law in the land, yes."

"You like being a petty arm of the law under the authority Denida appointed?" Loki blurted out without realizing it. *Why did I ask that?* He eyed the sky. *Queen?*

Claus lowered his hand to his holster, tightening his fingers around his gun's grip. "Move it!"

Loki raised his eyebrows and turned his focus onto the giant Gate. "What if I want to go there, first?"

Claus lifted his gun, aimed it at Loki, and pulled the trigger, but Loki vanished. Claus dismounted his horse and searched around Loki's horse with his gun drawn. Finding nothing, he surveyed his surroundings, and his eyes locked on the giant Gate.

"Over here!" Loki stood next to the Gate, waving.

Claus ran to the Gate, his face turning red with exertion. When he reached Loki, he doubled over, gasping for air. "Freeze… where… you… are."

"The queen's world is behind this Gate, you know."

"Your queen, again? Enough of that nonsense. This Gate is blocked off for security purposes. Your queen isn't beyond it, nor is anyone else's."

"Are you sure about that?" Loki extended his hands. "You want to cuff me again, don't you?"

"You'd just make them disappear again," Claus snarled.

"Probably." Loki arched his neck. "I wanted to see the Gate Denida used, and now I have."

"I hope it was worth it, because I don't care." Claus dragged Loki with him, leading him up the hill and into a house.

"Wait!" A guard standing watch inside held out his hand. "The sheriff's occupied."

Claus flinched. "This is important; I've come to-"

"There's more important business than a lawman's report."

"No," Claus hissed. "I must see Robert; I have a prisoner."

The guard shook his head. "Sorry, Sir, but no can do. Just lock up the hoodlum."

"You sure are an important sheriff," Loki jested.

Claus gritted his teeth and yanked Loki out of the building, continuing down a dirt road. He handed him to another set of guards in front of a jail, then spun and stomped off.

"Leaving so soon? Such a shame, you never even got to show me to your boss." Loki shrugged. "Guess you must like the feeling, having been both Denida's and Medusa's lapdog before this." Loki shuddered. *It happened again. Who's Medusa?*

Claus stopped and shot Loki a death glare. He strolled back, turning his eyes to the guards. "Excuse us for a second."

The guards nodded and trekked back to their checkpoint.

Claus sighed. "Medusa was an archdemon, not someone under my control-"

"But you failed because of her," Loki sneered.

Claus glanced at the guards on the other end of the building, then threw a punch at Loki.

Loki fell to the ground and struggled to his feet. "Oh, yeah!" He grinned joyfully. "That fire, how I've missed thee." He straightened up. "Don't you hate Lord Denida for thwarting your plans? He's the reason you're in this wasteland, right?"

Claus snatched Loki and slammed him into the bars. "Denida was never worthy of being called a lord."

"Is Little Evil better?" Loki muttered.

Claus loosened his grip. "Little Evil was the reason I failed."

"You won't lose this time," Loki gloated.

"What do you mean?"

A surge of Loki's tongue overtook him again. "Lucifer no longer cares about Denida. Vengeance is all that matters to him. My queen wants Denida's human form dead. If you help with that initiative, Earth will be yours."

Claus's mouth hung agape. "That's impossible. No queen can-"

A light appeared next to Claus. It shone brightly, and time froze. Henna stepped forward from the light with open arms. "Hello, my child."

Claus drew his gun. "I'm not your child. Stay back!"

"No? Guess who I met; you might remember him." Henna lifted her hands and an image appeared between them, depicting a rendezvous with her and Denida.

Claus gripped the gun tighter. "I don't care who you know."

"Maybe you will like this, then." Henna's eyes grew intense with a rainbow shade, and the image morphed into another one, depicting a barren street with carriages and horses passing by.

"This is very different." A Claus in the image stood beside Denida and gazed around.

Denida put his hand on Claus's shoulder. "I hope I'm not making a mistake. Take care of yourself, Claus." He walked a few steps before vanishing from the image.

"I remember this." Claus waved his arms. "But if you're not a demon, and you're not from the Underworlds, what are you? Are you Loki's queen?"

Henna lowered her hands, terminating the image. "Am I?" She turned to Loki.

Loki smirked. "Claus seems to believe that dark magic is the strongest magic."

"Really?" Henna's focus returned to Claus. She smiled vibrantly, and the color in her eyes intensified. "How can I show you this, then? It's not by darkness or light, but rather, a more complex magic." A silvery light formed in front of her, started to take shape, and the image finally reappeared.

In the image, Denida stood beside the giant Gate.

Robert ran up to Denida. "Is something wrong?"

"I left an old friend in your world. Can I trust you to keep an eye on him for me?" Denida whispered.

Claus trudged through the fog, making the image dissipate. "I already knew Robert was watching me for Denida. Don't waste my time with old news. Have a good day!"

Henna stepped closer to Loki. "Was this part of your plan, Loki?"

"Not at first, but it worked, didn't it?" Loki grinned.

"Come." Henna snapped her fingers, and they vanished, only to resurface in front of Claus's horse.

Claus rummaged through a pouch on the saddle. He peeked up for just a moment, before focusing on it again. "You again, Lady?"

Henna tilted her head to the side, where Loki stood waving.

"What?" Claus tore his gun from its holster.

"No." Henna clenched her fist vaporizing the gun.

"How did you do that?"

"I used *my* magic."

Claus frowned. "What do you mean your magic?"

"It's a magic that precedes light and dark magic. I can grant you anything you desire, Claus, if you help me." She glanced at the house. "Unless you enjoy being babysat?"

"You want me to kill Denida's human form, but I'm trying to-"

"Make amends?" Henna smiled tenderly. "That must be so boring, when I can grant you a power stronger than the Darkness's, and yes, a chance to kill Denida, without all the pesky consequences."

Claus stepped closer. "Without… how?"

Henna extended her hand. "Do we have a deal? Will you kill Denida's human form for me?"

"You can grant me the power to prevent them from stopping me?"

"If you wish to assist me, it won't be a concern." Henna's smile widened. "Which path will you choose? Earth, or here, the Wild West?"

"I…"

"Claus?" Robert strolled out of the mansion behind them. "Who're they?"

"Um…"

Loki shot Henna a glance. *This can't be good.*

"I'm Henna." She extended her hand.

Robert shook it after a slight hesitation. "I've heard that name before." He tapped his fingers on his chin.

Loki shifted on his feet. "No," Henna's voice rang in his head.

"We're just wishing Claus well on his travels in your world." Henna winked at Claus.

Robert shrugged. "I think an old friend mentioned your name. Could you possibly know Denida?"

Henna glowered with bright rainbow eyes. "Why don't you ask him?"

"Denida told me that he'd be away with his wife for a while."

"For now," Loki sneered.

"What?" Robert clenched his fists and faced Claus. "Detain both of them; there's something off about this whole thing."

Claus raised his eyebrows. "Why, they aren't criminals, or-"

"They threatened Denida."

"No, they didn't," Claus insisted. "Loki just said Denida might not always-"

Robert whipped out his gun. "When it comes to Denida, there are always people who are up to no good."

"No!" Claus blocked Robert's aim and tore his gun from its holster. "I don't care about Denida; he never did anything good for me."

"He saw the greatness in you."

"The greatness?" Claus extended his gun. "You mean he learned how to take advantage of me."

"Trust me; he would never do that. They're only here to hurt him, like all the demons before them."

Henna rested her hand on Claus's shoulder and stepped in front of him as Claus shifted aside, gun still raised. "Do I look demonic?"

"Whatever you are, Lady, I know you are suspicious."

"Oh, I am," Henna smirked. "But you are insignificant to me. I don't have time for this." She flicked her wrist, and the giant Gate lit up with a blinding light.

Robert gazed at the silvery glow emanating from it and spun back to Henna. "You!"

Henna tilted her head. "More drama? Fine." Her eyes flickered into a rainbow shade, and she teleported behind Robert. "I would hate to have you in my world, so sleep well." She rested her hand on Robert's forehead and pulled his head back.

Robert slumped to the ground.

"Why don't I show you my world, Claus?" Henna stepped past Robert's body.

"What shall I do with him?" Loki wrinkled his nose at Robert.

"Let him sleep. He may have company, soon, so he will need his rest before the storm." Henna locked arms with Claus and strolled to the Gate.

"You activated that Gate? I thought the Gates can't power on without a main device."

"It's different from the other Gates." Henna put her finger over Claus's lips. "This one works with a magic that only I possess."

"But-" Claus peeked at Robert.

"Choices, Claus. Robert's made his choice and he'll always protect Denida. I can grant you the power to stand above anyone, if you let me show you my world."

Claus followed Henna through the Gate.

"Go to Earth," Henna's voice rang in Loki's head.

# Chapter 13- All for Henna

When Henna appeared within the Gate's world, people swarmed her and bowed in adoration. "Don't you wish to have people treat you this way?" She glanced at Claus.

Claus gazed around. "What exactly is this place?"

"Home," Henna beamed. "- but also, where I can grant you powers, if you kill Denida."

Claus bit his lip. "But why do you want him dead?"

"I don't put all my eggs in the same basket, Claus. That would be foolish."

"Wait." Claus approached Henna. "You have more people on this mission? Who else-"

"Do you want to help me, or shall I take you back to the Wild West, where you already showed your true colors to Robert?"

Claus's eyes widened and locked on someone. "Daniel?"

Henna snapped her fingers, and a boy strode up to her, stopping in front of her. "Yes, my Queen?"

Henna pointed at Claus. "Daniel, say hello to my friend. He's going to help us bring your dad here."

"Claus? I remember you!" Daniel waltzed over to Claus and smiled softly. "Will you really help us?"

"How is this possible?" Claus scratched his head. "Denida and Nina's son, Daniel, is here?"

Henna spread her arms. "This is where dead souls go, Claus. I seek to bring the death I endured to the three who wronged me. I will grant powers to anyone who can help me."

Henna spread her arms. "This is where all the dead souls go, Claus. I seek to bring the death I endured to the three it belongs to. I will grant powers to anyone who can help me."

"Denida killed you?"

"No." Henna chortled. "Shaddai and Azal did, but you'd know them better as God and Lucifer."

"Why Denida, then?"

"He has a path he needs to take."

Claus turned around and took several steps forward, then stopped. "No, this doesn't add up. How did you come to this?"

"I am the goddess of all the gods in your world."

Claus pursed his lips. "How, then?" He shuffled back to her. "How did you become a goddess in the first place? Was your family divine, too?"

"Demons are swarming on Earth, so it may-"

"No, you're avoiding the question. You don't want to tell me how you became what you are?"

"I could always return you to your certain doom in the Wild West." Henna raised her eyebrows slightly, then flicked her fingers, and time around them froze. "You don't have the power to demand anything from me."

"I didn't-"

*I hope Destiny gives him the worst fate, but if not, he could be useful.* Henna's eyes intensified into their rainbow shade. "I will show you, and you can choose your path."

"Yes, if you reward me after I succeed, I will show you that I deserve the power." Claus clenched his fist.

"More than Shaddai, at least." Henna lifted her palm, creating a silvery veil in front of them.

It showed a dark void, where stars and dust shot through the universe. The image zoomed in on a lonely rock drifting in space. A much younger version of Henna laid still. After a few minutes, her fingers twitched, and she sat up, examining the empty space as far as the eye could see.

Henna shifted onto all fours and started to crawl. After the first movements of her legs, the ground in front of her collapsed and broke off the rock. She spun around to go the other way, only to have that section smash off, as well.

A silvery ash enshrouded her, and she watched different versions of what would have happened if she had gone left, right, or backward, or never moved at all. The possibilities flooded her mind. She clenched her hands tightly in front of her chest as the many variations of time flashed through her mind.

A silvery light emanated from the dark sky. "Fate's course is flexible. It's up to you to ensure that it runs smoothly."

"B-but… how can I?" Henna stuttered.

"We created you to oversee the many destinies that will unfold, for the universe, and you, personally. Only you can see these paths, but interfere with balance, and we will replace you."

"Oversee?"

"Destiny courses within you and empowers you. We'll be watching." The silvery light burst and smashed into her, making even more possible futures burn through her mind, turning her eyes a rainbow shade.

The image faded, and Henna gazed at Claus. "I have never heard that voice either before or after that moment, but I always knew the possible outcomes of any event. I still do, just not as many as before."

"Wouldn't sending me to Earth to kill Denida qualify as interfering?"

"Aren't you a logical one? Everything I've done up until now has made me realize that I can interfere, and that light and voice won't stop me."

"But Destiny shows you the paths, so couldn't it just lie?"

"It would have replaced me already, instead of showing me falsehoods."

"If I succeed, what will my destiny be?"

"Your destiny?" Henna snickered. "It depends. Your success sees you ruling Earth, your failure leads to your splashing death, and there are some other options depending on your exact choices." She flicked her fingers, and time resumed.

Claus rubbed his hands together manically. "In that case, when do I start?"

Henna rested her hand over his forehead, and a silvery ash enveloped Claus's head. "You're ready for your path."

Claus sniffed, then flinched. "I feel different. What now?"

"Time to see Loki." Henna grabbed Claus, and they teleported to Earth.

Loki waved as they appeared in front of him.

Henna stared at him sternly. "Loki will assist you, but remember: Denida's heart must be removed before he breathes his last breath." She folded her arms. "And Susan from the Underworld is here to protect him."

Claus licked his lips. "Am I allowed to kill Susan, too?"

Henna's eyes narrowed. "Denida comes first. Then, we'll talk about Susan. Until then, do not harm her; it will only infuriate Denida." She signaled Loki and waved her hand. "I shall anticipate good news." Henna teleported away through the pathway to her castle.

Nina gazed at the throne.

Henna cleared her throat, appearing before Nina.

Nina spun to face her. "My Queen, you wished to see me?"

"Yes." Henna sat on her throne. "You wish to have your son in your arms again, correct?"

Nina sprang to her feet and rushed forward.

Henna raised her hand, locking Nina in place.

An image appeared between them of Henna standing beside Nina's son, Daniel. Henna ruffled his hair.

Henna clenched her fist, terminating the image.

"Daniel!" Nina fell to her knees.

"You wanted to see him, and now you have."

Nina sniffed and wiped her tears, her eyes as red as plums. "I'm keeping Denida from Susan, so could you let me-"

Henna dismounted her throne and knelt beside Nina, resting her hand on Nina's shoulder. "I thought about that; it must be hard. I can't give him to you yet, but I can let you visit him."

"What-" Nina gasped. "Really?"

"Yes, but I do need something from you, in order to let you see him: Denida's ring."

"His ring?" Nina lowered her head, eyeing the floor. "He would notice…"

"Shame, I guess you're happy waiting to see Daniel until I bring him back, then." Henna shrugged and returned to her throne. "That time is nearing. It should be in a few years… or decades."

"No." Nina staggered to her feet. "I'll get it; just be ready to take me to him." She trudged out of the castle.

*The time has finally come for the end game…* Henna smiled widely.

***

Nina hurried with ever-increasing speed to Azal's house. Inside, she gazed at Denida.

"Nina?" Denida approached her. "I feel better, now. Whatever that was, it felt exactly like magic. Maybe there's something with this place. It is the world Lucifer and God came from, after all." He kissed Nina's cheek. "Where were you? I searched all over for you."

"I- I needed some air. That goddess you told me about was here; it was unreal."

Denida ground his teeth. "I know. I thought she only appeared here when summoned. Seeing as that's not the case, we should go. This place isn't safe."

Nina shook her head. "I doubt she'll be back."

"You don't know Henna. Restraint isn't in her vocabulary. I once believed that she'd disappear, too, until I realized how manipulative she truly is."

Nina folded her arms. "How so?"

Denida arched his neck. "How do you feel about what happened to Daniel, now?"

*Does he know?* Nina's eyes widened. "He's gone. We're here to find each other and move on." She stepped up to the door and rested her hand on the handle.

"Nina." Denida grabbed her hand and lifted it. "I wanted to undo Daniel's death, so I rebuilt the time machine."

"What?" Nina tore her hand free. "Why are you bringing this up, again? I still don't understand why you didn't just bring him back in the first place. That aside, I thought the time machine was a one-time thing. It still works?"

"Yes, but it requires Henna's material." Denida swallowed. "Even so, I see, now, that if I had stopped Medusa, it wouldn't have changed a thing. She was just a pawn."

"The Darkness," Nina stated scornfully.

"No, Henna told her to. Medusa tried to discourage Henna." Denida gritted his teeth. "But to no avail."

Nina grabbed Denida's arms to prevent her knees from giving out. "Henna wanted him dead, no matter what." She stared into Denida's eyes. "Can you get me some water?"

Denida gently released her and stayed beside her momentarily, before heading into the kitchen.

*That little witch! How dare she? No, she will pay for this after I get Daniel back my way.* She plopped down.

Denida returned with a glass and handed it to Nina.

Nina took the cup from her husband and sipped from it. "Are you certain that Henna caused that?"

"Yes, but…" Denida shrugged his shoulders. "I still haven't figured out what she would gain from his death."

Nina placed her water on the table. "Maybe you were right. We should go back to the Underworlds."

"Really?" Denida's eyes lit up.

"Henna won't stop," Nina hissed. "We should get as far away from her as we can."

"Good idea." Denida sprang to his feet. "I'll pack. Can you make sure we don't forget anything?"

Nina sighed, burying her head in her arms as Denida moseyed around, collecting their belongings. She peeked up to see him leaving, and a wide smirk crossed her lips. *Henna's material, huh? I may need to take the ring for myself.* She followed Denida, but stayed in the doorway while he packed.

Denida grabbed the duffle bags and spun to exit the room. His eyes filled with shock at the sight of his wife. "Nina, are you ready to go?"

Nina strolled up to Denida and kissed him tenderly, her hand on his arm. "Let's go home."

Denida embraced her and clenched his fist with the ring. A silvery aura enveloped and teleported them back to Dynasty.

"Feels like it's been forever." Denida surveyed their surroundings. "No one's here. Let's go home." He held Nina's hand, and they strolled to the front doors.

The butler stopped tidying the lobby and stared at them, wide-eyed. "You're back?"

Denida chuckled. "We weren't going-"

Nina lifted her hand. "We're still spending time on us. Pretend you haven't seen us."

Denida peered at Nina, puzzled. "They'll know we're back when we start spending time-"

Nina elbowed Denida's shoulder. "The cabin."

Denida wrinkled his forehead. "What cabin?"

"Where we caught Claus?" Nina sneered.

Denida scratched his temple. "Yes, she's right. Just forget you saw us." He grabbed Nina's hand and teleported to the cabin.

Nina clapped her hands. "We'll take some time to find ourselves here, without any interruptions from Henna or anyone from the Underworlds!" She took Denida by the hand. "Why don't I show you what love feels like." She led him inside the cabin and pushed him onto the bed, climbing up next to him.

***

"Somebody is having fun," the High Sorcerer sniggered. He turned away from the window and took in his surroundings. "So, this is the fabled Dynasty." He meandered through the forest, eventually exiting on the other side.

Dynasty basked in the bright afternoon sun.

*I think I'll wait here.* The High Sorcerer arched his neck. *Guess I'll see which of your futures will come to pass.*

Horses trotted outside the stables as stableboys tidied the dwellings.

The High Sorcerer approached the enclosure. He held out his hand for the nearest horse. *Come.* He blew air on his hand, and the silvery whisp flew forth with a soft silver color, landing on the horse's back.

The horse stomped up to him. The horse stopped, starting to graze in front of the High Sorcerer, who petted the horse compassionately. "Aren't you a nice one?" His hand rested on the horse's mane.

"Hey!" Nina flew out of the forest and rushed to the horse. "Get your filthy hands off my horse."

"Oh?" The High Sorcerer turned to Nina. "This must be Angel." He winked. "You appear to be in a hurry. Is it worth it to stay with your horse, or can this urgent matter wait, I wonder?"

Nina bared her teeth and shoved her left hand into her pocket. "Who are you?"

"I'm like you."

Nina laughed. "Me?" she mocked. "That's funny. I have nothing in common with someone as irritating as you." She climbed over the paddock railing and grabbed Angel's reins to lead him back to the stables.

When she reached the stables, she handed the horse to one of the stableboys. "Put him inside." She walked to the Dynasty estate.

"Denida must miss you." The High Sorcerer leaned against a wall as Nina turned the corner.

Nina grunted and continued past him.

"I guess you don't wish to talk." The High Sorcerer shrugged. "I suppose I should talk to Denida about you and Henna."

Nina stopped, as if frozen in place. She clenched her fists, and with one swift motion, she spun around, charging at the Sorcerer.

The High Sorcerer clapped his hands, and a silvery dust appeared. When it subsided, he was gone.

Nina reached for the dust, rubbing it between her fingers. "That's Henna's magic," she whispered under her breath.

"Yes." The High Sorcerer appeared behind her. "I told you; I'm like you. The only difference is that I have a different mission."

Nina lowered her hand. "Does Henna know you're here?"

"She knows what could happen here because she sees all possible paths."

Nina peeked in the direction of the cottage. "What exactly is your mission?"

"It is mostly to direct the Warlock."

Nina grumbled. "No, why has your mission brought you here?"

"Why are you asking me what you already know?" The High Sorcerer tilted his head.

Nina's hand searched her pocket. "I can't fail."

"There's only one way you can succeed; you must've realized this."

Nina closed her eyes and nodded with a deep sigh. "I'm aware." She opened her eyes. "Henna."

Henna manifested in between them, and she leered at Nina. "You've got something for me?"

Nina lifted her hand from her pocket, revealing a shiny ring. She held it in front of Henna's face. "I can see Daniel, now?"

"In exchange for that, yes." Henna extended her hand.

Nina handed the ring to Henna.

Henna closed her hand, and a wide smirk appeared on her face. "Thank you." Henna turned her focus to the High Sorcerer. "You can proceed with the next step; Denida should be waking up, soon." She tightened her fingers around the ring, emitting a silvery shade that rendered Nina unconscious.

The High Sorcerer folded his hands and lifted them to his chin. "Denida's weak enough to kill."

# Chapter 14- Darkness's Will

The Commander squinted as the demons led him into Hell. *The Darkness here is denser than I have ever experienced.*

"Halt!" Bael commanded the demons leading the Commander. He stepped up beside the Commander. "You're not going any farther." He flung the Commander into a crowd of souls.

Bael gloated as he roamed through the crowd, passing the Commander, and stopping at a group of demons. "Where's Denida's colonel?"

The demon lifted his finger above the crowd. All the souls darkened into a sea of silhouettes, except for one individual, who glowed.

Bael grinned. "There he is."

"No." The Commander blocked Bael's path. "You'll have to go through me."

"You think I wasn't planning on that?" Bael snickered and threw out his arm, expelling a dark cloud that hurtled the Commander into the crowd. "Remember your place." He spun to the Colonel.

*Bastard!* The Commander jumped up. "I said stop."

Bael halted and faced the Commander. "Do you have a death wish, Human?" His eyes reddened.

"I'm a soldier from the Underworlds," the Commander hissed.

"I suppose we have something in common."

"Don't make me laugh; I'm nothing like you." The Commander spat on the ground.

The red in Bael's eyes turned crimson, and Darkness adorned his silhouette. "You're right; I wouldn't die, as you-"

"Bael!" The Colonel shoved to the front of the crowd. "You were looking for me?"

The Darkness around Bael subsided. "I was, but your boy seems to want my attention."

"Commander, stand down!" the Colonel scowled at Bael. "No problem, now."

"You want to delay his death? How nice of you."

"Prevent, you mean." The Colonel clenched his jaw.

"Everyone here is going to die." Bael extended his arms.

The Colonel surveyed the crowd. "Shouldn't they become demons, instead?"

"Time's changing. When strengthening the Darkness is all that matters, demons are inconsequential," Bael gloated.

"Denida escaped," the Colonel grimaced.

Bael's eyes intensified. "He was nothing."

"Little Evil was nothing?" The Colonel frowned. "I thought Lucifer was training him, and your demons knew that?"

Bael forced a smile. "Your point? You're not him, and you will *never* see him again."

The Colonel shrugged and pointed upwards. "Denida and I defeated the Dark Angel, Danyel. I know Denida escaped from Hell. The Darkness even showed him to me, his human side, at least." The Colonel gritted his teeth. "What I mean by this is, if he can get out, so can we, especially now when everything is in disarray."

Bael sneered. "You sure are cocky for a meager soul." The Darkness around him intensified with each step he took in the Colonel's direction. "The master may be gone, but Darkness is here, and it's growing with each soul we take."

The Colonel flinched and stepped forward. "There's one thing you've forgotten."

"From you?" Bael mocked.

"When the cat's away, the mice shall play."

Bael's eyes narrowed in confusion. "Mice?"

"Other demons vying for power."

"Enough of this!" Bael lifted the Colonel off the ground. "The Darkness is too strong, here."

"Darkness?" The Colonel signaled to Naphtali, who grabbed Bael's arm. "You mean the entity that wanted to kill your master and replace him with Medusa?"

"No one dares to oppose the Darkness." Bael flung the Colonel into the crowd.

*I need to help him.* The Commander's eyes scrutinized his surroundings.

Bael gestured for the other demons to grab the Colonel. They followed Bael to the front of the crowd, where he spun around to face them. "This is the end of Little Evil and all his cohorts." He raised his arm, and Darkness encircled it.

The Colonel tried to jerk free, but the demons tightened their grip on him.

The Commander's eyes landed on a familiar face. *Naphtali!* He dashed through the crowd. "Naphtali, you were a demon before; do you have any idea how to get out of here?"

Naphtali glanced at the Commander a nervously. "There's no escape. We're all going to die, here."

A dark cloud formed above the Colonel. It morphed into a face. "Stop!" The cloud materialized into a shape of a man right in front of the Colonel.

The demons released the Colonel and stepped back.

"You might be strong enough to kill everyone here, including Lucifer, but we are here," the figure insisted.

"You could be strong enough to kill everyone here, including Lucifer, but *we* are here," the figure insisted.

"What do you want? Are you Lucifer?" the Colonel asked disgustedly.

The figure's face changed into a disembodied mouth without a face. "Lucifer's time is up. We can stop him together, if you possess the strength to stop all this?"

"Stop the Devil? Aren't you the one enabling him, and why would I help the likes of you?"

"You have strength, and it would benefit both of us."

"Where is the Devil, anyway?" the Colonel snarled.

"I'll take you."

The Colonel stomped his foot. "Negative, I need Naphtali, the Commander, and my troops with me."

"As you wish." The dark figure dissipated into the cloud, and the demons nudged the Colonel and his specified party to a giant mansion, shrouded in Darkness.

"Where are they taking us?" The Commander peeked at Naphtali.

"Lucifer's mansion."

*This can't be good.* The Commander noticed a row of demons behind them. *We're surrounded.*

Demons shoved them through the double doors. They entered a room where a Gate stood centerstage.

"Oh my god," Naphtali gasped.

The Darkness wafted in through the windows and hovered just below the ceiling. "This is the way to Lucifer," sounded from above.

"He's in Heaven?" The Colonel sounded doubtful.

"Yes." Bael shoved the Colonel into the room. The rest of the soldiers followed them. "You know how this works; you all have to enter together."

The Colonel pointed at the ceiling. "What about that?"

The Darkness materialized in a cloud next to him, taking the shape of a body. "I shall join you."

"The Darkness can adopt a physical form and get into Heaven?" The Colonel touched his forehead with his fingertips.

"Yes," the word from above lingered in the air.

The Colonel cleared his throat. "Let's get a move on."

The demons powered up the Gate, brightening up the room.

Bael extended his arm, and a fireball emerged from his hand. "Move it, or else."

Naphtali pushed the rest of the troop into motion, increasing his pace the closer he drew to the Gate.

When they exited on the other side, angels flew across the sky. The Commander approached the edge of the cloud they stood on, but a magical cone became visible, preventing him from advancing.

The Colonel stepped through the portal last. "So, what do you-" His eyes widened. "The Darkness's body is gone?"

"Sir." The Commander saluted. "Probably because we're in Heaven."

"What do you mean, Commander?" The Colonel turned to the Commander, but his eyes only widened as angels soared above them. He trekked closer to lean over the railing, stretching to glance down. Underneath them, he spotted a cluster of demons barraging Heaven's walls, attempting to break in.

Naphtali waved. "There are stairs over here."

"Hold it!" The Commander marched over to Naphtali. "I'll lead the way." He tiptoed down the stairs.

"The dagger's power will not allow them in."

*Who's that?* The Commander paused and squinted down the stairs.

"Peter."

*That voice… the Darkness's must've made it, after all.* The Commander and his troops retreated up the stairs. "Sir." He saluted the Colonel. "The Darkness is downstairs."

"We must stop it! Follow me, Commander." The Colonel descended the stairs.

Saint Peter jumped in front of the individual from earlier. "Stay back, my Lord!"

"Relax." The Colonel raised his hands. "We've just come from Hell. The man behind you told us to come here."

"We sealed the Gate from Hell."

"Sealed?" The Commander shook his head. "Impossible, we just came from through it."

The man behind Peter stepped past him. "Hello, I'm God. As far as I'm concerned, it's sealed. That aside, you said say I told you to come?"

"Yes, you were right beside me, but you vanished when we stepped through the Gate."

God gritted his teeth. "I think I understand what's going on here…"

"Great!" The Colonel clapped his hands. "So, what do you want us to do?"

"You're not welcome here." God turned to Peter.

"But you told us to kill Lucifer in exchange for our freedom!" The Colonel attempted. "That doesn't make any sense."

"Yes, it does," Peter insisted. "The Darkness broke off from God. It used to be part of him, so it looks like him, and sounds like him."

"That makes more sense." The Colonel hung his head. "Well, we're just passing through, so we'll be on our way."

"We can't just go," Naphtali blurted out.

"Damn, you're stupid," Peter mocked.

"Who's this idiot?" Naphtali shot Peter a death glare.

"I'm the keeper of the Pearly Gates. And you, clever joe?"

"Peter." God raised his hand. "Get rid of them!"

*Get rid of us?* "Wait; we're from Denida's underworld. We're just trying to get home," the Commander interjected.

"I liked Denida." A man hiding behind God rejoiced.

"Jesus." God nodded to Jesus. "Go downstairs."

Jesus grinned at the Commander before prancing down the stairs.

"Denida, again?" Peter remarked scornfully.

"And how do you plan to get rid of us?" The Commander stepped in front of the Colonel. "You can't just exile us while demons are trying to break down Heaven's doors."

"No?"

The Commander reached for Peter's robe. As if his touch triggered something, they all reappeared outside the Pearly Gates, with no sign of Peter.

Lucifer tilted his head. "Colonel." He jerked the Colonel off the ground and smashed him into the Pearly Gates. "Why're you here? You've got two seconds to talk." He tightened his grip around the Colonel's throat. A dark cloud manifested, drifting from Lucifer toward the Colonel.

"The Dark Angels helped me escape Hell, but I have returned to serve you, Master." Naphtali staggered to his knees.

Lucifer released the Colonel, who tumbled to the ground, coughing.

"Serve me, here?"

"I've already been inside Heaven. You want to take it-"

"Wrong!" Lucifer screamed, the sound louder than any in Heaven. His eyes darkened to the shade of black holes. "Why were you inside Heaven, and how?"

Naphtali swallowed, then shifted his gaze to Lucifer. "The Darkness, which looked like God, led us here. We entered through the Gate atop a tower."

"A tower?" Lucifer frowned, glancing into the cloud. "So that's where he has it."

"Master?" Naphtali's jaw trembled.

"Our Gate led you there, with the Darkness's help?"

"Yes." Naphtali lowered his head.

Blue flames enveloped Lucifer's body. "The Darkness doesn't do anything, without getting something in return, so what did you give it?"

"I don't know." Naphtali shook his head, which gleamed with sweat.

"Then I guess some torture will get your lips moving."

"Luci, I have your answer." The Commander stepped forward.

"Luci?" The fire around Lucifer intensified. "I think I will start by torturing you."

"It mistakenly assumed a former demon could replace you." The Commander straightened up.

The fire around Lucifer's body extinguished itself. "That's so nice, but it doesn't get us inside."

The Commander licked his lips and surveyed their surroundings. *The Gate-*

"What about the Gate?" Lucifer twiddled his fingers, as if on the edge of a revelation.

"We can use the Gate to enter Heaven through that tower." He pointed at the tower in Heaven, towering high into the clouds above them. "If you know where the second Gate is, that is-"

"I'm the Lord of Darkness; of course, I know where it is." Lucifer bragged. "Bring them!" He flung his arm around the Commander and took flight over the clouds.

The Commander peered at the tower, scrunching his forehead up in confusion. *Did they use magic to hide the Gate?*

They touched down again, and a Gate down the road of clouds outside of Heaven came into view.

The Commander turned back to see the others joining them. He could see the Pearly Gates in the distance. *That's not too far…*

"Your life is ticking away as you stand there," Lucifer jested.

The Commander shot Lucifer a strained smile before approaching the Gate. "We need this powered on, somehow."

"Like this?" Lucifer thrust his arm out, sending dark energy hurtling through the air. It darkened the clouds until it reached the Gate, which powered on instantly.

"Yes, like that." The Commander continued to the Gate. He knelt to examine its main unit. *Interesting…* "Colonel, can you help me with this? Denida showed you how." He waved his hand.

"Colonel." A demon rubbed his hands together and grabbed the Colonel, pulling him close.

Lucifer shot a beam of Darkness at the demon holding onto the Colonel, vaporizing the demon. "Go help that Commander of yours, unless you wish to join him in Hell."

The Colonel knelt beside the Commander, shaking his head. The Commander pointed to some writing in the cloud in front of the Gate, then pushed the Colonel over onto the writing, smudging it.

"You're right." The Colonel peeked back at Lucifer. "Bring Naphtali; he knows how to do this."

Lucifer turned to Naphtali, and the demons holding him swiftly backed away.

"I'm going." Naphtali waved his arms and dashed over to the Gate. As he neared it, the Commander stood and shoved him in front of the device. In the next second, the Commander pushed him down into the clouds.

"Goddamn, imbeciles," The Commander grunted and approached Lucifer.

"You want more to join you?" Lucifer glared at his demons. "Are you sure you can do this?"

"The Scientist escaped, didn't he? Perhaps you knew him as Jack?" The Commander chuckled.

"Take whomever you need, but if you fail me, you will spend eternity in Hell… all of you."

The Commander guided the remaining soldiers to the Gate.

"Azal." A dark cloud surfaced beside Lucifer and molded itself into a humanoid shape. "You do realize that they're pulling your chain?"

"We're finishing this, now," Lucifer jeered. "You just don't want me to kill your creator."

The cloud grew and surrounded Lucifer, brewing with an intense gust as it expanded in size.

*Now's our chance.* "Let's go!" The Commander signaled for everyone to follow him, and they ran through the Gate.

The cloud intensified, creating a black spot in the middle of all the white clouds.

***

"I made you what you are, and I can take that away, too," the cloud spoke with an intense voice that rang loudly, echoing off the clouds.

"You swore you'd help me get Heavani back, but you failed me!" Lucifer lunged into the cloud, but it shoved him back, sending him smashing into the clouds behind him.

"Weakness shouldn't be rewarded."

"Weak?" Lucifer clenched his fists tightly. He switched into his demon form, and the anger emanating from him made him grow magnitudes larger. "I am not weak." He threw himself into the cloud, cutting a hole in the Darkness with his fiery body.

"Better. Go bring this anger to Shaddai," it sounded from the Darkness, which swirled into the sky and vanished, reappearing in Hell. It lingered above Bael.

Bael's eyes widened and gazed up at the cloud. "Yes, Master?"

"The Colonel failed to penetrate Heaven," the cloud rasped. "We trust you to make him regret failing us."

Bael knelt. "Where are they?"

"The Wild West."

"Understood," Bael smirked with his head still touching the ground. "I won't fail you."

"He must die before he reaches his own Underworld."

Bael shrugged, taken aback. "His own world?"

The dark cloud swirled around Bael, creating a whirlwind until the cloud enshrouded him. An image of a giant face appeared on the inside of it. "Little Evil is in that world; We can't have him learning what the Darkness is doing there."

"He's just a has been," Bael mocked.

The cloud pushed behind Bael, wrapping around his throat. "You are a demon who's supposed to serve us. If you cannot, we can easily eradicate you."

"No, no, no, I will make sure he doesn't return to Denida."

"You would be smart to; anyone who fails us forfeits their life." The dark cloud retreated into the sky.

# Chapter 15- Denida's Ring

Denida wiped the sleep from his eyes. "Nina, what do you-" He glimpsed her side of the bed and stopped mid-sentence. *Wonder where she is?*

"Nina?" Denida climbed out of bed and wandered through the cottage. "Nina?" He scratched his head when he finished checking the last room. *This is peculiar…*

"She's not here, Denny." Gabriel appeared and hunched over next to the fireplace.

"Gabriel, why are you here?"

Gabriel straightened up. "I've followed you since you were small. You vanished for a few days, yet now you are back. Where did you disappear to?"

"If you know where everybody is, where's Nina? Did something happen to her?"

"She headed back to Dynasty, but I don't feel her, anymore."

*Why?* Denida sat in a chair in front of the fireplace.

"Earth is the only place I can't locate someone right away, but I didn't *feel* you anywhere."

"I was in Henna's world with Nina."

"What?" Gabriel knelt beside to Denida. "How is that possible? That world was destroyed."

*That's right… Gabriel never found Craym again, following Henna's death…*

Gabriel watched his fingers. "I couldn't find it because it didn't exist; Henna destroyed it."

"You can…" Denida gaped at Gabriel. "- read my mind?"

Gabriel looked up. "I'm not supposed to?"

Denida stroked each of his fingers compulsively and stared down at his hand. *It's gone.*

"What's gone?" Gabriel frowned.

"The ring!" Denida slammed his hand to his chest, feeling the necklace, pulling it out from under his shirt. *At least Henna's necklace is still here.*

Gabriel's wide eyes locked on the necklace.

"Maybe I dropped the ring?" Denida twirled around and rushed to the bedroom, running his hand through the rug by the bed. *Nothing.* He slumped to the floor and buried his head between his legs. After a moment, Denida jumped up and sprinted into the other room, where Gabriel now stood by the fireplace. "You can feel when there are changes in magic-"

"Not your ring. Its power is beyond my capabilities." Gabriel straightened up. "Where do you last remember having it?"

"When Nina and I were… no." Denida shook his head. "I must have misplaced it."

"Okay, but said you were in Henna's world. Can you show me that?"

Denida frowned and showed Gabriel his hand. "Do you not see what's missing, here? I can't take you until I find the ring."

"The necklace," Gabriel muttered. "If what you've said is true, Henna showed you how to enter Craym, but deliberately kept us away."

Denida lifted his necklace and gazed at it.

"The ring has to be here." Gabriel smiled reassuringly. "No one could get close enough to you to take it, when only you and Nina were here."

*Nina couldn't have, could she?* "No." Denida shrugged and slid the necklace back under his shirt. "There is no reason to go to that accursed place."

"Perhaps Nina-"

"No," Denida hissed. "She can't even get there without me."

"Maybe seeing Henna's world and feeling her magic can help me sense the ring? Her magic covered her world, if I remember, correctly. If not, four eyes are still better than two."

"Forgot I can only see through one?" Denida joked.

"Sorry, I only-"

"Forget it." Denida waved his hand dismissively. "I'll take you, if it means that much to you, but the world is devoid of life." He approached Gabriel and extended his arm.

Gabriel took Denida's hands.

The necklace under Denida's shirt glowed through his shirt, teleporting them away from the cottage. They reappeared in Henna's world.

Gabriel slowly stepped forward with his mouth hanging open. "This really is…" He walked past Denida, eyes wandering.

"Gabe, where-" Denida hurried after him. After a few minutes, he slowed his pursuit, as Gabriel neared a familiar row of houses.

Gabriel paused at the front door, as if rooted to the spot. "This was my house," he whispered.

Denida forced a smile. "The residence far away from Lucifer's and Shaddai's houses, I remember."

Gabriel peeked at him. "That's right, I forgot Lucifer showed you, once." He clasped his hand around the door handle and yanked it open, sauntering inside.

Denida turned his eye to the castle. *I hope this doesn't last long.* He strode to the door but stopped with a wide eye as silvery ash appeared before them. *Henna.*

"What brings you back, my child?" Henna's eyes turned warm. "Gabriel's house? I wonder…" She passed through the door.

*Oh, crap.* Denida bolted after her.

Gabriel examined a picture frame in silence. "I miss them."

"They miss you, too." Henna lifted her hand. "You want to come and see them with me?"

Gabriel peered at her. He laid the frame down slowly. "I don't belong in your world, and you don't belong, here." He spun to face her. "Why does this planet still exist? Is anyone here, or did you kill them all?"

"You mean your parents? When you, Shaddai, and Azal murdered me, you killed everyone in this world."

"I did nothing. Shaddai killed you."

Henna shrugged casually. "But you followed him. Azal didn't stop him, either. That's why Destiny condemned him with Heavani's fate. Take your chance before my offer is void."

"No deal." Denida stomped past Henna and stood beside Gabriel.

Henna raised her eyebrows. "Denida, why does this concern you?"

"I'm here because you think I can avenge you, but I can't, even if I wanted to." Denida wiggled his fingers. "The ring is gone, but I'm sure you already knew that?"

"It was one of Destiny's possibilities. At least the necklace still enables you to visit Craym." Henna's eyes glowed with rainbow colors.

*Why are her eyes glowing, now?* "Where is it?" Denida shot her a death glare.

Henna turned her focus to Gabriel. "You can still choose your path. Which option will you pick?"

"I'll never abandon my friends!" Gabriel asserted.

"I see. I wonder which one you will choose now that they are on opposing sides." Henna winked. "In that case, you are not welcome here, anymore." She blew a speck of silvery dust from her hand. It enveloped Gabriel, and he vanished from sight.

"What the hell?" Denida bared his teeth.

Henna rested her hands on her chest. "Don't worry; your friend is fine. Gabriel is back with Shaddai."

Denida flinched. "And Nina, where is she?"

"Your wife?" Henna tilted her head.

Denida grabbed Henna's arm. "If you don't help me find Nina, I'll never even consider helping you with your prophecy."

"I see many paths of destiny. One measly life doesn't matter in the grand scheme of things." She peeked down at Denida's hands. "Release me now, or shall I do to you what I just did to Gabriel?"

Denida released her. *Dammit.*

"Being crude now, too?"

Denida bared his teeth. "Without the ring, everyone can read my mind, so why not? I have to find it." He wrapped his hand around the necklace. Silvery ash enshrouded him, teleporting him back to his Underworld.

***

*One step closer.* Henna drew in a deep breath and returned to her world of dead souls.

Nina sat, chatting with her son.

"Daniel!" Henna called, and he ran to her.

"Wait!" Nina reached out, but she missed Daniel's shirt by a centimeter.

"Was it nice seeing your mom?" Henna ruffled Daniel's hair. "She may be back to see you again, if she wants to see you badly enough, that is." Henna tilted her head. "Run along, now; I need to talk to your mom."

Daniel waved to Nina, before scampering along.

"No!" Nina jumped up.

"Stay." Henna raised her finger, freezing Nina. When she lowered her finger, Nina's movement returned.

Nina dropped to her knees. "Why?"

"I told you that you were free to see your son, not that you'd have him back, yet." Henna leered at Nina. "You are not done, but you should be cautious. Denida knows the ring is missing."

"His loss." Nina chuckled.

"It will be yours, too, if he realizes you took it. If you want to have Daniel again, you'll make sure he never finds out."

"Fine." Nina gritted her teeth. "Just give me the ring and-"

"That isn't an option. The ring was the price you paid to see Daniel. You used it, so that's off the table." Henna tilted her hand. "It's a shame, really."

"Why the hell would you ask for it, knowing that?" Nina hissed.

"My reasons are irrelevant. If you fail, there's always Nylah."

"Not if she dies." Nina gloated.

Henna smiled and closed the distance between herself and Nina. "If she dies by your hand, Daniel will follow; you have my word on that. You don't want to fail me, no matter what."

"Then you'd have nobody left to keep them apart." Nina stepped back.

"Denida won't need it. We're approaching the time." Henna marched after Nina.

"Wait." Nina extended her arm. "How am I supposed to keep Denny in check?"

"That's for me to know and you to figure out." Henna snapped her fingers, and her magic teleported Nina back to the Underworlds. *Good luck with Denny. You'll need it.*

***

*This is bad. How could Denida's soul mate...* Susan stared at the car.

"I don't get it. How could Nina… Jacob and her were always close, so I get her wanting to avenge him, but she knew magic?" Den sat in the car, chatting with Sus. He turned his head to Susan. "You," he hissed. "You know something, don't you? What true colors was Nina talking about?"

Susan sighed. "Everything has just been a trip down the crapshoot since I came here."

"She learned in the Underworlds, where my soul is, too, right?"

"It doesn't make sense." Susan lowered her head. "The magic she used…" She arched her neck. "It can't be. That was Nina's human form." She shook her head. "Nina knows magic, but her human shouldn't know it, unless…"

Den squinted, making Susan avert her eyes. He took her hand and held it to his chest. "Unless?"

Susan pushed down her queasiness.

"Pretty please?" Den gazed into Susan's eyes.

"Henna," Susan muttered.

Den pulled back. "H-Henna?" he stuttered. "No…" He stepped back until he stumbled over his feet. "She can't." Den's face grew as pale as a corpse.

Susan stood, intrigued. "You know of Henna?"

Den gritted his teeth. "In my dreams, I've imagined that she was the worst, worse than Lucifer. You think Henna has something to do with Nina?"

"I don't-"

"Maybe we should request backup then?" Den blinked.

Susan shook her head. "We can't; that demon took the device from the Gate."

"But we killed their leader."

*He has a point; the Gate might be accessible again.* "It may not be enough, but you're right; it's worth a try!"

Den and Susan returned to the vehicle, and Susan turned the engine on to race down the road and across town.

Den glanced out the window as they sped past dead bodies filling the streets, and demons in the process of slaughtering even more humans. He clenched his fist in front of the window.

Sus rested her hand on Den's, making him unclench his. She intertwined her fingers with his.

Susan watched Den and Sus gazing tenderly at each other in the rearview mirror. *How can they be so close on Earth? It's surreal.* She parked behind a store.

Den glanced out the window. "I thought we were going to the Gate? It's by the lakes."

Susan chuckled. "You would know that." She faced Den. "But we shouldn't get too close, in case there are demons, so I will go-"

"I'm coming too." Den insisted. "Sus, I'll be back soon. If anyone comes for you, just run and I'll meet you back at the school." He and Sus shared a tender embrace.

Susan neared them. "I don't think that's a good idea; the demons want you dead. Besides, I need to use the Gate, so-"

"Please, Susan? I really need to see if it's as real as it has felt in my dreams?"

Susan tightened her jaw. "Denied."

Den peeked over at Susan. "Are you sure you want to leave us here, defenseless, where the demons might detect us?"

Susan looked over at Kate and Jakob and gritted her teeth. "Alright, but stay behind me." She exited the car with Den trailing behind her, continuing down the road to the lakes.

Demons trekked from the forested path leading to the Gate into the street.

Susan shoved Den behind a parked car. "Demons…" She turned back. *Don't see us…*

"Find them!" A demon marched out from the trees in his demonic form, followed by his cohorts.

"This can't be good." Den scratched the top of his head.

The demons scanned the road in the direction of the car, Susan's hiding spot.

"Where should we look, Master? We already checked that school."

The demon clenched his jaw and turned to the others. "Find their friends and family. Search everywhere. I want them all dead, especially Denida's and Susan's human forms."

*Maybe I should take Den back to the others.* Susan lowered her head. *No, too risky, they may notice us.* "Stay behind me. We must get to the Gate." She snuck forward, weaving behind parked cars for cover.

Den followed her cue and shadowed her.

Susan eventually reached the last vehicle, closest to the demonic figure, and crept into the tree line.

Den hesitated to gawk at the demon, before following Susan into the forest.

Susan gestured for Den to stay low to the ground. She carefully sauntered around the branches. After a few minutes of navigating the woods, she exited on a path. "The Gate should be nearby."

"If it's where I imagined, it would be behind that lake." Den pointed at a path with overgrown shrubs spreading out onto it.

Susan stepped in front of Den and followed his finger with her eyes. "Alright, let's try it." She trudged down the path.

Demons appeared up ahead.

*No, I must protect Den!* Susan froze abruptly. She reached back, but turned when she didn't feel Den.

"Hi, Missy." A demonic being stood with his hand clamped around Den's throat. "Thanks for saving me the trouble of looking for you."

The demons spread out.

"You thought you could go back to the Underworlds? Earth is ours, now." The demon flung Den to the ground. "You'll never return."

The demons surrounded Susan and Den.

Susan assumed a defensive stance in front of Den. "You'd better stay back!"

The demons stormed her.

Susan grabbed the first demon and hurled it back into the others, but even more demons attacked, knocking her off her feet.

Den ran to assist her, dragging her away from them. "Stop!" he commanded; his fist raised.

"Never," the demon gloated. "Kill-" He gasped and glared down. A sharp metal object impaled his chest. He clenched it, holding it in place. "Who the-"

"Me." Sus stepped in front of the demon and kicked him in the groin. When his grip loosened, she tore the metal rod out. "Den!"

Den turned to Sus confusedly, and the demons swarmed her.

Sus tossed the chunk of metal at the crowd of demons, and it slammed into the first row of her attackers, before falling to the ground and rolling.

Den darted over to grab it before the demons noticed where it landed. "Hey!" He scraped the metal on the ground. When the demons noticed, he readied it like a baseball bat.

The demons shifted their focus from Den to Sus, and then back to Den. "Denida," one of them growled.

"Yes, don't you want to be the one to kill me?" Den raised his eyebrows with a confident smirk.

Susan pushed herself up. She stared down the path in the direction of the Gate, just able to make out the top of it, towering over the trees. A dark cloud hovered around it. *It's that way, but we can't. We've gotta get away from here.*

Susan stumbled to Den, wincing with each step. *There are too many demons.* She gritted her teeth and sprinted as fast as she could.

Den held the metal in front of him like a sword, keeping the demons at bay, and guarding Sus behind him.

Susan grabbed the metal object and nudged Den and Sus forward.

"Why are we leaving?" Den peeked back.

"The Gate is enshrouded in Darkness. I need to take you somewhere I can keep you safe."

Susan stopped as they turned a corner and leaned up against a wall, peeking back around it.

Den saw a demon holding Kate and Jakob up and yanked the metal rod from Susan's hand. He used his full weight to thrust it into the demon's back.

*Den killed a demon?* Susan gasped.

"Susan?"

Susan investigated the body. *But how can I keep Den safe like I promised Denida? He's so reckless!*

"Master Sergeant!" Den screeched. "We have to go before they find us. Maybe there's somewhere that no one-"

Susan blinked. "Yes, we must go, and I know where, too." She climbed into the car with the children and accelerated, speeding away.

"So where, now?" Den scratched his forehead.

Kate shrugged. "The demons will just follow us."

"Not here." Susan turned sharply and they skidded down a side road. "This is a place with a magic shield on it."

"A shield?" Den frowned.

"Yes, Jack, a demon, shielded his island to prevent magic from being used on it." Susan stepped on the brake and watched the rearview mirror. "Jack is already dead, so Nina and you, Den, are the only ones who know about it, now. I will protect you there."

# Chapter 16- The Wild West

The Colonel scanned the horizon.

"Sir." The Commander saluted him.

"A storm is coming." The Colonel squinted.

"You think the demons will follow us?" The Commander looked back at the Gate.

"I meant the wind is picking up." *But he's right.* The Colonel shuffled through the crowd of soldiers, knelt in front of the Gate, and disconnected the device.

Naphtali watched the Colonel and knelt beside him. "What are you doing?"

"Disabling this Gate is the only way to prevent demons from coming here." The Colonel returned to the Commander and handed him the device. "Here's your chance to prove yourself."

"Sir, yes, Sir." The Commander shoved it inside his backpack.

Naphtali rubbed his hands together. "Where do we go, now?"

The Colonel smiled. "There's a Gate like this that leads to Earth."

"Where?"

"I don't know; I never asked Denida." The Colonel licked his lips. "We'll do some reconnaissance, find a town, and ask there."

"How? There's nothing but barren land as far as the eye can see." Naphtali stretched his arms out emphatically.

"We'll just have to try and hope luck is on our side." He beckoned with a large gesture. "Let's move it, on the double!" He strode away and lifted his hand to his forehead, shielding his face from the gusts.

*Very windy...* The Colonel led the troops across the barren plain. He raised his arm to shield his face from the thick dust blowing across the plains.

After hiking for a few hours, the sandstorm subsided, revealing a mountain up ahead. "That's our destination!" He plodded down a dirt road, approaching it.

"I sure hope there is some life, here." Naphtali grumbled.

*Is that a mine*? The Colonel squinted, trying to make out something in the distance.

"*Click, click, click.*" Guns cocked on all sides, as men surrounded them with their firearms trained on the soldiers.

Naphtali tugged the Commander's sleeve. "Should I use magic?"

The Commander shook his head. "Not yet."

"You can't have our ore!" A man screamed from the front of the civilian line.

The Colonel saluted. "Mister, we're not after that. We've come for assistance. I'm a colonel from another Underworld. Who might you be?"

"I'm the foreman of the mine up ahead. Now tell me what 'assistance' you've come for before my miners gun you down."

Naphtali clenched his fist, and Darkness encircled it.

"No." The Commander grabbed Naphtali's arm. "The Colonel's got this."

The Colonel rested his hands on Naphtali's shoulders. "We're not a threat. We came through a Gate, and we're just looking for the next one, but we need directions there, or to the nearest town." He glanced over at the armed men in the bushes. "Perhaps you could ask them to lower their guns before we have an all-out war? All it would take is one restless finger..."

The foreman rubbed his hands together. "Then you'd better leave before that happens."

"We don't know where to go." The Colonel clenched his jaw.

"Go back where you came and turn left. You'll come to a small town." The foreman gestured with his arm.

The Colonel spun around to face his troops. "You heard the man; move out!" he sauntered past them.

"Told you." The Commander smirked at Naphtali and continued after the Colonel. The soldiers followed him.

The Colonel took the left fork in the road, heading down a dirt path.

"Sir." The Commander caught up to the Colonel. "What is the plan when we reach the town? The residents might be as aggressive as the miners."

"You still haven't regained my trust, Commander. You disobeyed a direct order, but you did help us escape, so we'll see if you can redeem yourself." The Colonel shot the Commander an icy stare. "Get back in line!"

"Yes, Sir." The Commander saluted and retreated to his place in formation.

After a while, a town appeared in the distance.

"Halt!" The Colonel spun to face the soldiers and signaled with his hand. "Commander and Naphtali."

They stepped to the front of the troop, where the Commander greeted the Colonel with a salute.

"Naphtali, we're going into town." The Colonel pinched the bridge of his nose and closed his eyes momentarily. "Commander, set up camp." He turned to Naphtali. "Shall we?"

Naphtali started to talk but closed his mouth without a word. He nodded and followed the Colonel's lead into town. He peeked back after a while and rubbed his nose. "Can I ask you something?"

The Colonel nodded with a soft smile. "What is it?"

"The Commander, why-"

The Colonel grimaced. "We'll reach the town, soon."

"Yes, but the-"

"I don't want to talk about him," the Colonel grunted. "When we get back to our Underworld, he will face consequences."

"I get that, but-"

"No!" The Colonel stomped his foot. "Enough." He continued down the town's main road. *This is a more of a settlement than a town. I hope they know something, here.*

The Colonel halted at an intersection. He peered down each road. *Bingo.* "Follow me." He darted across the street and continued to a set of doors leading into a sheriff's office.

"This is idea bad idea!" Naphtali flailed his arms.

The Colonel ignored him, continued through the doors, and approached a man sitting behind a desk. "Hello."

The man wrinkled his nose and tipped his hat. "That's a weird getup. What can I do for you?"

"I'm looking for a Gate and hope you could help me."

The man snorted and grabbed a toothpick from the table, before leaning back in his chair. "You know you're talking to a sheriff, right? I've got more important stuff to do."

The Colonel hunched over the desk. "I came to you because you're the sheriff. Besides, this is a small town; how much trouble can you have, aside from pilferers at the mine?"

"I have other problems, like idiots coming in here and wasting my time. My question is: should I lock those sorts of pests up or wait for them to show themselves to the door?" The sheriff hunched over his desk.

Naphtali sauntered through the door. "Sorry, there was a ruckus in front of the saloon next door. I had to get past them."

The sheriff withdrew a set of handcuffs from his desk drawer and placed them on the desk. "Are you staying or leaving, Mister?"

Naphtali's focus flitted between the Colonel and the sheriff.

"You won't help me?"

The sheriff stood up. He took his toothpick out of his mouth and laid it on the desk next to the handcuffs, which he grabbed. "I guess I'll help you think."

"Negative, we're leaving." The Colonel nudged Naphtali out of the office.

The Colonel interlocked his fingers in thought. "You mentioned a bar?"

Naphtali nodded and pointed at the building next door.

*It's worth a shot.* The Colonel strode through the swinging doors and up to the counter. "Hi… I mean, howdy."

"Howdy Partner, what are you having?" the barkeep asked.

"I have a question."

The barkeep grabbed a glass and sat it on the counter. "This is a bar, not a library."

"The Gates. There are two of them, and one isn't too far from here. Where's the other?"

"Two? Don't you mean three?" The Barkeep stowed the glass under the counter. "If you're not a patron, get out."

Naphtali strolled up to the counter. "Please just tell-"

The Barkeep banged his hand on the counter. "Paying customers only, so unless you buy something, no."

"You know what I can do?" Naphtali lifted his arm and clenched his fist, his eyes becoming as dark as coal.

The barkeep retreated toward the wall. Darkness shone around Naphtali's hand, and the barkeep ducked under the counter.

Naphtali thrust his arm to the side, hurling Darkness at the wall. It shattered some bottles in its path.

"Naphtali, stop!" The Colonel commanded.

Naphtali shrugged and lowered his hand, ending the havoc. "We might as well use my magic."

The Colonel bared his teeth. He leered over the counter. "Last chance."

"Why do you…" The barkeep stood and held his hand over his mouth, his teeth clattering. "The Gates stand near Sheriff Robert's residence."

"You said Sheriff Robert?"

"Yes, the chief of law in our world."

The Colonel slammed his fist on the bar. "How do we get there, and what was that about a third Gate?"

"The one near here is the first. The Darkness used to reside way past this town, and there are two Gates there, now."

Naphtali cleared his throat. "I can *sense* where the Darkness used to be potent."

"Then we don't need you." The Colonel turned to Naphtali. "Let's get back to the others."

They exited the bar, marched down the road, and out of town, where the soldiers had set up a stronghold.

The Commander greeted them as soon as they approached. "Made progress?"

"Yes." The Colonel tilted his head at Naphtali. "Darkness used to surround the second Gate, so Naphtali can show us where it is."

"You can do that?" The Commander wrinkled his forehead in disbelief.

Naphtali flashed him a tiny smile. "Darkness leaves a trail. Anyone with basic training in dark magic can follow it."

"Commander, Prepare the troops for departure," the Colonel commanded.

Naphtali led the way, and everyone followed him across the plains, passing through settlements and towns on their path. Suddenly, Naphtali halted and sniffed the air. "It was definitely here."

"Here?" the Commander asked doubtfully.

Naphtali pointed at the hill. "Should be just past that."

The Commander shrugged. "We're in the middle of nowhere."

"Yes, but this isn't your call." The Colonel shoved past the Commander and ascended the hill.

On the other side of the hill, a sizable unit of armed guards patrolled a giant Gate, which towered into the sky.

The Colonel peered around. "It's definitely here," he stated.

The Commander and Naphtali joined him, observing the guards.

"Shall we join you, Sir?" The Commander asked.

The Colonel eyed the Commander. "We're all going." He descended the hill, advancing to the checkpoint, where the guards readied their sidearms. The Colonel stopped before he reached them and saluted. "I'm not a threat; I'm Denida's colonel."

A guard glanced over at a colleague to his side. "Denida…"

"I'm not sure if now's the right time." The other guard shifted on his feet.

"Denida knows him, so this guy may be able to help find the guy who shot the sheriff."

*Shot the sheriff?* The Colonel perked up. "Pardon me, but did somebody shoot Sheriff Robert?"

The Colonel gazed at the Commander.

"Claus, from your world," the second guard hissed.

"Sir?" The Commander's teeth dug into his lip, chapping it, while he retreated.

The Colonel reached for the Commander's arm. "It couldn't be our Claus." He shook his head in disbelief. "He can't be here." His fingers dug into the Commander's arm before the Colonel turned to the guards. "Is he imprisoned?"

"Imprisoned?" the second guard scoffed. "That little prick disappeared."

*Is Claus running amuck in this world, now?* "Is Robert…"

The first guard repositioned his gun. "He's recovering."

"We must find Claus before he does more damage. He wouldn't stop there. May I see Robert?"

The first guard waved his sidearm. "Only you, Colonel. I'll take you to Robert before we decide anything." He escorted the Colonel through the checkpoint. They passed an average-sized Gate and ascended a hilltop.

The Colonel stared at the Gate. *That must be the one we're looking for, but it looks-* At the hill, an even wider Gate captured his attention. "Wow, that must be the one we saw on our way here. It's colossal."

"That's the new Gate. Denida told us to monitor it, so we have, ever since it appeared." The guard approached a mansion standing on the hill's peak.

The lawman guarding the building let them through without question. *These guards must know each other.*

The Colonel's guide continued down the hall to an elevator. "This leads up to Robert's office."

As the elevator arrived on the top floor, the Colonel and the guard exited it.

Robert sat, slumped over, at his desk. A bird in a cage next to him stretched its wings. He glared at the bird. "I'm awake."

"Sir?" The guard saluted. "This guy says he's a colonel from Denida's world."

"John!" Robert rubbed his forehead and smiled. "Is Denny here, too?"

The Colonel flinched. "No, sorry. I'm here with my task force. We're trying to travel through the Gates."

"Of course, I will get it ready for you."

The Colonel gritted his teeth. "Pardon me, but I heard that Claus shot you. It couldn't have been our Claus?"

Robert stood, holding onto the desk to steady himself. "Thanks for bringing him here," he addressed the guard. "I will take it from here."

The guard nodded. "And his troops?"

Robert's fingertips tapped the desk. "Let them in."

"Yes, Sheriff." The guard tilted his hat and exited the room.

With a loud sigh, Robert leaned back in his chair. "Claus didn't shoot me; nobody did."

The Colonel opened his mouth, but he couldn't muster any words, so he closed it again.

"Denida wanted to give Claus a second chance somewhere far away from his own world and Claus did very well, until they came for him."

"They?"

"Loki, I think, but he didn't come close to Henna."

The Colonel's eyes widened. "Henna is here?"

Robert sighed. "Unfortunately. She turned on that giant Gate and used a spell to knock me out."

*Then we can't leave, yet.* "What exactly is that massive Gate?"

"Denida said it led to Henna's world, where dead souls reside."

"You think that is where Claus went?"

Robert lowered his hands to the desk. "I hope not; we would have no way to follow them, but you needed to use our Gate to Earth, right?"

The Colonel's limbs tensed, and he shook his head. "Negative, if Claus is here, we need to find him, first." He clenched his fist. "Do you still have an active link to my world?"

"Yes, why do you ask?"

"I want to send a warning, and see if Denida has returned, yet."

"A warning about what? Demons?"

"Yes, the final fight between good and evil has begun. That's probably why Henna was here."

"Sounds ominous." Robert rose and grabbed his cowboy hat. "Let's see if we can find my former sheriff."

# Chapter 17- The Colonel

The Colonel glanced over the balcony, focusing on the giant Gate. *Why wouldn't Denida mention this to me, especially with Henna's connection to it?*

"John?" Robert tapped his fingers on the wall. "We're ready."

The Colonel followed Robert into to a back room, where several law enforcement officers stood around a screen.

Robert cleared his throat. "Anyone here?"

"Yes," a voice responded from the feed.

*Dan?*

As if conjured by the Colonel's thought, Dan appeared on the monitor, waving. "I believe you say 'howdy' there." Dan tilted his head. "Colonel, is that you?"

The Colonel knelt in front of the robot. "Affirmative, is Denida back?"

"No, but I hope he will be, soon." Dan's brow creased with worry.

"That's a long time for him to be missing."

Dan lowered his head. "I know, but why do you need him? Are you ready to head back?"

The Colonel slammed his fist on the desk. "Demons are running amuck throughout the Underworlds. Denida should stop slacking off and come back; he knows the most about how to protect our world from a demon invasion!"

Dan's eyes widened. "What do you mean they're in the Underworlds?"

"They are trying to take control everywhere!"

"I see. Thank you." Dan nodded. "I have an idea." He jumped to his feet and charged out of the room.

"Um…" The lab technician on Dan's side stared at the door. "I guess we're done with the broadcast." He reached over to a control panel and killed the feed.

*Dammit. I needed to ask about Claus.*

Robert pursed his lips to rise into a reassuring smile. "Guess that's that. Shall I take you to the Gate, now?"

"Gate, yes, but not the one leading to Earth, take me to that giant one."

Robert put on his hat. "In that case, follow me." He descended the elevator and continued outside to the giant Gate, which disappeared into the clouds. Robert slowed as he neared it and turned to face the Colonel. "It appeared after an earthquake, back when Denida was here."

The Colonel crouched in front of the main unit. "It doesn't have a device in it." He ran his fingers over the surface of the Gate. "Is the entire Gate made of Henna's material?"

Robert frowned. "Don't ask me; I've only been keeping watch over it."

*It feels like the same material. Wait.* The Colonel examined the base of the Gate, where the device was on the other Gates. "What is this?"

"That's where you insert the key," Robert stated matter-of-factly.

The Colonel gazed at Robert. "You sound pretty sure about that."

"Denida found the key."

*Interesting.* The Colonel stroked his chin. "So Denida used this Gate?"

"He brought Nina, too."

"What did they find on the other side?"

Robert tilted his hat and scratched his hair. "When Denida described it to me, he said, 'Nina needed to see something.'"

*Something… what a weird phrase to use.* "I need my Commander." He trekked back to the checkpoint.

The Commander stood awaiting his return with their other soldiers and Naphtali.

The Colonel whistled. "Everyone, follow me." He spun around and headed back to the Gate, stopping beside Robert.

"What is going on?" Naphtali asked timidly.

"You'll see." The Colonel smirked.

The Commander saluted the Colonel. "We're here to serve, Sir."

"Hand me the device." The Colonel extended his hand.

"Sir?" The Commander stared at the Colonel's arm.

"From the Gate, Commander."

The Commander's eyes widened. "Sir, yes, Sir." He pulled the device from his bag and handed it to the Colonel.

The Colonel whipped in a around the Gate, where he knelt and ran his fingers across the device, then the Gate. *I was right; it is the same.*

Silvery ash fell from the sky, freezing time for the Colonel. Even the leaves, waving in the breeze stilled.

Henna appeared and glanced at the Colonel, then his soldiers. "Enjoying your discovery?"

The Colonel drew his gun.

Henna lifted her finger, and the gun jerked out of the Colonel's grasp. It landed at her feet.

The Colonel grunted. "Who are you?"

"I think you know the answer to that."

"Henna," the Colonel sneered. "What do you want?"

"You have something of mine." Henna's eyes fell on the device. "I want it back."

The Colonel pulled the device closer to his chest. "Why would I give this to you? You'll let the demons enter this world."

"I don't care about the demons. That object contains my magic, so I want it."

The Colonel arched his neck. "Fine, but Claus is my price. Give him to me, and you can have it back."

"A demand?" Henna peered at the frozen soldiers. "Are you sure you-"

"You don't scare me. I won't comply just because you know some magic." The Colonel gritted his teeth. "You're just like Lucifer; we won't succumb to the likes of you."

"Some magic?" Henna laughed. She sauntered back, increasing the distance between herself and the Colonel.

Henna folded her fingers. "Since you chose this path, allow me to demonstrate." She lifted her left hand and unclenched it before squinting. The rainbow shade in her eyes intensified.

The giant Gate lit up.

"Still think I'm just like Lucifer?" Henna smiled far too sweetly.

*Uh oh.* The Colonel raced away from the Gate, just as it started shaking and levitating above the ground.

Henna wrenched her arm to the side. The Gate followed her motion and jerked to the side. She smirked at the Colonel as she lowered her hand, setting the Gate back down where it had been.

"Now you've seen what I can do, little boy." Henna blinked and teleported behind the Colonel. She snatched the device, and blew a gust of wind from her lips, sending the Colonel rolling across the dirt. She ran her hand over the device, and it vanished.

"What the hell did you just do?" The Colonel clenched his fist.

"I took back what's mine."

"You'll never do anything like that again!" The Colonel rolled over and grabbed the gun Henna had taken from him. He squeezed the trigger repeatedly.

The shots impaled Henna's torso, filling her with holes.

*How is she still standing?* The Colonel raised his eyebrows and charged at her, firing until the gun clicked, empty. He tossed it aside and increased his pace.

Henna flicked her fingers.

The Colonel froze mid-step.

Henna glared down at her chest. The bullets fell to the ground, and her wounds healed instantaneously. "Odin!" she called.

An eight-legged horse descended from the sky, landing beside her.

"Ye called, my queen?" Odin bowed from atop the horse.

"The Colonel." Henna tilted her head indicatively. "Do it."

Odin glared at the Colonel. "As you wish." He pulled the horse's reigns and ascended into the sky.

*Come on, move!* The Colonel tried to get his limbs to obey, while Henna paced around him.

"Allow me," Henna smirked and flicked her fingers.

The Colonel's motion returned, and he slumped to the ground with a loud grunt.

"Time for everything to commence as normal."

"Henna." Sherrif Robert pulled his gun from its holster.

The Commander's eyes widened. "Fire!"

Henna's rainbow eyes shone brightly, and the bullets slammed into an invisible barrier, shattering on contact.

The Commander charged forward. He slammed into the barrier. "Naphtali, break through this with dark magic!"

Naphtali eyes blinked rapidly before they settled on the barrier. He rested his hands on top of it. Darkness started swirling around his palms.

The Colonel jumped up and lifted his leg, then lowered it again. "Urgh." He banged his hand against his chest. *What is this?*

"Your end is nigh. At least your soldiers get to witness it, now." She smiled at the Commander. "You should find this fun; it will shape your destiny."

The Commander banged his fist into the invisible barrier, then started kicking it.

"You can shield yourself from bullets?" The Colonel flinched but forced himself back to his feet. "You won't be able to protect yourself when I break your neck-" He gagged, clutching his throat. "What… is… this..." Sweat dripped from his forehead.

"Naphtali, break through, now!" The Commander screamed.

"I can't." Naphtali lowered his arms, cupping his hands together in a self-soothing manner. "My magic isn't even making a dent."

"Dammit." The Commander bit his lip.

The Colonel wiggled his fingers, but they moved in slow motion. *What's happening to me?*

"I can answer that." Henna leered. "All your souls throughout the Underworlds are dying, one by one."

"You're only making me stronger…" The Colonel glared at Henna, his eyes darkening with hatred. He lunged, knocking her to the ground. "You monster!" He punched her in the face repeatedly, increasing his strength with each strike.

"Yes." The Commander pressed his hands up against the barrier. "Keep it up, Colonel!"

Henna shot the Commander a condescending smirk and lifted her arms. A silvery ash locked the Colonel's hands in place. "I can see why Azal never liked you." She extended her palms, making the Colonel levitate. Henna rose and thrust her arm to the side, sending the Colonel smashing into the barrier.

The Colonel grimaced and met the Commander's eyes through the barrier.

The Commander nodded. "We'll get you out; I promise. Just keep-"

Henna's silver magic transformed into a sharp object. She impaled the Colonel from behind.

Blood gushed from the Colonel's wound, and the corner of his mouth. He peered down at it with wide eyes. *So this is how death feels…*

Henna teleported to the Colonel. "One more thing, for our audience." She shoved her hand into the wound and ripped out the Colonel's heart.

*Shi…*

Henna hurled the heart into the barrier, which tore it apart, leaving behind a gory mess.

***

The Commander hyperventilated, his rage rising. "Witch!"

"Aren't you sweet…" Henna winked at the Colonel's body. "- unlike somebody."

"It won't end like this." The Commander gritted his teeth.

"Oh?" Henna's eyes shone rainbow. "Forgot I called Odin?"

"And I care?" The Commander drew his gun.

"Well, he did complete my request by killing all the other versions of the colonel, so you might care."

"You!" The Commander loaded his gun. "You can't stay in there forever."

"That only shows how ignorant you are." Henna walked to the giant Gate. It powered on, growing increasingly brighter as she approached it. Henna stopped in front of it and spun to wave. She disappeared through the Gate.

As soon as Henna vanished, silvery ash enshrouded the Gate, which became opaque, then transparent, before fading altogether, making the barrier disintegrate.

Robert charged to the edge of the chasm where the Gate used to stand. He gawked over the edge, into the pit, waving his gun. "It's really gone."

The Commander clenched the Colonel's head tightly, before closing the Colonel's eyelids with his fingertips. *I'll avenge you, Sir.* He pushed himself up and marched over to Robert. "If that witch ever comes back…" He poked his finger into Robert's chest. "- you'd better tell us."

"Of course." Robert stepped back from the edge.

"Good, now, you offered to take us to the Gate to Earth?" The Commander glanced at the gaping hole again.

Robert sighed with a nod. He led them to the other Gate, standing near the hilltop.

Naphtali repeatedly shook his head. "We shouldn't go. Denida wouldn't expect to find us on Earth. Shouldn't we stay in the Underworlds to rendezvous with him?"

The Commander grunted. "Don't worry; we're just cutting through Earth and going straight to the next Underworld." He licked his lips. "Robert, remove the device after we leave. Keep it under lock and key, just in case she returns."

Robert tapped his holster. "You've got it."

The Commander nodded. "Colon-" He inhaled deeply, slamming his fist into a tree beside him. *Dammit.* He arched his neck and saluted Robert.

"Don't worry," Robert assured the Commander. "I'll make sure he gets a proper burial."

"Thank you." With a sigh, the Commander turned to his troops. "Let's go home." The Commander trudged to the Gate. It lit up when the Commander and his soldiers approached it. Robert waved and tipped his hat when the Commander peered back, as they marched through the Gate.

The Commander arched his neck on the other side, noticing a cloud above them. *Are the demons here, too?* "What's that foul odor?"

Naphtali shifted nervously on his feet. "The Darkness is so strong that it smells just like the air in Hell."

"No." The Commander shook his head. "That's impossible." He stepped into the street, noticing corpses scattered all over the pavement.

"Jesus…" Naphtali gasped.

The Commander turned on his heel and ran back to the Gate. He dropped to his knees and yanked out the device.

"Sir?" A soldier frowned. "Wasn't Robert doing that on his end?"

"We can never be too careful." The Commander shoved the device into his backpack and stood up, clapping his hands. "Move out! We need to find the other Gate and get home ASAP."

Naphtali moseyed over to the Commander. "Maybe-"

The Commander faked a soft smile. "Don't worry; humans could be responsible for this Darkness."

"No." Naphtali rolled his eyes. "It's too strong; it has to be demons."

"We'll be careful, but we need to get back home." The Commander inhaled deeply. *Without the Colonel…*

They all marched down the road, but after a few steps, they heard a chorus of screams up ahead.

*What was that?* The Commander stopped in his tracks.

"Help!" An elderly man limped into view.

Demons swarmed him within a second.

One demon met the Commander's gaze. "Fresh souls to harvest." He dashed down the road.

*Uh oh.* The Commander turned on his heel. "Disperse!"

"Enough is enough; I'm done running." Naphtali clenched his fist.

*What?* The Commander gaped in disbelief. "Naphtali, no!" he yelled.

Naphtali slammed his hands together and his eyes reddened with Darkness, as blackness encased his body. He thrust his arms out, expelling dark, pulsating energy. It, smashed into cars, sending them flying into the demons approaching the troop. The demons continued pounding down the road, and Naphtali's eyes intensified into a flaming red hue.

"Naphtali, stop!" the Commander shouted. *He's not listening.* The Commander surveyed his surroundings, his eyes stopping on the nearest parked car. *Of course.* He raised his dagger and shattered the window, so that he could rip the door open. Inside the car, he honked the car's horn.

"*Honk, honk, honk,*" rang out, making Naphtali's fierce, red eyes soften. When he noticed the Commander, he lowered his arm, relenting. Naphtali frowned at the destruction he had caused. "I did that?"

The Commander slowly approached him. "Yes, you saved us with dark magic."

Naphtali buried his face in his trembling hands.

"Naph!" the Commander called. "We need to go before more demons come."

"Go?" Naphtali looked up.

"Yes, unless you want to go on another Darkness-infused rampage?"

"No, never." Naphtali swallowed. "But do you even know where the Gate is?"

The Commander flinched. "It's by Paradise Lakes, close to where Denida's human side lives."

Naphtali rubbed his chin. "I um… don't make me revert to that ever again. The Darkness will cloud my soul; I can feel myself succumbing to it."

"Don't worry, we've got you." The Commander turned back to the soldiers. "Times a wasting; let's go."

# Chapter 18- Finding the Ring

*It has to be somewhere…* Denida rummaged through furniture, ripping drawers out of dressers, and searching under couch cushions. He slammed his fist into the wall. *Nothing…* He plopped down, leaning against the wall, for what felt like an eternity.

"Denny?" Nina appeared in the doorway, eyeing the mess he'd made. "What happened?"

Denida grumbled. "My ring's gone."

"It's probably-"

Denida stomped his foot. "I've gone through everything and it's not here."

Nina stroked her hair and smiled at Denida. "Alright, but I'd better clean up."

"Wait." Denida approached Nina, resting his hand on her shoulder. "When did you last see my ring? Did I have it when we arrived?"

Nina tapped her fingers on her leg. "Maybe, but I don't remember when I last saw it."

"Dammit. Where is it?" Denida scrutinized the room with his arms crossed.

Nina stroked Denida's cheek. "Don't worry; you'll find it." She pecked his cheek and gently tugged his shirt's neckline to reveal the necklace. "You still have the necklace."

*The necklace... that's right.* "You're the best!" Denida pulled out the necklace and stood in the middle of the room. *Show me any trace of your magic.* Denida stroked the necklace with his finger.

A silvery light surrounded the necklace and everything in the room became grey. Denida rushed through the cottage. Every room was just as bland as the living room.

*It's really gone.* Denida returned to Nina defeatedly, but he abruptly stopped in the doorway, as if he'd been stabbed in the chest. He pointed his finger at his wife, shaking. "Nina?"

Nina stopped tidying the furniture and turned to Denida with a calm smile. "Yes?"

"You're... silver."

Nina frowned. "I'm what?"

"There are traces of Henna's magic on you. How could that be?"

Nina peered at her clothes. "I'm appalled that you think I'd have anything to do with its disappearance." She turned her back and tightened her grip on the couch cushion. "Maybe it's leftover from when she stopped by on Craym, or when you brought me to her giant Gate to see Daniel?"

*That doesn't make any sense.* Denida rubbed his forehead with his fingertips, before raising his head. "Her magic doesn't linger that long."

"How else would you explain it? She's not touching me, right now." Nina mused.

*Yes, how would I?* Denida rubbed his hand on his neck. He glimpsed his hand and lifted the necklace from under his shirt. He grabbed it. *Of course.*

"Denny?" Nina's eyes widened.

Denida shoved the necklace under his shirt and kissed Nina on the cheek. "I need to return to Dynasty to call Dan." He exited the cottage and trotted to Dynasty, cutting through the forest on its outer perimeter.

"Lord Denida." A stableboy stood next to a roll of hay and waved his arm.

Denida continued pacing.

"Denida!" the stableboy raised his voice to a yell.

Denida rolled his eyes but turned to approach the stableboy. "Hello there."

"How's Lady Nina?"

Denida sighed. "She's well, thank you. Is something wrong?"

"No, Lady Nina and that woman seemed preoccupied, so I wanted to make sure everything was okay."

Denida felt a stabbing sensation in his gut. "Woman?"

"Yes, and an older guy."

Denida's upper lip twitched. "Thanks." He dashed to Dynasty's main building, where he meandered down the hallway, with only a single glance back, before stopping in front of a bookcase under a staircase. He pushed a button to reveal a secret monitor. Denida entered a code, and a scanner identified his iris, before revealing a secret entrance.

A dark passage adorned with cobwebs stood before him.

Denida wrinkled his nose at the state of the corridor and turned on a light at the foot of the stairs. He strolled through the passageway to a room, where wide monitors lined the walls next to a dust-ridden machine. He wiped the filth from its keyboard and screen before powering it up. *This time machine had better* work.

"*Beep,*" sounded from the monitor, and a red blinking light flashed around the power button, lighting up the otherwise dim room.

Denida sighed, removed his necklace, and placed it on a sensor. *I hope it works as well as my ring.*

The beeping stopped, and the time machine continued booting up.

*I don't want to travel back in time; I just want to figure out who was with Nina.* Denida deselected the option to travel, instead entering the date and location for a view-only interaction.

Silvery ash endowed the machine. An image of the stables appeared on the screen. The timestamp on the image began to regress until it stopped altogether. The image at the preset timestamp showed a horse grazing and a man approaching its enclosure.

*It can't be...* The man emitted a stream of a familiar silvery ash, and Denida squinted, hunching closer to the screen. *Henna's magic!*

"Hey!" Nina rushed over to the horse. "Get your filthy hands off my horse."

The man on the screen turned to face Nina.

Denida almost lost his balance. *The High Sorcerer? How?*

Nina led her horse to the stables, with the Sorcerer tailing her.

"Denida must miss you." The High Sorcerer leaned against a wall, as Nina stepped into the stable.

Nina moseyed farther inside, ignoring him.

"I guess you don't wish to talk." The High Sorcerer shrugged. "I suppose I should talk to Denida about you and Henna."

Nina stopped, tense like a statue. Suddenly, she clenched her fists, spun, and charged at the Sorcerer.

The Sorcerer vanished in a silvery flash.

*Enough of this...* Denida gritted his teeth and reached for his necklace.

"Does Henna know you're here?" Nina's voice sounded as Denida's fingertip touched the necklace.

Denida frowned and turned back to the screen.

"I'm aware." Nina opened her eyes and stared at the sky. "Henna."

Henna appeared in between them, sneering at Nina. "You've got something for me?"

Nina reached into her pocket and withdrew Denida's ring. She brandished it with a smirk.

Denida, shaking with rage, yanked his necklace off the sensor, and stormed up the stairs. He stomped down the corridors and across the field to the stables.

"Hello, Denida." The High Sorcerer leaned up against a paddock.

"High Sorcerer." Denida blinked. "What brings you here, and how did you even get here?"

The High Sorcerer approached. "The Gates."

Denida smirked. "Impossible, they're one-way."

"Not if you mess with them. Would you like me to teach you how?"

Denida quirked an eyebrow. "Why are you here? Is something wrong with the Warlock?"

The High Sorcerer clapped his hands. "You guessed it, but you have your ring, so you can take us back to my world swiftly, right?"

Denida flinched. "What's wrong with the Warlock? Is she hurt?"

The Sorcerer arched his neck. "Demons are invading."

"Invading?" Denida rolled his eyes. "I don't have time for that; I have someone I need to see." He shoved past the Sorcerer and strolled through the forest.

The High Sorcerer stretched out his arms, and an energy shot flew from his hands, bursting toward Denida.

Denida whirled around with wide eyes, his necklace shining. It had automatically created a shield around him, which vaporized the spell. "What the hell are you doing?"

"I had to get your attention. I knew the necklace would create a barrier, and I really need your help."

*He was with Nina, too. Maybe he should tag along.* "If it's that important, okay, but I need to see Nina, first."

"Promise you'll help me afterwards." The Sorcerer intertwined his fingers. "Please?"

Denida beckoned and continued through the forest with the High Sorcerer behind him.

He stopped in front of the cabin and smiled back at the High Sorcerer with his hand still resting on the doorhandle, then marched through the threshold.

Nina hunched over a table with a dust rag. "Denny, you're back!" She approached with her arms outstretched for an embrace, but her eyes landed on the High Sorcerer, and she froze in her tracks. "Who's that?"

Denida glanced at the High Sorcerer. "This is Nina." He rubbed his forehead. "Are you sure you don't want to say hello?"

The High Sorcerer and Nina both stepped forward and hastily greeted each other with tension in their arms during a handshake.

*That looked uncomfortable.* Denida caressed Nina's hand. "You should be happy; I figured out what happened to the ring."

The High Sorcerer chuckled.

Nina twitched and shifted the rag to her other hand. "How so?"

Denida paced around her to close the door. "I checked our time machine."

"Oh." Nina resumed cleaning the table. "I thought the time machine requires the ring?"

Denida leaned up against the doorframe. "You would think so..." He lifted the necklace from under his shirt. "- but this also contains Henna's magic, like many other things." He pointed at the High Sorcerer. "You used her magic, too."

"My god, so this guy took the ring?" Nina gasped.

"No, Nina, you had the ring." Denida scowled at Nina.

"Me? No, I would never-"

"Really?" Denida bared his teeth and grabbed the necklace, holding out his other arm. An image formed in the center of the room, depicting Nina showing the ring to Henna.

"You need to understand-"

"No!" Denida slammed his hand against the door. "Both of you have helped the worst creature alive."

"But she can bring Daniel-"

"Daniel?" Denida smiled sadly. "You think she would give you anything?" He relaxed his hands and peered over at the High Sorcerer. "Do you have a sob story, too?"

"No, I've always served the queen."

"Really?" Denida frowned. "You must be from her world, then."

"I am," the High Sorcerer stated slyly.

Denida tilted his head. "But you weren't worthy of becoming a god?"

"She has a different purpose for me, just like she does for you."

Denida squinted. "Me? Don't lower me to your level, but sure, I'll bite; what's your purpose?"

The High Sorcerer sauntered over to Nina. "Shall we?" He clenched his fist. Silvery ash hovered around it. "The queen sees all the possible futures, so she must know of this one."

Nina licked her lips. "Denny, we can still-"

"What?" Denida murmured. "Save Daniel from the force that killed him? I don't think so." He rested his left hand on his necklace. "You're both finished."

"Finished?" The High Sorcerer scoffed. "You'll have to beat us, first." He plunged his arm out. Silvery ash enveloped the room in a silvery shade.

"You think that'll get me? I have the same power, thanks to the necklace." Denida smirked.

"Get you?" The High Sorcerer chuckled. "No, I just disabled the necklace's magic," the High Sorcerer grinned.

Denida's eyes widened as he tightened his grip on the necklace.

The High Sorcerer and Denida stepped into the middle of the room with their eyes locked.

Nina eyed the door before turning back to Denida.

The High Sorcerer's body flared up, until he was ablaze. He jabbed his fiery fist forward.

Denida jumped back, baring his teeth. He thrust his arm out, casting white magic at the High Sorcerer. His combatant crossed his arms, creating a wall of fire in front of him. It devoured the white spell. The fiery wall spread until it filled the room.

Denida rolled behind a chair.

The High Sorcerer flung his arm in the direction of the chair, setting it alight.

Denida retreated behind another chair. With a deep breath, he sprang to his feet, charging at the High Sorcerer, only to stop dead in his tracks. *He's gone.* Denida's eyes panned the room.

"Over here, idiot." The High Sorcerer knelt next to the fireplace. He grabbed a log and tossed it.

Denida jerked back to avoid the incoming log, but it struck his shoulder. Denida lost his balance and tumbled to the floor.

The High Sorcerer ran over and pounced on Denida, punching him.

Denida lifted his hands to shield his face, but he could only block a fraction of the oncoming strikes. Blood drenched his face.

Nina flipped her hair to the side. "High Sorcerer? You can clear the magic seal, now. You've got him."

"No, he's still breathing. We can use dark magic."

Nina thrust her arm at the door. It flew off its hinges, letting the light from outside illuminate the room. "Guess you're right." She bared her teeth.

Denida's hands had stopped resisting.

"Henna had a purpose for you, which you are ignoring," Nina growled.

"I'll get to it after this." The Sorcerer grinned menacingly and extended his palm. A holy dagger appeared in his hand. He lifted the dagger above his head and thrust it downward.

Nina grabbed his arm before it reached Denida.

The Sorcerer's forehead creased. "What the hell do you think you're doing?"

"I'm guaranteeing that you can't impede my mission." Nina tightened her grip on his arm. The High Sorcerer's wrist reddened until his grip on the dagger loosened enough for Nina to yank it from his hand.

Denida crept backward, increasing the distance between himself and them.

"What the fu-" The High Sorcerer strained. His eyes turned crimson.

"I need to stay in Henna's good graces…" Nina ran her fingers over the blade. "- and this can kill anyone."

"Thanks for pointing out the obvious. I intend to use it on Denida, so give it back." The High Sorcerer reached for the dagger expectantly.

Nina sniffed. "The mission Henna gave me is different."

"Henna knows this is a possibility." The High Sorcerer neared Nina. "She isn't stopping us, so this must be her divine will. She will come out on top, with or without Denida."

Nina nodded slowly. "You have a point." She extended her hand, offering the weapon.

The High Sorcerer smirked and reached for the dagger.

Nina pulled it to her chest. "But before I do, I want to say this." She tapped the blade on her chin.

"Of course," the High Sorcerer grunted. "What is it?"

"I will get my son back."

"Of course, you will." The High Sorcerer attempted to snatch the weapon again.

Nina sidestepped and grabbed the High Sorcerer's arm with her other hand. She shoved him up against the wall. A picture frame on the wall thudded to the floor. "Then why not just do this the Darkness's way?"

"Good idea." The High Sorcerer crossed his arms and thrust them forward.

Nina held up the dagger, dispelling the dark energy hurtling in her direction. She cloaked herself in a dark aura, which threw the High Sorcerer out of the cottage, slamming him into a tree trunk.

The High Sorcerer groaned and lifted his arms, slamming Nina into the cottage wall, dislodging the dagger from her grasp.

The High Sorcerer hustled back inside and reached for the dagger on the floor. He winked. "Time to die."

Denida shifted on his feet. "But we go way back."

The High Sorcerer scoffed. "Only because Henna commanded me to support you. Things have changed."

Nina charged through the door.

The High Sorcerer spun around and grabbed her throat. "You think a weakling like you can fight me?"

Denida tiptoed, keeping his eyes fixed on them.

The High Sorcerer's hands emanated Darkness, which started to devour Nina.

Denida stood and focused his hands. A surge of white magic flickered on his palms. He threw the energy at the High Sorcerer, sighing with relief as the white spell swallowed the High Sorcerer's dark magic.

Nina sneered and jabbed her Darkness-enveloped hand through the High Sorcerer's body. She ripped out his heart and blood sprayed on the floor. Nina tossed the heart into the lit fireplace and grabbed the dagger.

Denida's eye tracked the blade in Nina's hand. "I know both dark and white magic, so if you plan to use that on me, it won't go well for you."

"I guess we can talk, now." Nina giggled. "After all, killing you would violate my mission."

"Really?" Denida cleared his throat. "And what mission would that be?"

Nina raised her eyebrows. "Why would I shoot myself in the foot by telling you?"

"Fine." Denida shrugged. "Just remember; Henna will never reward you, even if you succeed."

"No?" Nina sniggered. "Then why did she give me something when I gave her your ring?"

Denida jumped up and bared his teeth. "Probably because you need the ring to unlock the Gate to her world."

"What Gate?" Nina squinted.

"Remember, the one that appeared in the Wild West Underworld, where we saw Daniel?"

Nina straightened up.

"As I said, she's using you."

"You're wrong. We're at the end game, and you and…" Nina gritted her teeth. "Goodbye, Denny." She stormed out the door.

"Wait!" Denida pursued her through the room. When he reached the High Sorcerer's body, Denida almost slipped on the blood-soaked floor, but he leaned on the table to steady himself. He slowed his stride to the door.

Sunlight shone on the forest's branches and leaves. Denida turned around in all directions, but Nina's marked absence only became increasingly apparent with every frantic glance. Deep inside Denida's chest, concern turned into crushing pain. *She's gone…* He glanced at the High Sorcerer. *What did Nina mean by the end game, and who was she talking about?*

***

The High Sorcerer frowned at passing bystanders. "Am I back in Henna's world of dead souls?"

"Yes." Henna folded her hands.

"Why am I here?"

"Why do you think?" Henna approached the High Sorcerer. "You failed me. Nina tore your heart out."

The High Sorcerer scratched his nose. "I'm sorry, my Queen. If you send me back, I can-"

"Stop." Henna raised her hand and readied her fingers. "You tried to kill Denida before he carried out my will."

"But…" The High Sorcerer shifted on his feet. "He figured out who stole the ring."

"I know, but your actions have created the opportunity for the worst version of fate to unfold. In other words, you have not earned the right to be here." She extended her hand, and a pile of silvery ash appeared. "You know what you must do."

The High Sorcerer nodded. He held out his hand, and Henna let the ash drip onto his hand. "I won't fail you again."

Henna smiled, and her rainbow eyes lit up.

"As you wish, my Queen." The High Sorcerer lifted his hand above his head and let the ash fall over his body, vaporizing him immediately.

# Chapter 19- Realization

*Luci...* Gabriel's stomach knotted as he watched his old friend trying to smash through the Pearly Gates. Eventually, he sighed and with a flash of light, Gabriel ascended high above the wall into Heaven and landed atop the tall tower.

God and Peter stood in front of the Gate.

"You shouldn't have killed Heavani, but it's not too late. We can still mend things with Luci." Gabriel folded his arms.

"Lucifer is trying to break through the Pearly Gates, so that option is gone." God smirked.

"No!" Gabriel approached God. "Luci realizes that the Darkness has been using him."

"Gabriel," Peter snarled. "It's nice of you to join us, but we don't need Lucifer's lapdog." He stepped in front of God.

God laid his hand on Peter's shoulder. "Leave us."

Peter nodded and shot Gabriel a glare before descending the stairs.

Gabriel sighed. "I don't know why you like Peter, but more importantly, why was that Gate moved to the tower inside of Heaven? Queen Henna could enter through that."

God flinched. "No, I've sealed it with white magic, but Henna doesn't concern me; the Darkness and Azal do."

*Azal? I haven't seen that name for Lucifer in a long time.*

"Yes, your friend will stop at nothing before-"

"Can you blame him? Heavani died because-"

A bright light illuminated God's silhouette. "You don't want to finish that sentence, old friend."

Gabriel swallowed. "Henna is a much bigger threat. You know she still blames us for her death."

"I know Henna is baiting Lucifer. Enough time has passed; one of us has to go, and better him than me."

"We were all friends before Henna died. You trusted Lucifer more than anyone," Gabriel attempted to reason with God.

"He betrayed us. Our friendship is as dead as he will be after one of us or Henna gets to him." God peered out to the horizon. "Lucifer will keep trying to break into Heaven. Make him stop, or he will die."

Gabriel's eyes wandered, until they rested on the Gate. "Henna has contact with Denida. Maybe-"

"She believes Denida can help her kill us. You are not to contact him. If nobody else is willing to stop Azal, I'll do it myself." God transformed into a bright white stream and descended into Heaven.

Gabriel leaned over the railing and buried his head in his hands. *Lucifer loved Heavani more than life itself; he'll never give up…*

***

Denida tapped his fingers on the wall as his soldiers carried the High Sorcerer's body out of the cottage.

"Here, stay hydrated." The butler handed Denida a water bottle. "What happened here wasn't your fault."

"Wrong," Denida grunted. "Everything's off and I didn't see any of it coming." He swallowed the water and wiped his mouth with his sleeve. *I should inform the Colonel about Nina.* He glanced around. "Where's the Colonel, anyway?"

"The butler cleared his throat. "He's… um…"

"What?" Denida squinted.

"Dan should be able to explain, Sir.."

*Dan, right. He's at the HQ.* Denida handed the butler the empty bottle and waved to the soldiers. "I'm heading back with you."

The car rocked as it traversed muddy dirt roads, but as soon as it skidded onto the main road, the ride became smooth.

"It won't take long now, Sir." The driver smiled.

The car stopped in front of the headquarters, and a soldier opened the door for Denida with a salute.

Denida scratched his temple. "Thank you." He jumped out and strode inside the building.

"Sir." The receptionist sprang to her feet. "You're back?"

Denida rubbed his finger where his ring used to be, and wrapped his other hand around his fingers. "Where's Dan?"

"He should be in your office."

Denida forced a smile and trudged upstairs, making a beeline for his office.

When Denida entered his secretary's office, her eyes glowed. "Sir, we've missed you."

Denida scanned the waiting room. *No one's here.* He turned to the secretary. "Is Dan in?"

"No, Sir. Dan left to meet with the Galaxy Counsel."

*The... why would Dan see a council that ensures peace throughout the rest of the universe?* Denida's gaze stiffened. "Why would he go there? The council doesn't care about the Underworlds."

"I would need to check his notes on your computer." The secretary nodded toward Denida's office.

"Thanks, I'll take it from here." Denida marched through the door. He sat in front of the computer, turned it on, and flipped through the papers on the table while it turned on. *Nothing here...*

"*Beep,*" the login screen flashed.

Denida placed the papers on his lap and logged in, scrolling through the computer's folders. Finding nothing, he clenched the papers and slammed them on the desk with his other hand. Denida laid his head on the desk. *What's that?* His eye landed on a page. Reaching for it, he saw that the page was a printout with "GalaxiCo" on top of the page.

Denida laid it on the table and reached for the keyboard. He typed "g-a-l-a," and "GalaxiCo" appeared before he even finished typing. *Why would Dan have searched for this in the first place? They don't have time to address matters in the Underworlds.* Denida rolled his eyes and reached for the intercom, but his focus landed on a heart-shaped picture frame with a photograph of himself and Nina with their son, Daniel. Denida heaved in a prolonged sigh, before slamming the picture facedown on the desk and marching to the door.

The secretary sat, typing away. She raised her head from the keys. "Sir?"

"Make sure no one enters my office and…" Denida gritted his teeth.

"And?"

"Initiate a search for my wife, Nina."

The Secretary gasped. "Your wife's missing?"

"Worse, she's in cahoots with Henna." Denida strained to smile. "More importantly, where's the Colonel?"

"You don't know?"

"Why does everyone keep asking that?"

The secretary cleared her throat. "Dan sent him on a mission."

"A lot has transpired while I was away. I suppose I should reconvene with Dan at the council."

"Oh, should I prepare the spaceship?"

Denida shook his head. "I will use a faster method." He stepped out of the office and reached under his shirt as he strode through the door. His fingers wrapped around his necklace and Denida shut his eyes.

Silvery ash enshrouded Denida and teleported him away from the HQ. He resurfaced in a crowded city. People plodded about, bumping into each other, nearly knocking Denida off his feet.

Denida retreated to the side of the walkway, pausing to catch his breath, and looked in both directions. A wide road stretched onwards to his left. A grand skyscraper stood to his right. He strode through the bustling crowd and entered the building.

Dan stood in the lobby, conversing with an older individual with a bushy tail.

*Must be someone from the council.* "I found you." Denida tapped Dan on the shoulder.

"Denny?" Dan's eyes widened. "You're back! and here?"

"I am, but why are we here?" Denida clenched his jaw. "And where did you tell the Colonel to go?"

"That's…" Dan's eyes met the older man's again.

"Sorry, where are my manners." The man smiled and offered his hand to Denida. "I'm Costa, the chairman of the Galaxy Council."

Denida shook Costa's hand and tried to pull back, but Costa's grip remained firm.

"It's nice to finally meet the infamous Denida."

*Infamous?* Denida frowned. "You know me?"

Costa winked. "Unfortunately, no, but Vice President Dan has told me all about you and the dangers ahead of us."

"What dangers?" Denida raised his voice. "Henna?"

"Who?" Costa raised his eyebrows.

"No, the demons," Dan clarified.

"What about them?"

Dan turned to Denida fiercely. "The Colonel followed their trail."

"Why?" Denida's stomach turned inside out. "Where did it lead?"

"To the Wild West."

*How?*

Dan shrugged. "Susan went to Earth after we saw demons on the monitor there, too."

"All this happened in my absence, and nobody told me?" Denida demanded.

Dan shook his head. "We would've if we had known how to get in contact with you, but you went somewhere we couldn't reach you." He sighed heavily. "But you two are back now, so-"

Denida took Costa's hand and shook it once more. "It was nice meeting you, too. Until next time." He used his free hand to pry his other free of Costa's grip and nudged Dan out of the building.

"Wait! We need his help."

Denida blocked the door. "With demons? We've got bigger problems."

"How can there be bigger problems than demons?" Dan asked.

Denida removed his gloves and spread his fingers. "I'm missing something." His eyes locked on Dan's.

"Where's the ring?"

"Gone." Denida slipped back into his gloves.

"It can't be; you always wear it."

"I always had Nina too, but she's been working for Henna all along. She swiped the ring."

"How is that possible?" Dan rested his head in his hands.

"I have been asking myself the exact same thing." Denida shook his head slowly. *Hopefully she comes back...*

Dan raised his head with wide eyes. "Are you going to confront Henna about Nina double-crossing you?"

"Good idea; I will be back." Denida tightened his grip around his necklace, teleporting himself to Henna's castle.

The building boasted its iconic rainbow shades. Denida took a few steps into the room, examining it, before stopping in the middle of the floor. "Henna, show yourself. I know you're here!"

"Welcome back, Denny. I've been expecting you." Henna appeared next to him.

*Sure, let's go with that.* Denida rolled his eyes. "Then you know what I want."

"You've come to help me set things right with Azal and Shaddai?" Henna tilted her head, bearing a crooked smile.

*She's still calling them by those names.* "So much for your accurate predictions." Denida shook his head. "Now, about Nina-"

"Yes, you have a beautiful wife."

Denida's eyes darkened to a charcoal black. He ripped his glove off and wiggled his fingers. "Did you ask Nina to take my ring? Want the necklace, too?" he snarled.

Henna chuckled and folded her hands. "So, she chose that path, I see."

Denida gritted his teeth. "She's not helping you anymore; it's over."

"Oh… she isn't?" Henna looked up at the twin suns. "You'll stop her?"

"Neither of us are helping you. Your vengeance will never come to pass. Lucifer and God are too busy to give a rat's ass about you and your ridiculous prophecy."

"And you do not think this is all part of the agenda?"

Denida clenched his fist.

"I wouldn't, if I were you," Henna spoke into Denida's thoughts.

"Nina won't continue helping you once she accepts that you caused Daniel's murder. This manipulation will end."

Henna nodded. "Daniel's death really helped to motivate Nina, especially after you brought her to Daniel. I really must thank you for that," Henna smirked. "Nina wants something that only *I* can grant her, which has been the case even before Daniel passed away, so you won't get her back for nothing." She raised her eyebrows. "I can, however, bring her back to you, if you help me set things right with the entities you call God and Lucifer."

"Heh," Denida scoffed. "You think you can convince me to do that? The Darkness tried, and failed, to use Lucifer to defeat God, so why would you succeed?"

"That's because the Darkness came from the darkness in Shaddai's heart."

Denida grumbled. "You think you're any better? You've been deluding Nina into thinking she will get our son back."

Henna ran her fingers through her hair. "So, it's still a no, then?"

Denida twiddled his fingers and Darkness started to coil around them. "Remember Medusa?" He glared at Henna.

Henna's face wrinkled in confusion. "The Archdemon?"

"Yes, she killed Daniel, and you put her up to it," Denida accused her.

"Why would I care what happened to your son? I don't get involved with Destiny's affairs."

"Still blaming Destiny for everything? You wouldn't be dead if you always could predict fate, you know!"

"Maybe my death served a purpose." Henna tilted her head. "But you doubt my powers?"

Denida shook his head. "I'm sure you can predict… some paths, but I'd wager that Destiny keeps some details from you, just as you withhold information from Nina. That's why you sometimes need to interfere, like when I saw you commanding Medusa."

"Fascinating theory." Henna flipped her hair behind her shoulder. "Fate is always with me, so I knew this was an option that Nina could choose."

"Really?" Denida furrowed his brow. "Then explain why I had to summon you, when you always want to talk to me every chance you get?"

Henna teleported right in front of Denida's nose.

She stood so close that Denida could feel her warm breath. "Yes?" he sidestepped.

"I gave you the necklace. Why would I do that if I wanted to take something from you?"

Denida inhaled.

"Taking the ring would oppose fate." Henna's smile returned. "So don't worry, I would never work against you."

Denida's heavy breathing ceased, and he stared straight into Henna's eyes. "Really?" he sneered. "That's interesting. What I saw in the time machine contradicts what you're telling me, now. But you didn't know that, so perhaps you're also unaware that Nina now possesses one of your holy daggers."

Henna's wide smile stiffened, and she turned away. "That doesn't matter. Your Lucifer and God will kill each other, with or without your help." She whipped her face back to focus on Denida. "You can get your soulmate back, if you help me before it's too late."

*Soulmate?* The Darkness around Denida's hands dissipated. "You're right; Nina is my soulmate, so I don't need your help." He raised his eyebrows. "We're done. Like Lucifer said to me; you are no longer welcome in my presence!" Denida stormed out of the castle. He grabbed his necklace and teleported back to the Underworlds.

Denida appeared in his office. He turned on his heel, and suddenly feeling weaker, he stumbled through the door, and continued through the secretary's front office.

"Sir?" The Secretary stood up.

Denida ignored her and swept through the office, continuing down the corridor to Dan's office.

Dan sat, paging through stacks of papers with sweat running down his forehead.

"You look busy," Denida chuckled. "Have you reached the Colonel?"

"The… Colonel… he's…" Dan stuttered.

Denida rested his hand on Dan's shoulder. "Take your time. What's wrong?"

Dan turned to Denida with teary eyes. "He's dead."

*Dead?* Denida's mouth hung open. He shook his head in disbelief and stepped back until he fell into a chair. "That's not… possible."

"I'm sorry."

Denida raised his head. "How?"

Dan shook his head. "Robert didn't say."

"It happened in the Wild West? Were demons involved?"

"I don't know; I only heard that the Commander and the rest of his troop continued onward to Earth, but I can't reach anyone on Earth."

"Keep trying. Our contacts there must be busy." Denida rubbed his eyes.

"Before you go, bring this." Dan withdrew a device from his desk's drawer. "This brings you back home from anywhere."

Denida glared at it. "I haven't used one of these in forever."

Dan stood and forced the device into his hand. "Henna already took the ring, so the necklace is your only contingency plan. I'm giving you this device, just in case anything happens to the necklace."

"Fine." He shoved the device into his pocket. "I will eradicate those demons myself." He stormed out of the office, rubbing his necklace. With a deep breath, he teleported to the Wild West and stomped forward.

# **Chapter 20- The Rendezvous**

Denida hunched over to pick up an old picture frame beside Robert's bed. He smiled softly as his eyes skimmed the picture of younger versions of himself and Robert. He put the picture down.

Denida combed his fingers through his hair. *He must be near the Gate.* He wandered through the mansion and out the front door, peering at the sun. *I forgot how hot it can be at high noon.* He pulled his necklace out from under his shirt, teleporting to the hilltop in front of the Gate to Earth. A cross stood at the top of the hill. Denida stepped back. *Is someone buried here?* He shrugged and descended the hill, approaching the checkpoint.

"Halt!" A guard lifted his gun. "State your business."

Denida slowed down and raised his arms. "I'm Sheriff Robert's old friend."

"He's expecting you?"

"No." Denida lowered his gaze. "But he knows me well. I was his pupil, Sheriff Denida."

"Sher…" The guard gasped and lowered his pistol. He swiftly holstered it on his belt and saluted Denida. "Sorry, Sir. Go ahead; he's in the building up the path. Just take a left turn when you reach the Gate."

Denida shot the guard a crooked smile as he marched past him. After a short trek, he reached more armed guards stationed around the Gate. He arched his neck, gawking at the massive estate towering above everything from the hilltop. *Lars's estate… thank heavens, that demon is dead. Lars would've been an ace in Lucifer's revenge ploy.* He pushed his thoughts aside and continued to the mansion.

"Halt!" A guard stepped in front of the doors. "Robert isn't taking visitors."

"He knows-"

"No one, no exceptions," the guard insisted. "Retreat now, if you know what's good for you."

Denida rubbed his mouth. "This is vital."

The guard shook his head and cocked his gun. "I don't care. Leave now or you'll get to enjoy some time behind bars."

Denida tore off his glove. "Can't you see…" He bared his teeth. "Never mind." Denida swiftly put the glove back on and raised his hands in defeat. He strolled down the hill. Before he reached the bottom, he crouched beside the path, burying his head in his lap. *The ring increased my ability to perform strong magic myself. This necklace makes it feel like I'm borrowing some of Henna's magic. I guess I should get used to white and dark magic instead of relying on it. After all, Henna repossessed the ring, so it must only be a matter of time before she takes the necklace, too…*

"*Stomp, stomp, stomp.*" Denida turned to the sound, eyeing the man approaching him. *That's the sheriff I followed to see Robert.* He jumped up to follow the sheriff up the hill to the mansion. "Wait!"

The man jumped back in surprise. "Yes?"

Denida's eyes widened. *Doesn't he remember me?*

"You'd better remain vigilant, after what happened to Claus."

Denida's mouth dropped. "What happened to Claus?"

The sheriff tilted his head and shifted his hand to his holster, resting it in front of his gun. "Don't you work here?"

"Not exactly, don't you remember me, Clay?" Denida forced a smile. "Denida? We met with Robert."

"Ahh, Robert's apprentice." Clay's hand drifted away from his belt. "It's been a while. How are you?"

Denida scratched his forehead. "It's been rough. You're on your way to see Robert?"

Clay nodded.

"I was just on my way there, too, but had to stop to get pebbles out of my boot."

"Yeah? Then come along." Clay gestured with his arm and trudged to the mansion's front doors.

The security guard stepped out of the way for Sheriff Clay, before stepping in front of Denida. "Not you."

Clay glared back. "He's with me. I don't think Robert would like it if we left Denida waiting."

"Den… ida?" The guard retreated, allowing them to enter.

Denida pressed the button on the wall to call the elevator. "What exactly happened to Claus?"

Clay tapped his foot against the wall. "It's not my place to answer that; you'll have to Robert."

Denida rolled his eyes and hurried inside the elevator.

"Visitor, visitor," Sheriff Robert's parrot squawked.

Robert peered into the room from the balcony. "Who's there?"

"Miss me?" Denida raised his eyebrows. "I'm here to get an update on Claus and my colonel."

"Ahem." Clay laid a packet of papers on the desk. "I just came to bring you my report." He tipped his hat and ran back to the elevator.

Denida roamed around the room. "Nice parrot you've got. Is it new?"

"It used to stay with my niece, Lindsay. She treasured it."

"Was?" Denida frowned.

Robert fed the parrot through the bars of the cage. "My sister felt it was time for her to stop fantasizing about going on adventures with her parrot; she needed to grow up."

"That's a shame; pets help you grow up…" Denida's voice trailed off and he cleared his throat. "But Claus? Sheriff Clay mentioned him. Is he still here?"

"Claus is…" Robert slumped into his chair. "There's no nice way to tell you this, but Henna was here with Loki, and Claus left with her." He licked his lips. "She killed your colonel."

"What?" Denida stared, wide-eyed. "That can't…"

"Wait; you're telling me that your Commander hasn't reached your underworld, yet?" Robert bit his lip. "The Commander left through our Gate hours ago."

Denida clenched his hair and yanked it. "Where is my colonel?"

"What do you mean, where? He's dead."

"His body," Denida hissed. "Is it here, or did Henna take it with her?"

Robert hunched over the table. "I buried him atop a hill."

*That grave…* Denida collapsed into a chair, opposite Robert. "That little witch!" His eye turned to Robert. "Thank you, I'll go find the Commander." He sprang to his feet and stormed out and down the hill.

A cross stood next to freshly turned dirt. *It's a grave after all.*

Denida knelt, resting his hand on the dirt with a deep sigh. *I'm sorry, my old friend. I may not have been able to do much, but there's one thing I can still do.* He clenched his jaw and pushed himself up. "Henna!" he screamed at the top of his lungs.

A silvery light flashed in front of him. Henna appeared as it faded. "Have you changed your mind, yet?"

"No." Denida bared his teeth. "My decision is now final."

Henna frowned. "Have you forgotten that I know the threads of fate?"

Denida clenched his shirt. "I don't give a damn about your threads of fate nonsense!"

"You're upset…" Henna tilted her head. "-meaning you will either be stupid enough to think you can kill me, or-"

"Wrong, I just see clearly, now." Denida ripped off his necklace and chucked it on the ground. "You wanted your ring back; you got it. Want it or not, you have the necklace, too."

Henna frowned. "But you haven't completed the prophecy yet."

Denida's eyes turned crimson. "Then I guess you've got to get your ass moving if you want to accomplish anything, because you're on your own."

Henna extended her hand, and the necklace flew up into her open palm. "If you're certain?"

Denida clenched his fists. "You crossed the line when you killed John."

"I see." Henna folded her fingers over the necklace. A silvery ash surrounded her, and she vanished.

*I should find out what happened to the Commander…* Denida's shoulders slumped. With a heavy exhale, he took the device out of his pocket and used it to reappear in Dan's office at the headquarters in his home world.

"Denny?" Dan gasped. "What brings-"

"You were right about this device." Denida lifted it above his head. "I have a favor to ask. Can you continue to oversee our underworld?"

"Still?"

Denida nodded. "I need to go to Earth. We need all the help we can get with God and Lucifer's war."

"That's why I tried to proposition Costa. He leads the Galaxy Council, after all."

Denida grunted. "I know I said we need all the help we can get, but that's a bit extreme. I'm going to use the Gate to Earth; is it functional?"

"Why not just follow the link to your human side?"

"Lucifer severed our connection at birth, remember?"

"Right." Dan cleared his throat. "Why are you going?"

Denida tapped his knuckles on the desk. "The Commander has been there for hours. I've got a sinking feeling in the pit of my stomach that something is wrong."

Dan turned to Denida, puzzled. "Why?"

"I don't know, but I need to check." Denida flashed Dan a faint smile and waved before strolling down the corridor.

Denida approached the Gate, which stood in the center of a laboratory. "Power it up, please?"

The lead researcher signaled to the crew.

The Gate lit up, only to abruptly power down.

The lead researcher's eyes widened, and he turned to his crew. "Who shut it off?"

The crew chattered among themselves.

"Well? It doesn't just shut off by itself."

"But, Sir," one of the crew members insisted.

"No!" The chief kicked the wall. "Turn it back on!" He turned to face Denida and imitated a smile. "Sorry, Sir. We'll have it ready, soon."

The Gate flickered on again, but just like the first time, it powered off immediately.

The chief whipped around. "What-"

"Stop," Denida stated calmly. "It's not their fault. It won't turn on if it doesn't have enough power."

"Excuse me?" The chief furrowed his brow.

"Something must be wrong with Earth's Gate."

"On Earth, Sir?" The chief wrinkled his nose.

"Our Gate is fine, so…"

The chief cracked his knuckles. "We have no choice, but to find a way to get you through. Don't you need to go to Earth?"

*Yeah, don't I, but maybe I can find another way.* Denida shook his head. "I'll find a way. Just make sure everything is functional on our end." He exited the room and leaned against the wall. He tapped his teeth in thought, before continuing.

Dan exited his office, as Denida turned a corner. "I thought you went to Earth. You can't be back, already?"

"Our Gate couldn't connect with Earth's counterpart."

"Really?" Dan's eyes narrowed.

Denida nodded slowly. "Without the necklace, I'm stuck."

"Wait; that's not the only way." Dan shrugged. "You may not be connected to your human side, but even you know any soul can venture to its human form without using the Gate."

"You're right," Denida muttered under his breath. "Seeing as our souls are severed, I often forget that I can get to Den because I don't feel him." Denida closed his eyes tight for a moment. "I told them to make sure our Gate is up and running, so make sure you get their report."

"You're going, then?"

"Yes, since the Commander hasn't returned, something bad must've happened." Denida clenched his hand and lowered his head to meet it. *To the school on Earth…* His body grew pale until it vanished, reappearing within the school. *Is anyone here? These are school hours...*

"*Bang.*" A fierce sound echoed from outside.

Denida sped to the door. Bodies lined the grounds, from the school's steps to the streetlamps. He knelt next to the closest body. *This person was killed with dark magic. Is my human side okay? And is Nina really my soul mate?* Denida inhaled heavily. *She must be; Henna just manipulated her with Daniel's death, but surely I'll get some time here to see our human forms together and that'll be all the proof I need.*

A dark cloud flew overhead and took shape in front of him. "Welcome home, Denny."

Denida gritted his teeth. "Are you the infamous Darkness?"

The Darkness created a vortex that devoured all the bodies littering the ground. With every body it consumed, it grew. When all the bodies had been swallowed, it settled as a dense cloud with two crimson eyes glimmering against blackness.

"What do you want?" Denida bared his teeth and clenched his hands so tightly that his nails dug into his skin.

"Even the mightiest, like Henna, are powerless against the Darkness. We wish to help you."

Denida rolled his eyes. "No thanks." He headed for the road.

"We can take you to your human side."

Denida spun around. "He's in Hell?"

"No, we don't want him. We only wish to help you."

"You just want Lucifer's replacement, and it's safe to talk here because he can't come to Earth."

Denida flung out his arm. "Darkness caused this carnage, not humans."

"We can help you, before Henna reaches the child."

"The child?" Denida recoiled as the realization struck him. "Den?"

"We can shield him from Henna and Loki."

Denida's eye darted from side to side, finally resting on the cloud. "And what do you want in exchange for that info?"

"Just to show you-"

"No!" Denida thrust his hand forward, hurling a light spell at the cloud. It penetrated the cloud, creating a hole the size of his fist.

The Darkness ascended into the sky, where it lingered. "Guess that is a no… such a shame. Guess we shall deplete your human side's energy, then."

"You won't succeed."

"No? Our demons almost had him." The Darkness swept over the clouds, stopping on the school's rooftop. "We'll only extend this offer one more time, Denida."

"Want my answer?" Denida folded his hands tightly. "Here it is." He shot a wide ball of energy out of his hands. It bolted through the sky and smashed into the rooftop, narrowly missing the dark cloud, which split into small pieces and floated away.

*Time to get some backup from the Gate.*

Denida strode down the road. When he came to an intersection, his eyes locked on a demon across the way.

The demon waved his hand. "Hey, you! I'm coming over there." A dark cloud helped him levitate above the road. He landed on the sidewalk.

Denida grated his teeth. "Yes?"

The demon chuckled. "Guess you've already seen someone levitating with dark magic. What a shame."

"Who are you, and what can I help you with?"

"Oh." The demon snickered. "The divine Darkness craves your soul energy."

Denida ripped off his glove, bearing his hand. Think *you* can beat me?"

The demon frowned. "What's your hand going to do for you?"

*Frack it…* "Walk away, or you'll regret it!"

"Why?" the demon mocked. "Humans can't touch me."

"Human? I'm no human."

"Really?" The demon eyed Denida from head to toe.

Denida thrust his hands out, expelling an expansive ball of light magic through the sky. It collided with the demon.

"Cursed angels." The demon folded his arms, and Darkness enveloped him. "Darkness shall always extinguish the light." His eyes blackened as he flung a ball of dark energy at Denida.

Denida shielded himself by raising his hand to create a barrier of light magic, but the dark magic shattered it, and tossed Denida into a nearby building's brick façade. Denida stumbled away from the wall. *I need to remember that I don't have Henna's magic to protect me.*

"I don't think so." The demon tossed a ball of magic into Denida's backside, making him stumble to his knees.

Denida sized up the demon, who approached. Denida's eyes turned crimson.

The demon stopped, leering down at him deviously. "You can't get away. Many others, just like you, have already died."

Denida bit his tongue and closed his eyes. "You'll be the first demon I kill today." A fiery shade engulfed his silhouette, and a blue flame illuminated his hand.

The demon retreated a step. "What are you? First light magic, and now you're encased in dark magic?"

"You're right; light magic simply cannot compare." Denida slammed his fiery fists into the ground, creating a magic cone around them.

The demon's eyes widened as he stared at the cone. "This is high-level dark magic,"

Denida approached the demon.

"… meaning, when I kill you, the Darkness will flourish."

Denida sneered at the demon. "Still think you can?"

The demon arched his neck and opened his mouth. Darkness poured from it and surrounded the cone.

*Uh oh…* Denida's fingers fidgeted. A specter of light magic appeared around them, but before he finished the spell, the demon's darkness reached him and snuffed out the light magic.

The demon stood over Denida and tore open his shirt. He traced his index finger over Denida's chest, running it down his side, and eventually resting it on a scar. "This looks like a good spot."

"No…" Denida writhed. "If you rip out my heart, your master won't get my power."

The demon froze. "How do you know that?"

"Yes, how would I?" Denida smirked. His eyes darkened to the shade of charcoal, and a crimson fire covered his hand. He jabbed it into the demon's gut. "The name's Little Evil." He clenched his fingers around the demon's heart. The heat from the flames shattered the heart into a thousand pieces. The demon tumbled to the ground and the cone dissipated immediately.

Denida sniffed. *I'm not looking forward to journeying to the Gate with these demons here…*

# Chapter 21- Earth

Denida weaved down the road, carefully avoiding bodies strewn across the ground. He slowed to a halt when the lake came into view. Several demons patrolled the grounds. *There must be even more near the Gate.*

Denida rubbed his finger where the ring used to be and sighed. He clenched his fist and transformed into his demon form, with fiery, glowing eyes. *Now I'm ready.*

"Master." The demon in front of the lake bowed.

Denida ignored the demon and continued marching down the dirt path. *I should hurry.* His eyes narrowed, spotting the top of the Gate through the tree line. He scurried onward until he reached the clearing in front of the Gate.

Several demons surrounded the structure.

*What are they doing?* Denida squinted at the Gate and approached slowly.

"You won't beat me!" The Commander yanked himself free of demons.

The demons behind the Commander grabbed him by the throat. "There's no escape."

The Commander gritted his teeth and spat in the demon's face.

"You little…" The demon threw him into the side of the Gate and wiped his face.

The Commander's eyes lit up at the sight of the Gate.

"Don't get your hopes up," the demon gloated. "We removed its main device."

The Commander staggered to his knees and his eyes locked on Denida's. "Denny?"

The demon charged Denida, knocking him to the ground. "My, my, who do we have here? Little Evil, in the flesh." His grip on Denida's arms tightened. "Killing you will be such a joy." He fixed Denida's hand in place with dark magic and focused on Denida's shirt, ripping it open to reveal his chest. "No necklace? You're just as weak as your soldier boy." The demon smirked.

"We'll see about that." Denida's eyes darkened.

The demon placed his hand on Denida's scar. Darkness fluttered around the ribbed flesh, replacing the Darkness in his eyes with agony.

"Now!" the Commander screamed.

Soldiers charged down the path with sharp blades at the ready.

The demon jumped up and tossed waves of dark energy at the troop.

Naphtali appeared from the crowd. He deflected the magic and ran forward.

The demon created black holes beside him. Demons poured from the vortexes and sprinted toward Naphtali.

The lead demon and Naphtali stopped moving, both with dark glares.

"You think you can beat a demon?" the demon mocked.

Denida focused his eyes and a bright light emanated from within his scar, weakening the Darkness. He clenched his jaw and jerked his hands. His body shone radiantly, breaking the Darkness's grip. Denida ran his fingers over his scar, replacing even more of the Darkness with the light glow, repelling the shade from his body. He staggered to his feet and his eye fell on Naphtali, who sprawled out on the ground with the demon hovering over him.

"Little Evil… I'd stop right there, if you value your friend's life." The demon's hand hovered over Naphtali's chest.

Denida gritted his teeth. "Killing him won't honor the Darkness's desires."

Darkness flowed from the demon's hand to Naphtali's chest. "Are you sure about that? This one escaped Hell."

"Yes," Denida hissed. "- but I am the one who helped him escape."

The demon lifted his hand. "Are you offering to trade yourself for him?"

Denida gazed back at the Commander, licking his lips. "Yes."

"No!" The Commander dashed over.

Denida raised his hand. "This is my will, Commander." He approached the demon, stopping a few steps away from him. "Free Naphtali first. I know demons don't keep their word."

The demon clenched his fist and all the Darkness on Naphtali's body dissipated. "There." The demon charged at Denida, dashing clear through him. "What?" The demon spun around.

Denida materialized behind the demon. "As I said, you shouldn't trust a demon. That includes ex-demons." He thrust his hand into the demon's gut. "Cloaking and illusionary spells are basic dark magic." He tore out the demon's heart and hurled it across the road. *Demons are getting stupider every day.*

Naphtali sat up and wiped cold sweat from his face. "What do we do now? The Gate doesn't work."

"No problem," the Commander rejoiced. "Denida can use his ring."

"That…" Denida inhaled heavily. "No can do. Not until we check on Den."

"Den? But Sir, we've lost so many men. We should get backup first, so-"

"If I had the ring, I wouldn't need to use basic black arts, would I, Commander?"

The Commander gasped, staring at his finger. "But… what about your necklace?"

"Henna has both, so I am as weak as I was years ago, before Claus screwed us all over. Seeing as we're stuck here our top priority must be to protect Den. Heading back home comes second."

Naphtali frowned. "Where is he, then? We'd better leave the Gate before more demons show up."

The Commander's shoulders slumped. "We should check the school."

Denida shook his head. "I already checked there. There are dead bodies all around the school, but he wasn't among them, so he must have escaped."

"What about Nina?" The Commander rubbed his hands together.

*Nina? True, she wasn't there, either. Maybe... of course!* Denida turned to the Commander and nudged his arm. "You're a genius; they must be at Nina's farm." He guided them away from the Gate and out to the road. They eventually passed the school and continued farther, leaving town. Denida stopped at a dirt road. "It's at the end of this road; stay vigilant."

The Commander saluted and gestured for his soldiers to advance.

Denida arched his neck at the ravens croaking overhead. *I have a terrible feeling about this.*

The farm gradually materialized in front of them. Demons' corpses littered the estate.

"What-" Denida gasped. He knelt next to one of the carcasses. "Its heart has been ripped out."

"Don't worry; both of them escaped." Loki appeared in the doorway.

"Both?" The Commander frowned.

"Nina and Den. You're looking for them, right?"

"Yes, but-"

"I will take it from here." Denida shuffled in front of the Commander. "Loki, right? Why would someone from Valhalla be on Earth?"

Loki smiled brightly. "That's for me to know and you to-"

Denida rolled his eyes. "Translation: Henna. You have always reminded me of Claus, so I wasn't expecting a straight answer."

"Fine by me." Loki sneered. "But if you insist on not knowing what happened here and where Nina is, okay then." He waved his hand in the air.

The Commander lifted his finger. "I want to hear that."

Denida glared back. "Get in line, Commander."

"Your soldier sounds intrigued, but perhaps your men are living under tyranny?"

Denida gritted his teeth. "You were there when Henna killed my colonel, so you can't be trusted." He raised his brow. "Just like Claus."

"I still don't see the likeness." Loki rested against the side of the doorway. "I liked Claus when he was here, though."

Denida's eyes widened. "Claus is here, too?"

Loki shook his head. "I said was. He already left with Nina."

Denida charged forth and grabbed Loki, shoving him up against the house's outer wall. "Where did they go?"

Loki grinned. "You think you can get results with physical force?"

Denida kneed Loki and tossed him to the ground.

Loki crossed his legs and sat with his head resting in his left hand. "I'm a god. Have you forgotten that?"

"No, you're not; Henna granted Odin divinity, not you."

Loki jumped to his feet and extended his arms to his sides. A silvery silhouette started to form around him, slowly becoming thicker.

Denida backed up.

"Going somewhere? I guess that means you understand how little you know."

Denida lowered his head. "What did she bring you here for?"

Loki frowned. "You still don't understand?" He shook his head. "Then I can't help you. I can, however, tell you where Claus and Nina went, if you so desire that knowledge?"

"Yes." Denida tried his best to imitate a smile.

"They pursued Susan to the Scientist's old hideout."

*The Scientist?* Denida eyed Loki. "You mean Jack?"

"Who else?" Loki simpered. "But that is all I was told to tell you. If you want more, you'll have to come see me in Valhalla."

A flash of silvery light appeared, only to vanish with Loki in an instant.

Denida grunted and turned to the Commander. "We need to find Susan ASAP."

The Commander shrugged. "There are demons everywhere, Sir. This is dangerous, especially with Claus in their ranks."

"That was an order, Commander. Do you have a problem with that?" Denida shot him a piercing glare.

The Commander straightened up. "Sir, no Sir. I was just expressing my strategic concerns."

Denida stroked his finger. "Noted, but time's a wasting. Let's go."

***

"This is it." Susan shoved the giant steel fence. "*Creak,*" The fence opened slightly. *Is it rusted shut?* "Help me." She gestured to Den and the others.

Together, they pushed it just widely enough that they could shimmy through.

Kate frowned. "Are you sure this place is safe?"

"Yes," Susan stated harshly.

"… from demons?" Sus lifted her eyebrows.

Susan chuckled and threw out her arms. "This was a haven for a demon darker than any others. The demons here, now, would never look for us here, but if they were to, there's a tunnel that leads to an island where they can't use dark magic."

"Okay." Den clapped his hands. "Did they really vacate this building? It's quite an impressive estate to just abandon."

Susan shook her head. "Nobody's come here since Jack died; I'm sure of it."

"You're sure of it?" Den rolled his eyes. "Knowing is better than assuming; we'd better check to be sure."

Susan nodded with a meek smile. *Just like Denida…*

"Susan," Den's voice rang from the door.

Susan sprinted for the building.

Den, Sus, Jakob, and Kate stood, facing off against a group of teenagers, who had barricaded themselves inside. They had greasy hair and disheveled appearances.

Den peered at Susan. "I told you someone would be here."

"Who might you be?" Susan asked softly.

"*Klikt,*" metal clicked, and an old man appeared with a shotgun pointed at Susan. "This is our turf."

"Sir, you don't understand. We-"

"Those psycho things, we know. Why do you think we're here? We found this place first."

Susan lifted her hand. "Just wait a minute. I want-"

"*Bang,*" the shotgun shattered a window. "Last chance, Missy."

"Wow, Man," Jakob scratched his hair. "You're badass, but so is this lady." He pointed at Susan. "She's a master sergeant, who knows about a secret path to an island."

The man lowered his rifle. "What island?"

Jakob shook his arm. "The one with a magic barrier."

The man turned the gun back on Susan. "Is he right? Will it help with those freaks?"

Susan swallowed. "They're not freaks; they're demons… well, I guess 'freaks' is accurate. Yes, the island will be safe, as the Darkness can't sense us there."

The man rested the rifle on his shoulder. "I'm Tom. You going to take us there, or what?"

Susan surveyed the teenagers. *It couldn't hurt to have more people, if they find us…* "Alright…" She extended her hand to Tom. "- but only if you hand over that rifle. I'm not taking any chances."

Tom hugged the rifle to his chest. "And why would I relinquish it? You could just as easily turn on me."

"No island, then," Susan asserted.

"As you wish, Missy." Tom raised the gun again.

"No!" Den jumped between them with his hands up. "Let's just leave the rifle here for now, and you can come back for it after Susan shows you the island. Is that fair, Tom?"

Tom lowered the rifle. "Fine by me. What about her?"

Den smiled at Susan. "Sergeant?"

"Fine," Susan conceded.

Tom nodded and rested the gun up against the wall. He led the teenagers outside.

Susan snuck across the grounds, approaching the waterfront. She stopped suddenly, her eyes trailing the pathway to an old building.

Jakob frowned. "Su-"

Susan cleared her throat. "Jack had that demon, Danyel, lock us up inside that building."

"Why were you even here? Did some humans live out here?"

Susan shook her head. "I wasn't here for a person."

"Why then?" Den insisted.

"It's…" Susan rubbed her forehead. "Remember your friend, who went nuts after Jacob died?"

"Nina?" Den's eyes widened.

"Yes, like I said, her soul form is my close friend. She brought me here to avenge her son."

Den's eyes roamed around until they settled on Sus. "You and Sus are so similar. She has this inclination to do whatever she must do to protect everyone else, just like you."

Susan nodded with a sigh.

"If this souls-being-similar-to-humans pattern is the same in Nina's case, did her soul approach her human form and teach her magic?"

*Den has a point, but Nina has always been friendly, unlike what we saw from her human form. She even told Denida about my call at Dynas-* Susan gasped. *...or did she? I never reached the Underworld, and no one came looking for me...*

"You realized something, didn't you? I can see it written on your face." Den lifted his finger. "You've got that same expression Sus gets when something strikes her."

"It's not important. Let's keep moving." Susan clenched her jaw and hiked to a door, pushing it open. She knelt and picked up a flashlight next to the entrance.

Den sprang after her. "Wait, we didn't-"

"It's just on the other side of this tunnel." Susan descended the stairs.

"Give it up," Tom shook his head. "This sergeant of yours won't tell you anything." He gestured for the teenagers.

"Master sergeant, and the clock's ticking," Susan poked her head out of the tunnel. "The demons may not be able to detect us on the island, but they can on this side of the tunnel."

Sus approached Den and grabbed his hand. "Let's go."

Susan led the way with the flashlight she'd picked up, casting a meager light to guide them.

Den squeezed Sus' hand, bringing her focus to him. "Something wrong?" He tilted his head toward the light in front of them.

"I think so," Sus whispered. "- but if she's anything like me, she won't tell you."

Den pecked Sus' cheek. "But she might tell you, Princess."

"Uhm…" Sus retracted her hand.

"Please? She knows something; I can feel it," Den pleaded.

Sus swallowed. "Fine, but only because you asked… and because it may help us figure out what the hell is happening here." She slithered to the front of the group at a faster pace, only to slow down when she reached Susan. "Hi."

Susan glanced at her for just a moment. "You can tell him I'm not saying anything."

"Alright." Sus peered back at Den. "But why not?"

"We are in the middle of a demon apocalypse-"

"Puh-lease," Sus begged. "I know you're like me, so your pride wouldn't stop me from asking."

*Heh… I sure am clever.* "No can do. You're a human."

"You think that matters? Demons invaded Earth. How can we protect each other if we don't know everything?" Sus exhaled heavily. "We wouldn't want to trust the wrong person again, like that girl you know from your world."

"Jakob." Susan gestured. "Take Sus back there with you; it's too dangerous up here." She smiled coyly at Sus.

Jakob rushed up to Sus and returned her to Den.

"Sorry," Sus moaned to Den, as Jakob returned to his spot right behind Susan.

Den embraced her. "No, you did well, and I love you for trying."

Susan lowered her flashlight and pushed open a heavy steel door, revealing daylight.

"Wow!" Tom exclaimed. "You were right." He gazed around the forest in awe.

Kate cleared her throat. "Are you sure it's safe?"

Susan clapped her hands. "Den, can you please try to use magic for me?"

"Wha-" Den shot Susan a blank stare. "Me, magic? I'm human?"

"You're the human form of Denida and you dream about the Underworld. I'm confident in your abilities."

"Even if I could, why would I?" Den scoffed. "You *are* keeping stuff from us."

"You said it yourself; I'm like Sus. So would I really keep something important from you?"

"Perhaps not." Den kicked the dirt.

"Pretty please, Den." Susan batted her eyelids.

Den's shoulders slumped. "Fine, how do I use magic?"

"Simple." Susan stepped behind Den and grabbed his hands. "You fold them together and imagine a fire starting in between them. Keep focusing on that thought, and it shall appear."

"Focus?" Den asked doubtfully. "That sounds farfetched."

Susan sighed. "Trust me, what do you have to lose?"

Den folded his hands and closed his eyes. Faint sparks flickered in between his hands. but died down quickly.

"Was that magic?" Tom gasped.

"What?" Den opened his eyes and rubbed his fingertips. "They feel warm."

"Told you," Susan gloated.

Den gritted his teeth and rubbed his hands. "Can I do magic off this island?"

Susan tilted her head. "I'll teach you how."

# Chapter 22- Den

Denida bit his lip. The military had set a perimeter around a bus station, under the blazing sun.

"It's not like this where Den lived." The Commander bared his teeth. "These people have fortified their land."

Denida rolled his eyes. "True, but it won't save them. Bullets can't penetrate the Darkness." He shuddered. "I think they're preparing for what they heard about elsewhere, hoping they can stop it."

"He's right, Commander." Naphtali joined them. "Bullets can only knock down demons, but they'll get back up. The Darkness is impervious." He scratched his nose and turned to Denida. "Where do we go, now?"

Denida gestured away from the building. "This way."

They only managed to take several steps before armed forces surrounded them.

Denida raised his hands. "We're just trying to enter the city."

A soldier stepped forward. "The city is on lockdown."

Denida sniffed. "That won't do. We need to go-"

"Really?" the officer scoffed. "From where I'm standing, it looks like we're holding the winning cards." He motioned to the station. "I recommend you leave town before it turns into an inferno."

Denida ran his thumb over the finger that used to bear the ring. "But we need to see someone in town."

"No," the soldier retorted. "Everyone has been evacuated. The only people who stayed are under our protection."

"That's not possible." Denida stomped his foot on the pavement. "Susan is here, and she's not a resident."

The soldier chuckled. "Like you just said, that's not possible." He turned to his troops. "Enough of this, escort them back to the station."

The troops nudged the Commander and his troops toward the building.

Denida's eyes surveyed the area, as he followed his group. "We have to get into town somehow," he murmured under his breath.

"We can overpower them," the Commander whispered. "Just say the word, Sir."

Denida rolled his eyes. "Not everything can be solved with force. Didn't you learn that from the Colonel?"

The Commander's shoulders slumped. "How, then?"

*That's the million-dollar question, isn't it?* A thundering roar reverberated from above. Denida arched his neck to see that the sky had turned as dark as coal. "They're here."

Demons sprang through the station's doors and assaulted the nearest soldiers.

"Charge!" The officer drew his sidearm and started to empty the magazine into the oncoming demons.

A black hole manifested behind the soldier, and several demons appeared from it, charging at the officer and his men.

The officer whipped around. "*Click,*" his gun sounded. "Shi-"

The demons pounced on the officer, pinning him to the ground. They tore him limb from limb.

"Denny!" Naphtali waved his hands from across the road.

*Sorry I couldn't be of any help.* Denida heaved in a heavy sigh. "Yes, let's get to Susan." He sprinted down the road, into the city, with his soldiers in tow.

Denida led the trek across town, which now baked under oppressively hot sunlight.

Naphtali stopped and rubbed sweat from his forehead. "Are we almost there?" he asked hoarsely.

"It's across town, so it shouldn't be long. It's a building on a lake. A tunnel connects it to a remote island."

"You think Susan's on that island?"

Denida peeked back. "If she's clever, and I know she is, she would like-" His eyes locked on the building behind Naphtali.

"What?" Naphtali turned his head.

Denida pointed. "Someone was over there."

"Nobody's-" Naphtali's eyes glazed over, and he collapsed to the ground.

Denida rushed to Naphtali's side and knelt next to him, shaking him. *What happened?* "Commander, get over here!" He snapped his fingers and slapped Naphtali's cheek. "Commander?" He turned around. Everyone around him was on the ground, unconscious.

"They can't hear you." With a silver flash, Claus surfaced with Nina's human form at his side. Claus bore a wicked grin. "Missed me?"

"What did you do?" Denida jumped to his feet.

"No." Nina clenched her fist, creating a magic silhouette around them, blocking Denida's lunge. "They are only napping."

"Nina?" Denida wrinkled his nose. He put his hand on the cone. "Why aren't you with Den?"

"Den?" Nina scoffed.

"Yes, you were so close." A stabbing pain struck Denida's heart. *Aren't we soul mates?* "You were such good friends, Nina."

"Actually, I'm Nylah. Nina is just my weak twin."

"You know… Nina's soul? But … you're Nina's human form?"

"Correct, Queen Henna put me inside of her body, so I can carry out my mission."

Denida stepped back. "What would that be? Your twin stole my ring, so there's nothing left for you to take."

Nylah giggled. "True, I was originally just here to keep you and your soulmate apart, but things have changed. I have a new purpose, now."

Denida furrowed his brow. "Soulmate, you're right. We should-"

Nylah stood with her hands on her hips, shaking her head. "I never realized you were this stupid; maybe this will help you." She nudged Claus's shoulder and turned her back with a twinkle in her eye. "It's been fun." She vanished.

"Nina, come back!" Denida banged on the cone.

"You are fighting against the tide." Claus stepped closer. "Funny to see how far you've fallen."

"I haven't." Denida flinched. "How can you use Henna's magic? Are you her new lapdog? I thought you changed when I gave you another chance."

Claus smirked. "Change is for the weak; achieving my goal will get me what I deserve. Plus, I will get to watch your demise firsthand."

Denida raised his fists. "If you want that, then you'd better come out from behind your little shield and face me."

Claus shrugged. "Moi? I'm not the one tasked with killing you; Nylah is. She should have reached Susan by now, I think." Claus knocked on the cone. "Just a hint, you have to choose between saving Susan or everyone here. Choose wisely."

*Nylah…* Denida gawked at his soldiers. He returned his focus to Claus. "Henna won't beat me or grant you whatever she promised you for this fool's errand."

Claus rubbed his palms together. "You don't even know what she offered me."

"I don't need to; I know her." Denida thrust his arm out, hurling a ball of dark energy into the cone, which devoured the spell.

Claus tilted his head. "I see you've made your choice to defend these people. You even tried to fight me; I feel honored." He knelt and rested his hand on the ground. The cone dissipated. "This ought to make things more entertaining."

Denida's shoulders slumped. "You want to fight me?"

"I want to kill you, you mean," Claus gloated.

"Weren't you just saying that's Nylah's job?"

"Want to ask questions, or shall we end this?" Claus raised his eyebrows.

"Yes, I need to rectify my mistake; I never should've trusted you." Denida lunged.

Claus mimicked Denida's movements and chucked a glowing, silvery ball of energy at Denida.

Denida dropped to the ground. The ball whizzed past him and slammed into a parked car. The light vaporized the car, disintegrating it into ash. Denida sprang up and flung a ball of dark energy at Claus.

Claus cackled and thrust several more balls after Denida in quick succession. Denida jumped behind another car. He had to keep weaving, evading the attacks, and running from the cars being destroyed one after another.

Denida glared under one of the cars, searching for a glimpse of Claus's legs. *I can't stay here; I've got to get to Susan, but I can't leave the Commander and our troops.*

"*Boom!*" sounded from a car in front of Denida.

"You can't hide forever," Claus cheered. "Maybe I should have fun with your Commander."

Denida focused and sprang up.

Claus watched him with a wide smirk. "Ready to die?"

Denida tilted his head. "You can try."

"Oh, I intend to," Claus hissed.

"Really? Is that such a good idea? I'm pretty sure your 'master' won't like that."

"Master?" Claus chortled. "I don't have a master; I'm as powerful as I am 'cause I'm your downfall." Claus clenched his fist, and silvery energy sucked Denida toward him. Claus wrapped his fingers around Denida's throat.

Denida punched Claus's gut.

Claus gritted his teeth and flung Denida down the road, followed by silvery ash that hurtled through the sky, binding Denida's hands. Claus smiled as he stepped closer, his smile growing more wicked with each step.

Denida tugged and squirmed to free his arms.

"My magic is too strong."

"That's not-" Denida gasped and stared at his arms. "… yours." He lowered his head. "Henna!"

Claus's smile froze, and he slowly spun around 360 degrees, searching.

"Maybe she wants to join us?" Denida mused.

Claus sped to Denida, his hands starting to emanate silvery magic.

"Ahem," Henna materialized with a cough. "What's going on here?"

Claus shoved his hands behind his back. "My Queen, I'm just distracting Denida so that we can-"

"Killing me off, you mean!" Denida yelled.

Henna kissed her index finger, and the restraints on Denida's wrists disappeared.

Claus grunted. "He's better off restrained."

Henna turned her eyes to Claus. "That's unnecessary; he can't stop fate's trajectory. Your antics have delayed him long enough." She turned her attention to Denida. "Why don't you go to the others?" She smiled softly.

Denida squinted. "Just allow you two to get away? I don't think so."

"Us two?" Henna shrugged. "I no longer require Claus; he's already served his purpose." She rubbed her fingers together, and silvery ash materialized between them, thickening until she clenched her fist.

Claus frowned. "My Queen, what are-"

"*Click,*" Henna snapped her fingers, and a wave of silvery ash wafted through the air, encasing Claus. It turned his body into a pile of ash on the ground.

Denida's eyes widened. "But… he served you."

"He did, but how can I use someone who's so quick to betray me?" Henna extended her other hand and uncoiled her fingers, revealing the sparkling necklace. "I believe this is yours."

Denida glared at her hand. "Thanks, but no."

"Your loss, but Nylah will finish her mission at the camp, unless you do your absolute best to stop her."

Denida scoffed. "How?"

Henna closed her hand. "Since you're not ready for this yet, you should go see the others." She faded away with the necklace.

Everyone around Denida awoke from their slumber.

Denida gritted his teeth. "We need to move on the double! Follow me." He sprinted so fast that he almost lost his footing several times, but it didn't take long to come to a halt in front of the steel gates leading into Jack's estate. *Looks like somebody pried the gate open.* He exhaled heavily.

The Commander and the others joined him. "In there, Sir?"

Denida tilted his head. "Be ready for anything."

The Commander and his soldiers led the way inside. The grounds stood vacant and silent, completely lifeless.

Denida took a few cautious steps, while his alert eyes flitted about. *Something feels off, here; it's too quiet.* He gasped. "This way!" They marched across the grounds and descended the stairs into the dimly lit tunnel.

"Sir." The Commander's hand sought out the wall. His hand felt a shelf, and ran up onto it, stopping on a flashlight's rubbery shaft. He turned it on and waved it around. "Here." He handed it to a soldier and gestured for him to go first.

The group darted through the tunnel. Eventually, the soldier climbed the stairs on the other side and grabbed a door handle, but it didn't budge. More soldiers joined him and pried the door open.

The leaves outside blew with a fresh breeze, but that was the only sound. The island's stillness completed its abandoned vibe.

Naphtali scratched his cheek. "Do you really think someone's here?"

Denida frowned. "Yes, they're probably at the campsite." He waved his arm.

Denida led the Commander and his troops to the clearing Denida remembered Nina and Mara using. Their trek finally ended when they glimpsed the campsite through the tree line, but a sinking feeling grew in the pit of Denida's stomach. *Something's wrong.* He peered through the trees with bated breath.

Den and Sus sat next to a bonfire, making s'mores. Susan watched them from a distance and straightened up with a stretch.

Tom strolled up to the bonfire. "Look who I found." He stepped aside revealing Nina.

*That's Nylah.* Denida stepped forward, but the Commander stopped him with a hand on his shoulder.

"Sir, I know you said that's Nylah now, but Susan's got this," the Commander whispered. "Besides, if we interfere, she may take a hostage."

Denida bit his lip but nodded at the Commander. *He's right; she's unhinged enough to hurt someone if she sees us.*

Susan tensed and she rushed over to stand in front of Den and Sus. "Nina, how did you find us?"

"It was easy, seeing as it's the spot you and my soul used as a hideout."

"How would you know that?" Susan stepped closer to Nina.

"I'm just a little girl; there's no reason to be so intimidating," Nina recoiled.

"You killed a bunch of demons with Henna's magic."

"Whose?" Nina frowned.

"Maybe we should give her a chance? It is Nina, after all." Den tapped Susan's arm reassuringly. He gestured for Nina to come over to the bonfire. "We're making s'mores over a fire I lit with magic."

Nina winked at Susan. "Guess you're the only one who's wary, even with the barrier." She approached the bonfire.

Susan shot Tom an admonishing glare. "You can't just let random people in here."

"She said she knew you," Tom retorted.

"Yeah, but there was no reason to mention the barrier to her."

"The barrier?" Tom frowned. "She knew that on her own."

Susan's mouth hung agape, and she spun to the bonfire, only to find it vacant. Her eyes scoped the premises, and she spotted the others across the campsite. "Hey!" she hollered, but they all seemed immersed in a conversation. Susan sprang toward them.

"Hey Sus, I think your soul form needs you." Nina pointed at Susan.

Sus nodded and hurried over to Susan.

Nina smiled at Susan. Her grin widened into a wicked smirk, and she turned to Den. "I'm so happy that you're still safe." She unsheathed a blade and held it behind her back before hugging Den tightly.

Den clenched his eyelids so tightly that his forehead wrinkled. A flicker of a wind pushed Nina back.

"Den!" Susan bolted up to them.

Nina's smile froze and she charged forward, thrusting the blade into Den's side. She hastily yanked the knife free and ripped his heart out with a sick smile.

Susan smashed into Nina and shoved her up against a hut.

"Too little, too late to change his fate." Nina gloated.

"You'll pay for that!" Susan slapped her across the face.

Nina raised her arms to block Susan's next strike and swept Susan's legs. "Sorry, I don't have time to deal with you." Nina peeked at the bonfire to see Sus charging at her. Nina turned on her heels and fled.

Susan bolted after her.

*No...* Denida mouthed the word.

Sus' wails of despair broke the silence and disturbed the serenity of the lonely campsite.

Denida stumbled up to the campsite on wobbly legs. *I have to be sure...*

Sus whipped around with red, teary eyes. "Den, could that really be you? You look so much older." She rose to her feet and wiped her eyes. "Are you his dad, maybe?"

Sus' words sounded foggy and distant to Denida. His mind raced with shock and uncertainty. His eyes wandered, and his stomach sank at the atrocity before him. *No...* He shoved Sus out of the way, as rage and pain swirled in his gut, turning to nausea. His knees buckled and he slumped to the ground, right in front of Den's heart. Denida paled as he clambered over to the body on the ground. He lifted Den's head slowly and pulled it up to his chest. He clenched his fists so tightly that his knuckles ached. "Henna!" he screamed with eyes as dark and empty as blank, gaping voids.

# Chapter 23- The Twin

Susan knelt next to some branches in the forest, running her fingers across their cracked ends. *I'm still on track; she came this way.* She crept on with her eyes locked on the ground. She sniffed the air, and her eyes opened wide. *Is she approaching the beach? I need to stay focused, as the Commander said. She's not getting away from me.* Susan bolted after Nylah.

"I've been waiting." Nylah stood on the sand with her arms crossed.

Susan gritted her teeth, and her eyes drifted to the side, before resting on a pier.

"Memories?" Nylah chuckled.

"Nothing the likes of you would know," Susan chortled.

Nylah shrugged. "Henna told me about what happened here. She mentioned a demon, Jack, I think?"

Susan clenched her fists. "Do you have a point?"

"I thought it was a fitting place for you to meet your end."

"Really?" Susan drew her gun. "I think the odds are stacked against you."

Nylah tilted her head to the side. "Haven't you heard the saying 'don't bring a knife to a gunfight?'"

"It's not a knife." Susan cocked the gun.

"It is, when compared to magic." Nylah winked.

"You forget where we are? After Jack died, Denida recreated the magic barrier here because Nina started coming here to watch her human form, and he wanted to ensure her safety."

"The barrier can't shield you from Henna's magic." Nylah rubbed her hands together.

"That witch's magic won't save you." Susan clenched her jaw. "It wouldn't be this way if you'd just left us alone. Why did you kill Den, anyway?"

Nylah smiled wickedly. "I killed Den for the same reason that I'll kill you; it serves a greater cause for my queen." She launched a silvery spear of magical energy at Susan.

Susan ducked, and the magic slammed into a tree trunk, severing it. Susan steadied her gun with both hands and fired at Nylah.

Nylah created a cross with her arms and a silvery cone appeared, blocking the bullets.

Susan tossed the gun aside and charged at Nylah. Just like the bullets, she crashed into the cone with a loud thud.

Nylah lowered her arms and clapped her hands. The barrier faded. She lifted Susan off the ground.

Susan grabbed Nylah's arm with both hands and focused all her weight downward, so that she could deliver a powerful kick to Nylah's gut. Nylah gasped and loosened her grip. Susan dropped and swept Nylah's leg. She pounced on top of Nylah, and grabbed her by the throat, trying to squeeze the life out of her.

Nylah attempted to gesture with her hand, but Susan's grasp was so strong that she had trouble breathing. Nylah's face grew pale, so she trashed, slamming her fists against Susan's hands.

"Stop." Denida pulled Susan away from Nylah. His dark glare locked on Nylah.

Nylah crawled back and raised her hand. "Time for you-"

Naphtali grabbed her hand tightly. "I don't think so."

"Let me go!" Susan yanked free from Denida.

Denida raised his hands. "Stand down, Master Sergeant. That's an order."

Susan's lips twitched, and she eyed Nylah. "But…" Her knuckles whitened. "You don't know what she did."

"Of course, I do, but she's just another fool, blindly following Henna."

"Blindly?" Susan's fists relented.

"Yes." Denida spun around and approached Nylah. "We caught-"

Nylah smirked. "It doesn't matter."

"No?" Denida tilted his head. "You think Henna might help you, unlike the others whom she took advantage of: Nina, Claus, and Mara, to name a few?"

Nylah flipped her hair, so that it rested on her shoulder. "Good guess, but no. I'm a human, now. Do you really want to kill a human?"

Denida stroked her cheek. "You're something special." He clenched his jaw. "But if you don't tell me what I want to know, this will have to end. Nina screwing me over was enough for a lifetime."

Nylah blinked. "What do you want to know?"

"Why did Henna want my human form dead?"

"That's funny," Nylah mused. "You've asked for an answer I can't give you."

Denida bared his teeth and sauntered away, rubbing his palms together.

Nylah peered at Naphtali. "And you, Demon, do you want to try, too?"

*"Ex-demon."*

"Once a demon, always a demon."

Naphtali scratched his jaw. "Watch her; I'd better check on what's keeping Denny." He waited for Susan to grasp Nylah's hand before he dashed away.

"You disgust me." Susan dug her nails into Nylah's hand.

Nylah batted her eyelids. "Innocent, little me?"

"Witch!" Susan picked up some dirt and smeared it on Nylah's face. "You're a killer."

"Perhaps, but if Denida can forgive me for killing his human form, shouldn't you?"

Susan dug her nails in deeper. "Why should-"

Nylah rolled over, toppling Susan. She grabbed Susan's throat, lifting her other hand, which shone with a faint silvery light. "Want to join Den? Just ask."

Susan reached for her throat.

Nylah waved her finger, and a stream of silvery magic floated from her fingertip and smashed into a tree across the clearing, creating a massive hole in the middle of the trunk. "I wouldn't, if I were you," she smirked.

*Wow...* Susan's hand froze as her eyes remained fixed on the gaping hole. She cleared her throat. "What exactly do you want? They're gone, and you can leave. You don't need to hurt me."

"Leave?" Nylah sniggered. "Why would I do that? Do you know how many problems your existence has caused? Absolutely everything revolves around you."

"Me?" Susan frowned.

"Yes, but I can end that right here, right now."

"Nylah." Denida came to a halt just a few short steps away from them. "Don't do it; killing her won't-"

"It'll fix everything, wait and see."

"Really?" Denida bared his teeth. "What do you think will happen to you then? You can't seriously believe that I will just smile and let you be on your merry way."

"Not a bad idea," Nylah snorted and yanked Susan back. "But you don't have a say in this matter."

Denida clenched his fist, and his eyes darkened. "One wrong move, and I promise I'll rip your heart out." Darkness started swirling around his clenched fist, but it died down instantaneously. Denida waved his hand around and rested it on his waist. "Look around; you've got nowhere to go, and no one is coming to save you."

Naphtali circled them and paused behind Nylah.

"My mission was a success. Henna will-"

"Let you rot?" Denida furrowed his brow. "This is Henna's will?"

"I'm not sharing-"

"She doesn't even know," Susan mocked.

"Exactly, she did what Henna asked, so Henna no longer has a need for Nylah. I bet Henna never gave Nylah a secondary mission."

"She did!" Nylah raised her voice. "Henna wanted me to do what she did before with Daniel. Plus, are you forgetting that I've got Susan?" Nylah smirked.

"Henna doesn't want you to kill her, or you would have done it already." Denida took a careful step. "If you let Susan go, I can protect you."

"*Creak*," a branch snapped not far behind Nylah. She tossed Susan into Denida's grasp, knocking them both to the ground, and spun around. She raced deeper into the forest.

"You're okay?" Denida inspected Susan's stomach.

Susan grabbed Denida's hands. "I'm fine." Her eyes met Denida's, and her heart pounded. All the images of Sus and Den flashed through her mind, and her hand holding Denida's started to feel warm.

"She's getting away!" Naphtali stormed after Nylah.

"Right." Denida jumped up and hurried after them.

Susan rested her hand on her chest. *How is it possible that Sus and Den were so close?* She drew a sigh and peered at the trees. *Could we be-*

*"Ka-boom!"* The ground trembled, and a cloud of dust emanated from the woods.

"Denny!" Susan bolted toward the sound. She froze when she found herself surrounded by trees, and her eyes roamed around. *I need to find them, but where?* She tiptoed forward, trying not to make a sound.

Her eyes darted about until they fell on the source of the sound, a large tree with its trunk snapped clear in half. *Oh my god...*

*I must be getting close.* Susan lowered herself to her knees to crawl to the tree. Tiny bugs crawled on it, but silence persisted in the woodlands. Susan swallowed as she crawled to the other side of the tree, only to freeze as the sight of a lifeless human body made her stomach knot.

Susan's wide eyes scoped her immediate surroundings. *Who is that? Whoever killed them didn't take their heart.* She squinted, trying to make out the corpse's face. Branches creaked under her feet with each step. Susan drew in a deep breath and turned the body over.

*Naphtali? Thank god.*

"Aren't you sweet?" Nylah lifted Susan off the ground and swung her to the side, sending her rolling through branches on the forest floor.

Susan jumped to her feet. "Where's Denida?"

"You must be in agony, not knowing where he is, seeing as he means everything to you."

"I asked you where he is." Susan gritted her teeth. "If you hurt him…"

Nylah smirked. "I would never hurt him; my queen has plans for him. You, on the other hand, are a different story."

Susan's eyes wandered back to the tree.

"Don't worry, they're both napping."

Susan turned her focus back to Nylah. "Both? So that's what you did with Naphtali, but why?"

"So, we won't have any more interruptions."

"Why are you obsessed with me?"

Nylah shrugged. "I'm not; Henna is. Frankly, I don't see anything special about you. You seem like every other pathetic wannabe."

"You don't know me, but I know your sister." Susan sneered.

"Oh?" Nylah smirked. "Yes, I'll do what Nina could-"

"As if! You and your twin are nothing but vicious souls, using others for your own gain, but it ends here." Susan charged forward.

Nylah shot streams of silvery magic at Susan.

Susan sprang to the side. She weaved to avoid the onslaught of magic.

Nylah clasped her hands together and thrust them out. A barrage of magical daggers sliced through the air. Several struck Susan in the shoulder and leg.

Susan jumped behind a shrub and clenched her fist with a snarl.

"You can't beat magic, little girl."

Susan's fingers coiled around a rock, while the crunch of Nylah's footsteps approached. She jumped out, facing Nylah. Susan flung a rock. It smacked Nylah in the face, causing blood to gush from her nose. Susan bolted to Nylah and grabbed her, forcing her up against a tree. "It's not what we can do that matters; it's how we use what we've got."

Nylah clenched her jaw and spat in Susan's face.

The mucus on Susan's face morphed into acid, burning Susan's skin. She staggered back and smeared dirt on her face to absorb the acid.

Nylah lifted Susan from behind with her arm around Susan's throat. She ran her hand across Susan's face and her mucus evaporated like steam. "I already told you: you can't beat magic. You might as well-"

"I will never accept that!" Susan pried at the arm around her throat. Her hands loosened when she felt a warm sensation on her back. *My heart! She's gonna...* Susan's eyes darted about. She shifted her weight and dug her nails into Nylah's arm. The warmth on her back lessened. *It's my turn.* Susan stomped on Nylah's toes.

Nylah lost her grip on Susan.

Susan threw a circle kick, followed by punches directed at Nylah's throat. She jabbed Nylah repeatedly, hammering her back.

Nylah clenched her fingers in front of her throat, and a silvery shade started to appear, but sputtered out immediately, as Susan's onslaught forced Nylah to raise her hands to shield her face instead. She knelt in fetal position.

Susan grabbed and wrestled Nylah, trying to yank her from her protective position. She stepped back, eyeing their surroundings. *Naphtali...* Susan darted to Naphtali's side, where she crouched next to him and searched his pockets. *Where is it?* She felt a bulge in one of his pockets. She rapidly pulled the object from the pocket, smiling down at it. *His switchblade.* Susan jumped up and ran back to Nylah. Her face froze. *She's gone.* Susan's fingers tightened on the switchblade's shaft, as she listened intently.

"Over here," Nylah's singsong voice crooned from behind the fallen tree.

Susan raced to the other side of the tree but stopped so abruptly that she stumbled.

Nylah sat, hovering over Denida. "I could end it all right now." She traced her index finger over his neck. "All I would need to do is tear his heart out. Want me to do that?" She glared at Susan.

"No, of course not, if you hurt him-"

"Yeah, yeah. You'll kill me. Drop the knife, or I'll take my chances."

Susan gritted her teeth. Her fingers tightened around the shaft for a minute before she extended the blade and stabbed it into the fallen tree. She stepped back with her hands raised. "Now let him go!"

Nylah patted Denida's forehead and stood up. "Why would I do that?" Her silvery silhouette shone brightly.

"You knocked both him and Naphtali out, right?"

"Yes," Nylah gloated and closed their distance. "But I'm not done, yet." She lifted her arm and a cone appeared around the two women. "I need to finish what my sister couldn't. Then, I'll deal with Denida."

"Hurting Denny will work against you."

"Oh?" Nylah giggled. "Then explain how I was able to kill his human side without consequences." She extended her arms. "I don't see anyone trying to stop me. I just see you, here. Need a tissue?"

Susan bared her teeth. "You won't get a chance. You shouldn't underestimate me."

Nylah shrugged. "Look at the bright side; you may finally be together as soulmates in death."

Susan's eyes narrowed, and she stormed forward.

Nylah thrust her arm out, expelling a gust of wind, which sent Susan flying. She strode through the woodland and stopped in front of Susan. "I told you; you're fighting against the tide." Nylah flung her hand to the side.

Susan slammed into the fallen tree with a bang, reminiscent of wood splintering.

Nylah cupped her hair behind her ear. She neared Susan and grabbed her throat. Nylah raised Susan above her head. "Nina really should have done it right. You're a pathetic lit-" The cone above Nylah shattered, and her grip on Susan's throat loosened.

*We're not done.* Susan ripped the switchblade from the tree and stabbed Nylah's stomach. She quickly followed up by jabbing her hand at Nylah's gut. Without hesitation, Susan tore Nylah's heart from her chest. "Die!" She stomped on the heart with all her might.

Nylah's skin paled, and she slumped to the ground.

Denida and Naphtali jerked wide awake.

"What happened?" Denida pushed himself up to his feet and staggered over to Susan.

"No, don't come over here." Susan raised her arms.

Denida's eyes widened. "You killed her?"

Susan lowered her head. "I had to. She would have killed all of us."

"But…" Denida's jaw trembled. "She was just doing Henna's bidding. We could-"

"Come on; let's find the Commander." Naphtali waved his hand and led them out of the forest.

When they emerged from the forest, the Commander approached them, stopping in front of Denida. The Commander saluted. "Sir, you won't believe what we found at the camp." He uncurled his fingers, revealing a shiny metal object with the UW emblem engraved on it.

"The necklace," Denida wrinkled his nose.

"At least we can return home, Sir."

Denida grunted. "Henna got what she wanted… again." He snatched the necklace, tightened his fist around it, and hurled it into the woods.

The Commander cleared his throat. "Why don't we just make sure she can't succeed."

Denida wrinkled his forehead. "How?"

"She wants revenge on Lucifer and God, no?"

Denida's eye glazed over. "Yes."

"Well, why not get them to work against her?"

Denida rolled his eyes. "We can't. Not after what happened to Heavani."

"We can summon them." The Commander clenched his jaw.

"Hm…" Denida scoped the faces around him. "You might have an idea, there. I know what we need to do." He turned to Susan. "Master Sergeant, please retrieve the necklace."

Susan saluted and hurried to the forest, only to return a moment later.

"Here." Susan handed Denida the necklace.

"Commander, I need you to deliver a message to Dan; 'Contact Costa.'"

Denida took the necklace and slipped it over his head. His silhouette glowed. "Let's go home."

# Chapter 24- Last Attempt

Denida arched his neck, squinting. *Strong sun today.*

Naphtali coughed. "What do you need from me that's so important?"

Denida lowered his head. "Something no one else can do without raising alarm bells."

"What do you mean?"

Denida spun around to face Susan. "Henna is so focused on God, Lucifer, and me that I doubt she would consider you a threat." He unclasped his necklace and laid it on Susan's palm, before gently folding her fingers around it. "I know I can trust you, and it's time we pull the rug out from under that witch."

Susan smiled softly, followed by an official salute. "I'll protect it with my life."

Naphtali shifted on his feet. "So, what's your idea? You want me to teach your soldiers dark magic, or…"

"No." Denida turned to Naphtali. "I need you to bring me back to Hell."

Naphtali's eyes widened with fear. "No, no, no, that's not even possible."

"You must," Denida insisted. "I need to see Lucifer. You're an ex-demon, so you-"

"So are you," Naphtali retorted.

"The Darkness marked me, but you're a lower user of the dark arts, so you won't stand out."

"But Lucifer is in Heaven, trying to break through the Pearly Gates."

Denida snarled. "He'll fail. The Darkness is here, trying to build its power. Lucifer needs that strength. He can't succeed without it."

"I'm not…" Naphtali shook his head. "I am *not* going back there." He pointed an accusatory finger at Denida. "Can't you just summon Lucifer, if you want him that badly?"

"With all the demons swarming everywhere, I would need to use extremely strong magic to reach him, and I don't want to use Henna's magic." Denida winked at Susan. "I can't, now, even if I wanted to."

Naphtali frowned. "Why is it so imperative that you contact Lucifer, anyway?"

Denida sighed. "Lucifer is adamantly opposed to me even entering Hell, which is extremely alarming. Something's wrong, and it's getting worse."

Naphtali frowned.

"I know you said he's not in Hell, but he'll have to give up and go back, eventually. God's using Henna's dagger to seal Heaven. Not even Lucifer can breach a barrier made of Henna's magic."

Naphtali scowled, then cleared his throat and extended his arms. A dark aura covered his silhouette, encasing him.

Denida winked and stepped into the Darkness. "When you're ready."

Naphtali embraced Denida and the Darkness surrounded them, transporting them to Hell. Naphtali lowered his arms, his eyes focused on a fixed point dead ahead.

"Don't worry." Denida squeezed Naphtali's arm and stepped in front of him. *There's a lot more activity here than usual.* He clenched his fists, peering back at Naphtali. "Stay close." Denida strode down the path, as chattering demons swarmed the grounds, awaiting orders.

Naphtali turned back in the direction from which they came, and a cloud of Darkness glided toward them. As it drew nearer, it darkened the path. When it was right in front of them, it took shape.

"Denida," the cloud murmured. "You're back, and I see you've brought another escapee."

Denida pushed Naphtali behind him. "Yes, you wanted me to join you, didn't you?"

The eyes up in the cloud burned like radiant crimson jewels.

"But we need to…" Denida rubbed his jaw. "- see Luci. Is he still around?"

"Yes, he returned from Heaven a short while ago." An image of Lucifer's mansion formed in the cloud.

*I know where that is.* "Good, then we're ready." Denida strode through the cloud and down the path.

"Wait for me!" Naphtali ran to keep up.

Denida stopped in front of a dark mansion, identical to the one that had appeared in the cloud. He thrust his hand forward, and the giant steel doors opened slowly. He cautiously stepped inside.

"Denida?" Lucifer appeared through a dark cloud in front of Denida. "Welcome back to the land of despair." The doors slammed in front of Naphtali's terrified eyes.

"I'm only here to talk about your former queen, Henna."

Lucifer's eyes darkened to a fierce charcoal black. "She does not interest me. I am focused on God."

"But that's exactly what she wants." Denida stepped closer.

"So? He deserves to die for what he did to Heavani and me, regardless of what Henna wants." Lucifer clenched his fist, and waved his other hand over his chest, pulling Denida to him like a vacuum. He thrust Denida up against the wall. "But you've reminded me of something." He hastily ran a finger down Denida's shirt, ripping off the buttons, which clinked against the floorboards. Lucifer's jaw tensed. "Where is it? You're not wearing Henna's necklace."

"We need to end her vendetta."

Lucifer scoffed. "I don't care what she wants. Her magic is all that stands in the way of me settling the score with God, so where's the necklace?" His face leaned so close that Denida could feel his breath. "I told you that you aren't welcome here anymore, so either you give me the necklace, or you will die like Heavani."

Denida arched his neck. "I got rid of the necklace, so I can't give it to you, even if I wanted to."

"Lies." Lucifer's silhouette developed a malicious aura. "How did you get here?"

Denida shrugged. "Your demons have infiltrated the Underworlds, so I just used an ex-demon."

"Underworlds?" Lucifer ridiculed. "We're not stopping there; I need all the dark energy I can get, so we're harvesting all the souls we can."

"You're playing into Henna's hands."

Lucifer snickered. "Why do you keep mentioning Henna? God killed Heavani, so his imminent death is all that matters."

"By that logic, you could just ask Henna to let you through."

Lucifer's dark aura relented. "I considered that, but she won't stop with Shaddai's death, so it's not really a matter I want to approach her for."

"You know, Henna warned me about Heavani's death before it happened."

"Henna has always had this annoying way of predicting the future." Lucifer pointed at Denida. "And you? You think I don't know what the Darkness wants from you?"

Denida shook his head. "I don't care about the Darkness. I just wanted you to realize that you're helping to fulfill Henna's-"

Lucifer smashed Denida up against the wall, his hand hovering over Denida's side. "I know what she wants. I just don't care."

Denida's teeth chattered as the scar on his side burned.

"Killing you is easy…" Lucifer moved his hand closer to the scar but paused with his hand over it. "- but I haven't forgotten that you also gifted me with the opportunity to see Heavani, even if only for a little while, so I shall extend mercy, for now. Just know that if I ever see you again, I'll finish what I started." He grabbed Denida's head and kissed his forehead. "Goodbye, Denny."

Darkness swarmed Denida, teleporting him back to Dynasty.

A very jittery Naphtali appeared a few steps away. "What the hell happened?"

Denida shrugged. "Did the Darkness bring you back, too?"

Naphtali's shoulders slumped. "I sure didn't do it on my own. When you entered that mansion, and the doors closed with you inside, I tried with all my might to open them." He lowered his head with a deep sigh. "I even attempted to use dark arts, but they wouldn't budge."

*If Lucifer doesn't listen, then I need to try something else, but what?* Denida scratched his nose.

"Ahem," Naphtali cleared his throat. "I told you it wouldn't work. Shall we go see the Commander, now?"

"The Commander?"

Naphtali threw up his arms. "Yeah, you sent him to talk to Dan about some Costa guy."

*Costa… of course!* Denida snapped his fingers. "Right, we need to see Dan." He led Naphtali to Dynasty.

"Sir?" The butler welcomed them when they reached the lobby.

Denida smiled. "I need a car. Can you prepare one, please?"

Naphtali frowned. "You know where Dan is?"

"Yes, he should be at the HQ. Follow me." Denida strode outside after the butler, stopping in front of a parked vehicle.

"Sir." The driver saluted and opened the back doors for them.

Denida gestured with his hand. "After you."

As the car sped down the road, Naphtali scratched his cheek. "You really think Dan can help?"

Denida glanced to the side. "Trust me; I have a plan only he can help with." He smiled wickedly.

"What if it doesn't work? The demons are gaining ground. We aren't strong enough to stop them, not with how strong the Darkness is becoming."

Denida clenched his fist. "Failure isn't an option, Naphtali."

A flash appeared in the sky, followed by a low rumble. Rain began tapping the windshield, a few drops at a time, then quickly evolving into a downpour.

Denida blinked rapidly. *God, that...* He heaved a sigh. *Hopefully, the demons won't come here.* He unclenched his fist and tapped the seat in front of him. "We'd better slow down. We don't want to get in an accident."

The driver slowed down for the duration of the trip. Finally, he parked the car right in front of the HQ. The driver stepped out into the pouring rain and opened the door for Denida.

Naphtali stepped out of the car. "Crap!" He lifted his arms over his head and ran for the building. When he reached cover, he shook the rain out of his hair.

Denida darted over to him and squeezed his hair dry. "That was a torrential downpour." He marched through the front door and continued to the elevator.

"Wow, this place is huge." Naphtali gawked at the interior as he paused beside Denida.

"*Beep.*" The elevator arrived.

Denida led Naphtali inside. When they reached their floor, he marched down the corridor with focused determination, not stopping until he reached a massive door. He peeked back at Naphtali and flung the door open. "Dan!"

Susan sat opposite Dan. "Denny?" Her eyes narrowed in puzzlement. "I thought you left?"

"It didn't work." Denida stepped into the room. His eye fell on his necklace, shining on the desk. He blinked and turned his focus to Dan. "Can you get me in contact with your friend?"

Dan raised his eyebrows. "Friend, what friend?"

"Costa."

"From the Galaxy Council?"

Denida rested his hand on Susan's shoulder. "Can you take Naphtali with you? I need to talk to Dan."

Susan saluted and jumped up.

"Wait!" Denida snatched the necklace off the desk. "I want you to wear this at all times." He slipped it around her neck. "Don't tell anyone. You are to wear it and protect it with your life."

"Yes, Sir." Susan shut the door behind herself and Naphtali.

"We need another way to stop Henna." Denida spun around. "Lucifer didn't listen, but we must stop this war. Costa's council is our last chance." Denida frowned. "I'm going to travel there on a ship momentarily. Can you set up a meeting for me?"

"Why not just use the neck-"

Denida stomped his foot. "We're not using any more of Henna's witchcraft!" He drew in a deep breath. *I need to calm down.* He closed his eyes for a few seconds before opening them again.

Dan met Denida's eye. "I'll set it up."

Denida smiled broadly. "Thank you." He marched to the door and opened it, but froze suddenly. "Prepare for a demon invasion while I'm gone." He waved and strolled out the door, continuing to the ship to take him to the Galaxy Council.

***

Nina watched Denida's spaceship take flight. *When the cat's away, the mice shall play.* She licked her lips as she gawked up the HQ. She tied her hair up in a ponytail and folded it under a hat. Nina strolled into the building. Her left hand rested on the High Sorcerer's holy dagger that she'd hidden under her shirt. Nina smiled at the secretary in the lobby with her bright green eyes, but swiftly continued past her to the stairwell.

Nina examined the stairwell. *It's safe.* She lifted her shirt and wrapped her fingers around the holy dagger's shaft. Silvery ash covered her, creating a protective aura around her. She spun around and trekked through the door, moving past the secretary, who looked straight at her, but didn't seem to recognize her. Nina stopped among a crowd, waiting for the elevator.

"*Cling.*" The doors slid open. The crowd started to file inside.

Nina glanced over her shoulder before following them inside the elevator.

The higher the elevator ascended, the emptier it became.

Nina checked the current floor number. *It's the next stop.*

The doors chugged open, and Susan stood outside. She stepped back, so people in the elevator could exit.

Nina's thumb caressed the blade. She lowered her hand and scurried out of the elevator with her eyes locked on Susan. Her gaze remained locked until the elevator started moving again. Nina closed her eyes. *There was something different about Susan. I'd better hurry before she comes back.*

Nina bolted down the corridor to Denida's office and through the doors into his chambers. She sat behind his desk and turned on his computer, gazing at the screen with rapt focus while it booted up. Her eyes fluttered to a facedown picture frame. With a shaking hand, she stood it up and saw the photo of Denida and herself together with their son.

*Daniel…* Nina reached for the frame and stroked the image of her son. *Mommy will be with you soon, no matter what it takes.* She smiled, then returned to focus on the screen and logged in with Denida's password.

*Where would he have it?* Nina scratched her temple and tried to search through a few folders, but none of them had the information she sought. She slammed the dagger into the desk with so much force that the picture frame tumbled over, and her aura vanished. *I don't have the time for this! I have to find out where Hen-* Her breath hitched, and she leaned in closer. In the search field, she entered, "H-e-n-n-a."

Over a hundred search results appeared.

Nina gritted her teeth and added "Gate" to the search, narrowing it down to three results. She hastily clicked the first result, which mentioned an association between Henna and the Gates. Nina clicked back and selected the second result. "…Giant Gate appears next to the second Gate in the Wild West…" She smirked. *So that's where it was.* Nina stood up just as the door creaked open, and her gaze met Susan's.

"N-Nina?" Susan stuttered. "Why are you-" Her eyes trailed around the room.

Nina's fingers coiled around the dagger's shaft, and she vanished.

Susan spun around worriedly. She retreated to the door, bumping into it. Her hands felt around behind her, and she closed the door, locking it. "You won't get past me, even if you hide like a sissy."

Nina slammed the dagger into the desk again, becoming visible. "You wanted something?"

"What're you doing all this for?"

Nina rubbed her fingers on the shaft. "You would understand if you had ever had a child."

"But this is a little extreme. You can still return to Denida."

"No, I'll do whatever it takes to get Daniel back." Nina's jaw clenched. "I'm getting what I need."

Susan flinched. "For Henna?"

"Henna?" Nina scoffed. "She's too obsessed with vengeance. I'm going to bring my son back."

Susan's mouth hung agape. "But he's dead."

"Nothing's eternal," Nina insisted. "Henna died too, yet she is still here. Daniel can be, too." Nina bared her teeth. "I was in her world, and I saw him."

"No." Susan shook her head. "This is wrong; this isn't natural. He's dead and should remain so."

"You'll understand if you have kids." Nina pointed the dagger at her. "Let me pass."

"Or what?"

"I don't want to kill you, but I'll bring him back by any means necessary." Nina tilted her head. "I'll kill you if I have to."

"What happened to you? I thought we were friends." Susan drew her pistol and pointed it at Nina. "Now you want to kill me? I guess we'll see which one of us goes first."

"Relax." Nina shifted her foot defensively. "No one has to die. You can just let me go, and we can forget all about this. As you said, we're friends."

Susan shook her head, her eyes locked on Nina. "That isn't happening. You crossed the line when you gave the ring to Henna."

Nina ran her fingertips over the top of the blade's shaft. "I could just have vanished and snuck out of here, but I revealed myself to you because of what we had, remember? I saved you from Claus."

Susan inhaled deeply, then clenched her fingers around her gun. "That was before-"

"No, it wasn't. I've always served Henna." Nina laid her hand over her chest. "I know you care. I know that, deep down, you understand, and because of that…" She lifted her other hand from the blade and folded her hands in front of her. "- I'll tell you what Henna wanted me and my sister to do."

"Like that's gonna be a big revelation." Susan mocked her. "We all know Henna just wants revenge on God and the Devil."

Nina smirked. "While that's her primary goal…" Nina met Susan's gaze. "- that's got nothing to do with my mission."

Susan lowered her gun. "What do you mean?"

"Henna gave me a mission involving *you*."

"No." Susan raised the pistol again. "You're just making things up now, so that I'll let you go," she hissed.

Nina sighed and clenched her hand around the blade's shaft, vanishing along with the knife.

"I don't need your help, Susan," Nina's voice echoed throughout the room.

Susan darted into the room and jabbed at the air around where Nina had been, only to whip around with her gun raised. "You can't hide from me."

"I'll tell you my mission because you helped me out with Jack: Henna wanted me to keep Denny away from his original destiny."

Susan swung her arms throughout the room.

Nina jerked the gun from Susan's grasp. It flew across the room and smashed through the window.

Susan gasped. "How-" Cold air blew next to her left ear, but no movement followed. "I can't move! What did you do?"

"You are his soulmate, his destiny." Nina tapped Susan's shoulder, restoring her movement, before jumping through the window, surrounded by a silvery cloud.

# Chapter 25- Galaxy Alliance

A gust of wind blew the leaves in the Wild West, as a silvery glow appeared beneath the branches. It shone as brightly as a star, only to fade, revealing Nina.

She shifted her feet and surveyed her surroundings. *Time to inspect the Gate.* She spun around, only to feel a sucker punch to her gut. A gaping hole in the ground stretched out in front of her.

*Where the hell is it?* Nina's heart sank as she approached the edge of the chasm. *Did it fall? No, that's impossible. Henna must have moved it.*

"*Clippity-clop.*" A posse appeared on horseback.

Nina jumped back and wrapped her fingers around the holy dagger, vanishing from sight.

Several soldiers dismounted and marched over, stopping in front of the hole.

The soldier in front glared back at the cluster of armed men, clearing his throat. "Sir?" He pointed at the chasm. "It just up and vanished."

"How?" Robert moved through the crowd to the front. When nobody answered, he turned to man who'd spoken. "Sheriff Clay?"

Clay shrugged. "I wish I knew." His eyes turned to the hole. "Maybe Henna cloaked it?"

Robert grunted. "Can't it have fallen underground?" Robert stretched his head, gazing down into the pit.

"No, Sir. It levitated twice, but it didn't return to its initial spot the second time." Clay scratched his beard. "A strange silvery light enveloped it, and it completely disappeared."

Nina bared her teeth and trudged forward, stopping between Robert and Clay. *Is it gone. or invisible?* She gritted her teeth and folded her hands around the dagger. She sheathed it and thrust out her hands. A silvery tint coated them.

A gust of wind pushed Robert, Clay, and their companions forward. They tumbled into the gaping hole, and their horrified screams echoed in the chasm.

Nina shrugged. *Guess Henna moved it, after all.* She spun around and strolled past a crowd forming around the hole.

Nina stepped out into the field, heading away from the crowd. She sighed deeply and stabbed the holy dagger into the ground. "Henna!" she screamed at the top of her lungs; her eyes fiery with rage.

Henna materialized in front of her. "I see you've found one of my holy daggers?"

"You're damn right I did." Nina grabbed the dagger and straightened up. "Why did you move the Gate?"

"You expected me to leave it here?" Henna blinked. "It wouldn't have helped you, anyway. Do you think I didn't see this possibility? You need Denida's ring and a holy dagger to access the Gate, if you aren't me…" She folded her hands in front of her face. "- and you are not me."

"This dagger can kill all your gods, including you." Nina lifted the dagger. "Have your so-called visions shown you that possibility?"

Henna tilted her head. "I've seen you attempt that, but just like Denida, you fail."

"Really?" Nina lowered the blade. "That's a shame." She lunged, but Henna vanished and reappeared behind her.

"As I told you, I already saw this option."

Nina's eyes fluttered, she stabbed the knife into the ground and knelt beside it, lowering her head. "Please, My Queen, I just want Daniel back." She lifted the dagger and extended it to Henna. "I'll give you the dagger, if you let me take him home."

Henna ran her index finger down the blade, disintegrating it. "You think offering me my own dagger will help you gain favor with me?"

Nina raised her eyes but kept her head down. "My Queen, I did what you asked."

Henna spun around. "Yes, I no longer need you. Now that your mission is complete, you'll never see me, or Daniel, again." She met Nina's gasp with a sickly sweet smile. "You're a pathetic being. You chose this path, so live with it."

A bright, silvery light surrounded Henna. Nina charged into it, but it vanished as soon as she reached it. "No!" Nina slumped to the ground, repeatedly punching the dirt, as tears fell from her eyes.

***

The spaceship carrying Denida docked, and he exited the ship.

"Denida!" Costa scurried over.

"Costa, why're you here?"

Costa nodded. "Dan told me to expect you."

"So, you came to pick me up yourself?"

Costa shrugged. "Your name precedes you."

Denida smiled cautiously. "Alright, after you." He gestured with his hand.

Costa led him to his mansion.

Denida's eyes continually darted around as they walked.

"Is something wrong?"

"You're leading the Galaxy Alliance, yet don't have any security?"

"You find that strange?" Costa chuckled. "Should I have security?"

"Are you serious?" Denida retorted. "With your status, you should be protected against-"

Costa turned to Denida. "Are you saying I can't defend myself?"

"It has nothing to do with whether you can or can't." Denida bared his teeth. "Their job is to protect-"

"Protect me?" Costa snarled. "The world contains both good and bad. If I cannot handle whatever life throws at me, then that only means that my time is up."

Denida stepped back. "That sounds irksomely like Henna."

"Who?"

"The former queen of Craym. Apparently, you two have the same point of view."

Costa shrugged. "Perhaps, but it isn't her philosophy. It's a common perspective on my home planet."

*That's right; he's not from the Underworlds.* Denida clapped his hands. "Since we're on the subject, the clash between Heaven and Hell will affect the Alliance."

Costa heaved in a deep breath. "Not just the demons, but Henna, too?"

"You're quick on the uptake."

"If I weren't, the Alliance would have replaced me a long time ago."

Denida raised his eyebrow. "So, you'll assist us then?" He held out his hand.

Costa gaped at Denida's hand. "President Denida, are you expecting me to give you something?"

Denida chuckled. "No, it's a custom in my world to shake on a deal, and you can call me Denny."

"In exchange, you must go through the proper channels to gain the council's support." Costa stroked his chin. "That said, overexaggerating the impact of these happenings in order to get the council's support will be unacceptable." He stepped closer and stared into Denida's eyes before he extended his hand, and a flash of light emanated around it. "Those are my terms. We will be bound to our agreement by our soul energy, or no deal."

*Like a blood contract.* "Fine, if that is what it takes." Denida clenched his fist, and a dark aura encircled it.

Costa lowered his hand. "Don't use the dark arts. Use the energy within you."

"I don't have Henna's necklace," Denida gritted his teeth. "- and that wouldn't be 'energy within me,' either."

Costa shook his head. "Yes, there are conduits for magic, like a special device, jewelry, weapon, but also, our very essence, our souls. Why else would the Darkness, which you know by heart, want to harvest souls?"

Denida furrowed his brow. "The soul doesn't emit magic until it's harvested."

Costa raised his eyebrow. "Are you sure about that?" He folded his hands, and a wave of energy wafted from his body and levitated above his head.

Denida shifted on his feet, watching the energy above Costa's head. The energy hovered above Costa, before returning to his body. Denida swallowed. "I can't believe I'm asking this, but how do you do that?"

Costa lifted his hands and took ahold of Denida's. "Just focus on your breathing. Look within yourself and ask the essence of your soul what you truly desire."

Denida clenched a fist, then blinked and extended his hand. "Alright." He folded his fingers around Costa's hand and closed his eyes. "Please, soul," he muttered.

A weak aura materialized and hovered over Denida's body. It mirrored Denida's actions and shook soul-Costa's hand before both souls remerged with their bodies.

"I think we are ready to head to the council. I trust you know how to persuade them?"

Denida shrugged. "I just don't understand the point of having a council when there's a leader."

"The council exists to keep a leader in check. The Alliance will not take my word as law," Costa chortled. "Our Alliance is like your democracy. I'll do my best to support you, as promised, but we won't get anywhere if you can't convince them to get behind your cause, per your side of the deal."

"As their leader, can't you veto their decision if this goes badly?" Denida asked.

"We're a democracy, but not a tyrannical one, besides vetoing is a thing of your world, not ours."

Denida followed Costa as he led the way to the council, which stood in the town center, surrounded by more security checks than Dynasty had.

Costa raised his hand and turned to Denida. "This is as far as I can take you. The rest will be up to you." He patted Denida's shoulder. "Good luck." He wandered into the building.

Denida scratched his cheek. *This won't be as easy as I thought.* He entered, and an usher guided him into the council's expansive boardroom. Every leader of every planet in the universe seemed to be in attendance. All the leaders were different species. While most were physically present, others attended through holograms.

"Order!" Costa lifted his hand, and a light flickered throughout the room. "I declare this Galaxy Council meeting open. Welcome everyone, from near and far," he announced from the far edge of the room, now wearing a flashy outfit.

"Why the last-minute meeting?" An individual with three arms banged them on a desk. "We weren't supposed to convene until next week?"

"I called this meeting." Denida shoved through the crowd and stopped in the center of the room, where everyone could see him.

"You? A petty human?" a scaly man mocked.

Denida stared at the man. *His eyes have a silvery glow.*

"Silence Victore!" Costa demanded. "Yes, the leader of the Underworlds is here to address an issue."

"Why?" Victore hissed. "The Underworlds are just the soul realms of an underdeveloped planet."

"Because a problem we're facing in the Underworlds affects the entire universe." Denida ambled over to Victore, gazing into his eyes.

"What problem? If you want to ruin your planet, that's none of our concern."

"I'm here because of Lucifer, God, and most importantly, Henna."

"Heh." Victore smirked. "Yes, your planet has plenty of bad seeds, but you have yet to tell us why this concerns the rest of us?"

Denida faced the entire room. "The Darkness grows stronger by harvesting souls. It has reaped so many souls on my planet that it's only a matter of time before it spreads to your worlds." Denida rested his index finger on Victore's desk. "Where have I met you before? Hell? Valhalla? Craym?"

Victore rolled his eyes. "Your charismatic attempt to feign familiarity with me won't sway the council." He turned his focus to everyone else in the room. "Anyone else have a demon problem? Aside from the demon in front of us, speak up if you've ever even seen a demon."

Denida glanced around, listening to the deafening silence.

Victore banged his fists on the table, his scales shaking with the impact. "Master Costa, we thank you for bringing him here, but I propose we reject this silly request. Demons have never been a problem outside of the Underworlds, so they're of not concern for us."

Costa lifted his hand. "Wait; I haven't-"

Lights displaying minus symbols flashed in front of each participant.

"Wait!" Denida stomped his foot. "I know I've seen you somewhere."

"You can drop the act, now. The majority has spoken." Victore leaned forward. "Guess you should stay out of galaxy affairs, 'One Eye.'"

Denida clenched his fists. "If I was the man I once was."

"What would you do? Revert to your 'demon' form?" Victore cackled.

Denida clenched his fingers around the edge of the table.

Victore nodded. "Yes, I know who you are, but not because we've met. Logic dictates that we should never listen to the likes of you. After all, once a demon, always a demon."

"Costa!" Denida yelled. "Henna sent gods throughout the universe. I urge you-"

Costa leaned back in his chair. "Sorry, Mr. President." He gestured for the guards to remove Denida.

"What? No, we can't be done."

The guard gazed over at Costa, who nodded. The guard clapped his hands, and Denida reappeared outside the building.

*The hell?* Denida spun around to the building.

Guards in front of the building stepped in front of the door. "Authorized personnel only."

"Yes, I was just in there."

"Your pass has been revoked, sorry."

"But-"

The guard lowered his hand to his belt. "We won't allow you to pass."

Denida raised his hands in defeat. "As you wish." He retreated. *Who else can help me if they won't? Gabriel?* He hastened his stride and wandered until he found a desolated area.

"Gabriel, are you here?" He arched his neck to the sky. "Please?"

Gabriel appeared from a flash of light in front of him. "Strange place you're summoning me to. This must be important."

"It is. Lucifer's war with God must be stopped."

"You called me here to tell me that?"

"You know both of them. You can talk some sense-"

Gabriel cleared his throat. "Lucifer can't breach the Pearly Gates, so they have time to make up."

Denida sighed. "But they won't. Henna will not allow that, and you know it." He bared his teeth. "You know she's after you, God, and Lucifer."

"Henna?" Gabriel flinched. "We've kept her at bay this long and we'll continue to do so."

"That's what you think." Denida cleared his throat. "Maybe there's still a way to change fate's trajectory. Come on; I know how you can assist me."

"You are already on your path." Gabriel smiled softly. "All you need is talk to them."

Denida frowned. "I don't know anyone with a connection to her." His eyes widened. *Wait, maybe Odin?* He looked back at Gabriel, but he had already disappeared. Denida grunted. *Fine.* He reached for the ring on his finger before cursing under his breath. *Wonder if I can summon Odin, too?* He eyed the sky.

Denida threw up his hands and called at the top of his lungs. "Odin!"

Several clouds gathered in the sky, becoming increasingly menacing, until an eight-legged horse descended from the clouds and landed on the surface. "You called?"

"I don't have the ring, anymore. Can you take me to Valhalla?"

"You access Valhalla with your soul, not the ring." Odin extended his hand. "But since I'm here now, of course. Come hither."

Denida grabbed Odin's hand. Odin pulled him atop his horse, and they ascended into the clouds.

# Chapter 26- Loss at the Council

Sleipnir descended through the clouds and came to a halt on Valhalla.

"Welcome back, Father." Thor bowed and helped Odin off his horse. He scowled at Denida. "You brought a visitor."

"That he did." Denida jumped down. "I have come to talk to you and your father, and anyone else who will listen."

"By your word." Odin waved his hand at Thor, who bowed and ran off. "Come hither." He steered Denida into his grand hall. Odin strode to his throne and sat down. Odin extended his arm, and two ravens landed on his arm.

*Where did those come from?* Denida licked his lips. He shifted his focus throughout the room, seeing people starting to gather.

The two ravens hopped from Odin's arms to his shoulders, where they rested. "How may we aid thee, Denida?"

"I've brought everyone," Thor announced from the back of the room.

Denida clapped his hands. "Odin, Thor, everyone here, you know about your queen, Henna."

Indistinct mumbles sounded from the crowd.

"Silence!" Odin leapt up and slammed his scepter against the ground.

Denida cleared his throat. "Th-thank you, Odin."

"It's not for thy benefit. We do not discuss our queen with outsiders." Odin rested in his chair. "Anything else?"

"Else?" Denida mocked. "Lucifer and God will do everything they can to kill each other, regardless of how many lives they take in the process, and are willing to involve as many worlds as they see fit. You must care." Denida tilted his head and gazed at the crowd. "That's got nothing to do with your queen."

"You have my condolences, but we can't help you." Odin fed the ravens some nuts.

*What?* "I know you're from her world, like they are, and innocent lives are at stake."

Odin continued stroking his ravens, unfazed.

"Odin?" Denida trudged forward.

"Enough!" Thor blocked him. "You have overstayed your welcome."

"Her vendetta will fail."

Thor turned his head, and a hint of a grin appeared on his face.

"I saw that. Do you find these matters funny?"

The ravens took flight and hovered above Thor's head.

Thor nodded and turned to Denida. "I do. You, as the President of the Underworlds, are asking us to defy our queen, for a problem that is your responsibility to solve. Are you really that inept?"

"Lucifer showed me his past experiences with Henna on Craym. I know you served her once, and I know you dislike God, but this goes beyond-"

Thor cleared his throat. "We don't act out of contempt."

"Ahem." Odin tapped his knuckles on his throne's armrest. "My youngling meant that it's time for you to return to the Underworlds."

Denida arched his neck, watching the ravens circling just under room's ceiling. He flashed Thor a smile and held out his hand. "No hard feelings, I hope."

Thor removed his glove and shook Denida's hand.

*Big mistake.* Denida pulled himself close to Thor, grabbed the hammer from Thor's belt, and stepped back. "Still think I'm inept? This contains all your power, and-" His fingers stroked the hammer's shaft. "This is Henna's alloy."

"You little…" Thor's eyes shone with a silvery shade.

*That's where I saw those eyes.*

Thor stomped his foot. "You think you have some power here, just 'cause Henna took a liking to you and ordered us to cooperate?"

"Did she?" Denida raised the hammer with both his hands wrapped around its shaft.

"We turned your predecessor down, on her behest. He was in control of all the Underworlds at the time, and then Lucifer took his life. Perhaps you'll meet the same fate, kid."

"Thor!" Odin rose. "Relinquish that hammer, Denida."

Denida tightened his grip on the hammer. "You turned the president away, on Henna's request?"

"Yes," Thor gloated.

Denida bared his teeth and swung the hammer.

Thor raised his hand, slowing the hammer's momentum, until it rested in his hand. "Thank you."

Several deities surrounded Denida, including Odin, Thor, and Loki.

Denida raised his index finger. "Your queen won't approve of you hurting me."

Thor lifted his hammer. "Perhaps, but she always has several contingency plans. In the grand scheme of things, your death wouldn't ruin anything."

Odin lifted his scepter. "No, our queen has an agenda for him, now." Odin banged the scepter against the floor. "Good tidings, boy."

The bright light emanated from the scepter and flung Denida into the wall, turning his world black.

Sus knelt in front of a newly dug grave, her hand caressing the dirt.

"Sus…" Kate rested her hand on Sus' shoulder.

Sus shook off Kate's hand. "Don't bother." She turned to the crowd. "The demons are still here. It's just a matter of time before another one of our friends dies…" She peered at Kate. "- unless we're ready to take them on."

"Wouldn't it be smarter to run away?" Jakob whipped his long hair behind his ear. "Susan and her friends left, and Den is gone. We've got nothing left to fight them."

"The demons are everywhere. There's nowhere left to run." Sus grabbed a branch beside her. "We'll have to fight them ourselves."

"With a branch?" Jakob rolled his eyes.

"Yes." Sus smashed the branch into a tree, cracking the stem in two.

Jakob gaped, stepping back.

"No," Kate remarked. "Den's death proved that resistance will get us killed."

"So, we should just lie down and let them kill us?"

Kate lowered her head. "What are you suggesting?"

"We have to stop running and take our planet back." Sus glared into Kate's eyes. "They'll never expect it."

"No way, I'm out." Jakob darted off.

Sus squeezed Kate's hand. "We'll send them packing."

Kate bit her lip. "Just the two of us? I don't know…" She withdrew her hand and stole a glimpse in the direction Jakob had run. "We can't even persuade our friend."

"I feel wrong not finishing what Den started." Sus drew in a deep breath, held it, and exhaled slowly, as she sat beside the grave. "I know I didn't know him long, but we were close. It was like, I just knew him."

"A crush can hit fast," Kate whispered. "But time will make it better."

Sus raked her fingers through the dirt and tightened her fingers around the earth. She clenched a fist and tightened it with all her might, before slowly releasing it.

"Sus?" Tom stood over her with his hand outstretched.

*Why is here? At least he doesn't have the gun, like when we first met him.* Sus frowned but noticed Jakob hiding behind him. "Don't worry; I won't seek out the demons. Kate's already discouraged me."

Tom tilted his head to Jakob. "Yes, Jakob told me about what you said, and I'm not here to discourage you. In fact, I want to help."

*What?* Sus' mouth opened in bewilderment. "Come again?"

Tom knelt. "Den's dead, and he isn't the only one. The time for change has arrived."

Sus closed her mouth. "How? There's so few of us."

"This is about quality, not quantity." Tom smiled and handed Sus a gun. "Besides, I've got an idea, seeing as that woman who looked like you taught you how to kill the demons."

*Den did too.*

***

*What happened?* Denida's eyelids fluttered, and he held his hand up to block the light. He slowly opened his eye and turned his head, inspecting his surroundings. He noticed a figure sitting on a nearby bench. "Gabriel?"

"You're awake; good morning." Loki clapped. "I wish I were Gabriel. He tends to get involved in everything."

"Loki? What are you doing here?"

"I can't just come to say hello out of the goodness of my heart?" Loki smiled, only to let loose with a peal of laughter. "Okay, even I can't believe that. Odin expelled you from Valhalla, revoking your welcome." Loki meandered over to Denida. "It's similar to what happened to that last president, actually."

"You're well-informed." Denida sat up.

"Information is power," Loki winked. "Plus, I have some intel you may like."

"And what do you want for it?"

"Perceptive, aren't you? The Darkness doesn't care about upsetting the power balance anymore, so how can one gain anything? It must be knocked down a peg. By helping you, I'll be helping myself."

Denida clicked his tongue against his teeth. "I'm listening."

"You were at the Galaxy Council, correct?"

"Was that Victore guy one of Henna's cohorts? He had the same eyes."

Loki stared at him emptily. "No, she doesn't have anyone in the council, but the Darkness has launched its attack on the universe."

*Interesting...* "We're in the Underworlds now, right?"

"Correct," Loki chuckled.

"In that case, you can teleport through the universe, right?"

"Yes, you can use Henna-"

"No," Denida hissed. "It's time to change. I need to learn how to use my own magic."

"Souls can materialize anywhere. I can teach you how to use your soul's energy."

"Thanks, but no thanks. Someone's already teaching me that." Denida patted Loki's shoulder. "Just wait and see; I'll destroy the Darkness, I assure you." *Galaxy Council, please take me.* He closed his eyes, furrowing his brow with focus. After several minutes, an aura emerged above him, only to fade again. Denida tightened his jaw, and with a deep breath, he tried focusing again. The dim aura reappeared. He closed his eye and cold sweat appeared across his forehead. After several minutes, the aura vanished again, and Denida dropped to the ground. "Why can't I do it again?"

"Again?" Loki snickered. "Soul energy isn't like Henna's magic. Just like a human body, it needs rest."

"Then how do I recharge it?"

"You want the mighty Loki's help? How intriguing!"

"Can you help me or not?" Denida snapped. "Time is of the essence, here."

"Yes, it's quite simple. You have been on Earth and seen humans meditate, right?"

"Yes." Denida frowned.

"They've got it right, in theory, but it's more beneficial for souls. It restores the spirit."

*He'd better not be pulling my leg.* Denida grunted and assumed the lotus position.

"Clear your mind." Loki folded his arms. "Forget everything around you."

Denida grunted and allowed his mind to relax. The world around him faded out.

"Ahem." Loki cleared his throat after several minutes. "That should be sufficient."

Denida stood. "Okay, I'll try again. Thanks for the help." He closed his eyes and breathed slowly. *Take me to the Galaxy Council.* The aura swiftly appeared above him and pulled him through the universe. His soul stopped in front of the Galaxy Council building, where it remerged with his body. *Guess Loki was right.*

"Not you again. We said no entry." The guard from before stepped in front of the door. "Either leave-"

Denida stepped to the door, but his knees quivered like butter. He leaned against a tree to steady himself. "Or else? I've come with a concern about the planet, Craym. Ever heard of it?"

"I told you." The guard growled. "We can't let you in, unless they're expecting you."

"They are waiting for me."

"Oh?" The guard raised his head. "About this Craym place?"

Denida shook his head. "No, Costa wanted to ask me something about the Underworlds, but since you won't let me in, I guess it'll have to wait."

"Costa? The council's leader?"

"There's another one?" Denida raised his eyebrows.

The guard snickered. "Costa couldn't have issued you a pass because they're still in session."

"Strange, he told me it was urgent." Denida shrugged. "Oh well." He spun around.

"Wait!" The guard grabbed Denida's sleeve. "I'll make an exception this once. Go on in."

*You don't need to tell me twice.* "Thank you." Denida hurried through the doors, running down the corridors. He snuck into the spectator room, despite the "in session," sign above the door. The room overlooked the council from a balcony. He stared at the attendants. *Looks like some of them have left.*

"Thank you for your attendance." Costa bowed. "I hereby declare this meeting-"

"Not yet!" Denida hollered from the balcony and jumped down, extending his hands, hoping to use his soul's energy to cushion his fall. The aura appeared in front of him, slowing him in his descent at first, but halfway down, it vanished. Denida tumbled on the floor. *Dammit, I guess I've used too much.* He staggered to his feet with a bitter face and turned to the room. "Hi."

"Denida, are you okay?" Costa's eyes widened.

Denida waved his hand dismissively. "May I address the council?"

"You already had the floor."

Denida lifted his finger. "I have vital, new information." His focus turned to the remaining council members in the room. "It affects all of you."

"No." Costa blinked. "You may request an audience again, but seeing as you hail from an underdeveloped planet's underworlds, you aren't permitted to hijack this one, when we've already given you the floor."

Denida arched his back. "But I'm not just the leader of an underdeveloped place; I've got another one: Craym."

Costa lowered his hand. "Fine, you may speak, but only if it concerns that planet or an existing member planet. Your underworlds are a forbidden topic."

"I'll honor those terms." Denida's smile widened to reach his ears.

Costa peeked at the guard next to him. "Gather everyone again, since this should involve them, now."

Denida tilted his head. "Is it that easy to do?"

Costa rested his hands on the table in front of him. "It should only take a few minutes."

Over the following minutes, holograms appeared in almost every seat in the room.

"This guy again?" Victore mocked as soon as he appeared. "His very presence violates the council's rules. I demand his removal." His eyes brightened as he stared at Denida. "Plus, I vote to charge him with trespassing, if he ever comes back."

"Ahem." Denida raised his hand. "If I may?"

Costa nodded.

Denida faced Victore with a soft smile. "First of all, you seem to think of my presence as a security breach, but Craym is not an underdeveloped planet, far from." He frowned. "Secondly, I've been given the floor, so I'm not trespassing. I welcome you to challenge me if you wish, but as a former demon, who escaped and led the Dark Angels, I assure you, I'm not a pushover."

"Craym's deserted and desolate," Victore rebutted.

"Some former residents of Craym are still alive and well." Denida faced Costa. "Should I bring them before the council?"

Costa stretched his back and leaned over his desk. "That won't be necessary. The council still acknowledges Craym as a developed planet, despite its lack of current residents."

Denida folded his hands. "In that case, I'll proceed."

"Anything new, or are you just enjoying the attention?" Victore hissed.

Denida ignored him. "I was originally here regarding an issue that I believed could be impacting the whole universe. However, Mr. Victore successfully convinced everyone that it was only an issue for the Milky Way Galaxy -"

"Wrong!" Victore pounded his fist on his desk. "I said it only affected his underdeveloped planet, and its soul dimensions."

Denida promptly turned to Victore before Costa could object. "You bring up a good point, Mr. Victore. You believe it only affects my world, correct?"

"Denida, you agreed that we wouldn't turn this into a discussion about your underdeveloped planet," Costa interjected sternly.

"Your incompetency as a leader is the problem," Victore ignored Costa, addressing Denida as if he were the only one in the room.

Denida tapped his upper lip with his finger. "Interesting… and why do you believe I'm not suited to handle the problem?"

"Tch," Victore sneered. "You seized power from your former Dark Angel friend in a coup. That isn't an election; it's a power grab."

*Gotcha.* Denida strolled around the room, still tapping his chin. "That's a fascinating point, considering only a small group of residents knows about that." He stopped next to Costa's table and crossed his arms. "Who gave you this information? My son? Lucifer? My colonel?"

"How does it mat-"

"Wait, wait!" Denida interjected. "Sorry, my mistake, they're all dead, except for Lucifer, so maybe I should be asking why Lucifer has someone here?"

"I'm not a demon." Victore's eyes glowed with a silvery shade. "I think you're mistaking me for yourself."

"Your eyes… I thought only Henna's appeared silvery, until Loki told me that she doesn't have any followers in the council."

Costa jumped to his feet. "What are you implying?"

Denida rested his hands on Victore's desk. "You're an agent of the Darkness, aren't you?"

Costa furrowed his brow. "What are you talking about? His eyes aren't even dark, and you're harassing a member of this council."

"His eyes threw me off, too. I wondered if he could be here on God's behalf, but God detests Henna, so he would never send someone to look like one of her servants."

Victore raised his finger. "Lucifer started the war against-"

"Against God, but I'm ruling Lucifer out because he's only had one goal since long before I even met him; he wanted Heavani back."

"You just proved my point, thanks. Good thing you never became a lawyer," Victore gloated.

"Did I?" Denida lifted his hands. "Lucifer isn't the only player in Hell; there's also the Darkness, my prime subject. If the Darkness is behind this, the trials facing my planet have spread beyond my planet to the entire galaxy."

"Nice theory." Victore licked his lips. "But it lacks proof."

"The Darkness came from God's innate hatred and jealousy, which is why it contains some of the magic Henna granted God. That's how you have that silver glow in your eyes. Lucifer couldn't give you that, so the Darkness did."

Victore stared around at the faces of the holograms and people in the room. Their expressions appeared doubtful.

Costa clapped his hands, and a white light surrounded him. "Mr. Victore, show us the essence of your soul, so that we can discount this theory."

"What?" Victore squinted. "I will do no such thing."

"It will set your colleagues at ease."

"And violate my privacy?" Victore hissed.

Costa clenched his fist, expelling a beam of light which created a barrier around Victore. "Guards!"

"I'm just a hologram, remember? I'm safe at home, where you'll never find me," Victore smirked. "Maybe the time has come to crush this alliance, while we take over the universe."

Gasps echoed throughout the room.

"Is this what you wanted, Little Evil? Henna wants to kill God, Gabriel, and Lucifer, but she doesn't care about the Darkness. It decided to take on a new face."

"You?" Denida clenched his fists.

"I'm in the real Hell. I hope we'll never meet, for your sake. Consider this a kindness; you'll know your way around when you die." His eyes flickered from silver to crimson. "Goodbye." The hologram disappeared.

# Chapter 27- The Darkness

*The Darkness sure has grown.* Denida rubbed his forehead. "Doesn't somebody know where Victore is?"

Costa closed his eyes. "I'm afraid not." He slowly reopened them. "But the council agreed that this threat impacts the whole universe, so we will find him. It'll just take some time."

Denida grunted. "Please let Dan know if you make any progress, and we'll do the same." He gritted his teeth. "Take care, Costa. I hope we won't be too late to fix this." Denida tilted his head before spinning around to exit the council's building. He waved to the guard outside, but before the guard could respond, Denida had already strode away from the entrance.

"In a rush?" a feminine voice spoke from behind him.

*I know that voice.* Denida whipped around.

Henna waved her hand. "My dear Denny, how nice it is to see you again on this blessed day."

Denida scrunched his nose. "Henna." He clenched his fist and lunged at her.

Henna teleported to where Denida had been standing. "Is something the matter, my child?" Her eyes widened.

"You killed my colonel." Denida's jaw clenched.

"We've been over this." Henna smiled.

Denida breathed heavily. "You say that like you didn't kill him."

"Oh, do you want him back?"

Denida charged at her, but she teleported back to where she had been originally.

Henna tilted her head. "If you want him back, you know what I want in exchange."

"Don't!" Nina jumped out from the bushes. "It's exactly what she promised me, but she never followed through."

"Nina…" Henna's eyes shone with a bright rainbow tint. She smiled and focused on Denida again. "Ignore her. She-"

"Ignore me? I'm going to be here until you give Daniel back to me." Nina pointed accusingly. "I deserve it, for bending fate in your favor, and you promised."

Henna's smile stiffened, and she glanced at Nina. "If you'll excuse us."

"You need to honor our deal!"

Henna whipped her head to face Nina. "In that case, allow me to be crystal clear; I have no desire to talk to you, and I will never give you Daniel!" Her rainbow eyes intensified and expelled a stream of colorful energy. The magic shot through Nina, vaporizing her, leaving behind an energy cloud that hovered above the ground.

"You… killed… her because… she wanted… to talk… to you?" Denida stuttered.

"Not exactly." Henna lifted her arm and the energy cloud returned to her hand. "I sent her to another part of the universe, where she won't be a nuisance."

Denida eyed Henna's extended arm. *But… the cloud…*

"That was just her potential to use magic. You just watched me remove it." Henna retracted her arm. "You should thank me; this benefits you, possibly more than you realize."

"You won't coerce me into doing what you want, no matter what you try. I would rather die than continue this sham. Find someone else to manipulate to create your destiny." Denida closed his eyes and teleported through the universe, reappearing in front of the cottage at Dynasty. He sighed, overcome by an almost tangible loneliness, before plodding through the forest toward the central estate.

A brilliant light flashed between two trees and Henna appeared. "We weren't done talking."

"Yes, we were." Denida strode past her.

"Nina was wrong about one crucial detail."

Denida halted. *I'm going to regret this.* He turned. "Alright, what was she allegedly wrong about?"

"I didn't task Nina with manipulating fate. Her goal was to ensure that you wouldn't choose the worst destiny possible for me, and it usually worked."

"Usually?" Denida frowned.

Henna smiled gently. "There were a few times that you still chose the least favorable path for me. In those cases, I had to make... modifications. For example, you became the leader of the Underworlds." She tilted her head. "That was the worst possible scenario, and there was nothing I could do once it happened, but it worked out in the end because I gave you Craym."

"Everything's always under your terms, isn't it?" Denida raised his eyebrows.

"I'm just a bearer of destiny, who can tell you about the possible-"

"Wait a minute." Denida stomped his foot. "You can see the paths of fate, so you knew that there was a possibility that I would be chosen to rule the Underworlds."

Henna's smile soured. "Sometimes there are too many paths."

Denida rolled his eyes. "Enough of this garbage. We both know that you're here for your revenge ploy. There's no deeper meaning than that." Denida spat on the ground. "Which begs an interesting question, by the way." He stepped closer. "Why didn't you stop God and Lucifer from killing you in the first place? You must have foreseen that possibility."

"You think you deserve an answer to that question, when you clearly don't want to get involved in the aftermath?" Henna's eyes narrowed and started to glow with rainbow colors.

"Want to know what I think?" Denida sneered. "I don't think you could foresee that-"

"I see all the possible ways fate can change."

"Do you?" Denida bit his tongue gently. "I know you can predict some events, like you did with Heavani. The question is: can you see the paths that impact you?"

"That's for me to know, and you to find out, if you accept your destiny."

"Destiny?" Denida grinned and stopped a step away from Henna. "You realize that if you get what you want, Heaven and Hell will be no more. All of God's angels will scatter, and all the dem-" He heaved a sigh. "Actually, no, Hell won't die. The Darkness is taking over, and who's going to stop it? Everyone who can stop it is on your hitlist."

"God's hatred created the Darkness. When he's no more, the Darkness will die."

Denida sneered. "Think so? I thought you said you could see all the different paths. The Darkness has developed its own will. It's been trying to replace Lucifer forever, and I think that it has succeeded."

"You do not know all the paths that I have seen, but I can tell you the Darkness's fate, if you want." Henna extended her hand.

Denida leered at Henna. He pushed past her and ventured into Dynasty, not stopping until he reached the secret door under the staircase, leading to the chamber below.

Denida slumped into his chair in front of the wide monitor, rubbing his nose. *Henna can't be allowed to win. If I can't get her to help me, then the council will have to stop the Darkness.* He connected the monitor to Costa's feed in the council.

A soldier appeared on the monitor, his face dirty and rugged. "Hello."

Denida's eyes widened. "What's going… is Costa around?"

"I…" The soldier peeked to his side before wiping his face. "I'm not at liberty to disclose that information. May I ask who's calling?"

"Denida." Denida hunched over closer to the monitor. "What's going on there?"

"Nothing." The soldier shifted on his feet.

"Wait!" Denida leaned forward as the soldier moved out of frame. "I was with the council when everything with Victore happened. I need to talk to Costa about-"

"*Screech!*" a light source emanated from the middle of Denida's secret room.

Denida grabbed a gun attached to the bottom of his desk and pointed it at the light.

Several pillars of light shot up, creating an oval circle in the room.

*Demons? No, that's impossible; Dynasty has a magical barrier.*

"Hi, Denida." A hologram of Costa appeared in from the first pillar. His hair was uncharacteristically disheveled.

"Wha…" Denida lowered the gun and rose from the chair. "What's going on?"

Costa inhaled deeply. "Victore, the Darkness, all of it…"

"What happened?"

"Demons attacked the council."

Denida's mouth widened. "Demons? Victore's or Lucifer's?"

"We don't know," another voice emanated from one of the holograms behind Costa.

Costa cleared his throat. "Does it matter? The Darkness is controlling the demons, regardless of who sent them."

Denida ruffled his hair. *This isn't good.*

"We can't let them grow stronger." Costa gritted his teeth. "You have experience with the Darkness, Denida."

Denida nodded. "However, the Darkness came from God … Shaddai, I mean, so there's really only one way to kill it."

"Tell us!" the leftmost hologram demanded.

"Henna's magic can destroy it, but she won't help us. If we had the necklace she gave me…"

Costa rubbed his hands together. "If God dies, won't the hatred die with him?"

Denida shook his head. "The Darkness seems to have achieved sentience, so I don't know if that would work."

"If you don't know for certain, wouldn't that make it worth trying?" Costa frowned. "We can kill God and-"

Denida flinched. "Kill God? No."

"Denida, we're talking about the fate of the universe here, not just your underworlds. It's one death, to save the universe."

Denida shook his head. "We'd be playing right into Henna's hands."

"Your personal vendetta against her aside, we're still talking about the fate of the entire universe, here." Costa lifted his glowing hand. "If she wants him dead, can't we make a deal with her? We can kill God, and she'll help us deal with the Darkness."

"She's not exactly known to keep her promises, even when she gets her way," Denida grunted. "And we're still not even sure if killing God is a viable solution."

Costa sighed. "I know this is a serious matter, Denida." He licked his lips. "And I know we're acting on a maybe, but a maybe is better than nothing. God won't die in vain."

A knot formed in Denida's stomach. *I'm sorry, Shaddai.* "Deep down, I know you're right; we're out of options. Even so, I should tell you that Henna already told me that she doesn't want to deal with the Darkness, so I wouldn't expect her to uphold the bargain, but I'll attempt it."

"Thank you." Costa bowed, and all the holograms dissipated.

*Guess we need to outsmart Henna.* Denida stowed the gun under his desk, then climbed the stairs, exiting the chamber. He continued outside, where he slogged through the forest, not stopping until the cabin came into view. "Henna?" He gazed into the sky. Silence weighed on the air, so he repeated her name with a shout, "Henna!"

A flicker of silvery light flashed in front of him. "You called?" Henna appeared where the light had been.

"Yes." Denida rubbed his fingers with this thumb, but stopped after a moment, gazing at his wedding ring. He licked his upper lip. "I need to know for certain: if you succeed, and Go- Shaddai dies, what will happen to the Darkness?"

"That still?"

"Yes." Denida closed his eyes.

"If you kill his soul with the necklace, it will kill all of him, including the hatred that you call the Darkness.

"Fine." Denida stiffened. "You want me to kill him? My price is the ring that Nina stole from me." He extended his palm.

Henna smiled at his hand. "You think I'll give it back to you?"

"You want Lucifer, God, and Gabriel dead. My necklace is insufficient."

"That's a valid point, but there's one essential fact that you're not considering."

"Which is?"

"Well…" Henna smirked. "None of the destinies I've seen show you killing all of them yourself. In fact, I've only seen you kill one of them, and we're moving toward that path, now."

"One?" Denida gloated. "Are you sure that's going to happen?"

"What do you mean?"

"You could be mistaken, misinterpreting it, perhaps?" Denida smirked. "Or perhaps the actual path just hasn't revealed itself, yet. Are you sure you want to take a chance based solely on what you have seen, or would you like more options to manifest?"

Henna glared at Denida for what felt like an eternity. She clenched her fist and slowly opened it, revealing the Underworlds ring. "This will come with a price. Like you said, Denny, are you willing to take that risk?"

Denida's face remained cold, not showing any emotion, but inside, his heart sank. "What's your price?"

"In exchange for this ring, you will kill all of them. Shall you fail, you will die."

Denida reached for the ring without hesitation.

Henna rested her hand on top of his. "Not until you give me your answer?"

"If you say A, you gotta say B, so yes, you win." Denida bared his teeth.

Henna tilted her head down and her eyes narrowed. Without another word, she vanished, leaving the ring on Denida's palm.

Denida scrutinized the ring. *This is the real deal. Why would she get Nina to take it, only to return it to me so soon?*

"Because you just sealed your fate," a low, but familiar voice sounded from some nearby bushes.

Denida swiftly slipped the ring on his finger and whipped around. "Reveal yourself!" He readied his hand.

A man stood up, revealing his face.

"Gabriel?" Denida's eyes widened. "Why are you hiding in the bushes?"

"You had a visitor, who doesn't exactly like me, as I'm sure you've noticed."

"How do you have time to be here?"

"Time is irrelevant."

Denida shrugged. "Lucifer and God are preparing for a faceoff, and you're here? Don't you need to be in Heaven, or Hell, for that matter?"

Gabriel glanced at a flower. "No, I…" He raised his head. "You know Lucifer, Shaddai, and I go way back, but neither of them are listening to me." He peered back over his shoulder. "Even you know where this is going, but that knowledge is worthless. Lucifer has become overcome with hatred, and Shaddai refuses to accept accountability for Heavani's death."

*What?* Denida shifted on his feet. "Aren't you God's archangel?"

Gabriel raised his index finger. "I urged them to make peace one too many times, I suppose-"

"Then you're here to request my help?"

Gabriel tightened his jaw. "There's only one way forward; neither of us can change their minds."

"But that's-"

"Queen Henna must have predicted this."

Denida led Gabriel into the cabin, handing him a bottle of water, and led him to the chimney.

Gabriel sipped the water and stared into the flames. "It's cozy."

Denida hummed and sat beside him. "What are you going to do? Henna wants you dead, too, and you can't just disappear."

"I know." Gabriel met Denida's quizzical eye. "I thought that if neither God nor Lucifer would listen, I'd just need to think of another solution. There must be a way to get them to see reason."

"Gabriel." Denida leaned forward. "Maybe you just need to accept the fact that the point of no return has come and gone."

"There's still time," Gabriel insisted.

"You can stay here for as long as you need, old friend. I need to take care of something, though." He exited the building and grabbed the doorframe to steady himself. He sighed. *I don't care what Henna says; this is the worst possible outcome.*

# Chapter 28- The Susan Issue

Denida flung Dynasty's door open and turned his head, narrowly avoiding a collision with Susan. "Susan? I was just on my way to see you."

"Must be kismet, seeing as I was coming to see you," Susan mused. "I ran into Nina at the HQ."

Denida's face stiffened. "We have bigger concerns-"

"No." Susan shook her head. "Nina is never going to stop on her own. We have to do something."

Denida flashed Susan a weak smile for a second, then met her eyes. "Trust me, she's a low priority, now. Henna intervened and handled Nina singlehandedly. Besides, the universe faces a much more significant threat than Nina's selfishness." He put his hands together and held them in front of his face. "Please, I need your help."

"With wha-" Susan gasped. "The ring? I thought Nina stole that for Henna."

"She did." Denida wrapped his other finger around the ring. "However, I…"

"No." Susan stepped back. "You didn't."

"Henna and I made a deal to-"

"I don't care what," Susan hissed. "Why would you be that stupid?"

Denida stiffened. "As I recall, it wasn't that long ago that you asked me to see what sort of knowledge and help we could get from Henna."

Susan bit her lip. "Yes, but that was before I realized just how deep Henna's manipulation runs." She closed her eyes tight, blinking back tears. "I always thought of Nina as my best friend, but that witch had a hand in everything, including that."

Denida sighed. "I understand, but we need to stop the Darkness, and Henna's the only one with the power to intervene."

"Yeah, because we can really trust her." Susan rolled her eyes.

"Susan." Denida shifted his feet. "You have to believe me; I know what I'm doing. This is the only way to stop the Darkness, and I have a contingency plan."

Susan whipped her hair to the side. "The Darkness is a threat, but Henna is worse."

"Exactly." Denida raised his finger. "Henna's so distracted by her thirst for revenge that she'll do anything to achieve her goals, and won't even realize that she's really just helping us with the Darkness."

Susan folded her arms. "Did you want to see me just to tell me this?"

"This war will continue. Nylah killed my human side, but you still have yours."

Susan shrugged. "By some miracle…"

Denida nodded. "That's not important. All that matters is that I want you to remain safe, so please, go to Earth, and protect Sus."

"What… no!" Susan's jaw tensed. "You can't do this by yourself. You need-"

"The council will work with me. Together, we stand united. We'll beat the Darkness and put an end to all of this. But I…" Denida heaved a deep breath. "I can't lose anything, or anyone, else. We must keep our remaining human forms safe, by any means necessary, and you…" Denida gazed into Susan's eyes. "You're the only person I trust with as much faith as I have in Dan, so it must be you. I need your assistance."

Susan gulped, then nodded. "I'll take care of Earth." She smiled softly and teleported to Earth.

Denida stood perfectly still, watching as she disappeared. Once she was gone, he glared down at his ring, stroking it with his thumb. *Time to defeat the Darkness.* He clenched his fist and teleported to the HQ, where he materialized in front of Dan.

"Back again?" Dan frowned.

"It's time to get down to business." Denida leaned over the desk. "The council and I agreed to unite forces in a coordinated attack against the demons."

Dan blinked. "How?"

"With this." Denida held up his hand, brandishing his ring.

Dan leaned in close and examined the ring. "Your underworlds ring? I thought Nina gave it to Henna."

Denida withdrew his hand and scratched his nose. "Yes, but I got it back."

Dan leaned back in the chair with huge eyes. "How did you manage that?"

"That doesn't matter." Denida waved his hand dismissively. "We need to prepare. Raise our systems to high alert and get me the Colon-" His jaw tensed, and he exhaled heavily. "The Commander, I mean. Where is he?"

"I think he and Naphtali are preparing soldiers for a possible attack on the HQ's barracks."

"Take me there, please."

"Why? Can't you use the ring?"

"Dan."

Dan smirked and rose from his chair. "Don't get your knickers in a twist. Of course, I'll take you." He led Denida out of the operations building and into the military complex. They cut across the grounds to the training area behind the barracks, where several platoons of soldiers stood in formation at the far end of the field.

A dark, condensed cloud hovered above the units, despite the sunny blue sky stretching as far as the eye could see.

"Naphtali!" Denida ran to the soldiers. He snapped his fingers, expelling a burst of silvery light from his palm, tearing the cloud asunder.

The soldiers stepped aside, revealing Naphtali and the Commander at the head of their group.

Naphtali's eyes widened. "Is something wrong?"

"No." The Commander stepped forward. "I'd recognize that accursed magic anywhere, but how did you use it?"

Denida marched through the crowd, halting in front of the Commander. "I retrieved the ring." He glanced at Naphtali. "What do you say we vanquish the Darkness once and for all?"

"I wish," Naphtali mused.

"We've got the means, now."

Naphtali frowned. "How? The demons are everywhere."

"We can be, too." Denida rejoiced. "We have troops; we just need to lead them." He turned to the Commander. "It's time to put your experience to use."

The Commander tensed. "The demons have spread across the Underworlds. They're already on Earth. We've run out of time to train and we're not ready."

*No reminder necessary.* "Just prepare your troops to move out. We'll join forces with another unit, and these soldiers will get all the practice they need." Denida winked at Naphtali.

"Pardon my question, but how will we connect with the council's forces?"

Denida stretched out his arm and swirled it in a circular motion, creating a circle of silvery ash in front of him. It cut a hole in the air, creating a portal to the Galaxy Council's planet.

"Denny?" Costa waved from within the visage.

"Hello, Costa." Denida smiled. *It worked.* "My unit will prepare your troops." Denida turned to the Commander. "When you're ready?"

"Sir." The Commander saluted. He faced Denida. "I know you're planning to start tackling the demon problem while we're training with them, so this might be useful." He removed a sheath from his belt and presented it to Denida before turning to his troops. "Soldiers, march!" He led them through the portal.

As the last soldier stepped through the portal, Denida dismantled it with a flick of his wrist and examined the sheath the Commander had given him. *His combat knife? He sure learned a lot from John.* Denida smiled, affixing it to his belt.

"What about us?" Naphtali asked shakily.

Denida eyed Naphtali. "We're going to kill the Darkness."

"We're going to Hell?"

Denida shook his head. "No, more and more souls are appearing in Hell by the second. We need to cut off the Darkness at its source: the harvesters."

Naphtali shifted his foot. "You're referring to the demons on Earth, then?"

Denida wrapped his arm around Naphtali's shoulder and clenched his other fist, teleporting to Earth. Denida and Naphtali appeared in the middle of a road with abandoned cars and corpses from curb to curb.

Denida flinched, despite having seen this sight before. "Come on; we need to find Susan."

Naphtali peered down at a dead body. "She's probably dead, like everyone else."

"Not Sus, Susan. Death is not an option… yet."

"Don't you see all the carnage?"

Denida nipped his tongue. "Susan's more determined than anyone I know. She won't go down with the demons so far ahead."

"Ahead?" Naphtali threw up his arms. "Even if you're right, there's no way of knowing where-"

"Follow me; I know where she is." Denida stepped over the first corpse and sauntered down the street.

Naphtali rolled his eyes and followed close behind.

Denida stopped in front of a school. "I feel her presence inside."

Naphtali examined the school and then turned back to Denida. "I sense someone in there, but…"

"Yes. I understand your 'but.' I feel something else inside, too."

Naphtali drew in a deep breath. "Only one way to find out what it is."

Denida clenched his fist. He grabbed the door handle and stepped inside. Negative energy turned the air opaque with a gut-wrenching miasma. Denida caressed his ring as he tiptoed forward. "Follow the Darkness," he whispered.

Naphtali nodded but stayed a few steps behind Denida as they trekked down the corridor.

Denida led them down several hallways, glancing into rooms as they passed, but his stride remained consistent. As if keenly aware of Susan's whereabouts, he continued methodically until he turned a corner, where he suddenly froze and clenched his fists.

Naphtali darted for the wall beside Denida. "Are you sure this is a good idea? The Darkness is extremely intense."

Denida raised his hand and uncoiled his fingers. Silvery ash wove around each of his fingers, and a voice from around the corner became more audible.

"… you will pay the price, little girl."

Denida gritted his teeth and jumped out. "I don't think so!"

Three demons stood before Denida. Blood soaked their arms.

"Denny?" it sounded softly from farther away, beyond the demons.

*Susan...* Warmth filled Denida's stomach. He charged at the demons.

A flurry of dark energy surged through the sky. Naphtali redirected it with a wave of magic, making it crash into the wall.

The demons grabbed each other's hands to focus their power, creating a force that transformed the room into a pit of darkness. With their combined power, the room remained murky, even with daylight filtering in through the windows.

Denida froze as a bolt of energy slammed him into a wall. His eyes narrowed. "Naphtali, get ready." Denida folded his hands, caressing the ring with his thumb, as his dead left eye turned red and scanned the Darkness in front of him.

Naphtali frowned. "Do you see some-"

Denida unsheathed the Commander's combat knife and stormed forth, slashing the knife carelessly into the oncoming Darkness.

"*Thud.*" The blade struck something.

Denida pulled back on the knife's hilt, but it remained stuck. He reached out to examine whatever lay before him. *Just a cabinet...* He yanked harder and the knife came free.

A gust of wind surged through the void.

Denida turned a corner and stood with his back against the wall.

A demon appeared and inspected the deep stab through the cabinet. "Peculiar," he muttered.

Denida tiptoed forward and held one hand over the demon's mouth as he slashed its side with the knife. He let the demon fall and tore its heart out.

Another demon hurled a ball of vicious energy at Denida. It collided with him and slammed him up against the wall.

"Why don't you watch me kill your little girlfriend." A third demon raised his Darkness-imbued hand.

Denida clenched his hand and expelled a humongous stream of silvery magic, which tore through the Darkness and vaporized the demons on contact. He heaved in a deep breath. *Guess the ring has its strengths.*

"Denny!" Susan sprang forward with her arms out, ready to launch herself into an ecstatic embrace, but she stopped short, just before she reached Denida. "Sir." She saluted him. "I have some bad news, Sir."

"You look to be okay, so that can wait." Denida cleared his throat. "You need to lead us to your human form ASAP. That's our top priority."

"But Sus is probably where Den… where your human form died."

"Then allow me." Denida pulled Susan close to his body.

Susan's cheeks reddened. "Denny…"

Denida extended his arm for Naphtali, who took his hand.

A silvery aura enveloped them and teleported them away from the school. They reappeared in front of a freshly dug grave.

Naphtali's eyes flickered.

Denida knelt before a makeshift grave and stabbed the blood-soaked dagger into the dirt. "She's not here. Do you feel her close by?" he asked.

Susan rubbed her nose. "I think she's this way." She led them to a large wooden shack, just beside the grave.

"Are you sure she's here? I don't feel any Darkness in the air." Naphtali leaned in to Denida.

Denida smiled. "Trust me."

Susan stopped in front of the building. The grounds seemed vacant, and eerily silent.

"Stand your ground, Naphtali." Denida grabbed Susan's hand and guided her inside the building.

"We can do-" People huddling around inside stopped speaking to face Denida and Susan as soon as they stepped inside.

"He looks like-" a voice muttered from the crowd.

"Was it his son?" another remarked.

"Hi." Susan waved to Sus.

"No!" Sus ran through the room to them. "I know why you're here, but we won't stop fighting the demons."

"I'm not asking you to." Denida glanced around the room. "Quite the opposite, actually."

"We don't need your help. We've already captured one on our own." Sus smirked. "Show him." She pointed into the room.

The crowd stepped aside, creating a path to the middle of the room. A bound demon sat in the center of a glowing pentagram that had been drawn on the floor.

"We're well on our way to figuring out how to stop them."

Denida raised his eyebrows at Sus. "What if you don't need to?"

Sus furrowed her brow. "What do you mean?"

Denida took a single step, closing the distance between himself and Sus. "Demons come from souls carrying hatred in their hearts."

"Ha!" Sus rolled her eyes. "So, what are you suggesting? We should kiss them and try to talk it out like a bunch of six-year-olds?"

"Not exactly." Denida chuckled. "Hatred has a weakness, and I have the means to help you harness it."

Susan cleared her throat.

*Susan?* Denida turned to her. "Something the matter?"

"I don't know if I should say…" Susan's eyes scanned the room, noticing the many gazes glaring back at her. "Your ring may be able to kill the demons, but we'd have to do something more permanent for these people in the long run, so that they can continue to protect themselves after we leave." She arched her neck. "You know as well as I do that the demons will come back with renewed vigor, as soon as they get the upper hand."

Sus retreated with a single step. "We're fine, thanks. We can take care of ourselves."

"Listen!" Denida raised his hands.

"No," Sus hissed. "You won't stop us. They killed Den and our families." Sus waved a shotgun in the air. "We've learned stuff since you left. I wonder…" She lifted the gun and pointed it at Denida's face. "- what would happen if I shot your eye out?"

Denida shook his head. "I assure you, that won't work on me, but if you'd just listen-"

"Perhaps Susan, instead?" Sus shifted the gun toward Susan.

*No.* Denida clenched his fist and teleported in front of Sus. "No, I'll make you a deal."

Sus squinted. "What deal?"

Denida unclenched his fist and removed the ring from his finger. His aura became fainter the second he removed it from his finger. He stretched out his hand with the ring on his palm. "This is the only thing that can stop the demons. You may have it."

Sus lowered her gun and approached Denida. She eyed the ring and glared back up at Denida. "You think a stupid piece of jewelry will help? Don't insult-"

Denida shrugged. "It's not just-"

"No!" Sus lunged at him with a deafening shout. She shoved Denida aside and fired the gun. The slug slammed into Susan's arm.

Susan staggered to her knees with a grunt.

"Ugh." Sus flinched and lowered the gun.

Denida clenched his fist around the ring and reappeared beside Susan. He put the ring on his finger and held his hand over the gnarly wound. The muscle and bone started to recover under a silvery shade.

Sus strode over with wide eyes. "This feeling…"

Denida continued to hold his hand over the wound until it closed. He gazed up at Sus. "You wounded your soul, but she's fine now."

"You… healed… her," Sus stuttered. "But how?"

"There's a reason I offered you the ring."

Sus gritted her teeth and handed Denida the gun. "I didn't mean to-"

Denida laid the shotgun aside. "Please just hear me out, now."

Sus nodded. "Say whatever you need to say. Whether I take the ring or not will depend on what you tell me."

# Chapter 29- Lucifer's Plan

Denida sat at a table on Earth, fiddling with his ring. *I've come so far since I first got my ring here.*

"Denny." Susan sat next to him, rubbing the weariness from her eyes. "I contacted Dan. He said he'll set up a call with all the Underworlds."

Denida tapped his ring on the table. "Good work. I sent Naphtali back to take care of the Wild West World."

Susan leaned in close. "You sure Sus is on board with this plan?"

"You don't trust yourself?"

Susan shifted on the bench. "It's not that."

"You should." Denida smiled. "I do."

"Ugh." Susan rolled her eyes.

"What?"

"Well, if you must know, you've always been a bit naïve."

"Why do you say that?" Denida eyed her.

Susan turned her head.

"It won't bother me," Denida insisted. "Say what you want to say."

"Your infatuation with me is clouding your judgment." Susan covered her mouth as soon as the words tumbled out.

"My what?" Denida shook his head. "Susan, can you hand me the necklace?" He extended his hand.

Susan held her hand close to her chest. "Well, that's... I tried to tell you."

"Tell me what?" Denida jumped up.

Susan stared down. "Demons saw me outside of the school and swarmed me. There were too many of them for me to fight off on my own." She crossed her arms. "I thought I was a goner, but when they saw the necklace, a few of them snatched it from me. I was going to go after them, but a larger group chased me into the school."

*They must've really wanted it if they didn't kill Susan right away... or maybe they were scared that she'd use it if they fought her while she had it.* Denida licked his lips and his expression darkened. "We really needed that necklace, Susan."

"Am I interrupting something?" Sus waved her hand from a safe distance. "Your friend, Dan, said to tell you that they're ready."

*Perfect, time for me to do my part, too.* He took Sus' hand to help her sit where he had just been. "We'll continue this later, Susan. Please wait for me, here." He waved and turned away.

"You're leaving?" Susan stormed after Denida and grabbed his shirt. "Sus just set everything up and you're-"

Denida raised his finger to Susan's lips. "You and Sus have things covered here. I've taught her everything I can. Now, I need to go get my necklace back and fix everything else." He spun around and took a step, followed by another. Silvery ash surrounded his feet. By the third step, it engulfed him, and by the fourth, he walked into oblivion. As he exited a stream of silvery mist, he found himself in Hell. Demons stood all around him.

*Wow, I've never seen Hell this crowded before.* Denida lifted his finger and studied the ring before continuing his trek. The air was so heavy that it was hard to breathe. Within a few steps, the necklace's power called out to Denida from the Darkness. *Where can it be?* Denida squinted. *Does one of the demons have it?*

A fiery cone flared in the distance. All the demons spun to face it.

"Maestro!" A demon rushed past Denida, hurrying over to the crowd forming before the flames.

"It can't be," Denida whispered under his breath.

A figure with outstretched arms materialized from the flames. "The time has come to engulf Heaven in darkness."

A loud roar ensued.

Denida sauntered up to the mob, avoiding eye contact with the figure.

"Prepare to kill God and all his angels."

Denida arched his back. *Of course, Lucifer has the necklace.* "Reficul!" Denida hollered.

Hell fell as still as a tomb. All the cheering stopped and even the wind died down to nothing.

A chuckle emanated from the figure in the flames. "Denny in your soul form, how original."

"I don't need my demonic form ever again."

"Oh, no?" Lucifer snickered. "I know why you're here, but coming alone will cost you dearly."

"I don't need anyone else. I have myself and this." Denida raised his hand, brandishing the ring.

Lucifer teleported from the flames to stand next to Denida, where he leaned in close. "What you're forgetting, my former apprentice, is how much stronger Hell has become."

Denida's eye examined the demons surrounding them. "Quality over quantity."

Lucifer stepped back. "Perhaps, but you are 'persona non grata,' my former Little Evil." He raised his arm and clenched his fist.

The demons stormed past Lucifer. Before Denida could respond, the demons shoved him to the ground.

"You were saying weak, little Denny?" Lucifer's eyes reddened. "Bring me his ring."

The demons dragged Denida to his feet, one holding him by his throat. They ripped the ring from Denida's finger and handed it to Lucifer.

Lucifer scrutinized the ring and approached Denida. "Like I told you, you'll need your demonic side for this." He raised the ring to Denida's head. "Join me, and together, we can bring that little hussy and Shaddai to their knees."

Denida bared his teeth.

Lucifer gestured for the demon to loosen its grip around Denida's throat.

"Thank you." Denida swallowed. "But Naphtali is right. This will be the end of you, too."

"Oh?" Lucifer motioned for the demon to tighten its grip on Denida's throat. "How do you figure that, when my signal can kill you?"

"You… can't… use… those… objects… without me," Denida stuttered.

Lucifer stormed forward and grabbed Denida. "Why not? I'm from her world; you're not."

"Do you really think Henna would make magical artifacts that work for everyone, especially when she can see everything fate has in store?" Denida raised his eyebrows.

Lucifer released his grip on Denida and stepped back.

Denida shifted his jaw and rubbed his throat.

"You're going to help me, then. I recommend you bear in mind that you're nothing without her artifacts, so you would be wise to obey me."

Denida chuckled. "We're at the final stretch, Luci. I urge you to reconsider your path. Nothing will bring Heavani back. The Darkness will abandon you for your obsession, and Henna will end you, even if you kill Shaddai…" He sniffed. "- just like she wants you to."

The fiery glow in Lucifer's eyes intensified. "Shaddai killed Heavani. If I die, so be it. As long as I get to avenge my light, the only light I ever had, it'll be worth it."

*He's not listening to reason…*

"You're damn right I'm not," Lucifer took on his demonic figure. "And you'd better not fail me, puppet of Henna."

"I am not her puppet," Denida hissed.

"Your jewelry begs to differ."

"Everything has a purpose, Luci." Denida straightened up. "Heavani's fate, too. Hell, Henna even prophesized Heavani's death, remember?"

The dark cloud above Lucifer grew, becoming infinitely denser. It filled the sky with blackness, swallowing Lucifer whole, making him gargantuan and dark. Two bright red eyes shone like rubies from within the blackness.

Denida arched his neck. "You think that scares me?" He cleared his throat and raised his voice. "Remember the shit you had me endure as a demon?"

Demons lunged at Denida.

Denida drew in a deep breath and charged at them. He mumbled something inaudible, creating a swirl of magic around one hand. He jabbed his magic-coated hand into the first demon, ripping out his heart. He swiftly bit into the heart before attacking the next demon. His own figure darkened with each heart he bit.

Lucifer swung his arm into the demons around him, devouring them with just his touch. The rest of the demons scattered. He grabbed Denida and lifted him up.

*The hell?* Denida wriggled with all his might, but Lucifer's grip held fast.

"Prepare to invade Heaven!" Lucifer steadied his hand with Denida in front of his face. "You will help me, or we'll go to your world and kill everyone you hold dear. Then, we'll ravage Earth." Lucifer stomped to his mansion. An ever-growing crowd of demons tailed him, with more and more joining as he passed them.

Denida gazed down at the crowd, seeing nothing but a dark cloud of hatred and disgust. Eventually, a round shape appeared at the far end of the crowd, becoming clearer as they drew nearer.

Lucifer came to a standstill, lowering Denida to the ground.

Denida squinted as he touched the dark cloud around him. He struggled through it until he emerged from underneath. Demons surrounded Lucifer and Denida.

Denida arched his neck. "You can threaten me all you like, but no creature of your size can enter…"

The dense Darkness enveloping Lucifer dissipated, and he appeared in his normal form next to the Gate. "That much was obvious, Mini Evil."

Denida's gaze panned in a circle, taking in the demons surrounding them. He met Lucifer's eyes again for a second before bolting. He sprinted toward the closest demon.

The demon lunged forward, taking the bait.

Lucifer's eyes turned crimson, and the demon exploded into dust. The cloud above Hell descended and swallowed Denida. It flew back to the Gate in front of Lucifer, where it set Denida down, before the cloud ascended into the sky again.

Lucifer cracked his knuckles. "If you disobey me again, you will face the same fate as all these demons and your dearest friends." He extended his hand expectantly.

Denida stole a glance at the demons before taking Lucifer's hand. "You do realize-"

"The Darkness will replace me?" Lucifer grinned. "I'm well-aware that my end is nigh, but it doesn't matter. Heavani is gone, so I have nothing left. And karma must come around."

Denida rubbed his nose. "How do we do this?"

Lucifer held up the ring. "With this."

*Is he going to call my bluff about the ring and necklace?*

Lucifer shook his head. "No need, as you said, I already know deep down. I feel like she wanted me to know, just to mock me." He dropped the ring on Denida's open palm. "After you."

Denida clutched his fingers around the ring and approached the Gate's device. He knelt next to it, but paused, turning his head with wide eyes. "The ring's insufficient. Hand me the necklace, too."

Lucifer frowned. "You're not doing anything."

"I'm telling you, I can feel that the ring won't suffice. What I'm about to do will deplete the main unit's magic, so we only have one chance." Denida rolled his eyes.

Lucifer inhaled deeply. The cloud above them grew denser. He lowered himself to Denida's height and threw a punch, stopping just before striking Denida. He unclenched his hand as a dark light flashed, and the necklace emerged in his palm. "Fine."

Denida blinked and reached out.

Lucifer clasped his hand around Denida's fingers. "Fail me, and both Susan and Dan will die."

Denida met Lucifer's gaze, staring into his eyes for an eternity. He finally blinked and swallowed hard. "I would never allow that."

"Then you'd better help me." Lucifer released his grip.

Denida faced the Gate and held the ring and necklace in his left hand.

"Get to it!"

Denida slipped the ring around his finger and the necklace around his neck. He exuded a silvery aura, which pierced the darkness around him. He held his hand over the Gate's main unit, illuminating it.

The demons shielded their eyes.

Denida peered back at Lucifer. "Ready?"

"Yes," he hissed.

Denida shrugged. "Your demons don't look like they are."

"They will become ready when their lives depend on it." Lucifer stepped forward.

"Wait." Denida held up his hand in front of Lucifer's eyes, which deepened from crimson to blood red. "I'd better go first, to start the energy flow."

Lucifer grunted but yielded to Denida. "Then go, now!" His eyes narrowed.

Denida tightened his jaw and spun to face the Gate. He inhaled heavily and stepped through the Gate. An intense light vaporized the dark miasma, which had surrounded Denida, making him squint. But in the next millisecond, Denida whirled around to face Lucifer, who was only partway through the Gate.

"Heaven." Lucifer's lips twisted into a smirk.

Denida grabbed ahold of Lucifer's left arm. "What you seem to have forgotten, is that your Darkness is suppressed in Heaven."

Lucifer yanked his arm free. "I haven't forgotten. Why do you think I have so many demons on standby?"

"You?" Denida smirked. "I thought that was the Darkness's doing."

Lucifer scoffed. "You seem to have forgotten who I am."

Denida shut his eyes, and memories of Lucifer and Heavani flickered through his mind, followed by the image of Lucifer and God standing together over Henna's dead body. He slowly glanced at Lucifer. "It's a shame it had to come to this." He raised his hand and unclenched his fingers.

The Gate shut down before more demons could come through. Denida flicked his hand in the direction of the Gate's main unit, and it powered on again.

"I won't let you do this." Denida glowed silver with the might of the ring and necklace. He retreated a step and emitted a wave of silver energy, which tossed Lucifer and his demons back through the Gate. Lucifer's shocked, red eyes could be seen through the Gate as it powered down. *Sorry, old friend...*

# Chapter 30- Safeguarding

Denida glanced down at himself. *I have my necklace and ring. I can head back to Earth and-*

"Finally."

Denida spun at the sound of Peter's voice.

Peter slammed Denida up against the Gate, before jerking him forward again.

Denida's feet searched frantically for footing. "What the hell?"

"Your master can't help you here. God would like to have a word with you." He flung Denida into a bright white flash.

The light subsided, revealing the floor outside God's chambers.

Jesus strolled out of the chamber and knelt beside him. "Denida, you're in Heaven?"

Peter stepped out of another white flash and grabbed Denida, tossing him closer to the door.

"Stop!" Jesus stood in between Denida and Peter. "What are you doing to our guest?"

"Guest?" Peter mocked. "Leave this to the adults." He stomped closer to the door.

"No." Jesus blocked Peter yet again. "You'd better stop, or Father will hear of this."

"That's what I'm banking on." He clenched his fist. A surge of white energy slashed through the air, tossing Denida into God's chambers. Peter walked past Jesus and knelt next to Denida. "My Lord."

God towered over them in his enormous form, as he'd been watching over Heaven.

Denida held up his hand. "Wait; God, you don't-"

"Father, please tell him to stop treating Denida-"

God held up his hand. "Make sure this ruckus didn't cause any problems outside."

Jesus nodded and darted outside.

God frowned, staring at Peter.

"He came through the Gate… from Hell," Peter stated.

God shrank to Denida's height and approached him, extending his hand to help Denida to his feet.

Denida cleared his throat and stole a glance at Peter before accepting the assistance.

"No one can use that Gate without Henna's magic." God clenched his fist around Denida's fingers. "Are you Henna's new lapdog?"

Denida shut his eyes and exhaled heavily. "This ends now." His eyes slowly widened, meeting Peter's perplexed gaze, and he peered over at God. "Isn't it about time to stop regarding Henna as the Bogeyman? It's been eons."

"That's a bold statement for you to make in Heaven."

Denida blew in God's face.

The air flickered into a silvery shade, forcing God to recoil and release Denida's arm.

"How can you…" God continued retreating. "Henna's magic is inside of you?"

"No." Denida lifted his hand. "I just have her ring to help me fend off demons in the Underworlds."

"Her magic was in your breath." God grew pale, and a bright light enveloped him. "And there aren't any demons in Heaven."

Denida folded his hands. "As I said, I only just got the ring back from Lucifer-"

"Lucifer was here?" God's voice rang from the ceiling. He shrank to his usual size and faced Peter. "Monitor the Gate."

"Wait!" Denida rushed to God's side. "I already pushed him and his demons back into Hell."

"… he'll be back. Once he's found a way, there's no going back. And the Darkness will return with him when he does." God glanced across the room as Peter slammed the door behind him. "Little Evil, you are no longer useful to me, seeing as you are no longer welcome in Hell."

"That's-"

"You're not welcome here anymore, either." God clapped his hands, and the sound echoed throughout the room.

Denida grew seasick as the air rippled, like a wall-to-wall shade suddenly filled the room. As soon as the pulsation reached him, he closed his eyes and reappeared in the Underworlds.

Denida knelt in the grass. Bewildered, he stared around, but fields surrounded him. He ran his fingers through his hair. *What?* He lowered his hand, finding it to be drenched in sweat. *What happened? I was in Heaven, and...* Denida's eyes widened. *Lucifer's going to hurt Dan and Susan!* He quickly stroked his ring and reappeared next to the Gate on Earth. He whipped his head around to get his bearings before turning to the Gate. Still breathing heavily, he ripped the main unit out.

He turned to Sus, who sat next to the Gate, monitoring a screen. "Call all the Underworlds."

Sus spun to face him. Her face revealed a snarky quip on the tip of her tongue, but after a moment, she simply nodded and began to call the Underworlds on the monitor feed.

Susan approached with a furrowed brow. "Everything okay?" Her soft tone contrasted with the tension in their exchange.

Denida twisted toward Susan, his eyes frantic so frantic that he could feel the crease in his brow.

"We've got everyone!" Sus called out before Denida could speak.

Denida approached the monitor, sighing in relief at the familiar faces of his allies across the Underworlds. He cleared his throat and crouched down so that they could see him. "In ten minutes, all of you will remove the main units from your Gates." He ripped his necklace off, clutching it tightly. "Make your necessary preparations now."

Susan stroked her hair in a self-soothing manner. "Denny, what's-"

Denida rested his hands on her shoulders. "The situation is escalating. We must act, now." *Before Lucifer attacks.* He fiddled with the necklace, raveling its chain around his fingertips.

"Ready," Dan announced from the monitor, so suddenly that Denida jumped.

A chorus of acquiescence rang out from the Underworlds' leaders.

Denida's heart pounded hard in his chest. *Please, don't let Lucifer sense this before we're done.* He began counting down with as much passion as his shaky voice could muster. "In ten… nine… eight…" He clenched his fist, gripping Earth's main unit so tightly that his knuckles paled. "Seven …six… five... four…" The faces on the monitors all stared back at him so intently that confidence warmed his chest, adding strength into his voice. "Three… two… one… now!" He raised his fist, holding the main unit high in his hand for emphasis, as everyone ripped the main units out of their Gates.

"Done," Trey's voice stated from his feed.

Denida faced Susan with his jaw shaking. "Everything…" Denida arched his back.

"- is connected to the humans on Earth, so there's only one way to stop Lucifer and his demons."

Susan's eyes widened. "What are you…"

Denida slammed the necklace down onto Earth's device with a *"thunk."* The Underworld emblem appeared on the ground, illuminated by a silvery light. It expanded outwards in all directions, like a wave of energy, covering Earth in a bright silvery shade.

Everyone stood still with gaping mouths and wide eyes.

"You just gave Earth to Henna!" Susan lunged at Denida.

Denida stepped back with his hands raised. "No, Susan. I've just created a barrier that will protect Earth from every type of magic. I had to make it with Henna's magic because that's the strongest magic available to us."

"No, her magic could still be…" Susan's nose wrinkled, and she shoved Denida to the ground, striking him across the face.

Sus and Tom rushed over to separate them.

"Let go of me!" Susan screamed and wrested herself free, but with people stepping in between herself and Denida, she stayed still, gritting her teeth. "You didn't want to use her magic before you left, but now, suddenly you do. Henna has got herself a new lapdog after all." Susan spat on the ground.

Denida stroked his cheek and shifted his jaw. "Nice right hook, Master Sergeant." He slowly stepped through the crowd until he stood before her. "This was the only way to stop Lucifer from destroying Earth."

"Lucifer?" Susan mocked. "His demons have been a problem since long before you left."

"Unfortunately." Denida shrugged. "But I got the ring from him in Hell, so the danger is even more imminent." He jerked his face toward the monitor. "Have any demons come for you?"

"No," Trey remarked from a monitor.

"We're clear, too," Dan followed.

"In that case, there's only one thing left to check." Denida inhaled deeply and removed the ring from his finger. He placed it on the ground in front of him, stepping to the side. "That should be far enough…"

Susan and Sus exchanged a glance.

Denida knelt and interlocked his hands, while muttering something incoherent. He held his hands tighter. A small flicker of light formed around his fingers, only to die down after a few seconds.

Denida gritted his teeth and tried again, but it yielded the same pathetic result.

"Just use the damned ring!" Dan shouted from the monitor.

Denida wrinkled his nose and picked up the ring, sliding it onto his finger, but unlike before, when it made his aura bright, the ring only endowed him with a slightly silvery tint. *Her power still works, but it's weaker, which makes sense, seeing as the barrier uses her magic.* He smiled at the ring and peered over at Susan and the rest of the crowd. "The barrier is a success; magic can no longer be used on Earth." He bit his tongue, avoiding the Henna clause. *No need to worry them.*

"I don't know about that." Susan grabbed Denida's arm and pulled it upward. "Look, your arm still has a silvery glow."

Denida flinched. "Well, at least other magic can't penetrate it. I got the idea from Heaven, where a holy dagger containing Henna's magic keeps the Darkness at bay. We can use this in all the Underworlds."

"How?" Dan demanded. "Could there really be enough magic in her necklace and ring to-"

"You don't need those; Denida just used them to make a reinforced barrier on Earth." Naphtali appeared on one of the feeds. "I managed to make a simpler one here without his ring or necklace."

"Naphtali? I thought you were…" Denida turned to Susan in bewilderment.

"Yes, I'm still in the Wild West."

Denida's eyes widened. "Sorry, I'll use the ring to get-"

"Don't bother; you can't reject your destiny." Naphtali waved his hand dismissively. "I'm fine where I am, but I figured out how we can use the device's magic to generate a barrier on each world."

Dan snorted. "Yeah, 'cause it's not like we wouldn't have done that already if it was really that easy."

Denida cleared his throat. "Magic, Dan."

"Not all of us can do that, thank you!" Dan raised his voice.

"I understand that." Naphtali rubbed his hands together. "But it's fairly easy. Just take a main device from a Gate and reinforce it with your world's soul energy."

"That's it?"

"Dan, please get someone in our underworld who can use magic to try it." Denida leaned close to the monitor. "Everyone else, too."

Everyone scattered away from their monitors, and all that sounded from the feeds was indistinct clattering.

Susan moved closer to the monitor, stopping beside Denida. She grabbed his hand tightly, caressing it. "Do you think it will work?"

Denida shrugged. "I hope so." Denida's eyes dropped to the necklace. "I need to leave that here to keep Earth sealed. It would be a blessing if the rest of the Underworlds don't need to rely on the necklace or ring."

Naphtali rubbed his eyes. "You shouldn't have to use those here, but we're still testing the strength of the seal without them, just to be sure."

"It worked." Dan returned to the monitor with an exuberant smile. The other leaders followed, relaying the same good news.

"In that case, the only way to leave here is through the Gate, and a soul can only return to check on his or her human form, so I won't be able to come back after I use the ring to end this war." Denida shook Sus' hand. "Thanks for everything you did. Susan will stay to watch over the device, just in case." He smiled at Susan tenderly.

***

Nina ran her fingers through her long her and tied it in a ponytail. *This would be so much easier if I could still use magic.* She gazed at a spaceship through a pair of binoculars. Satisfied, she stowed the binoculars in her hoodie's pocket and zipped it up. Nina trudged toward the ship and joined a queue boarding the spacecraft.

Slowly, the queue shrank.

Nina surveyed her surroundings. *There must be another way abord.*

"Keep moving or I'll cut in front of you." A scaly man behind Nina frowned.

*What?* Nina's mouth hung agape at the silvery eyes boring into her. "Yes… yes, I'll move." Nina hustled forward.

"Victore is the name." The man extended his hand to Nina.

"Hello." Nina nodded, then turned back and took a step as the queue advanced.

"Ticket?" the clerk asked.

"I lost mine, so could I buy another?"

The clerk waved his hand dismissively. "No doing."

Nina folded her hands in prayer. "Please, it's-"

"With the demon invasion, everyone wants to leave, so we're fully booked. You'll have to leave the line." The clerk pointed to the side. "Now!"

"Nina, babe!" Victore hollered from behind her. "I found your ticket; it was in my pocket."

"You… found?" Nina glimpsed two tickets in Victore's hand. "Darling, that's great." She swiped the tickets and handed them to the clerk. "All's well, then?"

The clerk nodded and gestured for them to proceed.

"Nice, come on, Babe." Victore clasped Nina's behind, before taking her hand and strolling aboard the ship.

Nina peered back, scrunching her nose as she followed Victore. She pulled the ribbon from her hair as they boarded the ship and swiftly yanked her arm away from Victore.

"Don't you owe me some thanks?" Victore turned to face her.

"No." Nina pinned Victore against the wall and held the ribbon she had removed from her hair tightly against his throat. "Are you here to finish her work?"

"You can't do any real damage with that, you know," Victore mocked.

"Answer the question." Nina's eyes flared. "You're doing her bidding, aren't you?"

"Her bidding?"

"Killing me," Nina hissed.

"No," Victore chuckled. "Why would I kill a sweet thing like you?"

"Then what are you here for? And don't bullshit me; I know that you know something because you knew my name."

"Oh, I know you very well. You're the Nina who wants her son back from Henna." Victore's scales swayed. "Question is: would you accept the help you need to achieve your goal?"

Nina relented, stepping back. "From you? A man with silvery eyes..."

"Before you attack me again, the eyes are just to distract the easily distracted."

Nina snorted. "Yeah, like that would ever work."

"It worked on your husband," Victore sniggered. "He had no idea who I worked for until it was too late."

Nina bared her teeth. "And who do you work for?"

"The master Henna forgot about: the Darkness."

"Lucifer's?" Nina rolled her eyes.

Victore's eyes darkened from a silvery shade to charcoal. "Lucifer's the past. I'm the future."

"What are you after?"

"You." Victore leaned closer. "- if you want magic again, that is, or do you just want to keep playing stealthy with your binoculars and silly little ploys?"

Nina's eyes widened. "How?"

"The Darkness can grant you magic."

Nina scoffed. "I'm not giving you my soul."

Victore cleared his throat. "If you kill Henna, you can have your soul, and your son, who resides in her world."

Nina ran her tongue over her teeth. "I don't know how to reach her."

"We've got that covered." Victore smiled widely. "She needs her Gate to return to her world, but if the device is removed-"

"She'll come check on it."

"Precisely," Victore chuckled. "But you need to choose sides now, because she can move that Gate anywhere at will."

"I'm aware, but don't I need a knife or something to kill her?"

Victore crossed his arms. "You do. You're going to bring me the device from the Gate, and I'll transfer its power unto you, so that you'll be as powerful as she is." He held out his hand. "Do we have a deal?"

Nina glared at his hand. "I don't-"

"Surely, you remember how powerful the ring made Denny?"

*He's right; with Henna's magic...* Nina hastily extended her arm.

Victore wrapped his fingers around Nina's. "Remember our agreement; bring us the device, or we'll be forced to assume you're on Henna's side."

"Of course." Nina waved her hand lazily.

"If we get that impression, we'll have to welcome you back to Hell... permanently."

Nina gripped his hand tighter and dug her nails into Victore's skin. "If you're right about the Gate and dark magic, we have a deal."

Their hands shimmered with a dark aura, for only a second, before it vanished. Victore instantly clapped his hands. Darkness spread from his hands and surrounded Nina. "Now, we'll await Henna's death, and the return of your son." Victore lowered his hands, bearing a menacing grin.

# Chapter 31- A Mission

Denida scratched his temple and looked over at Costa. "Are you nuts?"

"We're out of options; the demons are spreading left and right, and you ended their reign in the Underworlds." Costa rubbed his hands together.

"Still." Denida shifted on his feet. "The council won't listen."

"They might, now. We're out of options."

*So, I'm their last choice.* Denida nodded solemnly. "Understood."

Costa trudged into the meeting room and banged his gavel on his podium. "The council is now in session."

The attendees' idle chatter died down.

Costa cleared his throat. "The demons have invaded even more worlds since our last session-"

"Victore promised to bring us peace, and we already know he keeps his word!" a voice yelled from the back of the room.

Hushed whispers of consensus echoed throughout the room.

"I think we should vote-"

"May I take the floor?" Denida stepped into view.

"Affirmative, the President of the Underworlds and Craym has the floor." Costa gestured to a podium.

Denida approached it, bowed, and cleared his throat. "It's an honor to be here again. I only wish it were under happier circumstances." His eyes flitted to Costa for acknowledgement. "You won't like what I'm about to say."

Denida cleared his throat before proceeding. "The Darkness must be stopped. We have succeeded in the Underworlds, but we need to join forces to crush the demons throughout the rest of the universe." Denida gritted his teeth. "Victore *must* be stopped."

"Impossible…" murmurs of uncertainty rang throughout the room. "If he falls, another demon will replace him."

"Then we will throw every single one of them out so that there's no one left to take his place!" Denida slammed his fist on the podium. "We'll drive them back to Hell and finish this once and for all."

"How?" Costa frowned.

"Mr. Chairman." Denida scowled. "A normal demon dies when you remove its heart."

Costa sighed. "Graphic… and inefficient, given that there are so many of them."

"I have a military that specializes in fighting demons. We can train your troops, too."

"The demons are wreaking havoc on our worlds. Let's vote on Denida's offer to assist our troops." Costa lifted his gavel from the podium.

"Wait, is it even possible to train everyone to win this fight?"

Denida tilted his head toward the voice. "My military and I removed them from my underworlds. If you want the same for your planet, shouldn't you rely on our expertise?" He held the dissenter's gaze for what felt like an eternity.

"All for…" Costa broke the deafening silence.

"Wait!" Denida interjected. "I know you all want to make a deal with Victore, but that is not an option." He clenched his jaw. "He is one with the Darkness, which is leading the charge against all your worlds." Denida turned to the attendees. "That's why he's absent, now; he's busy leading an attack."

Indecipherable whispers rose from the attendees again, as some turned to their neighbors.

"Order!" Costa banged his gavel on the podium again.

Denida scanned the crowd. *There are so many of them… so many worlds for Victore to target.* His stomach dropped as he wrapped his fingers around the edge of his podium. "Victore has access to all your planets. He knows all of you personally and he will stop at nothing to help the demons breach your defenses." Denida took a deep breath, which empowered him to continue. "Together, we can fight Victore, and destroy the demons once and for all."

Costa turned to the attendees as mutterings began rising in the hall again. He struck the podium with his gavel. "Let's put this to a vote."

Before Denida could utter another word, lights in all four corners of the room lit up, calling for silence during voting.

The attendees' podiums lit up as they voted.

"Interesting," Costa mused. "We have reached a decision." He banged his gavel on the podium and cleared his throat. "You have unanimously voted to declare this a state of emergency."

Denida's smile widened.

Costa eyed Denida. "May God favor us in this trying time."

"God?" Denida grunted. "I sure hope not."

Costa furrowed his brow.

Denida waved dismissively and turned to leave.

"Where are you going?"

Denida turned to Costa. "It's time for me to go to war, Costa."

Costa shifted his feet. "Why don't I join you?"

"Join… me?" Denida stuttered.

Costa nodded. "Given the council's will, I want to create a bright future for everyone."

***

A soldier cocked his gun and stared through its sights. After a moment, he fired at some cans. His first shot missed, causing him to wrinkle his nose in frustration. The soldier's eyes narrowed, and he attempted again.

"I don't think that'll work." Nina rested her hands on her hips.

The soldier lowered his gun. "Lady, this is a restricted area."

*Thanks for explaining Earth's obvious protocols.* "Why?" Nina gasped with her hand over her mouth.

The soldier shrugged and holstered his gun. "Let me show you the way back."

Nina followed the soldier toward the barracks. "What is that?"

The soldier turned back to see what she was pointing to. "The second Gate."

"But it's so tall, unlike the other one," Nina blurted out.

The soldier squinted. "Why are you so interested in that Gate?"

Nina flipped her hair over her shoulder. "I noticed that the first Gate has been disabled, but that one looks different."

The soldier scratched his temple. "We did disable the Gates, but to your point, that one is... odd. We can't get near it."

"Oh?" Nina's sly eyes focused on the soldier.

"See for yourself." The soldier handed Nina a pair of binoculars.

Nina squinted through the binoculars. The Gate stood on an elevated piece of land with a deep, circular chasm surrounding it *Thanks, Henna.* Her gaze drifted back to the soldier. "Are you planning to investigate that Gate?"

The soldier straightened up. "My commanding officer told me that the Gate vanished before and reappeared somewhere else, so we're just being careful so that it doesn't disappear again."

"If even an idiot can find it..." Nina sneered. "- I think we'll be good."

"Whatever your game is, I'm not playing it." He grabbed her arm and hollered to another soldier. "Sergeant, this girl's trespassing! Lock her up."

"Yes, Sir." The sergeant grabbed hold of Nina.

"Ma'am." The soldier saluted and strode back to the firing range.

"Come on, Miss." The sergeant pulled Nina's arm.

Nina's eyes trailed to the Gate. *If I still had magic, I would've been able to cross that chasm with ease.* She clenched her fist.

The sergeant passed several other soldiers and stopped in front of a building. "We'll sort you out, here. Please follow me."

Nina tapped her foot.

"Something wrong, Miss?" the sergeant inquired.

"I need to um… do some…" Nina flushed. "- lady stuff."

"Ah, the lavatory's over there." The sergeant pointed across the yard.

"All the way over there?" Nina gasped. "But the demons-"

"Demons?" the sergeant chuckled. "Don't worry; with the magical seal on Earth, demons can't use their sinister magic, here. I'll see you inside." He turned and entered the building.

*Fascinating… no one can use magic here, then.* Her eyes wandered across the yard. *What can lift me off the ground?* Her eyes fell on a truck filled with fatigues. She tilted her head. *It might do me good to blend in.* She scurried over and dug through it to find a uniform in her size, while continually peeking over her shoulder.

"How could you let her go to the lavatory unsupervised, Sergeant?" The soldier from earlier stormed across the yard, followed by the Sergeant and several female foot soldiers.

Nina snatched a uniform and tiptoed to the building they came from, where she rapidly changed and tossed her old clothes into a garbage can. *One problem solved…*

"*Bang!*" The front door slammed open, and the soldier rushed inside. "This is on you, Sergeant. Find that girl before she causes trouble, or it's your ass."

*Better his ass than mine.* Nina bit her lip, then straightened up, and casually strolled past them. She crossed the yard, where she continued to the armory.

"Ma'am." An armory guard saluted her.

Nina ignored the guard and continued inside, but paused after a few steps. She turned to face the guard. "Soldier, we need to get to the Gate, but there's a chasm around it. Do we have something that I could use to cross that gap?"

The guard shuffled into the room, passing her.

*What's taking so long… is this a trap?* Nina tensed and eyed the door, prepared to leave.

"Here." The guard returned and placed a bulky device in front of Nina.

Nina straightened her posture. "What the hell is that?"

"A jetpack, Ma'am. You said you needed to cross a chasm."

*Huh… that could work.* Nina rubbed her hands together. "Good work, Private."

The soldier quickly helped slip the jetpack onto Nina's back, before they stepped outside, where he taught her how to operate it.

Nina ignited the jetpack and set off in the direction of the Gate, soaring high above the ground.

The top of the Gate came into view. As she drew nearer, she could tell the top of it was at eye-level.

*Guess I'd better get lower.* Nina grew a wide smirk and descended.

The people on the ground grew from the size of specks to ants, to miniature humans, to full-sized adults as she descended. They turned their eyes upward. The scattered soldiers became full troops as she neared the Gate, but the perimeter of guards stopped meters shy of the chasm.

Nina descended until she was hovering in front of the Gate's main unit, where she set her jetpack to auto, so that she'd continue to levitate at a constant height. *Just in… what, where's the main device?* Nina growled through clenched teeth and studied the Gate.

Nina felt at the edge of the Gate. *It's all the material of the main Gate, so if I could just...* Her hand trailed the edge, searching. Nina froze as she felt a loose piece, which she yanked free. *Take that, you little witch. I told you I'll get my Daniel back.* Nina flung her arm to the jetpack's left handle and took a firm step down on the dirt.

The ground under the Gate trembled and gave way. The Gate still stood, floating in midair.

Nina pressed down on the jetpack's ignition to take flight. She soared through the sky until she was in a secluded area.

Nina descended and laid the piece on the barren land. She slipped the jetpack off and stared at it. *I wonder if even Henna's magic is sealed, here.* She shut her eyes and rested her hands on top of the fragment. A silvery stream encircled her, making her shine brightly. Nina slowly reopened her eyes. *Ah... her magic imbues me with knowledge, too.*

"I see now, so much knowledge. I don't need Victore, or his pathetic Darkness." Nina stretched her fingers out and clenched a fist. She rose and eyed her hand. A wave of silvery energy emanated from the device and seeped into her.

The device dimmed, becoming pale and rusty as the magic vacated it.

"Victore!" Nina called the demon's name with a devious grin.

Victore appeared before her, his eyes wide as he glanced about. "Where am I?"

"I summoned you to Earth."

Victore stared at Nina. "Did you find the device?"

"Oh yeah, you wanted this." Nina stepped aside, revealing the dull piece on the ground.

"Oh." Victore knelt beside it. "Wait; this can't be it. I don't feel any magic in it."

"The magic's gone," Nina giggled. "But if you miss it, here you go." She extended her hand and a stream of silvery essence shot out from her palm. It enveloped a tree, disintegrating it.

"Your eyes just glowed silver!" Victore stood up. "How did its power get into you?"

Nina leaned in close and whispered. "How do you think?"

Victore turned away. "Well, you still need the Darkness's help. Let me call-"

"Earth has a magic seal, now. Your dark arts are useless, here." Nina clapped her hands so loudly that Victore withdrew. "What a shame."

"If I'm here, the Darkness must be here, too." Victore clenched his fist, and a flicker of crimson appeared around it, only to fade instantly. "How can I be somewhere that the Darkness can't exist?"

Nina threw her hands out to the sides. "Henna's magic is supreme; I'm unstoppable."

"Why would you use her magic to summon me?"

Silvery ash surrounded the two of them, creating a dome.

"Why else?" Nina taunted. "The Darkness sent you to manipulate me, but I'm one step ahead, now."

"We made a deal." Victore grumbled.

"Deal-shmeal, the Darkness will leave me be once its errand boy is gone." Nina approached Victore.

"You clearly don't know us."

"No?" Nina raised her eyebrows. "I was married to Denny. You said you met him, didn't you?"

Victore backed up against the dome, keeping his distance. "Your husband couldn't stop us. What makes you think you'll manage?"

"Nothing can stop me," Nina rejoiced.

"Really?" A wide smirk appeared on Victore's face. "Maybe you want to rethink that?"

"I don't." Nina clasped her fists together, and the dome collapsed on Victore, dissolving him into nothingness. *Now I can focus on Daniel.*

Nina snapped her fingers and teleported such that she was levitating in front of Henna's Gate. She rubbed her hands together ecstatically. *Finally...* Nina extended her arms and her hands glowed as a shiny substance enshrouded her hands. It extended to the Gate, sparkling.

Nina smirked, but nearly as soon as she did, the glow died down. *What, how?*

"It won't work!" a voice yelled from the edge of the gaping valley behind Nina.

Nina whipped around.

Victore stood at the edge of the hole. "Hi, again. Guess you didn't expect me back so soon?"

"… or at all." Nina wrinkled her nose and descended to stand in front of Victore. "What do you mean by 'it won't work?' You and your Darkness assured me that this would get me my Daniel."

"The Darkness asked you to retrieve the device." Victore sighed. "You needed to give it to us, which you didn't do."

"What do you mean?" Nina gritted her teeth, shaking with white hot rage.

"The Darkness needed a large amount of Henna's magic condensed into a small object, which is why we needed the piece with the magic inside."

"Fine, I'll put it back." Nina spun around and flipped her hair from her face.

"Uhm… well, you'll see." Victore folded his hands.

*Is he trying to… wait.* Nina lifted her finger. "How are you even alive? I saw Henna's magic vaporize you."

"The magic in the device is not strong enough to kill a soul, especially one as powerful as Victore, but I guess I never told you that." Henna materialized out of thin air. "At least you know, now. Do you still think you're untouchable?" She boasted.

*How does…* "Just give me my son," Nina hissed. "I did everything you asked of me."

"That wouldn't be very fun. Besides, I told you, you'll never see him again." Henna peeked at the Gate. "You know, this is partly my fault. I should've removed the Gate altogether, after I let you and Denida see Daniel."

"Hang on!" Nina hollered. "That means you didn't see this possibility."

Henna smiled vividly. "Of course, I did, but I left it here, just to see if you'd take this path." Henna smiled mischievously. "So that I could do this…" She charged forth, passing through Nina, with a trail of silvery energy following her.

Nina rolled on the ground for a moment, before jumping to her feet. She flung her arm toward Henna.

"It looks silly when you don't have magic, anymore."

Nina rushed forward, clenching her fist tightly, and punched Henna's face.

Thick clouds formed above them, blocking the sunlight.

"You still have some fight in you." Henna straightened up and levitated above the ground. "Perhaps this will change that." She flicked her fingers.

The Gate sparkled and turned on.

"Daniel…" Nina's eyes lit up. "The jetpack!" Nina swung her head from left to right.

"You should say goodbye, as I no longer need a broken Gate." Henna snapped her fingers and the Gate powered down. It crumbled into miniscule pieces, which fell into the deep pit. Henna kissed her index finger, and a solid blue flame rose from the chasm.

Nina breathed heavily, clenching her fists.

"Let's kill her," Victore whispered to Nina.

Henna raised her eyebrows. "You're still here?"

"Yes, this little witch betrayed us. She has to pay."

Henna tapped her lip. "No, I don't think so. I'm done with our deal." She waved her hand dismissively, and Victore vaporized.

"He's gone, you… should… too…" Nina sputtered, hyperventilating.

"You distracted Denida, but you sure as hell can't anymore," Henna mocked.

"We'll see about that."

"Such anger." Henna teleported to levitate above the crater. "Keep it up; you have nothing left." She folded her arms. "Your sister killed Den, the Darkness thinks you betrayed Victore, and there's no more magic for you to acquire." She scratched her cheek. "I wonder how you'll succeed, or rather, fail."

"*Cough,*" it sounded from farther away. "May I intrude?"

Henna frowned. "Loki?"

"A henchman of yours?" Nina stared at Loki.

"I'm from Valhalla. I'm-"

"Loki." Henna vanished and reappeared on the ground next to him. "What are you doing here?"

*Valhalla…*

Henna swiftly turned her attention back to Nina. "You don't belong on Earth, anymore." She held up her hand and blew some grains of silvery ash in Nina's direction.

The magic darted through the sky, grabbed Nina, and yanked her away. When it vanished, she stood in a garden, surrounded by greenery.

*Where the hell did she send me?* Nina trudged down the garden's path. After a few steps, she froze. She tilted her head back to gaze upward. *Henna's glass castle? I'm on Craym!*

# Chapter 32- The Final Vote

Standing on a planet with demons swarming in the distance, Denida used his ring to conjure up soul projections of Susan, Costa, and the Commander. He ran his hand through his hair, thinking of what to say.

"Sir." The Commander saluted. "We're ready to proceed, on your command."

Denida turned to Costa. "How are you doing? We can ask others to participate in this war instead, if you've changed your mind."

"I would never change my mind on a matter of such great importance," Costa stated.

"Everyone, remember that you can shoot regular demons in the eye." Denida clenched his jaw. "But when it comes to the stronger ones, you'll have to tear their hearts out and crush them."

"Killing their souls." The Commander grimaced.

"We must do it, or the Darkness will win," Susan whispered.

"This war ends now. In two minutes, and counting, we charge." Denida waved his hand, and the soul projections vanished. He held up a pair of binoculars, just in time to see an onslaught of demons charging at him. *I hope I didn't underestimate the number of troops we'll need.*

Denida lowered the binoculars and turned to his soldiers. "Let's kick some demon ass!"

The soldiers clashed with the demons, their guns blazing at the demons' eyes. Soul energy from fallen demons wafted into the sky like an opaque fog.

Denida swallowed hard. *Showtime.* He grabbed a rifle.

"You won't need that." A smirking demon appeared in front of him.

Several other demons appeared, surrounding Denida.

Denida raised his gun.

The first demon's grin faded, and in a split second, they closed in on Denida, throwing him to the ground. The rifle fell beside him. The demons chaotically reached for Denida's ring, climbing on top of each other and shoving as every demon struggled to be the victor who would successfully remove it from his finger.

Denida attempted to yank his arm back, but the demons held it too tightly. *Damn.* He tightened his fist to hinder the demons. He peered in the direction of the soldiers. *No luck, just Darkness.*

"Allow me." The lead demon tried to wrest Denida's hand open.

Denida closed his eyes with a deep breath, before yelling, "Argh!" The force of his roar emitted a pulse of white magic, throwing the demons a few steps back.

Denida jumped up and raised his hand. A silvery wave surged through the sky, obliterating the demons. He wiped his forehead. *Hope it'll get easier from here...* A bright silvery light flashed right in front of him.

"Where are you going?" Henna manifested from the light with her arms folded.

"Henna?" Denida adjusted his grip around the rifle. "What are you doing here?"

"I just came to check on your progress, but I do not think God is here for you to destroy."

"No, but demons are here." Denida's eyes narrowed. "You want me to get Lucifer too, don't you?"

"Don't think I haven't seen this possibility!" Henna's voice hollered inside Denida's head.

"I'll get Lucifer's head after I deal with the demons." Denida bared his teeth. "If that is unacceptable, you can take your ring back."

"I have another idea." Henna smiled. "Why don't I free up your schedule?" She raised her arms, and a ball of silver magic formed in between them. She hurled it forward, and it expanded, disintegrating all the incoming demons, leaving the soldiers puzzled. "Guess you have time for Azal, now." She dissolved in a rainbow flash.

*Henna actually wiped them all out. Wait; I gotta go see the Commander and the others!* Denida waved his hand in a circle, creating a cloud of silvery dust, which he stepped through.

"Die!" A demon attacked Denida as soon as he exited the portal, knocking him to the ground. The demon gloated as he lifted his hand and thrust it downward.

Denida's ring flickered faintly, and a bright light tossed the demon back, leaving him rolling on the ground. He leered down at his hand. *Guess it still has the strength to protect me.* He jumped to his feet and raced after the demon.

The demon rose and charged at Denida, with dark magic oozing from his body.

They clashed, and silver light devoured the darkness, first brightening the blackness into grey, then slowly turning it silver. Denida smashed through the flickers of silvery ash and shoved the demon to the ground, where after he jabbed his hand toward the demon's chest.

The demon launched a wave of fire at Denida, scorching his hand, forcing him to recoil.

"Time to get serious." The demon spread his hands to either side. Several more demons appeared from black clouds that hovered in the sky. The clouds merged into a black mass of Darkness above Denida.

Denida spun on his heels, but it didn't take long before more demons appeared in front of him. Now surrounding Denida, the demons began closing in on him.

"You betrayed our master, Little Evil," the first demon hissed. "Face the consequences."

"Sorry, but I don't think so." Denida extended his hand and spread his fingers. A cloud of silvery dust covered his hand.

"Get him!" The demon gestured for the others to close in. The Darkness intensified as they drew closer.

The silver energy covering Denida's fingers faded. His eye widened, and he swiftly tried to conjure it again, but the demons threw him to the ground.

*How is this possible?* Denida swung his fist in the direction of the demons, but one demon caught it and snatched the ring. The ring shone brightly against the Darkness. Denida squinted, following the ring's path, until something swallowed it whole.

"I'll take the ring to the master. Bring us his heart," a voice sounded from the other end of the Darkness.

"Wait!" Denida writhed. "Give me the ring; Lucifer can't use it, anyway!"

"It belongs to the Darkness, now." A demon pushed Denida down. "All life in heaven dies tonight."

"Charge!" a muffled voice commanded.

A spear impaled the demon's skull from behind and exited through its eye socket. Several soldiers charged through the Darkness to attack the demons.

"Sir?" The Commander extended his hand to Denida.

Denida's eyes widened. "You're here, Commander?" He clenched his teeth. "They took the ring."

"The demons, Sir?" the Commander asked.

"If I knew which one, I would tell you." Denida began patting down the nearest demons' corpses.

"Sir!" The soldiers called as they pursued the second wave of demons.

"Sorry, Sir, but this takes precedence." The Commander grabbed his gun and followed his soldiers.

Denida watched the Commander. "Oh, thanks for saving-" *Dammit, too late, but it's true; this war takes precedence. I wonder how Costa's doing.* He raised his hand, freezing as his eye landed on his bare finger. *Right.* He turned in the direction the Commander had run. With a heavy sigh, he chased after the troop.

Many shades of Darkness hovered in the distance, some thicker than others. Denida set his course for the lowest concentration of Darkness. *It's faint there because that's where the troop is fighting it off!*

"*Bang, bang!*" gunfire roared up ahead, followed by a loud "*thud!*"

*Found them.* Denida increased his pace, but someone with a dagger threw him to the ground and held a dagger to his one eye. Denida grabbed his attacker's wrist. "Stop! It's me."

"The hell?" The Commander pulled the blade away from Denida's face. "I thought you left."

"I can't leave without the ring."

"Why don't you use your soul magic to go to-"

"Are you nuts?" Denida threw his arms up. "That's not the problem. If Lucifer has the ring, stopping the demons' advance might be impossible."

"Sir?" The Commander peered down at his dagger. "If I may ask."

"What?"

"We do have other means of protecting the Underworlds. So why does it matter?"

"But are our troops enough? Sure, they could be, but what if we're wrong?" Denida bit his lip. "We have to find a way, or all of this is pointless."

"Can't you just ask Henna's aid to retrieve the ring?"

Denida's eyes lit up. "You're right, I could ask her, just in case."

"Sir." The Commander saluted and sprinted after the demons.

Denida stood. He folded his hands and cleared his throat. "Henna!"

A flash of silver pierced the Darkness, and Henna appeared out of the light. Her vision panned to one side to the other. "I still don't see Lucifer here, so that mustn't be why you summoned me. Could it be because you lost your ring and the necklace?" She batted her eyes.

Denida rubbed his finger and nodded. "You probably know why."

"You want another ring?" Henna tilted her head.

Denida lit up. "Really?"

"No, I don't help failures, as you know." Henna blinked. "But we still have a deal, so you'd better find a way to fix this."

Denida bared his teeth for a second, before his expression contorted into a fake smile. "If Lucifer and God face off, only one of them will die, not both."

"Neither will die by the other's hand in any of the possible outcomes, I assure you."

Denida chuckled. "In other words, you still need me."

Henna glared into Denida's eyes. "Choose your path wisely; you're only one of my options." She faded away with a rainbow flicker.

Denida swallowed. *I'd better check on Costa.* He took a deep breath, focused his soul energy, and teleported to Costa's home planet. Denida appeared in front of the council's building. He assessed his surroundings and nodded before approaching the building. Unfortunately, his knees gave out, and he slumped to the ground. *I forgot how much energy it takes. I doubt I will ever get used to that.*

"Are you alright, Mister?" A man extended his hand to help Denida to his feet.

"Yes… the demons… they're…" Denida stuttered.

"Costa set everything in motion so that we could dispose of them," the man boasted. "Want to see the bodies?"

"No, sorry." Denida rested his hand on the man's shoulders to steady himself. "Thanks, though. Is Costa here?"

"Check the council room." The man gestured to the building. "Need me to take you?"

Denida shook his head. "No, I've been there." He trotted for the building, glancing over his shoulder at the man, who was heading in the other direction.

The silence in the building rang heavily in Denida's ears.

Denida found Costa alone in the council's chamber. "Everything okay? Why are you here by yourself?"

Costa turned to face Denida, revealing a bruise on the side of his face. Costa gently dabbed at it with a rag "What are you doing, here?"

"I see you destroyed the demons here." Denida lowered his head. "I'm here because we need to gather the council again."

"Now?" Costa lowered the rag. "But most of them are still fighting the Darkness."

"This is of the utmost importance."

Costa shifted on his feet. "More important than the demon invasion?"

"It's related," Denida grunted.

A hologram with a dark flame around it appeared in the center of the room.

Costa grabbed his gavel. Denida prepared a spell, which shone faintly, only to die down again. He grunted, raising his fists, poised to strike.

"Found you." An image formed in the dark flame.

*That voice…* Denida's tension disappeared. "Susan?"

"Affirmative," the feminine voice exclaimed as the hologram stabilized, revealing Susan's image.

The Commander cleared his throat. "Status update, Master Sergeant?"

Susan straightened up. "All the demons have left Earth."

"See?" Denida winked at Costa.

"No, Denny, it's strange. I checked almost everywhere, and they've cleared out." Susan paused for a second. "It's like the Darkness no longer cares about Earth."

"Unlikely," Costa grunted.

"Actually, she may be on to something. The Darkness has Victore, now. It knows Lucifer is a losing game." Denida bared his teeth. "It's time to strike and cut off the snake's head."

"Sir, is that-"

"We can't." Costas shook his head. "We'd be playing right into the Darkness's hand."

"And if we don't?" Denida furrowed his brow. "The demons in Hell empower the Darkness. This way, we'll cripple it. One down, one to go."

"Don't you mean two." Costa tilted his head. "Victore is there, too."

"Not if Henna's prediction is true, and God dies. Like she said: the Darkness came from God."

The Commander shook his head. "That witch…"

Denida laid his hand on the Commander's shoulder. "It can't be helped." He turned to Costa. "It's time to act, and we need the council's approval if-"

"What, to borrow their troops for a fight in Hell, the Devil's lair?"

Denida slammed his palm on the desk in front of Costa. "Lucifer has the ring with Henna's magic in it. Either we act now, or we pay the price."

"You're right." Costa rubbed his hands together. "I'll speak to the council and bring you back in afterward." He smiled softly.

The Commander turned to leave the room, spinning back to the door. "Sir?"

Denida stayed rooted to the spot, shaking his head. "There must be… we need them to understand the urgency."

"I'll make them understand." Costa clapped his hands. "Don't worry, Denny."

"I'll be outside if you change your mind and need someone who has experience with the Darkness." Denida followed the Commander out of the room and shut the door behind him. *I hope my trust wasn't misplaced.*

The Commander turned from the front door to face Denida. "Why don't we relax in the sunshine for a bit before everything turns-"

"I can't leave, and neither can you." Denida closed the distance between himself and the Commander. "Prepare everything for our attack on Hell."

The Commander gasped. "You mean in the Underworlds? Without the council's aid?"

"We won't have time to waste, so make preparations. We're going to war, even if we must go alone. If Hell falls, demons will return with a vengeance."

"Denida?" Costa's voice rang from the other side of the door behind Denida.

Denida glanced at the door and back to the Commander. "Secondly, call Susan and-"

"Susan, why? We have that magic barrier on Earth. Demons can't use dark magic there, anymore."

Denida bit his lip. "If the council says no, there's only one option left; we'll have to remove the barrier by taking the necklace." He met the Commander's gaze determinedly.

"Yes, Sir." The Commander nodded.

Denida entered the council's building, heading straight to their chambers.

"… and as I said, here is the man who knows more of the Darkness than any of us." Costa embraced Denida and led him to his podium. He gestured toward him. "If you please?"

Denida approached the podium, surveying the room with all the holograms lit up. *There are more attendees present than I've ever seen.* He looked back at Costa, who trembled with nerves.

"*Cough, cough,*" tore through the room, shattering the silence.

"The demons will be back." Denida clenched his fists and pounded them on the podium. "We must take this battle against the demons to the source of their power."

"The Darkness?" Costa asked.

"It's going to replace Lucifer with Victore, so we have to-"

Murmurs rang from the crowd, filling the dramatic pause.

"The Darkness has chosen Victore, in the event that Lucifer fails, but until he does, more demons will be harvesting souls to empower it." Denida gritted his teeth. "When Lucifer becomes strong enough to breach Heaven…"

"Heaven?" a hologram frowned.

Denida nodded. "The demons are only acting this way because of Lucifer's vengeance." He straightened his posture. "But his soap opera ends now."

"How can we stop this?" several voices asked in unison.

"We must go to Hell and stop the demons once and for all." Denida raised his fist in the air.

Chatter broke out among the holograms.

"We're not just cogs in the machine; we *are* the machine," Denida interjected swiftly, cutting off the idle discussions before he lost the crowd. -but only if we seize this opportunity, and act now, before the Darkness sends more demons."

The murmurs continued.

"I've been to Hell. I've seen the demons. I know what it's like." Denida lowered his head, scanning the floor before raising his gaze again. "Even now, even with all the demons, if we unite forces, we can win." He pointed at Costa. "Unless his faith in all of you is misplaced?"

"I don't think…" Costa shook his head.

"I've instructed my soldiers to prepare to invade Hell, with or without you. I am going with them, no matter what." Denida banged his fist on the podium. "But if I go alone, the demons will return, and my troops won't be available to lend assistance." He spun around and marched out of the room.

A thundering roar echoed in the distance.

Denida sighed heavily.

"What were you thinking? That was insane!" Costa stormed out of the building.

"Foreboding, isn't it?" Denida smirked.

"If it is so foreboding, then why are you smiling?"

Denida shrugged. "Have you ever felt like you had to do something different, if you want a fighting chance?"

"So, you think that was smart?"

Denida spun to face Costa. "They don't care about the Underworlds on my underdeveloped planet. Did I really have a chance of gaining their support without making them realize that the threat extends to their planets, too?" He patted Costa's shoulder. "I need to go prepare, now." He marched toward the hangar.

"Don't you want to know what they said?" Costa called after him.

"Their vote?" Denida turned to Costa. *It can't be.*

Costa's lips quirked up into a wide grin. "Another unanimous vote, they're ready to charge Hell on your command."

# Chapter 33- Inevitable Demise

*I guess Nina isn't coming back...* Denida stood in a corner of the room on the Galaxy Alliance's planet. He stared down at his wedding ring. *I... can't wait forever when the fate of the world is... at stake, now. She has her life and I have mine.* He sighed to build his resolve and slipped the wedding ring off his finger. He stowed it in his pocket, and his heart lightened. He stepped into the room next door.

Costa hovered over a group of individuals, concentrating on magic. He dashed over to Denida. "Is your former demon friend here, yet?"

"Not-"

"We need to hit Hell, now. Time is of the ess-" Costa pushed past Denida to cross the room.

Denida followed. "No, you see…" He stepped in front of Costa. "Naphtali wants to remain in the Wild West World."

"But we need him," Costa asserted. "Your necklace can-"

Denida intertwined his fingers. "My necklace is currently protecting Earth from magic. Naphtali can call in as a hologram to train your men."

Costa tossed his arms into the air. "Call him, then!"

Denida prepared the intercom and connected to Naphtali in the Wild West World.

"Time, Denny." Costa peeked at his watch.

Denida frowned. "Now that the Gates are deactivated, we'll need to use magic to get to Hell." Denida drew in a deep breath. "Naphtali's position in the Wild West is perfect, as that's where we'll be heading to cast a spell to get us into Hell, so that I can face Lucifer."

Naphtali's fingers twitched. "You want me to direct their spell into Hell?"

Denida nodded. "You've been in Hell, so know how to direct it there, if you don't mind?"

"Anything, as long as I'm not going there myself." Naphtali raised his eyebrows. "I'd prefer to never set my foot there again, but can you even get in after being exiled?"

Denida grunted. "I guess there's only one way to find out, my friend." He gestured to the crowd. "You just need to work with the wizards to figure out how to get us there."

"Wait." Naphtali held up his hand. "I gotta tell you something about-"

"Not now!" Costa stomped his foot and gestured to the crowd. "Get to it. You can catch up after everything's said and done, but we don't have time for that right now."

Naphtali shrugged. "Fair."

Costa patted Denida's shoulder. "This had better work."

"Don't worry; the Darkness is shifting, now. It's not focused on Lucifer, anymore."

"And if you're wrong?" Costa's eyes widened.

"That's why we've got Naphtali and a massive army."

Costa glanced at the Commander and the rest of the troops.

"Naphtali!" Denida raised his hand authoritatively. "Send us to various spots throughout Hell."

Costa clasped his hands. "It's time."

The Commander and the rest of the soldiers formed rows in front of the magicians.

Naphtali's hologram stood in the center of the crowd. He lifted his hands and folded them above his head, as his eyes turned crimson.

The magicians began to chant, and magic filled the room.

Naphtali lowered his arms, still with his hands folded, as the chant and the magic in the room intensified. The room started to darken like a black hole. Suddenly, a vivid red light appeared in the center of the room. Naphtali turned his gaze upwards. "Time for you to go, Denny."

"Go!" Denida darted into the light, followed by the Commander and his troops.

Denida surveyed his surroundings. The dense air hung heavily. "Let's get them." He gritted his teeth. *I need to get to Lucifer before something disastrous happens.*

The Commander readied his gun and waved his hand forward. "Move out, troops!" The Commander and his soldiers began charging through Hell.

After just a few steps, a demon jumped out from the shadows.

The Commander sidestepped to dodge the attack, before lunging. He jabbed his combat knife into the demon's eye socket and yanked it back out, before wiping the blade on his shirt. "Stay vigilant; the fight has begun."

Out of the corner of his eye, Denida spotted a familiar figure in the distance. He squinted. *Is that Gabriel?* He ran toward the figure.

"Sir, it's this way." The Commander gestured in the opposite direction.

Denida spun around. "You can deal with the demons. I'll catch up soon." He sprinted deeper into Hell's dark void. "Gabe… Gabe!" he hollered repeatedly.

A demon emerged from the Darkness. A silvery veil enveloped Denida's hand, as he thrust it forward.

The demon ducked and shot two balls of crimson flames in his direction.

Denida shielded himself with his silvery hand, extinguishing the flames.

Darkness enshrouded the demon, who tossed Denida on the ground and kicked the scar on his side repeatedly.

Denida bared his teeth and punched the demon's leg with all the strength he could muster, making the demon recoil. Denida pounced on the demon and thrust his hand into its gut, ripping its heart out.

A warm presence appeared behind Denida. He spun around, wide-eyed, fists poised. The warmth vanished, only to reappear over his lips.

"It's just me, Denny," Gabriel's voice buzzed in Denida's thoughts.

Gabriel appeared in front of Denida, with a bright glow around him.

"You're here, in Hell? Don't you know what's going on?"

"I do." Gabriel lowered his head. "Which is why I had to try to talk to them again. Wouldn't you do the same, if you were in my shoes?"

"I understand." Denida bit his lip. "It's just-"

"They're my friends."

"Gabe…" Denida held up his hands, gesturing like he wanted to grab Gabriel, but after a moment, he lowered his hands to his sides. "They won't listen; they haven't been listening."

"We were always a group of three; I just need them to remember those days," Gabriel asserted. "Azal's not ready to listen, but I will try Shad- I mean, God, instead."

"You want to go to Heaven?" Denida shook his head. "After leaving Heaven to come here? God won't welcome you back with open arms."

"The things you regret the most are the choices you don't make. Besides, I already returned to Heaven once." Gabriel smiled reassuringly. "Saint Peter was nowhere to be seen, so he and God must be up to-"

"Exactly." Denida stomped his foot. "They're up to their nefarious agenda, which they will carry out, if you return, just to spite you. So please, I implore you, don't go!"

Gabriel's eyes glinted. "You know all about my past with Lucifer and God. There is a reason I can move freely between Heaven and Hell." He rested a gentle hand on Denida's shoulder. "Trust me; I know my friends by heart." A bright light surrounded Gabriel, and he ascended into the sky.

Denida felt his heart pound. *This won't go well, but I-*

"*Bang, bang!*" gunfire roared in front of Denida, followed by tiny flickers of light, breaking the veil of black.

Denida squinted as he approached the sounds that became increasingly louder with every step.

"You're mine!" a man screamed from behind Denida.

Denida spun around, just in time to dodge the man's dagger.

"Denida?" The man in soldier fatigues withdrew his knife and saluted.

"Do I know you?" Denida asked.

"Naphtali sent my unit in to add coverage."

*Makes sense.* "We need to hurry." Denida stormed forward.

"Demons…" One soldier charged, with others following close behind.

Denida clenched his fist, and the Darkness thickening the air swiftly shrouded his hand as well. He thrust it in the direction of the oncoming demons. A huge burst of black energy thundered through the sky and smashed into the demons, disintegrating them on impact. Denida studied his hand. *Looks like dark magic is still strong here, even without the Darkness.* He turned to the soldiers. "Eradicate the demons! This ends, now," he commanded.

"*Bangs*" and "*thuds*" surrounded Denida.

Denida darted about, tearing through hordes of demons on his haphazard quest. Despite his chaotic wandering, and frantic search, Lucifer's mansion remained undetectable. His freneticism turned to frustration, which gave way to clarity. Denida stopped suddenly, heaving in a deep breath. *I need to be more systematic about this.* He bared his teeth, and his eyes illuminated the dark like crimson rubies. He inhaled deeply and pressed his fists against each other as tightly as he could, until they shook from exertion. A circle of dark energy formed around him. *Where is the strongest concentration of Darkness?* His bad eye darkened to coal, and he lowered his arms to his sides, heading in that direction.

A demon sprang out of the shadows, its arms shrouded in blue flames. It charged at Denida, who merely lifted his arm, freezing the demon mid-movement.

Denida continued his slow trek. As he walked, the air thickened, and a dark castle started to come into view in front of him.

A dark miasma covered the castle. The door stood ajar, casting the only light among the blackness.

Denida hesitantly approached the door.

"*Taz.*" The light in the doorway flashed more vibrantly for a moment.

Denida stopped in front of the door, peering through its narrow opening. His eye skimmed the floor, finding the main hall to be vacant, until his gaze landed on the Well of Memory. Beyond the well, he saw two figures, one on his knees, and the other hovering over him.

"… time to compensate for your son's failure." The standing figure, Saint Peter, raised his arm, and the holy dagger in his hand came into view.

"Wait," Lucifer commanded from his spot, kneeling before him. "You're doing exactly what Henna wants you to do."

"Ha!" Peter mocked him. "I never served that has-been. God's will is absolute."

Lucifer's face paled, and he crossed his arms, forming a cone of Darkness as a protective seal.

"Peter!" Denida leapt through the door.

"Den-" Lucifer's eyes met Denida's.

Peter thrust the dagger downwards. It pierced the cone and slammed into Lucifer's body, sapping the life from his eyes. Lucifer slumped to the ground.

Peter grinned at Denida and blew him a kiss. He then flew out the window, shrouding himself in a pillar of light, as he ascended to the sky.

Denida rushed to Lucifer's side as his body crumbled to ashes.

"Luci…" Denida fell to his knees, and grasped Lucifer's hand, which was the last part of his body that was still fully intact. "I'm sor…" Denida's eyes widened as he uncurled Lucifer's hand, revealing the dagger's shaft. *Maybe I still have some of Henna's power inside of me…* He swiftly jumped to his feet, holding his hand over the mountain of silvery ash.

A speck of silvery dust hovered under Denida's hand. It swirled away from the pile of ash and glided over to the Well of Memory, where an image formed.

***

Lucifer sauntered toward the former president of the Underworlds, who stood confidently, seeming to steel himself with the possible knowledge that he had no way to fight back, now. The fire in Lucifer's eyes glowed as he approached him.

"Why do you even want this child?"

Lucifer stopped. "That's a child who has more power than God and I combined. God wants to kill that child, but I'd prefer to use it." Lucifer wore an evil, devious smirk. "But you won't live to experience it." With fire surrounding his hand, he plunged it into the president's body and ripped out his heart.

The president collapsed at Lucifer's feet. Lucifer dropped the heart and knelt to pull the ring from the corpse's hand, but his eyes widened at the sight of the president's bare fingers. He checked the president's other hand and recoiled in confusion.

"Where is it?" Lucifer frantically searched the president's pockets.

"You won't find it." Gabriel approached him. "He was prepared for this, just as he always was."

Lucifer's face turned as black as the darkness around him.

"We need to talk."

"What?" Lucifer glared at him.

"God wants the child dead. If the child dies, God will know where his soul is."

Lucifer chuckled to himself. "Perhaps, but that won't help him. He'll still have to get past my demons."

"What demons?"

"The ones I'm sending to Earth to watch the boy." Lucifer walked away, vanishing in the Darkness, only to reappear on the outskirts of a garden filled with a plethora of lush vegetation.

"Azal, welcome back… or should I say, 'welcome home?'" Henna glanced up from a rose she was sniffing. "What brings you here? I thought you knew that my offer expired?"

Lucifer spat on the flowers. "I know the day will come when Shaddai and I both fall. My Well of Memory has shown me many possible outcomes, but they all end the same way."

"Then?"

"You already know, considering you have seen every possibility." Lucifer sneered. "Your chosen ones keep failing you."

"The time is not ripe, yet." Henna slowly twirled the rose under her nose.

"It could be riper, if you help me to ensure that Shaddai doesn't kill that soul's human counterpart."

"Fascinating…" Henna stood. "And how would that benefit me, when you have his soul in Hell?"

"If you assist me, I'll mentor him, prepare him…"

"For?"

"When the time comes, he'll escape Hell, and what I taught him will benefit us both." Lucifer clenched his fist and raised it into the sky.

"It's odd that you'd help me, seeing as your end will come, too." Henna grinned.

"Darkness resides in his heart. So, I'll take my chances."

"It's an interesting proposition, helping fate on its way. I'll bite." Henna extended her hand.

Lucifer grabbed her hand and shook it. Silvery ash swirled around their hands.

***

The image created by the silvery ash dissipated, and in its place, the well's water sloshed about. A Darkness-infused energy enveloped it. A silhouette formed in the dark ripples.

"If you see this, I guess Henna got what she wanted." Lucifer's voice spoke gently. "But don't feel bad, because I always knew this was going to happen one day." He tried to feign a smile, but his lips barely moved. "You could say that I was always paddling upstream, when it came to Henna, God, and the Darkness." Lucifer shrugged.

*How?* Denida peeked at the pile of ash.

"You'll need your ring, if you choose to face God."

The ring appeared, floating in the middle of the well.

"I hope I meet Heavani in the afterlife." Lucifer stared ahead with a dead gaze. "We're all doomed. I hope you don't choose the path that I know you will take, and suffer the same faith as the three of us."

The silhouette faded into the black pit of water.

Denida grabbed the ring. As soon as his fingers curled around it, the water splashed to the ground, and the Darkness's miasma lifted. He spun around and scurried to the mountain of ash, lifting his hand, and clenching a fist. *Come back!*

Denida's hand lit up, dissolving the ash.

Denida's knees turned to butter, and he slumped to the ground where Lucifer had been.

*Is there even any Darkness left in Hell without Lucifer?* He marched out of the castle. The world outside appeared vacant and silent. Denida drew in a deep breath, finding the air to be as clean as it was in the Underworlds. *It really is gone...* He heard a tremor behind him and whipped around to see Lucifer's mansion shaking. His eyes widened, and he stepped back, watching with wide eyes as it crumbled to the ground, leaving Denida's heart pounding heavily in his chest.

"Sir!" The Commander called from behind him.

Denida trembled. He turned to the Commander, as his legs threatened to buckle.

"What happened?" The Commander pointed to the rubble.

Denida shook his head, his heart thundering away. "Where are the demons?"

"They..." The Commander shrugged. "They all disappeared into thin air when the dark cloud lifted from Hell."

Denida recoiled. "We're the only life in Hell, now?"

"Sir, yes, Sir."

"Let's return to Costa, on the double." Denida waved his hand in a circular motion, and a silvery light glowed in its wake.

The Commander's eyes widened. "You got the ring back?"

"Yes, I'm going to need it." Denida ventured into the circle the ring had formed. When he exited it on the other side, he found himself back in the room with Costa and his magicians.

"You're back!" Susan rejoiced.

*Susan's here?* Denida nodded. "Hell is… no more." He waved his finger. "And I retrieved the ring, so now we can stop God, and put an end to this nightmare." He clenched his fist and extended his arm.

"Wait!" Susan rushed in front of Denida and grabbed his arm. "I must tell you something important."

"It can wait until-"

"No, Naphtali tried to tell you, too." Susan insisted. "It affects your ring, too."

Denida withdrew his hand. "Okay, what's so important?"

"You wanted me to go to Earth, remember?" Susan raised her voice.

*Why's she asking me that?* "Yes, to keep an eye on Sus, and the necklace." Denida chuckled.

"I went to check on the necklace, and the barrier is draining the necklace's magic, just as Naphtali feared."

"What?" Denida's stomach knotted, making him nauseous.

Susan nodded. "Naphtali said that the barrier in his world faded. All the Underworlds are going to follow suit. We're lucky the necklace contains more magic than the devices, because Earth's barrier should be able to hold up a bit longer, but still."

Denida turned to the magicians. "Where is Naphtali, anyhow? Isn't his hologram supposed to be here?"

Costa met Susan's gaze and stepped forward. "His hologram vanished."

"Vanished? Then I'd better go-"

Susan rested her hand on top of Denida's. "No, he isn't there. Someone else from his end confirmed that he up and disappeared."

"The magic barrier fading from the Underworlds is less problematic than it fading on Earth, as humans don't have the ability to fight magic with magic." Susan's shoulders slumped. "But you returned, so did things go badly in Hell?"

Denida's heart sank, and tears prickled his eyes. "Lucifer's dead." Denida heaved in a heavy sigh. "Saint Peter used a holy dagger to kill him for good. I'd guess it was the dagger that has been shielding Heaven, which means Henna and the Darkness can enter, now."

"What?" Susan rested her hands on her hips. "God sent that Peter guy to kill Lucifer? I hope you destroyed him for it."

Denida shook his head. He took her hand and stepped to the side.

"What's wrong?" Susan frowned.

Denida flinched. "I've been thinking… when this is over, maybe we should go somewhere… together?"

Susan's mouth started forming a smile but froze midway. "You're serious?"

"There's been so much death and destruction in the Underworlds that I just want to be with you, somewhere I can ensure your safety." Denida lowered his head. "Just think about it."

"That's why going to Heaven is so vital, now." Susan rested her hand on his.

"That's not…" Denida sighed and gestured at the magicians. "You'd better get everyone back from Earth and Hell." He strolled over to Costa.

"I'm guessing you wish to go to Heaven, now?"

"Yes, Gabriel went there while Peter was attacking Lucifer, so I have an uneasy feeling, now." Denida shifted on his feet.

Costa nodded in agreement. "I'll send the units in as soon as they're all back."

Denida looked at Susan forlornly before turning to Costa. "I'll need at least an hour." He created another circle with his hand and marched through the silvery hole that appeared. He resurfaced on a cloud.

Denida's eyes examined his surroundings. The majestic Pearly Gates stood in front of him. He ventured forward briskly, laser-focused on the gates. As he drew near, he slowed down. *Perhaps I can catch Peter off-guard.*

Denida's eyes widened as he snuck closer. *No one's here.* He surveyed his surroundings and tiptoed closer. He glanced over his shoulder again, before stepping through the gates with his hand clenched, ready to charge.

"I already told you: I'm not with Henna," Gabriel insisted. "She blames me just as much as she blames God."

Saint Peter rubbed his fists together.

"Ask God," Gabriel pleaded.

"Oh, trust me, I'm following his orders, and we're cleaning house." Peter chuckled. "Henna will be less likely to come here, once you and Lucifer are gone for good."

Gabriel shook his head and sighed. "That won't be enough for her."

Peter threw up his arm. "So be it, but you must die."

"Peter!" Denida shouted from where he stood. "Don't become God's errand boy."

Peter tilted his head. "Denida, how did you like my handiwork in Hell?"

Denida turned his head, scanning Heaven analytically. "I don't see any angels, here. Did you kill them, too?"

"Funny," Peter jested. "No, God is holding a meeting with them."

"Interesting." Denida's stoic expression slowly morphed into a smile. "Then I guess you have time for me." He hurled a stream of silvery energy at Peter. It enveloped Gabriel, shielding him within a cone.

"That won't keep him safe," Peter snickered. "He'll have to leave eventually. And you should know that light magic reigns supreme in Heaven." He threw a wave of light magic crashing into the cone, shattering it into a million tiny pieces.

Denida's eyes widened. *He's not bluffing...*

"Surprised?" Peter scoffed. "You're not as powerful as Henna, and neither the ring nor the necklace contains her full power. Did you really think that witch would ever give you something to even the odds if you're up against her?"

Denida stepped in front of Gabriel and extended his arms to either side, peeking back over his shoulder at his friend. "Hide!"

Gabriel clenched his jaw. "I'm an archangel and I don't-"

Denida spun around, thrusting his arms forward with so much force that his magical energy sent Gabriel flying backward, down the road, and out of sight. Denida turned back to Peter and lifted his finger. "I'm your combatant."

"Don't worry; I can always kill him later." Saint Peter tilted his head. "I always wanted a chance to kill you, anyway, so I wouldn't miss it for the world."

"Death by light magic." Denida raised his eyebrows. "Sounds fun, if you can beat me, that is." He smiled slyly and flung a stream of light magic at Peter.

Peter interlocked his thumbs and pushed his hands forward, sending a flurry of light magic bolting through the sky. It ripped through the stream and merged with the light magic, before smashing into Denida. "Enough small talk! It's time to die, Little Evil."

*Damn, that hurt.* Denida rubbed his behind and rolled behind a bush for coverage. He tiptoed out from his hiding spot with his eye fixed on Peter's movements.

"Running, now? Isn't it a little late to play chicken?" Peter calmly scanned his surroundings for any trace of Denida.

Denida peered down the street he'd sent Gabriel down. *Still safe… it's just me and Peter, and the Darkness won't lose to him.* He readied his fist and focused. His hand flickered with Darkness. *The hell?* He squinted his eyes and fired a weak stream of combined light magic and soul energy at Peter.

Peter bared his teeth and returned fire with white magic.

The two streams of energy clashed with each other, creating a flare that shone more vividly than the rest of Heaven.

Peter reinforced his energy by using his free hand to support his first. His energy began to devour the combined streams.

Denida clenched his jaw and focused on his hand. He spotted Peter's intense stare out of the corner of his eye. *Fine, I'll use Henna's magic.* He sighed and clenched his other fist, sending a blast of silvery energy hurtling at Peter.

The stream ran parallel to the white one at first, but gradually changed course, becoming closer to it, until the two streams combined, and slammed into Peter's light magic. Denida's combined magic intensified and tore through the light magic, lancing toward Peter.

Peter jumped to the side just in time to dodge the attack. The magic struck the ground where Peter had been standing, and black mist rose from impact.

"Looks like I can overcome your light." Denida chuckled.

Down the road, Gabriel came into view.

Denida approached Peter, pausing in front of a crate. *Peter?* His eye fixed on a shirt behind it. "This ends now!" He pounced on the shirt, but when his hands failed to make contact with anything solid, his eyes filled with fright.

Before Denida could react, Peter banged him over the head with a log, forcing Denida to his knees. Peter slammed the log forward again, hammering it into Denida's crotch.

"Ugh!" Denida tried extending his hand but could only muster a pathetic flicker of magic.

Peter snatched his hand and ripped the ring from Denida's finger. He tossed it down the road.

Denida gasped and tried to jerk free of Peter's grasp.

Peter clenched his fist and smacked it against the ground, creating a white cone, which barred them from escaping. "Go ahead and try your petty soul magic now," he chortled.

Denida began hyperventilating. "This… means neither of us… can use magic, now." He straightened his posture and stormed at Peter, slowly regaining control of his breathing.

Peter remained still as Denida charged at him. He stepped aside just before Denida reached him.

Denida crashed into the edge of the cone. He spun around to punch Peter in the face, but Peter retreated, grabbed Denida's arm, and slammed him into the cone again.

Peter swung his arm at Denida, landing a blow across Denida's face, causing blood to gush down the interior wall of the cone. Denida collapsed, again. Peter knelt next to Denida. "This seems like a good time to tell you that I made this cone to keep us inside, not to restrict magic." He lifted his hand, and light magic enveloped it. In a flash, he rammed it downwards.

Denida jammed his elbow into Peter's left foot with all his might.

"Goddammit!" Peter screamed, and the magic around his hand subsided.

"I thought we weren't supposed to take the Lord's name in vain?" Denida stood and grabbed Peter.

Peter threw a punch, but Denida ducked.

Denida swung back and headbutted Peter with crimson eyes. He jumped on Peter and threw punch after punch.

Peter caught Denida's fist as it came close to striking him for the umpteenth time and held it tightly.

A fiery red flame enshrouded Denida's other hand, and he struck at Peter with even more ferocity. His assault continued, until Peter's grasp loosened enough for Denida to yank his hand free.

Peter tried to deflect the blows, but the attacks came too rapidly, so he tried to conjure up some magic. His hand flickered with light magic, but Denida's fist smashed into Peter's gut, causing Peter's spell to falter. Denida's strikes intensified, as soul magic encased his fists to strengthen his blows.

"This is for Luci and Heavani!" Denida's fists became enshrouded in a crimson glow. He jabbed them into Peter's abdomen and ripped out his heart so fast that Peter didn't even have time to react. Denida held it in front of Peter with his hand, and a reddish hue encased his aura.

"Please don't!" Peter reached out.

Denida lowered his other hand onto the still-beating heart, and a blue flame engulfed it.

A single tear rolled down Peter's cheek, and the life faded from his eyes. As his expression turned blank, the cone dissipated.

Denida's eye reverted to its usual blue, as he stumbled down the street, where he encountered Gabriel.

"Here." Gabriel handed Denida the ring.

"Sir?" The Commander bolted up to Denida. "What happened here?" He examined Denida and Gabriel, and their somber faces. "Where is everyone? Is that… God?" He pointed to Peter's corpse.

"I wish." Denida slipped the ring on his finger. "I need to talk to God." He peeked at Gabriel. "Do you still want to join me?"

"… No." Gabriel stared intently at Peter's corpse and lowered his head.

Denida nodded solemnly. "Commander, stay here and keep Gabriel safe."

"What? But Sir, shouldn't we all go-"

"No," Denida ordered steadfastly. "If I don't return. come after me, but…" He hugged Gabriel. "I'm sorry." He trudged down the road with his eyes locked on the tallest tower in Heaven. *I hope you're ready, because I'm coming for you.*

# Chapter 34- Nina's Last Attempt

A swarm of butterflies fluttered about harmoniously. Nina's soft eyes tracked their movements. *So sweet, just like my life will be, when I get Daniel back.* She shifted her attention to Henna's castle. *I wonder if her residence has a means to leave this forsaken lump of vegetation.* She plodded toward the glass dwelling.

"*Twig,*" thin branches caught on Nina's shirt and snapped, as she cut through the woods, brushing against trees.

Nina's gaze shifted left and right, but her trajectory and pace remained unencumbered. After what felt like much too long, Nina sighed with relief and ran up the steps to the castle's main entrance. Her heart sank, as she meandered across the glass floors and rummaged through the meager belongings in each room she came to.

*There's nothing here.* Nina sighed heavily and exited the castle. On the steps, she frowned, as anxiety created a lump in her throat. *Can I really be stuck here?*

The sky above the castle suddenly clouded over, turning an ominous shade of grey.

Nina furrowed her brow. "That weather seems peculiar," she whispered to herself.

The sky darkened, and a menacing presence filled the air.

Nina shifted on her feet, breaking her intense focus on the sky.

"My dear, Nina," a haunting, familiar voice echoed from within the castle.

Nina spun to see Victore, and a shiver coursed through her core. "You're here?" she gasped.

"Henna sent me here. She finally did something right." Victore smirked wickedly.

"We can talk about this." Nina slowly descended the stairs.

"Talk?" Victore cackled. "You must be mistaking me for someone who wants something more than your death." His eyes turned to coal, and he pointed to Nina. Several demons appeared from pits of blackness in the garden in front of the castle.

"Demons?" Nina glared at one of the demons, a sparkle in her eyes. "That one's wearing clothing from the Underworlds. Are you borrowing Lucifer's demons, now?"

"The Darkness reclaimed all the demons." Victore gestured to the demon, who Nina seemed interested in. "Naphtali, come here."

Naphtali sauntered over to Victore. "Yes, Master?"

Victore snapped his fingers and Naphtali knelt beside him. "This is one of Hell's former demons, Naphtali. He escaped Hell with the Dark Angels, but he couldn't escape the Darkness." Victore scratched Naphtali under the chin like one might do to a dog.

"A former demon? Does that mean Denida-"

"Little Evil." Victore grabbed Naphtali's arm. "Lucifer saved your ex-husband's soul by taking him on as a protégé. Unbeknownst to us, Little Evil never belonged to the Darkness."

Nina giggled.

"But I don't need him to kill you, my dear." Victore thrust his hand into Naphtali's gut and ripped his heart out. He crushed the heart in his hand.

Nina gasped and turned on her heel. She darted back up the stairs, past Victore, and through the castle's foyer. The demons chased after her, practically on her heels.

*Left, right, left...* Nina wove through the castle, darting through rooms and corridors. *Damn, they're keeping up.* Her eyes widened to the size of teacups, as she encountered a locked door at the end of a long hallway. She began hyperventilating and rapidly whipped her head around, searching for an escape. She tried to pry open the door at the end of the corridor. Her knuckles turned white from her grip. *Come on... budge!* Nina bit her lip, turning away from the door, sporadically searching for an exit. Two demons stood in the corridor, blocking her only escape.

"*Clap, clap, clap,*" slow clapping echoed throughout the extravagant hall.

"Nice try, little girl, but this ends here." Victore appeared next to the demons. "You thought you could escape me? What stupidity."

"Wait!" Nina lifted her shaky hands. "Henna… I can help you beat Henna."

"Can you get any stupider?" Victore tilted his head to the demons. "Bring her soul to our master."

"Lucifer doesn't want me; he knows me." Nina smirked.

"Lucifer?" Victore stepped in front of the other demons. "I guess you don't know, so allow me to enlighten you. Lucifer and his Hell are no more."

"No… more?" Nina's heart pounded in her chest. "You're pulling my leg, right? I can see that there are demons right here, and demons come from Hell."

Victore wrinkled his nose with disgust. "I have replaced Lucifer. This is a new beginning."

"That's impossible. He's the reason that the Darkness has been growing, and-"

"Oh?" Victore raised an eyebrow. "Haven't you realized that the Darkness anoints its charge?"

Nina's legs quivered. "…but Lucifer-"

"The Darkness has forsaken Lucifer." Victore spread his arms and smiled wildly at his demons. "Get her."

The three demons darted down the Hall.

Nina remained rooted to the spot, as the demons charged at her. Her rapid heartbeat tracked their approach in milliseconds.

"*Creak,*" the door behind Nina opened.

Nina peeked back. *How?* She shook off her stupor, leaping into the room. A giant mural of Henna decorated the far wall.

The demons rushed after her, before she could close the door, but each demon vaporized into silvery ash upon crossing the threshold.

Nina peered down at the three piles of ash in the doorway.

Victore's smile stiffened. "How the-"

"Watch it." Nina waved her index finger. "You're about to take your lord's name in vain."

"You little…" Victore stomped down the corridor.

Nina swiftly slammed the door and searched for its lock. *This door doesn't have a lock? But I couldn't open it, before…*

Victore kicked the door open. "You need to be faster than that."

As Victore stepped closer to her, Nina retreated. Her heavy breaths intensified. "Something weird is going on."

Victore rubbed his hands together. "I know; the Darkness hates the fact that you're still alive."

"No, the door was locked, but there's no way to lock it." Nina shrugged. "See for yourself."

Victore rolled his eyes. "You expect that to work on me? I thought you had more brains than that."

"She's right," a playful, masculine voice spoke from behind Victore.

Victore spun around and shoved the man who had spoken up against the wall. "And you think I care? Do you really want to intrude on my moment of unrivaled bliss?"

Nina clicked her tongue against her teeth and eyed the door. *No, they're too close; I wouldn't make it. Maybe I could egg Victore on?* "Do I know you from somewhere?" She faced the man.

The man sneered. "You will." His body turned slippery, and he slithered from Victore's grasp to shimmy up next to Nina. "My name's Loki. I'm from Valhalla."

*Valhalla?* Nina gasped.

Loki closed her mouth with his index finger. "Yes, the two of us served the same master for a long time… or should I say, the same goddess?"

Victore stared from his empty hand back to Loki. "If you are with Henna, why're you here? If it's to kill Nina, get in line."

Loki stepped closer to Victore. "No, thank you, but while I am here, do you want to know how your demons died?"

Victore wrinkled his nose. "That little witch set us up."

"Eh?" Loki glanced at Nina and laughed. "You're funny. You think a garden-variety soul can kill three demons without laying a single finger on them?"

"Then how?" Victore demanded.

"You own the demons, no? Darkness devours their souls."

"I'm waiting for an answer, not a riddle," Victore retorted.

"This is Henna's castle. She died in this very room."

Victore sighed. "Last chance, Valhalla Boy. Do you have anything to offer, outside of a history lesson?"

"Henna's magic seals this room, such that only her magic can enter, except for you, it seems." Loki raised his eyebrows. "Do you understand, now?"

"So what?" Victore crossed his arms. "Lucifer died, and she'll have God soon. Once that happens, Henna and the Darkness will be all that remains." A wide smirk appeared on his face. "Maybe I'll start by killing her two defectors, unless you wish to join me on the winning side?"

"Who said I was a defector?" Loki tapped his upper lip and turned to Nina. "Did you tell him I was? 'Cause I know I never said it."

"I…" Nina shook her head.

"Well, there's no one else here but you, then." Loki turned his head to face Victore. His pupils flickered with silver specks, and he held up his hand to blow some silvery dust at Victore. It flew in perfect silence, until it reached Victore. In a split second it sucked him out of the room and down the corridor. The door slammed shut and locked, leaving Nina and Loki alone in the room.

Nina cleared her throat. "You do realize that Henna dumped me here, right?"

"I do." Loki approached the mural on the wall and examined it. "Fascinating…"

"Like Victore asked, why are you here, if you know that she's abandoned us here?"

Loki traced his finger along the lines of Henna's face. "I met your hubby in Valhalla."

"Ex-hubby." Nina approached Loki. "But I'm sure you're already aware of that."

"That's correct." Loki turned to Nina. "You're a clever girl, and I see some essence of me inside of you. We can help each other."

Nina shook her head dismissively. "I can't use magic anymore, so I doubt it."

"No, the thing about you that reminds me of me is-" Loki's eyes lit up. "…how you still press onwards, even when Henna screws you over seven ways from Sunday."

"I have just reason." Nina flipped her hair to her other shoulder. "Throwing Victore out was awfully sweet of you, but we can't stay in here forever."

"We can leave, as soon as you agree to help me."

"You sound exactly like Henna," Nina jested. "Everything on your own terms."

"Yet, I won't penalize you if you say no, but would you really want to?" Loki lifted his hand and blew on it. Silvery ash flickered on his palm.

Nina peered at the door. *I suppose anything is better than Victore.* She arched her neck. "Alright, what do you need?"

Loki leaned in close to Nina. "Henna. I need to win her favor and I have an idea that you can assist me with."

"I can't." Nina marched over to the door. "I'll take my chances with Victore."

"Why?" Loki clenched his fist and threw the dust at the door. It flung wide open. "You really want to face that?"

Victore rubbed his hands together greedily as he rose from the floor. "I knew waiting for you would pay off."

Nina flinched at the sight of Victore "No, but Henna will kill me if she sees me again. Whereas, I've got a chance, here."

Loki raised his hand. The corridor elongated into a hallway that stretched as far as anyone could see.

Victore grumbled and bolted forward, but no matter how many steps he took, the distance between Victore and the room stayed the same.

"I only need you to agree, as your words alone would be enough to get her attention. She'll kill the Darkness for good." Loki met Victore's puzzled eyes. "In exchange, I'll tell you how to get your son back."

Nina waved at Victore. "It's been fun." She blew a condescending kiss in his direction.

"Try to stay alive, for now." Loki's eyes flicked silver. He grabbed Nina, and silvery dust enshrouded them. They vanished from the castle and, when the dust settled, they reappeared somewhere new.

"Where are we?" Nina brushed herself off.

Loki smiled and pointed at the sky. "We're on the outskirts of Valhalla."

*Huh?* Nina trained her eyes on the sky. Lush greenery dangled from atop a cloud. "Okay, and how do I get Daniel back?"

"I need to approach Henna. After I've had an audience with her, I'll show you where you can convene with her."

"And tell her what, exactly?" Nina folded her arms. "I already told you that she doesn't want to see me."

"You tell her about the Darkness's new master's intent." Loki chuckled. "That will show her how valuable I-"

"Yeah, yeah. What about me!" Nina raised her voice impatiently.

"After we talk to her, she and the rest of her gods in Valhalla will be so busy dealing with Victore that I'll be able to sneak us to Odin's Gate to her world." Loki's eyes drilled into Nina. "- but this will only work if you help me succeed."

"Victore already gave me that line." Nina waved her hand dismissively. "Daniel is the only thing that matters, so don't worry."

Loki nodded excitedly and his eyes flickered silver. In a flash of light, he ascended into Valhalla.

Nina watched him rise, until he was as small as the head of a pin. *If this works, I'll get my prize without Henna.*

Nina folded her hands and began pacing back and forth as the hours ticked away. *He'd better hurry up.*

A flash of silvery light sparkled, and a hologram of Loki's likeness appeared. "Nina?"

Nina shook a stray hair off her face. "Yes?"

"Can you tell Henna what you saw on Craym?" Loki folded his hands pleadingly.

"Are you referring to how Victore rejoiced over the fact that Henna played right into his hand by letting Lucifer die?"

Loki nodded. "And?"

"And, once God is also gone, the demons can conquer everything?" Nina asked doubtfully.

"Why are you asking instead of telling?" Henna stepped into the frame. "You're starting to be a real pain, Nina."

Nina fiddled with her hair. "I thought you already knew how everything was going to play out?"

"I know what you plan on getting for this, but attempting to manipulate me didn't work for Claus, and it won't work for Loki." Henna grabbed Loki by the ear and shoved him to his knees. "One more failure to you, Nina." Her hands clamped Loki's temples.

Loki vaporized into a massive pile of silvery ash.

"Once God dies, I ought to end Daniel, for good." Henna waved her hand, and the hologram vanished.

*That...* Nina stood, trembling. She gritted her teeth as her eyes locked on Valhalla. *I have to find a way up there before Henna can get back to her world!*

# Chapter 35- Final Confrontation

*I must be getting close.* Denida followed the sound of chatter around the corner. When he arrived, he noticed God standing in the center of a crowd of angels.

"Denida." God lifted his arms in a welcoming embrace. "If I were Lucifer, I would say that my prodigal son has returned." He lowered his arms. "This is a glorious day. You should join us in celebrating the wonderful fact that the Darkness is no more."

"Celebrate…" Denida ambled forward, and the angels stepped back, clearing the way to God and Jesus beside him. "Hello, Jesus."

Jesus smiled and waved at him.

"Gabriel is missing the festivities…" Denida smirked and gazed into God's eyes. "- so is Peter."

"Don't play coy; you're in Heaven, now." God stepped behind Jesus and rubbed his shoulders. "I know you killed him."

The angels gasped.

"He was going to kill Gabriel… you know, your friend?" Denida raised his eyebrows. "And worse, Heaven is no longer safe. Henna can just waltz on in, now."

God shrugged. "She doesn't know that Peter used the dagger to kill Lucifer."

"Then you must have forgotten about her power to see the different strands of fate," Denida mocked him. "And you must know Lucifer's death won't be enough to appease Henna, not when she wants you dead, too, Shaddai. You killed her, not Gabriel, not Lucifer."

"Um… Father?" Jesus lifted his head toward God.

God caressed Jesus' cheek. "Everything's alright." He knelt beside Denida and whispered. "Why are you here? Still playing Henna's lapdog?"

Denida chuckled. "I was never her lapdog."

"Then you should know that there's only one righteous god, and you're trespassing in his domain." God clasped his hands. "My children, our meeting is adjourned."

The angels dispersed, leaving only God, Denida, and Jesus in the room.

"Did you not hear me rescind your welcome?" God demanded irritably.

"I did, but we need to discuss how to end this conflict with Henna peacefully."

"That doesn't concern you." God rested his hand on Jesus' arm.

"Don't you have someone else to get rid of me, now that you've lost Peter, Gabriel, Lucifer, and Heavani?"

"Jesus, can you show Denida out of Heaven once and for all?" God expanded to an impossible size and stood in the tower, monitoring Heaven.

Jesus nudged Denida forward. "Please?"

"You're still obeying him?"

Jesus glanced at the ground. "Father has flaws, just like the rest of us. I won't fail him again."

"Again?" Denida turned to Jesus. "How have you failed him before? You've followed his every whim."

Jesus shook his head. "Saint Heavani and her son Daniel… I still remember her sweet, tender smile."

Denida scrunched his nose. "That wasn't your fault."

"She isn't here anymore, is she? As Father's first son, I should have protected-"

"Stop!" Denida grabbed Jesus and stared him in the eyes. "Heavani, Lucifer, and their son died because of God, not you."

"How? Father never left, so I don't know how he could have done that."

*Of course not, he's too scared ever to leave and risk running into Henna.* "Heavani died from a curse that killed her the moment she set foot outside of Heaven." Denida clenched his jaw. "God's curse."

Jesus inhaled deeply. "Are you here to kill Father?"

"I… come on, let me bring you to Gabriel." Denida took Jesus by the hand and began to lead him away.

"No." Jesus yanked himself free and stepped back, close to where God's form ascended into the clouds. "I'm not going anywhere, but you are." He raised his finger, pointing at the doorway. "Get out!"

"I can't." Denida turned his head. "I have to get him to-"

"To what, die?" Jesus shifted on his feet. "Memories are made, and some may be forgotten, but we all must live life to the fullest." He stretched out his hands. "And that is why I'll protect Father, just as he would protect me."

Denida rolled his eyes. *I'm not getting anywhere with him.* He lifted his hands in defeat. "Alright, you win. I'll leave."

Jesus' frown transformed into a broad smile. "You've come to your senses."

Denida arched his neck to look at God. "It's a shame, though…" He clenched his fist and held it up to his mouth. He extended his arm, resting his hand over Jesus' eyes. Silvery dust covered Jesus' face, and he slumped to the ground.

Denida heaved in a sigh and carried Jesus over to the far wall, where he gently placed him on the floor. *I'm sorry to make you sleep through this.*

"Shaddai… God, whatever you call yourself now," Denida muttered as rage built inside his chest. "Stop hiding like a coward and face me!" He screamed.

God's response came in the form of a deafening silence.

"You want me to summon Henna?" Denida rubbed his hands together, smirking.

A whirlwind of white magic flashed in front of him. As it faded, God stood before him, at his normal height.

God scanned the floor, until his eyes came to rest on Jesus. "The fact that you killed him won't get a response out of me, you know."

"Ki-" Denida clenched his fists so tightly his knuckles paled. "He's sleeping, not dead…"

"By Henna's magic, I see," God remarked. "I don't need her magic to kill a mere soul, you know. I'll show you, if that's what you really want."

Denida ran his hand over his face. "I'm not here to kill you, but Saint Peter killed Lucifer, on your command."

God glared at Denida with bright, white eyes, but his face remained stony.

Denida's fists trembled at his sides. "Peter tried to kill Gabriel for you too, so I killed him."

God remained as still as a statue.

"Henna wants you and Gabriel dead. We've already lost Lucifer. It's about time we end this feud, once and for all." Denida sighed and shook his head. "You can finally do something right and give yourself to Henna, so that she'll spare Gabriel, who wasn't even there when Henan died."

"Are you done?" God waited for Denida to nod before he continued. "How can you have been Azal's apprentice, and Henna's chosen one, when you are the epitome of stupidity?" God snarled. "I would never sacrifice myself for anyone, and if you really thought I would, you should consider the fact that you're even stupider than you look."

Denida drew in a deep breath.

"You are here, after all," God added, before Denida could speak.

Denida shook his head solemnly. "That's not why I came. Don't you see? Everything comes back to your selfish attempts to attain power for yourself. It started with you and will end with you, one way or another." He thrust his hand forward, firing a wave silvery magic.

God crossed his arms, vaporizing the incoming attack. "You're forgetting where you are, little boy." He grew to his impossible height, and a bright light enshrouded him.

Denida squinted against the light's intensity.

God lowered his giant hand and wrapped his fingers around Denida, lifting him up to his face.

Denida tried to wrest free from God's grip, but the fingers around him tightened as he squirmed.

"I warned you that I don't need anything special to kill an itsy-bitsy ant like you." God peered out at the horizon.

"Wa…" Denida closed his eyes as he endured the crushing agony. "Killing… me…"

"Would anger Henna?" God's grip loosened. "Why would it? You're not her only weapon, nor are you her first."

*Her first?* "What are you talking about? She doesn't choose our paths; destiny does."

"Believing in that malarkey only shows how naïve you really are." God drew his hand closer to his face. "Haven't you realized that she doesn't know which version of fate is the one that will come to pass?"

Denida bared his teeth. "Of course, I have, but I'm not here on her behalf."

"You could have fooled me," God snickered. "Enlighten me; why are you here, ring-boy?"

"I thought you were the all-knowing Father?" Denida tilted his head and eyed God.

God tightened his grip so tightly that Denida cried out in pain. "Last chance."

Denida panted for air. "…You killed Luci…"

"Your point? I also killed Heavani and Lucifer's son." God moved his arm back. "But enough toying with you." He tossed Denida high into the sky. Denida flew through the sky and plummeted into the clouds beyond the Pearly Gates.

Denida crawled a few steps before struggling to his feet. He slammed his fist into his open palm and vanished, reappearing in front of Heaven's Pearly Gates. He stomped through the gates, heading straight for God's chamber.

"Denida?" Gabriel exclaimed. "I thought you were…" He pointed at God's chamber.

"He threw me out. Literally."

"But Henna's ring." Gabriel panted. "How could he…"

Denida shrugged. "White magic is strengthened here, as you know, and he happens to be the most powerful wielder of it." Denida held his hands together in front of his lips. "But you need to stay here, where he won't kill-"

"God bolstered my white magic once, so that I could repel Henna's attacks on Heaven, and he never undid it." Gabriel approached Denida. "Let me join you."

Denida's eyes widened. "I don't…"

"We must put an end to this madness. Shaddai was my friend, but he had our best friend killed. I can help you with my reinforced white magic."

Denida nipped his tongue. "I want to argue, but I know I can't do this alone, so I must accept your help."

Denida and Gabriel strode to God's chamber.

Denida's eyes scanned the room as when they entered it. Hs gaze came to rest on Jesus, still sleeping against the wall. Denida pointed to Jesus. "Be careful; Jesus is still in here."

Gabriel nodded. "Shad, you're still in here?"

A bright flash appeared in the center of the room. When it vanished, God stood in its place.

"Gabe." God grinned maniacally. "You've come-" He stopped mid-sentence, as his eyes landed on Denida. "You're back?"

"His presence doesn't matter." Gabriel stared at God with innocent eyes. "How could you? Azal was our friend. We made Heaven for the three of us. We played together as children. I..." Gabriel's hands trembled. "You could've made up."

"Times change, Gabe." God extended his arms to his sides and a bright light encircled him.

"Denida, now!" Gabriel dropped to his knees and folded his hands in a praying pose. White magic enshrouded him.

White magic wrapped around God, who grew gigantic.

Gabriel had lowered his head in his praying hands, and his white magic fused with his body, allowing him to grow to God's size.

*Holy...* Denida backed up to where Jesus slept, shifting his focus between God and Gabriel, as they kept growing taller and broader.

God's face darkened. "Gabriel, you have more magic than I thought."

"I only have what you granted me."

God tilted his head. "That was my biggest mistake."

"And mine was supporting you for this long, but that ends, now." Gabriel flung his giant arm into God's cheek, and Heaven rumbled with the impact.

God socked Gabriel in the stomach, and again in the jaw. A waterfall of blood cascaded to the floor, creating a puddle.

Denida threw himself over Jesus to shield him from the blood pooling on the floor.

Gabriel headbutted God, who stumbled into a wall that collapsed under his weight. The ground trembled, and more blood rained down onto the clouds, which absorbed it like sponges. Below the clouds, scarlet rain drizzled from Heaven.

God staggered to his knees, and stretched his hands, grabbing Denida and Jesus. He stood and lifted the hands next to his face. "Shrink down, or they'll both die."

Gabriel stood locked in place, huffing. "… Fine." He folded his hands and raised them to his lips. His excess white magic ceased, causing him to shorten. "There!" He kissed his hand. A stream of white magic flowed from his hand and surrounded Jesus.

Jesus' eyelids fluttered open, and his eyes widened. "Father?"

God flung Jesus through the air, and he smashed into a wall. Jesus slumped to the ground, unconscious.

Gabriel rushed to Jesus' side.

God lifted Denida above his head. "Time for you to die, for good."

"What about Gabriel?" Denida pinched God's hand and wrist repeatedly.

God glanced at Gabriel. "I'll deal with him, after he watches me kill you, Lucifer's apprentice, as I did Lucifer."

*He doesn't feel it…* Denida leaned his head over the giant fingers to plan his next move.

"Wait; I should show him close-up." God placed Denida on the floor across the room from Gabriel. He lifted his leg and stomped with enough might to make Heaven's foundation tremble, but Denida escaped the blow by rolling to the side.

Denida jumped up, wrapping his fingers around God's pants, and began climbing.

"No, you don't!" God swatted at his pants. He struck Denida, who fell off, but Denida flailed and managed to grab ahold of the material again before he dropped too far.

Denida resumed climbing, holding on as strongly as he could, to avoid falling again.

God started shaking his legs.

Denida passed God's knees. God cupped his thighs, and long bursts of white magic formed a ring around his leg and shot downward, pushing Denida off.

Denida hurtled toward the ground.

Gabriel fired a stream of white magic at Denida, which smacked into him, just before he hit the ground. It tossed Denida in the opposite direction, and he collided with God's stomach. Denida recovered quickly enough to grab God's shirt and he twirled his hands around the fabric to reinforce his grip.

God shifted his gaze to Gabriel and tossed a barrage of white magic at him. It knocked Gabriel off his feet, and he slammed into the wall, out cold.

Denida watched in horror. From the corner of his eye, he noticed God's incoming knuckles, and he leapt to the side, where he quickly turned around and crawled under God's shirt.

"Where are you?" God slapped himself all over, trying to squash Denida like a bug.

Denida crawled up the inside of the shirt, with his back to God's skin, trying to avoid making contact with it. Every few seconds, he pressed his face up against the shirt to locate the shadows of God's fists through the material. One open hand smacked mere centimeters below Denida's legs. Denida wrapped his arms around the shirt to brace himself for the impact. He pulled back, glancing down at the red mark on God's skin. *That was too close.* Denida wiped sweat from his forehead before climbing higher.

"Curses!" God started to unbutton his shirt from the top.

The light from outside immediately filtered in. *I don't have much time; this had better work...* Denida ripped the ring from his finger and hurled it at God's chest.

When the ring touched his skin, God's fingers stilled. A silvery flash engulfed God's skin, disabling his white magic, so God shrank to his normal size and disintegrated into a mound of silvery ash.

Jesus and Gabriel awoke from God's spell, and they, along with Denida, approached the pile of ash. Denida knelt next to it.

A rainbow flash lit up the wall behind them. "Perfectly done." Henna saluted Denida. "Now you only have Gabriel left." She turned to Gabriel with a sickly-sweet smile.

"Never." Denida jumped in front of Gabriel and raised his hand. *Oh yeah, the ring…*

"I see that you chose the path where you don't have any of my magic on you, anymore." Henna shrugged. "… seeing as the necklace is elsewhere."

Jesus pushed forward and launched a flurry of white magic at Henna, but it dissipated before reaching her.

"I guess you didn't realize that with Shaddai's death, light magic is no longer strengthened in Heaven. I'm sorry, my child." Her eyes flared up with a rainbow tint. She pecked her finger and pointed to Jesus. A silvery shade encased him and dissolved him into ash.

Denida tilted his head to Gabriel, with his teeth bared. "Use the magic you have as an angel to escape. I'll distract her and meet you at Dynasty." He turned to Henna, a fierce hatred in his eyes. "Now that God's dead, is the Darkness gone, too?" He tilted his head. "It did emanate from him, like you said." He strolled across the room.

Gabriel tiptoed out of the room.

"No, it broke free from him a long time ago." Henna smiled softly, and her eyes turned rainbow. "Perhaps you should retrieve the necklace, before the barrier sucks all my magic out of it," she stated matter-of-factly. "You'll need it to kill Gabriel."

"I said never!" Denida's eyes flared crimson.

"Destiny sees you either killing Gabriel, or watching everyone you've ever cared about die." Henna raised her palm and blew silvery ash on Denida, sending him to Earth.

# Chapter 36- The End

Henna stepped through a magical portal in Odin's Grand Hall. She turned to Odin, who slouched on his throne with his head and shoulders slumped. *Is he really still upset over Loki?* "Odin!" she called.

"My Queen." Odin lifted his head, and she could see the tears in his eyes, sparkling in the room's light.

"God and Lucifer are no more."

"I see," Odin whispered demurely. "Then we-"

"Yes, we're relocating Valhalla to my world. After Gabriel's death, I will no longer require gods outside of my realm."

"You want everyone from Valhalla?" Odin's eyes stayed locked on some point dead ahead.

"Ahem." Thor stood in the doorway.

"Do come in, my child." Henna lowered her head to Odin's ear. "Everyone and everything will be in my world, including Loki, who's a permanent resident, now." She made a mental note of how far into the room Thor had walked. "But you should definitely keep Loki in line, because if he dies by my hand again, it'll be for good." She put her finger to her lip and disappeared, leaving a rainbow in her wake as she traversed through the dimensions until she came to one in particular.

Demons ran around chaotically in a world with a crimson sky, bathing the entire world in eternal dusk.

Henna weaved between the demons and strolled toward a giant crowd of them in front of her.

Victore lounged on a foam couch in front of the mob. A dark cloud hovered above him, in the shape of a person.

"I see the Darkness has outlived God." Henna crossed her arms. "With all due respect, well done."

The dark cloud bolted into the sky and expanded, filling the horizon.

"There's no getting rid of you, is there?" Victore sat up, glaring at Henna. "How did you find this place? The master sealed it away with magic."

"Nobody can hide from the messenger of Destiny."

Demons encircled Victore and Henna.

"Maybe I can't hide, but I can end this." Victore snarled.

Henna's eyes surveyed the demons. "Do you really think this meager army can defeat me? Have you forgotten who I am?"

"Are you forgetting where you are?" Victore retorted.

"No, but Lucifer's death gave you this power, so you should show me some gratitude."

The demons started closing in on Henna.

"Destiny will smite you." Henna raised her finger at the demons.

"Your power may be supreme when you're literally anywhere else, but this is the new Hell, and the world's new capital." Victore extended his arms to both sides and fused with the dark cloud from above, increasing in size and mass.

"That would ruin the equilibrium."

"Think I care? Our era starts now." Victore clenched his fists, and the sky turned a fiery crimson. The demons lunged at Henna.

Henna teleported to a spot farther away from the attacking demons, but like bloodhounds, they spun on their heels and charged at her. She raised her palm and blew on her hand.

A giant wave of silvery dust floated toward the demons, but most of it blackened to charcoal before reaching them. By the time some of the dust reached the demons, it had weakened into a mist, which the demons ran right through, as if it weren't there at all.

*How is that possible?* Henna blinked.

"Just to remind you, our Achilles heel is light magic, not your silvery crap." Victore bore a wide smirk. "Looks like your predictions aren't as strong as they used to be. Has your beloved Destiny forsaken you?" he mocked.

Henna's eyes turned rainbow colors. "We'll see about that." She charged forward and smashed into the demons with a silvery flash.

The demons withstood her attack and shoved Henna to the ground, only to lift her back up and drag her to Victore.

"Kneel for our master, weakling!" The demon holding her pushed her down.

"Guess the power dynamic has changed." Victore lowered his arms. "It's shocking that both God and Lucifer feared you like naughty kindergarteners fear their teacher. I don't get it."

"Because…" Henna tried to wrest free. "- Destiny, my creator, does exist, and it will return the moment things become unbalanced. That's why both God and Lucifer had to die; it ensured that magic and power would remain balanced."

Victore rolled his eyes. "I'll take my chances with your Destiny." He waved his fingers as he approached her.

"If you think tearing my heart out will be enough to kill me, you're sorely mistaken."

"Perhaps, but I will enjoy it, and it'll send you back home where you belong, with God and Lucifer." Victore scrunched his nose and jabbed his hand into Henna's stomach.

Darkness ripped into Henna, tearing a gash in her stomach.

Henna crossed her arms, creating a silvery barrier, which deflected the Darkness's assault. She glared at her stomach in utter shock. *I'm bleeding?* She ran her finger across her stomach, healing the wound, and stared at Victore. "This isn't over!"

Henna spun on her heel and traversed through the universe until she stood in her realm, where she huffed for air. *That was too close for comfort...* Henna ran her hand up her side over the wound that had already vanished. *What does this mean for balance?*

Henna stepped forward and paused, as her eyes flickered rainbow, and visions began manifesting. Every path ended with the same image: Denida smiling with rainbow eyes. *No.* Henna clenched her fists. *Fate cannot replace me. I must stop this from getting further out of hand.* She teleported from her world to the cabin outside of Dynasty in the Underworld.

"Henna's vengeance must end." Denida tapped his knuckles on the table.

"That's impossible." Gabriel ran his hands across his face. "Both God and Lucifer, heck, even Jesus, are dead."

"It wasn't vengeance; it was balance." Henna poked her head in through the doorway.

Denida jumped in front of Gabriel with his hand raised. "No!"

"Oh? What are you going to do? Smite me with your soul magic? I see you didn't retrieve the necklace." Henna stepped into the cabin.

"God, Jesus, and Saint Peter are gone. Who else could lead Heaven? Did you come to kill Gabriel or to lecture me about the necklace?" Denida's eye tracked Henna's every move.

Henna held her finger up to her lips. "Neither actually… I've come to discuss creating an equilibrium with the Darkness."

"You need both light and dark magic to create that balance, and God, Jesus, and Saint Peter are all gone. Light magic is underrepresented for the first time, since the Darkness appeared," Gabriel remarked.

"Ah, but Gabriel, you have been friendly with both Shaddai and Azal, since you were children, and even after my death." Henna turned her eyes to Gabriel.

"I've learned from my mistakes, my Queen. The Darkness must be kept at bay."

Henna smiled. "I could kill you myself, but you have a point. The Darkness is stronger after all the soul harvesting and their new-"

"Victore," Denida interrupted.

Gabriel stepped out in front of Denida. "All my friends are dead, but I remember you making several deities back in the day." Gabriel knelt and closed his eyes. "I'm your servant, my Queen. You may kill me now, or use me, as you see fit."

Denida gasped. "Gabe, I…" His jaw trembled.

"I know you don't trust me, Denida." Henna lifted her finger. "As a sign of goodwill, I'll show you that I'm not all bad." She kissed her finger and waved it in front of her. *Bringing someone back is the easiest thing to do.*

A pentagram of silvery ash formed on the floor. When it subsided, a silhouette of a man appeared.

"Jesus?" Denida screamed.

Gabriel's eyes sprang open and shifted to Jesus, but the rest of his body remained still.

"To show that I mean this…" Henna gestured for Gabriel and helped him up. "Jesus can assist you, as you restore Heaven."

"In exchange for what?" Denida hissed.

*Will he stop poking the bear?* Henna turned to Denida with a rainbow tint in her eyes. "I was always a goddess, created to instate and maintain balance. Allowing the Darkness to exist, unchecked, will upset that balance."

Gabriel embraced Jesus as tightly as possible. Then, he pulled back and faced Henna. "Alright, but my power isn't as grand as Shaddai's was, so I'm still not strong enough to contend with Victore, let alone the Darkness."

"Leave that to me." Henna took Gabriel by the hand and led him outside, where she gestured for him to take a knee in the grass. "A long time ago, there was a path that would see you becoming divine, instead of Shaddai. Fate diverged, but now, we've come full circle."

Gabriel lit up. "Yes, my Queen."

Henna raised her hand. "Do you swear your allegiance to me, and to fate, on the condition that shall you fail, you'll forfeit your soul to your master?"

Denida and Jesus exchanged a nervous glance.

"I do," Gabriel quipped. "Peace will finally reign in Heaven."

Henna's hand trembled above Gabriel's head. *This is harder than I remember.* She lifted her other hand too, and a powerful silver energy shot into Gabriel.

Gabriel opened his eyes, which now contained a silvery tint. "I won't fail you, my Queen." He nodded at her.

Henna waved at Denida. "Toodeloo." She teleported to Valhalla and sighed in relief. *Thank Destiny, it's done-* She gazed up at the starry sky. *Intriguing...* She strode into Odin's chamber.

Odin and Thor were the only residents left in Valhalla. Odin sat upon his throne, and his son stood by his side.

"Are you ready?" Henna rubbed her eyes.

"Aye, my Queen." Odin rose and pulled Thor down on his knees to bow beside him.

"In that case, we're going home." *After I deal with the last little thorn in my side.* Henna teleported to the rock below Valhalla, sensing Nina's presence.

Nina stared intently at Valhalla.

"Isn't it fascinating?" Henna folded her hands. "You do know that it's impossible to set foot in Valhalla without an invitation, right?"

Nina glared at Henna. "I don't need to get in, so long as you're down here."

"True, but I just dropped by because I wanted to show you something."

"What's that?" Nina's eyes sparkled. "Are we going to make another deal, so that I can have my Daniel back?"

"The opposite." She pointed at Valhalla. "Pretty, isn't it? So much color, surrounded by nothingness."

"I guess?" Nina peered up.

"Too bad it's gone." Henna clasped her hands together, and Valhalla disappeared in a silvery flash, leaving behind a massive crater.

Nina's mouth hung open. "So, you've relocated it… I'll find it again, just like I found your Gate."

"No, it has returned to my world, back to your twin sister and your son, both of whom are serving me." Henna smirked. "Would you like me to send your regards?"

Nina lunged at her.

Henna levitated, ascending into the sky. A silvery aura enshrouded her, making her glow brightly among the inky blackness. "Toying with you has been quite entertaining, but enough is enough."

Nina panned the ground, and she scooped up a few rocks, which she hurled at Henna.

Henna raised her shoulders and the rocks struck her, but bounced off like they were made of cotton. "Nice message, seeing as this is our last rendezvous. Thanks for the entertainment, Nina." Henna faded to her world.

***

Nina doubled over, panting. *That old witch can't have gotten the better of me.* She stormed forward until she reached Valhalla's dismal remains.

Nina gritted her teeth as she strolled through the empty woods, staring intently at every shape, every shadow she encountered. *Nothing...* She felt a tinge of excitement every time something caught her eye, only to feel like she'd taken a punch to the gut when it turned out to be her imagination playing tricks on her. *There's nothing left...* Nina's knees buckled, and she fell into the dirt. She sat on the ground with a horrible, stinging sensation in her heart. *Was it all for nothing? Why couldn't she have killed me, instead of Loki? At least then, I would've been with Daniel.*

*I've got it!* Nina jumped up and scrounged through the woods for anything she could use to achieve her goal, but all she found were rocks, leaves, and some wild animals that scurried away from her. *Come on; there must be something...*

"*Creak, creak...*" the wind rustled some branches, and an old wolf lifted his head.

Nina smiled broadly. *Finally.* "Hi, little one. Am I on your turf?" She waved her arms up and down. "Come and kill me!"

The wolf sat down, watching her every movement.

"Attack, already!" Nina's eyes searched the ground. She grabbed some stones beside her and threw them at the wolf.

The wolf whimpered and dashed into the woods.

*Dammit.* Nina pursued it, but after a few minutes, she halted, panting for air. *Which way did it go?*

"*Creak, creak, creak,*" branches cracked behind Nina.

Nina spun around, ready to resume her chase.

A pack of wolves stood in front of Nina, and several more approached from behind her. *It's now or never. Daniel, Mommy's coming home!* She rubbed her hands together and sauntered forward.

"*Rustle.*"

Nina turned back, as several Siberian huskies fought off the wolf pack behind her. Nina shifted on her feet.

The dogs looked up and darted after the old wolf and the rest of its pack.

*Hell no.* Nina sprinted after them, following the trail of broken branches. The trail ended at a cliff with a ledge below it. Nina peered down at the ground. *A far drop? Fine.* Nina tore off her jacket and stepped away from the ledge, before running as fast as she could. She threw herself over the cliff and fell, smashing into the ledge below. A puddle of red formed on the ground underneath her.

Nina gasped and touched her head. *It hurts. Can I really be dead?*

"That you are." Thor stood before her, with his hand resting on his belt next to his hammer. "You do remind me of someone, but welcome to Queen Henna's world. Follow me."

"Um, wait." Nina jumped to her feet. "Since I died, perhaps I could see my son, who died before me?"

"I'll take it from here." Nylah stepped forward with a smile.

"Of course." Thor bowed to Nylah.

"Nylah?" Nina gasped. "You've sure got some say."

"That's what happens when you follow Henna."

"Great." Nina rejoiced. "Then you can take me to Daniel?"

"She won't need to." Henna appeared next to Thor.

"I'm here, so you can't prevent me from seeing him, anymore," Nina hissed.

"Killing yourself… I'll admit I didn't see this possibility." Henna snapped her fingers, and Daniel appeared beside her. "Nylah?" She gestured for Nina's sister to come to her side.

"Yes, my Queen?" Nylah neighed.

"Wait," Daniel pleaded. "Let me talk to my mom."

Henna's eyes flickered rainbow. "I see, so that's an option.  Alright, Daniel." She gestured for him to proceed.

*Daniel*... Nina extended her arms and Daniel fell into them. She hugged him as tight as she could. "I'll never let you go again." She shut her eyes, smiling joyously, but the bliss on her face could only express a fraction of the happiness she felt with every beat of her heart. "Ugh!" Nina suddenly felt a piercing pain in her gut. Her embrace loosened, as she glanced down at her abdomen. To her shock, Daniel had pierced her with a dagger. "W-why?"

Daniel ignored her and raised his head to look at Henna. "It's all for you, My Queen."

Nina gasped in disbelief, as Henna gestured for Daniel to stand beside her.

Nina reached for Daniel, but he strolled over to Henna.

Henna pinched Daniel's cheek. "Good boy."

"What the hell?" Nina screamed.

"Nina, you're still here?" Henna met Nina's eyes.

Nina gasped for air. "I tried... for so long... and yet..."

"I warned you." Henna rubbed her hands together. "This little game was fun while it lasted, but I'm tired of you, now. Goodbye, Nina." Henna snapped her fingers, and Nina dissolved into a silvery pile of ash.

***

Denida and Susan stood next to each other.

"I'm happy you decided to go to Earth with me." Denida caressed Susan's hand and kissed her tenderly.

"The results are in!" An aide rushed into the next room.

Susan stroked Denida's hand with her thumb. "Are you certain you're ready to resign?"

Denida retracted his hand and ran it through his hair. "I've thought long and hard about this since I asked you if you'd like to get away from the Underworlds with me. The more I see and experience, the more convinced I am that I've made the right decision." He gazed into Susan's eyes. "I can't risk losing you, and we can't use the Gates anymore, so now's the time to get away, if you'll still come with me?"

"I understand… and absolutely." Susan smiled. "I guess we'd better see the election results and say our goodbyes, then." Denida squeezed Susan's hand and they stepped into the room where all the candidates waited for the results.

Dan paced back and forth, only stopping periodically to check the wide monitor in the center of the room.

Denida stood in front of Dan. "You seem troubled."

"Can you blame me?" Dan fiddled with his fingers. "We're about to see who will become the next president."

"Denny!" Susan called from the monitor.

Dan covered his head with his hands. "Please, tell me they didn't elect the Henna-admirer!"

Denida tilted his head to the screen. "I think you should see this for yourself."

"Okay." Dan inhaled deeply and lowered his hands. He turned to the monitor. "89%... for *me?*" Dan almost collapsed, but he grabbed the side of a nearby table to catch his balance.

"That's what you get when you successfully lead the Underworld during a demon apocalypse." Denida patted Dan's shoulder. "You deserve it, so you'd better have a speech ready."

Dan straightened up. "Yes, I'm in charge now, but what about Nina? Did you ever find-"

"Dan." Denida swallowed. "She worked with Henna, who got everything she wanted. I'm sure she still has Nina under her thumb." He clenched his jaw. "Besides, we lost the Colonel and Sheriff Robert, and Naphtali never came back after he went MIA. Nina's disappearance is a tragedy, but we've lost so many other good men and women in this fight that she's still only one loss."

Dan rubbed his hands together. "I suppose, but remember, if you ever want to come back-"

"I'm done." Denida raised his hand. "I will remain with Susan, protecting her human form on Earth. It's where I want to be, where I need to be." He met Susan's eyes, and they shared a smile.

Dan nodded and stepped through the balcony door. Colossal applause erupted from the crowd.

"Are you certain you want to leave?" Susan hugged Denida. "Without your ring, or human form, this decision can't be undone."

"Yes, I'm sure." Denida closed his eyes and whispered "Gabriel" under his breath.

A bright, white light flashed, and Gabriel appeared with his silvery eyes and a sparkly silver aura. "You called?"

Denida's lips curled into a slight trace of a smile. "Yes, I did. Would you be able to help us get to Earth?" He pulled Susan close.

"Are you certain? It won't be easy for you to return." Gabriel folded his hands.

"Yes, we're going to watch over her human permanently. I've had enough of the Underworlds for a lifetime." Denida leaned in and whispered into Gabriel's ear. "Do you remember when you hinted that I should go to the Paradise Lakes all those years ago?" He smiled tenderly, appearing completely at peace. "I'd like to bring Susan there."

"Your wish is my command." Gabriel smiled. "I haven't had time to check on Earth since I took over Heaven." Gabriel rested his hands in Denida's and Susan's, and they teleported to Earth, appearing next to a tall tree.

Denida smiled at Susan. "I want to show you something." He took her hand and led her into the woods to a white rock. "I've always found peace right here, ever since I stopped here with Daniel on our journey home when we first trekked through the Gates." Denida gazed into Susan's eyes. "Now. it can be our spot." He leaned in and kissed Susan.

"I'm happy it's final-" Gabriel's smile stiffened midsentence. "Something feels wrong." He took both Denida's and Susan's hands and teleported to the other Gate.

Jakob rushed over to a desk next to the Gate, where Sus stood with Tom, who was wearing a suit. "Sus, here's Kate's update, regarding rebuilding our homes." Jakob handed Sus some papers.

Sus skimmed the pictures with a giggle. "It's nice to see progress."

"I see your human form is as capable as you are." Gabriel smiled at Susan. "However…"

"What's the matter?" Denida's heart sank.

Gabriel's eyes grew brighter. He swept up to the Gate and dropped his knees. He touched the Gate's device, which still sat on the grass. With a simple stroke of his fingertips, it crumbled, leaving only the necklace behind.

"Gracious…" Gabriel stared at the necklace, which had turned to dust, leaving only the chain intact.

Denida sighed. "We need to inform Dan that the magic barrier on Earth has fallen."

"That won't be necessary; I'll create one. We can't repeat the errors of yesterday, especially now that the Gates are disintegrating."

"Because Henna's gone?" Denida frowned.

Gabriel nodded. "But we are here." He crossed his arms, and a solid, silvery essence emanated from him, encompassing the entire planet, restoring the barrier.

"Finally, peace on Earth."

Gabriel nodded at Denida. "Forever."